# THE TRIAL OF LEE HARVEY OSWALD

ALSO BY WILLIAM ALSUP

*Such a Landscape!*

*Missing in the Minarets*

*Won Over: Reflections of a Federal Judge on His Journey
from Jim Crow Mississippi*

# THE TRIAL OF
# LEE HARVEY
# OSWALD

## A Novel

## WILLIAM ALSUP

NewSouth Books

an imprint of
The University of Georgia Press
Athens

**NSB**

Published by NewSouth Books
an imprint of the University of Georgia Press
Athens, Georgia 30602
www.ugapress.org/newsouthbooks/

Designed by Randall Williams
Maps by Laura Murray
Printed and bound by Sheridan
The paper in this book meets the guidelines for permanence and
durability of the Committee on Production Guidelines for Book
Longevity of the Council on Library Resources.

Most NewSouth/University of Georgia Press titles
are available from popular ebook vendors.

Printed in the United States of America
23 24 25 26 27 C 5 4 3 2 1

Publisher's Cataloging-in-Publication Data
Names: Alsup, William, 1945– , author.
Title: The trial of Lee Harvey Oswald : a novel / William Alsup.
Description: Athens, Georgia : NewSouth Books, [2022] |
Identifiers: LCCN 2022939656 | ISBN 9781588384690 (hardback : alk. paper) |
ISBN 9781588384706 (ebook)
Subjects: LCSH. Historical fiction. | Historical novels. | History—fiction. | Historical
fiction, American. | American historical fiction. | Presidents—Assassination
attempts—Fiction. | Attempted assassination—Fiction. | Presidents—Assassination
attempts—United States—Fiction. | Presidents—Assassination—Fiction.
LC record available at https://lccn.loc.gov/2022939656

# CONTENTS

# PREFACE

WITHIN NINETY MINUTES OF THE ASSASSINATION OF PRESIDENT
John Kennedy in 1963, the Dallas police had in custody the accused Lee
Harvey Oswald. Two days later, Oswald himself was shot and killed as he
was being paraded by police before the press. Jack Ruby was then tried for
that murder.

*The Trial of Lee Harvey Oswald* is a work of alternative history anchored
in the conceit that Ruby, at the last second, loses his chance to shoot Oswald
so that America gets the trial of Oswald rather than the trial of Ruby. While
this novel is fictional, it has drawn extensively on the evidence compiled by
the Warren Commission, established after the assassination to determine
how and why it happened. The Commission filled twenty-six volumes with
testimony, affidavits, diagrams, photographs, and reports. All of the physical evidence in this novel is from those twenty-six volumes except for one
note by Oswald that was described for Congress in the late 1970s. Most of
the testimony in this novel is also from those twenty-six volumes but some
passages are my own estimates, as will be explained in more detail in the
Author's Note at the end.

Readers will take from this work a fair, if slightly embroidered, understanding of the actual historical evidence for and against Oswald, will see
how excellent attorneys, then and now, prepare and try tough cases, and will,
if I have done my job, have a ringside seat at the legal drama that America
craved but never got—*The Trial of Lee Harvey Oswald.*

# Presidential Motorcade Route through Dealey Plaza

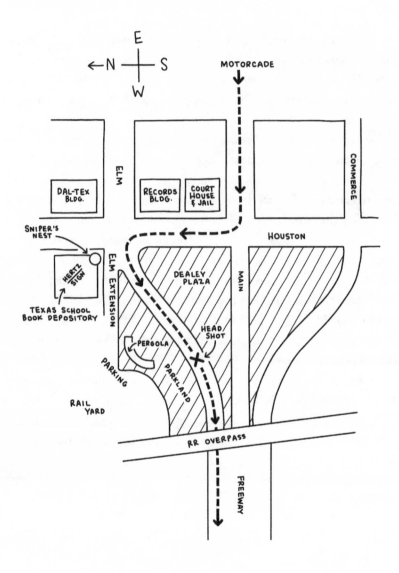

**Downtown Dallas and Oak Cliff**

# 1  FRIDAY, NOVEMBER 22, 1963

"When we get there, Abe, don't take notes. But remember it all and write it down later—tonight if you can," Miller said, working the clutch and gears. "He feels obliged. He's the attorney general of the United States."

The roadway lay empty.

"Everyone's at home now, vigil by television," Miller went on.

Abe Summer served as a career prosecutor in the Criminal Division of Main Justice, the nerve center of the United States Department of Justice. Herbert "Jack" Miller was Abe's boss, the assistant attorney general for the Criminal Division.

On the George Washington Parkway, they drove upstream along the Potomac. Abe rolled his window down a turn. In Washington, it had been an unseasonably warm day, the twenty-second. The evening air brought cool relief. Slanting light illuminated the parkland corridor. Late fall colors rested in rust.

Abe felt the enormity of the death of the president. He had admired his grace and judgment, the sense of elegance the First Family had given America—all obliterated in an instant.

Miller glanced at Abe, "You've never been out to their place, I take it."

"No," replied Abe.

"Jack and Jackie sold it to Bobby and Ethel. Needed it for all those kids. Old house, country style. You'll see."

They were led to a small study. Dusk glowed through a window. Beside book-lined shelves, Kennedy sat alone, jacket off, his shirt sleeves rolled up, his face drained of color, save for pink ringing his eyes. He didn't rise. He gestured to sit. They took seats. Condolences were given and acknowledged.

"I wanted you to come," said Kennedy, his jaw muscles tight, "because we can't, I can't trust Hoover. I trust you. We've got to get this right."

"Yes, sir," said Miller.

Miller summarized what they knew, then explained the scope of the

Criminal Division's response. The main item: The Dallas police had in custody a communist named Lee Harvey Oswald.

"I mean," resumed the attorney general in subdued but deliberate words, "we don't know how widespread this is—or even what it is. My first thought was that we might see, any moment, nuclear," he paused, "nuclear holocaust. But anything like that would've occurred right away. It's been hours now." He paused again. "The missile trouble in Cuba, if you think about it—that's when they would've hit us. Not now, a year later. So I don't think the Soviets are behind this."

Abe made mental notes.

"But Castro could be," Kennedy shifted his weight. "The president's made some tough speeches about Castro, one of them just a week ago—Miami. That's all public. What's not so public, but you should know," he hesitated, "is that the CIA's been trying for months to get Castro and Castro knows it. So maybe he got Jack first."

Abe had heard rumors about this.

"Has Castro claimed any credit?" Kennedy raised his eyelids.

"No, no one's claimed credit, but we've got information," Miller continued the thought, "that Sam Giancana had some part in trying to get Castro."

"That's very true," confided Kennedy. "So that leads to another possibility—maybe the one that worries me most—Giancana and his ilk. They think they got Jack elected in Chicago. It's true they've helped on Castro. They think we owe them. They're mad as hell that we've gone after Marcello, gone after Hoffa, and got Profeta."

The attorney general looked to Abe in acknowledgment. Abe had been the lead prosecutor in the Profeta case in New Orleans. No one brought up that Carlos Marcello, another Louisiana mobster, had been acquitted that very afternoon.

"They said, I think you know, they'd throw acid on my kids' faces—crap like that. I thought they might try something on me." Kennedy turned to the window, presenting a profile trimmed in gold. "But I never thought they'd try to get Jack."

Abe felt for Bobby.

"We got wiretaps up," answered Miller. "Nothing so far, but we're on it."

"Well, those people might be the best bet," Kennedy sank back in his chair. "Yes, sir."

"Who else could it be?" Kennedy looked to Miller for help.

"Exiles or maybe right-wing nuts," replied Miller. "Dallas is Ground Zero for right-wing nuts—John Birch Society and General Walker, those people."

"But," interjected Kennedy, "this Oswald's a communist, not an exile, not a right-winger."

The attorney general leaned in, his elbows on his knees, his hands in a delicate gesture. "Abe, what are we missing?"

"Hoover's saying," Abe replied, "that Oswald was a lone wolf." Abe immediately knew he'd said the wrong thing. He knew the attorney general despised J. Edgar Hoover, director of the FBI.

"Maybe," Kennedy interjected, "he's just a lone wolf but there's no way anyone could know that yet. Hoover's just trying to cover his ass." Kennedy made a slow fist. "The president got killed on his watch, so he's setting up defenses."

Kennedy shifted, "Jack, don't you think we need Abe down there? As soon as he can get there. Be our eyes and ears. Work himself into the case. Stay for as long as it takes."

Ethel appeared, signaled with a nod, then left, discreetly avoiding any glance at their guests. The attorney general apologized and gently asked to be excused. He had to go, he explained, to Andrews Air Force to meet Air Force One. They were bringing the president's body and Jackie home. "This will be," he ended, "the hardest hour of the hardest day of my life."

# 2 JACK RUBY

LITTLE LYNN NEEDED RENT MONEY. HER LANDLORD WAS BEING an asshole. She'd caught a ride all the way into Dallas on Saturday to get paid, only to learn that the strip club had been closed on account of the assassination. She'd had to borrow five dollars to get back to Fort Worth. She'd wasted the entire day and the five bucks too. All this she whined to Jack Ruby on the phone. He ran three burlesque bars in Dallas. She performed at his Carousel Club on Commerce Street in the hotel district.

"All right, all right. Fuck your landlord," he interrupted. "I'll wire you the money this morning."

So, on that Sunday morning, November 24, 1963, after another night of torment over the assassination, Ruby splashed his face, dressed in his usual dark suit, then stuffed his left pants pocket with a roll of cash, more than two thousand dollars. He cleaned his glasses, rubbed Vitalis into his receding hair, slicked it back, and adjusted his gray fedora. He popped another Preludin, slipped, as he regularly did, his loaded Colt Cobra .38 into his right jacket pocket, whisper-whistled for Sheba, then headed for the only Western Union in Dallas open on a Sunday.

He couldn't rid his mind of the red-on-pink image of the First Lady in her blood-soaked suit. He so regretted that he'd missed the president's last moments. That Friday, the twenty-second, at midday, Ruby had sat five blocks away at the office of the *Dallas Morning News* composing weekend ads for his clubs. As the president's life ended brutally, Ruby had had his mind on tits and ass.

It came as no surprise to Ruby that the killer had been a communist. Dallas reeked with racists, but the reds hated Kennedy, too. The assassin, Ruby had now heard over and again, went by Lee Harvey Oswald. From the accounts, Oswald was twenty-four, a loner, a misfit, a former Marine who had defected to Russia only to defect back. Oswald had worked at a schoolbook warehouse on the parade route. The news had played up the sequence that, forty-five minutes after the assassination, Oswald killed a patrolman who'd interrupted his flight. The Dallas police had charged him with both murders. From his club, Ruby had marched over to police headquarters around midnight that Friday and had seen Oswald as he got paraded out to the press as the killer. Ruby still smoldered over Oswald's smirk.

The scum dripped guilt. The radio delivered all the proof needed, even the fact that the rifle had been purchased by an Alek J. Hidell, an alias found in Oswald's own wallet. The front page of the Sunday *New York Times* called the proof "conclusive." Ruby ached over the shame now raining on Dallas. That was why he'd darkened the club, why he couldn't sleep. But he was on a mission now. He would save the First Lady the agony of a trial. A class woman like that deserved better. The Kennedys had suffered so much, too much; he also ached for them; they didn't deserve to suffer any more, certainly not a trial. Ruby knew how it would go—delays, crap excuses, lawyers twisting the truth 'til no one knew which end was up.

He intended to kill the man who had killed the president.

*Goddamn fucking red. Let's cut the shit and end it. Be a Jew with guts.*

From his apartment in Oak Cliff, he drove downtown. KLIF had reported that Oswald would soon be moved from police headquarters to the county jail, both places he'd drive by. Ruby had no family, but he had his dachshunds. Sheba, his favorite, rode shotgun. He expected to be captured. She'd be his defense. If he'd really premeditated to kill, wouldn't he have left her at home rather than stranded in a car? Ruby and Sheba crossed the Trinity River. Below, along its banks, Ruby could see the Negro shanty town in The Bottoms. On this sunny but cool day, blue-gray smoke curled up from tin stovepipes and melded into the breeze. Across the river, the huge Hertz Car Rental electric clock atop the Texas School Book Depository read 11:05. The viaduct brought them to the scene of the murder, Dealey Plaza. There, a vast garden of flowers, wreaths, candles, flags, and crepe-lined photographs of the president honored his memory. As he drove by, Ruby caught sight of two nuns on their knees in prayer. He groaned, then slammed his fist on the top of the wheel.

Across the street from Dealey Plaza at the Criminal Courts and Jail Building, Ruby saw a crowd waiting for the arrival of the assassin into county custody. He cruised another dozen blocks down Main Street, the same dozen blocks that had been the epicenter of the exuberant welcome for the president, still strung with bunting and banners. At police headquarters, another gathering waited to see the assassin leave police custody.

*Good—they haven't moved the asshole yet.*

Ruby swung left across the oncoming lanes of Main Street into a bare parking lot across from Western Union. He put his billfold and identification in the glove compartment. He left the car unlocked so they could retrieve

Sheba. He showed her a half-full bowl of water, but she wore a mournful look, knowing something was up. He cracked a window, told her he loved her, then jaywalked across Main to the Western Union. Inside, he filled out the money order form. When he reached the service window, he peeled off thirty dollars.

"Fuck him," Ruby muttered. The station manager ignored it. Ruby himself wasn't sure whether he meant the landlord or Oswald. Both, he supposed.

At 11:17 a.m., the station manager stamped the money order, saying it would go immediately to Fort Worth.

AT THE OTHER END of the block, Captain Will Fritz, veteran chief of the Dallas homicide bureau, didn't like the plan at all. His Stetson rested on a gray metal desk. In his dark suit, white shirt, and thin tie, Fritz argued with the newly appointed chief of police over the plan to transfer Oswald from city police custody to county sheriff custody. Usually, such a transfer was a ten-minute, uneventful process. But this time, the prisoner ranked as the most hated man in America. In fact, a call had already come in saying a group planned to kill Oswald. The chief wanted to transport Oswald those dozen blocks in an armored car.

The driver of the armored car, Fritz protested, worked for a private company. "What do we know about the driver?" he asked. If evasive action had to be taken or radios were needed or quick police work was called for, "the driver would be useless." The chief gave in and dropped the idea. Instead, they'd use a caravan of squad cars. The armored car would be a decoy.

But there remained a second problem. While escorting Oswald to the vehicle, the new chief wanted to vaunt Oswald through the basement, a space now crammed full of press. "Someone aiming to kill Oswald could hide in plain sight in that crowd," Fritz told the chief. The transfer should have been done already, unannounced, in the dead of night. The last thing Fritz wanted was to compound their failure to protect the president with a failure to protect Oswald.

The new chief shrugged his shoulders, saying it was "too late to change it"—the press already filled the basement, waiting for the show. Anyway, Fritz had been the one, the chief argued back, to insist on prolonging his interviews of Oswald in hope of obtaining a confession. That's why they'd missed a midnight run. So Fritz swore under his breath and told his team to cuff Oswald to a heavy detective. They'd all escort him through the clamor to a squad car waiting in the basement.

Finally, all was ready. With Oswald in tow, a wall of flesh formed, topped by the gray Stetson hats, headwear reserved by Dallas custom only for homicide detectives. En masse, they moved into the hallway by the elevator. From there they descended to the waiting throng of reporters.

RUBY EMERGED FROM THE Western Union station into the bright sunshine. He caught the faithful eyes of Sheba, watching him through a pane smudged with nose prints, then turned toward police headquarters, one block away, where onlookers spilled across the sidewalk.

The gun felt heavy, so he placed his right hand in his jacket pocket to hold it steady. Two days earlier on this very street, he realized, a vibrant young president had waved to the cheering masses. He'd do a great service for the First Family and the country if he could just get close enough. He'd kill the asshole—even if it meant getting killed himself. Ruby focused on the headquarters' garage exit, less than a hundred steps away.

*I'll be a Jew with guts.*

After a dozen steps, he heard a voice behind him, "Sir, sir, you forgot this."

Ruby looked back. The Western Union manager was hanging out the door, waving a receipt. Without thinking, Ruby retraced the dozen steps, snatched it, and resumed his march to police headquarters. Halfway there, Ruby saw a cruiser pulling out of the basement onto Main Street. An officer stood guard at the driveway. He leaned in to check the car going out.

Ruby arrived at the exit moments after the car had moved on, and the guard had little to do but watch Ruby approach. If only he hadn't gone back for the damned receipt, he thought, he would've arrived at the exit while the guard was attending to that cruiser and could've ducked unnoticed down the dark ramp into the basement. Nevertheless, Ruby started down the ramp, simply pretending he belonged there.

The guard called out, "Hey, you."

Ruby kept going. He heard the din of a crowd below.

The officer yelled louder, "You, on the ramp, I'm ordering you to stop."

Ruby ignored him. The officer scurried down to him and grabbed his right arm. Ruby stopped. In the dim light, he made out the name plate "*Roy Vaughn.*" Ruby still had his hand on his piece in his jacket pocket.

"Police and press only, sir. Can I see your press credential?"

Politely, he replied, "Roy, you know me. I'm Jack Ruby, from the Carousel Club." Ruby said that he just wanted to watch. But Vaughn insisted that he was under orders. "Sorry, Mr. Ruby, but you must leave."

"Here they come," someone shouted below.

The din exploded in pandemonium.

Ruby broke free. He hurried down the ramp, reaching the edge of the basement. He saw Oswald, wearing a dark sweater and bruised face, only a dozen steps away, Stetsons on both sides. Flash bulbs popped. Ruby heard him tell a reporter, "I'm just a patsy. They're violating my rights. Please, I need a lawyer."

Ruby's blood surged.

*Now—Be a Jew with guts.*

Ruby felt a grip on his right arm and on the neck of his jacket. Vaughn yanked him.

"I'm ordering you—get the hell out, now." Vaughn steered Ruby back up to the Main Street sidewalk, then pushed him out.

Ruby hurried around the building to the opposite Commerce Street exit, where another gaggle of spectators waited. He arrived just in time to see the caravan pull out. As one of the cars swept by, he saw Oswald in the back seat, surrounded by Stetsons. Ruby had no clean shot. His right hand remained in his jacket pocket. The caravan drove away.

Ruby wept.

As he wept, he saw, back down in the basement, a slim, tall brunette staring up the ramp at him.

# 3   ELAINE NAVARRO

AT THAT VERY MOMENT, A HALF DOZEN BLOCKS AWAY AT THE
Post Office and Federal Building, Assistant United States Attorney Elaine
Navarro yearned to pray at mass, but this Sunday she remained at work,
where she'd been since Friday. As Oswald headed for a cell on the sixth
floor of the county jail, she sat bone-dead tired and wiped the glass lens of
her black-rimmed spectacles with a damp handkerchief. Her boss, Barefoot
Sanders, across his desk, finished his half of a cheese sandwich.

"So, so hard to believe," Sanders said, crumpling the sandwich bag, "that
there's no federal crime in killing the president, not even treason."

"All the harder to believe," Elaine replied, "that Congress would make
it a crime to kill an FBI agent but not the president."

Sanders tossed the wad into a metal trash can. "Well, they damn well
better fix it now."

Elaine had been returning from Houston when she'd heard on KLIF
about the shots. She'd headed straight to the federal building to report for
duty only to learn that Kennedy was dead. She'd burst into tears, quieted
herself in the ladies' room, then turned to the task at hand. Sanders had
locked the door to keep out the press as they worked. Task number one
had been to ascertain whether or not killing the president even qualified as
a federal crime, then to identify other possible federal offenses that might
be used to hold anyone suspected of complicity.

In those first forty-eight hours, Elaine remained racked with grief, angst,
and fear. Was America facing an orchestrated attack—would a second or
third act follow? Who? Where might be next? Nothing was off the table.
One of the other prosecutors, Elaine knew, had brought his shotgun to the
office, just in case. They left a transistor radio turned on to catch the latest
alerts. She helped establish reliable lines of communication with the FBI,
Secret Service, Dallas police, and White House, all the while sorting out
the legal research.

She saw his stubble. His tie had long since been draped over his jacket
on the rack. They both still wore their clothes from the twenty-second.

They were the only two left. The radio, on low, carried the state ceremonies in Washington.

"You know," she noted quietly, "they said a while ago that the FBI knew about Oswald but didn't warn anyone."

"Knew about Oswald? No way. Hoover must be livid," he drawled. "Heads will roll."

He sipped his tea. The ice had melted.

*For those in peril on the sea.*

Through the open window Elaine heard the robust strains of an organ-and-choir performance of the Navy Hymn, drifting in from the First Baptist Church of Dallas on the next block, the largest Baptist church in the world. The pathos drew Sanders to the window. Elaine knew he had been a Navy man. He raised the window to its full height. Brilliance fell through. She figured all six hundred churches in Dallas, likely all churches in all America, brimmed over, reflecting on the gravity of that Friday and, as she'd been, praying for the future of the country. The banners that had welcomed the president, she'd seen on the sandwich run, still fluttered over Main Street. Placards reading "All the Way/JFK and LBJ/in '64" still littered the sidewalks.

"We were both out in the Pacific but, of course, never met 'til years later. He got back from that PT boat before I even got orders."

She could tell he was pausing until the hymn ended, respecting the moment. Elaine gazed past him, into the blue.

*Dear Father, Son and Holy Spirit, accept our president, comfort him and his loved ones,*" she prayed silently. "*Forgive us, God, forgive us.*"

She crossed herself.

*Glad praise from air and land and sea.*

The hymn finished.

"How else," she quietly asked, "can I help?" Her long dark brown hair brushed the arms of her glasses, sweeping past her ears in a ponytail. She'd reached a point of complete exhaustion.

"Nothing," Sanders replied, returning to his chair. "You've done way more than your share, Elaine. I'm proud of you. Go home, like everybody else," he said, looking at her squarely to show he meant it. "It's pretty clear Oswald did it. This is gonna be for the state people to prosecute, not us."

Gathering up her notes, she offered, "Can I help with the guy from Main Justice?"

"He'll be flying in for the officer's funeral tomorrow," Sanders answered. "Day after, I'm gonna meet with him. We need to give the district attorney our support. This comes straight from the attorney general."

Elaine kept quiet. That officer and his grieving family had been lost in the worldwide spectacle of the assassination. She appreciated the decency of the Department of Justice to send a federal representative to his funeral.

Sanders continued his thought, "You know, Elaine, maybe you oughta join us Tuesday. Take tomorrow off and rest. We'll then meet up Tuesday morning, say at 8:30 in Dealey Plaza? Right about Houston and Elm."

"I'll be there."

# 4   DEALEY PLAZA

ON TUESDAY MORNING, ELAINE ARRIVED AT DEALEY PLAZA WITH a head scarf and waited in the shadow of the County Records Building, hands deep in the pockets of her winter coat. Commuter traffic plus engine exhaust filled the streets. Pedestrians hurried to work. Commerce had returned to normal, she recognized, even as her gaze fell upon the hundreds of bouquets, roses, flags, and photographs still covering the lawns of Dealey Plaza.

She reflected on the state funeral the day before and its cherished memories, like the images of two salutes—one at the bier by the towering Charles de Gaulle, in khaki, who had stood for France in its darkest hour, standing now with America in its darkest hour, and one by the president's son, turning three that very day, saluting his father's flag-draped caisson. How it hurt to think of the president's son and daughter, now fatherless. Elaine knew how it felt.

Sanders found her, then said, "Elaine, here's our man from Main Justice, Abe Summer."

Elaine smiled.

"Abe, please meet our newest and prettiest assistant, Elaine Navarro."

Elaine took it in stride. She understood the rarity of women among federal prosecutors, even more so of minority women. She regularly got introduced with compliments. It was part of the territory, part of the job, she felt. One man, she expected, was usually trying to tell another that if you're going to have to work with a "girl attorney," a phrase in locker-room use within the Justice Department, she might as well be good looking.

"Good to meet you," replied Abe. She felt a firm handshake. Abe looked her in the eye, something she appreciated.

"I wanted to begin here," Sanders continued, his breath rising in the cold, "to show you the scene of the crime."

Elaine saw Abe staring upward at the already infamous sixth-floor window across the street at the Texas School Book Depository, a seven-story warehouse overlooking Elm Street, the window now closed on the frigid morning, bathed in slanting sunlight.

"Yeah, that's the one—one floor below the top floor, the corner window on our right," Sanders said, pointing. "The motorcade came through downtown on Main, turned right onto Houston for this one short block behind us, then they made a sharp left, just here, onto Elm. The limousine was open—no top, heading down toward that Triple Underpass. Then the shots came. Three shots." Sanders turned to his left, then gestured west to the railroad works crossing above Elm, a one-way street headed that way. "The last and fatal bullet hit when he got a little more than halfway to the tunnel."

Sanders motioned to walk in that direction. "Oswald had been in the Marines—scored pretty good with a rifle. He worked in that warehouse, a schoolbook warehouse."

Staying on the left side, they walked two hundred feet down Elm, out of the shadow and into the sunlight, along a gentle S-curve. Park lawns graced both sides of the roadway. They drew up halfway to the Triple Underpass, the triple part referring to the three roadways, Elm, Main, and Commerce, in order of nearness to the Depository, funneling under the tracks.

"By about here," Sanders said, pointing to the center of Elm a few yards away, "both the president and Governor Connally had been shot in their backs." They walked another thirty steps. "And, then, right there in the middle lane, the president took the shot in the head. Fatal, no way he could've survived it."

Elaine forced herself to take a deep breath. A soul, a beloved soul, an important soul, recently departed here. She looked back at the sniper's window. She felt the chill of a gunman at his perch, his sights aimed at them. The horror remained fresh, palpable.

"Just inside that corner window," Sanders repeated, looking back as well, "is where they found the three spent cartridges, on the floor. Three shots. Three spent shells. The rifle close by on the same floor. The FBI's already traced it to an alias used by Oswald."

Sanders looked at his watch, then said, "We should be going up there. They're waiting for you." They retraced their steps to Houston Street. As they did, facing into the morning sun, Sanders pointed to their center-right, diagonally across Dealey Plaza, to the corner at Houston at Main. "By the way, that's the courthouse and jail across the street from the plaza. The Sheriff's keeping Oswald's cell a secret. But we know it's on the sixth floor."

Can Oswald, Elaine wondered, look out a cell window and see all this, see the scene of the crime, see even us, right now? As they walked, Elaine studied the jail windows on the sixth floor. At one stood a motionless silhouette of a solitary figure. She refused to cringe.

# 5    THE TEXAS SCHOOL BOOK DEPOSITORY

ELAINE HAD DRIVEN BY THE DEPOSITORY MANY TIMES BUT HAD never paid it much mind—except for the giant Hertz clock on its roof, which she'd regularly relied on while driving over the river to work. It spelled out the time in light bulbs. She'd known it simply as a rust-colored brick building, evidently built around the turn of the century, in Romanesque Revival style, resembling a giant cube, seven stories tall, as tall as it was long and wide, about one hundred feet per side. Along each side of its seven floors were windows, seven sets of double windows on the Elm side.

The building stood not on Elm Street, but on the Elm Street Extension, a short, easily missed stub of what used to be Elm as it came westward from downtown straight across Houston. The official Elm Street now curved left, as it crossed Houston and headed down to the Triple Underpass. In between the two Elms lay a narrow strip of parkland spreading ever wider as the official Elm Street curved down and away, the green ending at the Triple Underpass.

They met Captain Will Fritz waiting with the Depository's superintendent, Roy Truly, at its front door on the Elm Street Extension. Elaine welcomed the warmth of the small foyer, a simple room with nothing more than a pay phone, a public elevator running between the first four floors, and an open stairway to the next floor. After introductions, Sanders excused himself.

Truly led Fritz, Summer, and Elaine rearward to the shipping and receiving department, a large open area also on the first floor. The company, a private firm, sold textbooks used in the Texas schools and had occupied the building since January 1962. Oswald's job, he said, had been to take a written order from the first-floor shipping department, then to go up to the appropriate upper floor to fetch whatever was in the order. One of fourteen such "order fillers," Oswald specialized in filling orders for books published by Scott, Foresman & Company, many of whose works resided on the sixth floor.

Truly showed them the back entrances, along the rear walls of the shipping and receiving department. Large cargo doors opened onto loading docks. Outside and beyond the docks, many employees, he said, parked in the undeveloped acreage between the Depository and the rail yard and, out of convenience, used the rear entrances.

"This old place got built," Truly gestured toward the rail yard, "back when it meant something to have a warehouse right by a rail yard."

In the corner nearest the rail yard (the northwest corner), close by the shipping and receiving area, stood an old wooden stairwell connecting all seven floors, cramped, even claustrophobic. Hard by the stairwell rose and fell two freight elevators, side by side, also connecting all floors.

Truly took them up the wooden stairway, telling how on the twenty-second, right after the shots, he'd taken an officer that way. At the second-floor landing, Truly said, "The officer saw movement right through that little square window on the door to the lunchroom, so he went over into the lunchroom and found Oswald buying a coke out of the machine."

Truly led them through the lunchroom door. They saw an ordinary red-and-white Coca-Cola machine. Elaine imagined Oswald standing before it, inserting a coin, extracting a coke, prying off the cap. "When I caught up to him, I told the officer that Oswald worked here, so he let 'em go and we resumed flying up the stairs."

Let 'em go? Elaine asked herself.

The stairway creaking, they climbed single file all the way to the sixth floor. The sixth floor proved to be a single, large, open room studded with dozens of support columns. It housed many stacks of cartons of schoolbooks. Along all four walls, tall windows dropped to within eighteen inches of the floor. Sunlight slanted through front windows. The support columns and stacks of cartons cast cold dark shadows toward the center, shadows relieved only by illumination from a few bare electric lights.

Catching his breath, Truly remarked that it would not have seemed strange that stacks of boxes, several high, had been shoved together. They'd been moving boxes around as they reworked the floor. So, no one would've thought there was a sniper's nest hidden among the stacks of boxes over in the corner farthest from the stairway. Truly gestured and they headed for that corner.

As they approached it, Elaine felt the weight of history. She sensed Oswald walking the same way, breathing the same air, smelling the same brick and timbers, taking in the same scene, contemplating his plan.

It turned out to be nothing remarkable—just an ordinary warehouse corner with plank flooring and unfinished brick work for walls—except for one thing: a window that offered a grand view of what was now the most famous presidential parade route in history.

Fritz spoke up, "That's where we found the three hulls," pointing to the crude plank floor in the sniper's lair. "Oswald could lean back and hide inside the corner with its brick work, then lean forward to see everything—most of all, to lean through the window for better aim down Elm toward the underpass. Some boxes even got arranged by the window to steady his rifle."

Truly stepped in to raise the window, saying, "The window was part way up—like this," producing a half-open window.

A cool gust rushed in.

Elaine crouched where the sniper had crouched. She held and steadied herself on a pair of vertical pipes running from floor to ceiling. She imagined the scene, the sunny day, the motorcycle roar, the applause, the cheering, the limousine, the Kennedys, the Connallys, their smiles and waves, their approach along Houston, their left turn onto Elm—and Oswald, lurking in this very place, his eye locked on the target, tracking left to right, his finger poised against the trigger, his mind processing wait-versus-fire, his ears listening for intruders, his lungs drawing the shallowest of breaths, his neck feeling his pulse, his name hovering on the threshold of eternity.

Another chill blew in, so Truly closed the window.

"Over there," Fritz re-commenced, pointing into the shadows in the direction of the stairs, "is where we found the rifle."

They headed that way, the way they had come, Elaine again picturing Oswald scurrying there, sliding the rifle among yet more boxes as he fled. Fritz knelt by the place, near the stairwell. "Right in there."

"Prints?" Abe asked.

"Several over by the window on the boxes," Fritz answered, "Oswald's. But the rifle was wiped clean. An old print of Oswald's was between the barrel and the grip."

"Wiped clean, you say?" Abe asked.

"Yes, sir."

"Why would he even care," Elaine queried, "knowing that his fingerprints were everywhere else?"

"Very good question, young lady," Fritz replied.

"Did he go down the stairs or down an elevator?" Abe asked.

"Stairs, we think, based on where we found the rifle and where the elevator cars were found later," Fritz answered.

"Going down, he probably heard me and the officer," added Truly, "starting up these stairs, so he ducked into the second-floor lunchroom and pretended to want a coke. If we hadn't been coming up, he'd gone on down and run out the back."

"Surely he knew you'd find the rifle," declared Abe.

"Yeah, I suppose he knew we'd eventually trace it to him," Fritz's twang showed. "Hiding it might've given him just enough time to get out of town."

"Or out of the country," added Elaine, exchanging looks with Abe.

"Yeah—with all of thirteen dollars in his pocket," ended Fritz.

On their way out, Truly said, "Listen, at some point, you oughta talk to our Virgie Rachley. Works on the second floor. She was standing on the sidewalk right out there on Elm as the president came by and saw a spark come off the pavement behind the car when the first shot rang out, like maybe the bullet hit the road or something, meaning missed the car. No one's interviewed her yet."

"She's saying a United States Marine missed the entire car on the closest shot?" Fritz seemed incredulous. "But, yeah, okay, we'll talk to her."

## 6   A RARE MOMENT OF NATIONAL WILL

"Welcome to Dallas, Mr. Summer," smiled United States District Judge Sarah Hughes. Abe saw a small woman with a warm smile navigate around her desk to offer a handshake. He and Sanders had just walked up from the United States Attorney's Office at her invitation. "I hope you'll both watch Lyndon's address to Congress with me."

Her black-and-white Admiral television was on but turned down.

She offered seats, plush ones. Federal judges earned a fraction of what they could make as lawyers but, Abe realized, enjoyed spacious and sumptuous chambers. On her desk Abe saw an oversized porcelain cup with baked-in lettering "Texas Demitasse," filled with pencils, plus an empty shot glass.

Typescripts of marked-up orders fanned across her desk. Abe knew she'd have no role in the Oswald case and appreciated her courtesy in greeting him.

"The judge," Sanders began, "was the one who swore in LBJ on Air Force One."

"I heard you were here, Mr. Summer, and I just want you to know how glad we are that you are here," gesturing for all to sit. She proceeded to give him a lowdown on the key players, saying that Henry Wade excelled as a prosecutor. "You'll like working with him." Wade's assistant, Bill Alexander, by contrast, was "a bulldog," she cautioned.

"I'm here for the duration," Abe said. "I'll help them any way they'll let me. Compliments of the attorney general."

They turned down an offer of coffee. The air in her office smelled fresh, even floral. No ashtrays were deployed.

Judge Joe Brown was keeping the Oswald case for himself, she went on. That "bothered" her as well as the civic leadership in Dallas. "We want a conviction that'll hold up on appeal." To show the world that Dallas remained a responsible city, not a circus, they wanted a judge up to the challenge. Brown, unfortunately, had a flair for "showboating." "He'd turned that Candy Barr trial into a spectacle," she said. Henry Wade, she added, had even told Brown to his face that the Oswald case "is too big for you."

Abe soaked it up in respectful silence.

"This whole thing's been so awful." The judge's face lost its vim.

"You know," Sanders confided, "we told 'em not to come here." Sanders fiddled with an unlit cigar. "I was with Lyndon and Lady Bird back in the '60 campaign when they tried to walk from your hotel, Abe, the Baker, over to the Adolphus. We had to wade through a vicious crowd of right-wingers—all women too, some in mink coats. They were crazed, absolutely crazed. One of 'em smashed Lyndon with a sign on a stick—tried to beat him. Lady Bird was terrorized.'"

Abe saw an inscribed photograph of JFK on the wall.

"Don't forget October," the judge added.

"Exactly, just two months ago, it got worse. Adlai came to town to talk about the United Nations but got roughed up—they even spit on him. So the mood was bad here. I worried myself sick over what they might try on

Kennedy. I advised the White House to take Dallas off the list. But it was already set. The president insisted on coming, specifically to Dallas."

"Why?" inquired Abe.

"Texas politics. The election. We were sure to lose the rest of the South on account of the Civil Rights Bill. We needed Texas. Our Senator Yarborough—he was at war with LBJ and Connally, hurting the party. So Kennedy came down to patch things up, to work on Texas for '64. If he'd left Dallas out, it would've looked bad."

"How, Judge, do you think, this new commission will affect things?" Sanders changed the subject.

"It'll," she said, "just put on more pressure for a quick trial. Here's the thing," she leaned in, "Earl Warren won't release any report that'll prejudge the verdict on Oswald. He'll wait 'til the verdict's in. But the other thing is Lyndon—you know Lyndon."

"It's about to start," the judge interrupted herself.

She leaned over to the admiral and turned up the volume.

"I was about to say Lyndon wants a verdict and that report, all before the convention. So I expect everything will roll right along. Now, let's watch."

Lyndon Baines Johnson, the new president, stood before a joint session of Congress. Wearing a face graven in sorrow, he slowly said, "All I have I would have given gladly not to be standing here today." He pledged to carry on the policies of the late president. With genuine passion and determination, Abe thought, he emphasized that the best way for America to remember President Kennedy was to enact his Civil Rights Bill. It had been languishing before Congress since the summer, the victim of conservative and diehard segregationist resistance. Thunderous applause greeted this clarion call. Thunderous. Sustained. A rare moment of national will. The judge glanced at her guests during the ovation.

It was November 27, 1963, the day before Thanksgiving.

Abe figured they all felt the same thing. In a molten moment in history, America seemed—very possibly but very possibly not—at the edge of a galactic shift, all hanging on whether Congress would—or would not—approve the most sweeping civil rights reform since Reconstruction. Johnson was calling for its passage as a remembrance of the fallen president.

At the end, the judge leaned to the set, turned it off, then quietly said, "If the Civil Rights Bill ever becomes law, my friends, an entire way of everyday life in America, day in, day out, will go by the boards. Segregation will vanish. Like in the movie, it'll be gone with the wind."

The two men nodded.

She ended the moment.

"Where will Mr. Summer have offices?"

"He's got two," Sanders answered. "We got one for him with us here but the FBI's got even more space waiting for him over in their building, an entire new floor just for the Oswald work."

"Now," she dropped her voice, "let me talk with you both confidentially. I had a girl-to-girl talk yesterday with Elaine, your new deputy, Mr. Summer. I explained to her this new assignment might seem like a back-stage chore but it would, in my judgment, wind up being the most important case of her career. That thought had already taken hold of her. She's very keen to do her god-awful best. She's got real talent, I tell you. I've seen how well she works up her cases in my court. Now, Mr. Summer, I must say this to you—Elaine will work herself to death if you let her. So please don't let her—take care of that young woman."

"I promise," said Abe, feeling immediately he'd sounded too casual.

"Elaine," the judge went on, "got the same crap I got in law school— teachers telling her that she was just taking up a slot meant for a breadwinner. So strike one is being a woman. Strike two is being Tejano. She puts in the extra effort to prove them wrong."

Abe replied deliberately this time, "I appreciate your telling me this."

A secretary interrupted to tell the judge she had a hearing to attend, so they all stood.

"Sanders," the judge clasped his arm, "you and I go back a long way, so hear me on this."

"I'm holding onto my wallet."

"Sanders, listen, I'm serious now. When you introduce a lady lawyer— do me a favor—there are so few of us, you know—tell how good they are instead of how cute they are."

"Yes, ma'am."

"They can already see how cute they are."

"Yes, ma'am."

"You know, Mr. Summer, I'm the reason Sanders hired Elaine. They all knew I needed another woman in the courthouse."

"It's an honor to meet you, Judge."

"Thank you both for visiting. Mr. Summer come by here any Friday afternoon and join us for some adult refreshments. Bring this old cuss with you. Elaine too. She's close to Jesus," the judge beamed, "but not quite a choir girl."

# 7 VOLVEREMOS

THAT EVENING, BEBE BOUDREAUX ORDERED HER OWN ADULT refreshment, Ballentine's over ice, saying it had been JFK's favorite. "Likewise," Abe added, "without."

A model with bare shoulders and a fur-lined corset circulated among the tables with a tray strapped to her tiny waist selling Winstons, Marlboros, Chesterfields, Camels, Newports, Tareytons, and Lucky Strikes. Reporters and camera crews filled the room, smoked, and laughed. Raucous Texas howls split the air. Bebe drank much but smoked little. She hated the way it made her clothes smell—like ashtrays.

Bebe had driven from New Orleans, then checked into the Adolphus Hotel on Monday afternoon. Mirroring the style of Louis XIV, the landmark exuded elegance, mansard roof and all. She'd heard Abe was in town and called him to meet for a drink.

"Very good to see you, Bebe," Abe raised his glass.

"Next year in Havana," she replied, raising hers in mock salute to the toast making the rounds.

She savored the first sip, a fervid streak down her throat.

"Which reminds me, Abe, you need one of these." She extracted a red-and-white bumper sticker that blared "Volveremos!"

"Just like General MacArthur," she grinned, "the exiles all have them."

"Gracias."

The cold slick of the frozen glass relaxed her. She luxuriated in the moment—here she was covering the case of the century and making shop talk in an upscale bar in the best hotel in Texas.

"You know, Abe, the whole exile thing was already our front-page story, virtually every day, but now, with Oswald and the assassination, it's boiling over down there."

He lifted his hand, like he already knew.

"Get this," she continued, "just a few weeks back WDSU put Oswald on the air to debate some Cuban, a guy he had a fight with, a fistfight on Canal Street."

Abe yielded polite wonderment.

"I heard the debate myself," she added. "Now, think about that, Abe, New Orleans heard a presidential assassin on the air."

"Who won?" Abe asked.

"You know, in a way, he did. He stayed surprisingly composed, even polite."

"What we're asking in New Orleans," she resumed, "is why Oswald came there—just up and left Dallas. He didn't have a job or place to land in New Orleans. He just picked up, then took his chances. Last Spring. Why would someone do that?"

She took a drink, only half expecting an answer. She knew Abe wouldn't say much, at least in public.

"Listen, Abe, just before coming here, I went by his dump on Magazine Street," she said. "You know how we got those double shotgun houses, long and narrow, like side-by-side barrels on a shotgun? Well, his little part was just one-half of one side. Narrow to begin with and he had only half of the half, in the rear. You entered through a side screen porch, stuck on like a sidecar."

"Plus a wife and kid," added Abe. "Cramped."

"Here's what I think," she revived her own question, "Oswald went there to make headlines as a Fidelista, to earn his stripes to get into Cuba. He *wanted* to get into that fistfight with an exile. It'd look good in his portfolio—help him get into Cuba. We got way more exiles per square foot than Dallas, so New Orleans was the place for him."

The cigarette woman glided by again.

"And you, Abe, what are you doing here?"

"This is a state prosecution, Bebe, but they'll need our help on some federal things, so I'm here to help, not to try the case."

"They should let you try this case, just like they should've had you on the Marcello case."

"No need. I'm happy in the background."

Leaning in closer, she changed the subject, "'The City of Hate'—that's the line about this town. It's ironic, don't you think," she half whispered, "that in a place so overrun by right-wingers, it'd turn out to be a communist that killed the most liberal president in history."

"Hard to figure," said Abe.

"But I hear Percy Foreman will come in and, listen, he's no commie," she leaned back. "I've seen him too."

"Yeah. He's very good," Abe added, "Hundreds of death cases. Puts the police on trial. His clients almost never testify. I'm surprised Oswald had the good sense to hire him."

"Are the communists paying his fees?" Bebe wondered aloud.

"Why don't you get an interview and ask?" Abe cocked his head. "I'd like to know too."

"I plan to," she replied. "Now, here's another thing I don't get, Abe."

She glanced about.

"Where in hell was Oswald headed when he killed that officer? He had so little money on him. Thirteen dollars, they say. He was just wandering along a residential street over in Oak Cliff. How the hell was he planning to get away?"

A middle-aged man wearing a dark shiny suit with horn-rimmed glasses walked toward them.

"I've seen this guy before," Bebe whispered.

Jack Ruby pulled over a chair and barged in. Ruby, she saw, was brawny with medium height, jowls, a strong nose, and slick receding dark hair.

"Well, allow me." He shook Abe's hand. Turning to Bebe, he smiled, "I'm Jack Ruby. I run the Carousel Club over on Commerce Street. Have we met before?"

Bebe smelled Vitalis.

"Not really, but please join us. I'm Barbara Boudreaux, Bebe for short. I write for the *Time-Picayune*. This is my friend Abe."

"A pleasure, Miss Boudreaux."

They remained seated. Ruby seemed impressed. Bebe, she knew, had East Coast good looks. Bebe could read a man and tell how she rated.

"I just wanted to invite you both to have a free drink on me," said Ruby. He handed each a card.

"Business must be good right now," Abe gave him an opening.

"Well, this is a Baptist town. You know them. They come with the Ten Commandments and a ten-dollar bill and they don't break either of them."

All three laughed.

"That's not what I hear," one-upped Bebe. "Anywhere you find four Baptists, you'll find a fifth."

When Ruby laughed, the cleft in his chin seemed to laugh as well. His eyes, Bebe saw, were small but burned with intensity.

"The trial," said Ruby, "actually has brought good people like Miss Boudreaux from all over. Look at this place. Packed. So, yeah, business is good. By the way, we got a class magician tonight. Plus our classy chassis. Starts at eight."

Ruby stared down at the "Volveremos!" bumper sticker.

"I gotta have one of those."

"I'll bring you one," replied Bebe.

Ruby beamed graciously.

"So, Mr. Ruby, what do you think about this trial?" she asked.

Ruby straightened his diamond cufflinks.

"He's guilty as hell and will burn in hell. Someone should've saved us all the trouble." His cheeks flushed, then his hands fiddled with his stack of free-drink cards.

"You should give Foreman one of those," Bebe advised. "Surely, he needs a drink."

"Percy's tried a few cases here and been a good friend of mine but now he needs a swift kick in the pants," Ruby made a fist.

Shifting, Ruby asked, "Perhaps one of you remember that benefit I did last year? I'm thinking of doing one for the widow of Officer Tippit. Whatta you think?"

"A very fine idea," Abe offered.

Bebe wondered how the widow herself would take the idea—strippers laying all bare for the fallen officer.

"Would you please bring our beautiful Miss Boudreaux?"

Abe yielded an ambiguous smile.

A pause developed, one a little too long. Ruby seemed to know it was time to leave. Nodding at the cards, he announced again, "Hey, remember, the first drink's on me. So pleased to meet a class act like you, Miss Boudreaux." He rose, bowed slightly to Bebe, revealing his diamond stickpin, and stepped away. Bebe raised her glass to Ruby as he departed.

"'Will burn in hell,'" Bebe mused, "Now, let's save that for the final headline."

## 8 PERCY FOREMAN

"Testing, testing, one, two, three," Attorney Karen Eisenstadt pretended to address secret listening devices buried in the walls as she and Percy Foreman waited in the interview room at the county jail. Karen was Percy's young assistant, a recent law graduate. Oswald entered as she mugged. He caught her humor and produced a half grin. He would warm to her sarcasm and cynicism. All shook hands, then got down to business. It was the morning of Wednesday, December 4.

Karen became surprised by Foreman's method. Instead of beginning by asking Oswald whether he did it or not, Foreman leaned into Oswald to say, "Lee, I need to say something right up front. We're going to go through everything—eventually. But we gotta do it my way. Please. My way's this. We'll start at the beginning. I'll ask you questions and we'll take a lot of notes. So that's one part. We'll eventually get to what happened on November 22 but it'll take a while. Not so pronto. Along the way we'll be telling you items of evidence against us as we learn them. When we tell you about particular evidence, it's best if you just listen—don't try to explain it right away. Not so pronto. Think about it, day after day. You need to focus on all the evidence, think about it, and eventually explain it when we get to that part of the story. Trust me on this. This is the best way."

Oswald clasped his hands around a thin plastic cone of a jailhouse coffee.

"Let's start with your childhood."

"The shits." Lee wiped his nose on his sleeve, then frowned. Karen could tell that Foreman disliked Oswald's affect. Foreman let it pass.

"Okay, let's go step by step. Who was your father?"

Karen saw Oswald glare.

"Died before I was born."

Your brothers?

"Robert. And a half brother, John."

"Sisters?"

"No."

"Mother?"

"Marguerite, certifiable." Oswald raised his eyebrows, widened his eyes, causing some pain from his injuries, then shook his head in commiseration with himself.

"Her line of work?"

"Supposedly a nurse. Fired from almost every job. God help those patients."

"Where'd you grow up?"

"New Orleans. Dallas. New York. An orphanage. She couldn't afford kids, so we got unloaded on an orphanage."

Lee looked at Karen. Fluid wet his swollen eye.

"Where was that?" asked Foreman, handing him his handkerchief.

"New Orleans."

"How long did you stay in the orphanage?"

"Two years, during the war."

He finished off his coffee, crumpled the thin plastic, then tossed it in the corner.

It went on like this. Sometimes, Oswald opened up, sometimes offered poignant memories, but usually just had smart-ass commentary.

From Lee and mainly Robert, his older brother, counsel, but mainly Karen, eventually pieced together his life, a story stamped with failure.

Oswald was born on October 18, 1939, in New Orleans. His father died two months before he was born. His mother, unable to cope, a cantankerous, controlling type, had more than a dozen jobs and was fired from half of them. The day after Christmas 1942, Marguerite placed Lee into the Bethlehem Children's Home where his brother and half brother already lived. This was not rare. The Depression had forced many parents to place children in orphanages (or with relatives). The orphanage made them eat everything on their plates, a rule that irritated Lee. In early 1944, Marguerite checked them out, then moved from New Orleans to Dallas, where she married someone but then constantly fought with him. Lee, however, loved the man. He was as close to a father figure as Lee would ever have. Marguerite moved in and out of her husband's house. In January 1948, they filed for divorce. Lee refused to testify at the trial, saying he would not know the truth from a lie. His brothers left home.

In 1952, Marguerite and Lee moved to New York City. The Rosenberg prosecution loomed large in Manhattan. Young Lee thought they were being railroaded into the death chamber merely because they were communists, not because they were actually spies. By then a young teenager, Lee threatened a relative with a knife, even punched his mother in the face. In public school, he missed most days of class, and when he did attend, became disruptive. After truancy hearings, Lee was remanded to Youth House for three weeks of psychiatric evaluation. He tested above average on intelligence, reading and math. But he remained a loner. When asked if he preferred boys versus girls, he said, "I dislike everybody." Rather than diagnose him as mentally ill (which would have meant mandatory institutionalization), Youth House placed him "on probation under guidance." Lee returned to regular school. There, he refused to salute the flag during the pledge of allegiance and continued to skip many classes. He refused help from teachers, saying he didn't need any help. Finally, a judge ordered that Lee be placed in a home for disturbed boys with mandatory psychiatric care.

So, in 1954, to avoid the placement, they fled back to New Orleans where Lee continued in his truculent ways. He attended classes at Beauregard Junior High School, then Warren Easton High School, both in New Orleans, and finally Arlington Heights High School in Fort Worth (after yet another move). He gravitated toward guns, reading, history, and communism. Curiously, despite his fascination with communism, Lee hoped to drop out of school to join the Marines, as his brother Robert had done. When he turned seventeen, he did just that.

A fresh start, the Marines. That was 1956, seven years before Dealey Plaza. As a Marine, Lee learned to shoot. He tested twice, qualifying once as a marksman, once as a sharpshooter, but never as an expert, the highest category. In the Marines, he taught himself some Russian. But Lee suffered from discipline problems and insubordination. He disliked the service. He applied for and obtained an early discharge based on a supposed hardship need to assist his mother.

But promptly upon early discharge, rather than assisting his mother, Lee went to Russia. If it was not defection, it was very close to one. There, the Soviets assigned him a job and a decent apartment. He married a pretty Russian named Marina. But soon Oswald grew tired of the Soviet regime, so with the consent of the State Department, he returned to America in 1962 with Marina and an infant child. He half expected to be received as a celebrity, then groused when no one took notice of his return.

After living a while with Robert in Fort Worth, Lee settled his young family in a cheap flat in Oak Cliff, just across the Trinity River from Dealey Plaza. Lee found only sporadic employment, the most meaningful as a trainee in a commercial photo darkroom in downtown Dallas, Jaggers-Chiles-Stovall. But he was fired from that job at the end of March 1963. Within a few weeks, the Oswalds moved to New Orleans, him first and then his family. There, he succeeded only in making a splash as a Fidelista, handing out leaflets for an outfit called Fair Play for Cuba Committee.

Oswald yearned to get into Cuba, so in September 1963, after only five months in New Orleans, he sent his family back to Texas, then got himself to Mexico City, where he sought a visa to enter Cuba. But the Cuban consulate in Mexico City denied the visa, another aching failure. He returned to Dallas in October 1963, broke and frustrated. By then, his marriage also had failed. He and Marina lived separately. She stayed in a Dallas suburb called Irving with a woman friend while he rented a room in Oak Cliff. He got a menial job in a warehouse, the Texas School Book Depository—a warehouse that overlooked what turned out to be a presidential parade route.

Lee reflected, "It's always better to take advantage of your chances as they come along," but Karen couldn't see any chance taken that had worked out for him. His brother, Robert, confided to her that Lee had a pattern in life, a pattern of trying at something, failing, and then doubling down on something bigger, failing at that, then doubling down again, and so on. Once in a tender moment, she imagined aloud to Lee that when "all of this was over," he might go back to school. Lee replied, "I don't need to go back to school. I already know everything."

 ## 9   JUST AS ADVERTISED

"Bob," Bebe asked, "how'd a young guy like you get to cover this case?" Her bench mate Bob Schieffer worked for the *Star Telegram* in Fort Worth. She was making small talk while they waited for court to start.

"Amazing luck, I guess," he toyed with his snap brim hat, "I was home asleep when the assassination happened, having been up late with some Secret Service agents at a bar. My brother woke me and said I'd better get to work because the president had been shot. I got to the newsroom—and let me tell you—pure pandemonium. A phone rang and I happened to answer. A woman asked if we'd give her a ride to Dallas. I said something like, 'Lady, this is not a taxi company and anyway the president has been killed.' The woman said she knew that but they were saying that her son had done it.

My jaw dropped. So me and another guy rushed out to her address, then drove Mrs. Oswald all the way to the police station in Dallas, talking with her all the way. A lucky scoop. So my paper let me stay on the case."

The judge entered. All rose and hushed.

"Please be seated," the judge said, then asked the clerk to call the case.

Almost simultaneously, a corner door aft of the bench opened where Oswald and three deputies entered. His ankles shackled and his wrists uncuffed, he wore striped jail clothes.

Counsel rose to make their appearances. A larger-than-life character in a perfect, dark-blue, pinstriped suit with a white shirt, gold cufflinks, and red tie, stepped forward.

"Percy Foreman for the defense, Your Honor. Good morning."

"Mr. Foreman, welcome back to Dallas."

"Thank you, Your Honor."

Through the packed courtroom, Bebe saw Abe in the front row, seated as a member of the public.

"How can I help the lawyers this morning?" the judge asked.

Alexander wormed his way forward, but Foreman kept the floor. "Your Honor, may I please raise three items? One, we need to schedule a bail hearing. Two, we need to schedule a motion to change venue. Three, we need to schedule a motion to suppress in-custody interview statements taken without counsel present."

"Mr. Alexander?"

"Good morning, Judge. Well, for our part, we want a prompt trial setting for jury selection. This is a capital case. It'll take two weeks to select the twelve. We ought to begin soon."

"What," the judge asked, "about bail, venue and—what was it? Suppression?"

"Bail? Come on, Judge, this is an exceedingly important capital case. It'd be unthinkable to grant bail. This man fled to the Soviets, then fled to Mexico, then tried to flee to Cuba, by our information. As for venue, it's simple. We ought to stay right here and try to pick the twelve, soon. If, after trying, you think we can't find twelve fair-minded jurors in Dallas County, then okay, we'll stipulate to transfer. But we ought to test the water here first."

"The interview statements?"

"We don't plan to use them."

"Mr. Foreman?"

"Plans can change. We want a firm order of exclusion. It's clear-cut under Texas law."

"Your Honor," Wade intervened, "we may be able to reach a stipulation on this. I recommend we pass on it for now." Wade evidently realized, as Bebe read the situation, that his position on the interviews, conducted despite a request for counsel, was weak, so he wanted time to work a trade. In the jailhouse interviews, Will Fritz hadn't extracted a confession, but she figured he'd heard a lot of provable lies.

"But on bail, isn't Mr. Foreman at least entitled to a hearing?"

By Foreman's side, Oswald stared at the judge, motionless, expressionless.

"Technically, maybe," Wade continued to preempt Alexander, "but, really, it would be nothing more than a fishing expedition to find out what we have."

No doubt true but it'd be a good thing too for a hungry press, Bebe thought, but even as she thought it, Foreman replied, "Bail is guaranteed by the Eighth Amendment, Your Honor."

"All right. The bail hearing will be next Monday, the sixteenth, at nine. We will also then hear the motion to suppress the interview statements.

"We'll get to the other motions in due course." The judge studied the red-and-black calendars on the wall to his right. "Jury selection will begin on Monday, February 24, at 8:30 a.m. We'll start the trial the morning after the last juror is sworn—unless a change of venue is granted first."

"Your Honor, thank you—now, one last item, if I may?"

"Yes, Mr. Foreman."

"Earlier this year, the United States Supreme Court handed down a decision by the name of *Brady v. Maryland*. That decision reversed a state conviction because the prosecution had possessed exculpatory evidence, meaning, of course, evidence helpful to the accused, but had failed to turn it over. Put differently, the decision made clear that prosecutors have a duty to disclose to the defense all exculpatory evidence in their possession—even without a court order. We need to have a discussion about how that will work in this case, especially since this is a large, large case. The files of the prosecutor must be very full—all the more since we understand the FBI and Justice Department from Washington are in the background supplying evidence to the prosecutors in this case. We all want, in other words, to make sure the rights of the accused under the *Brady* decision are honored."

"Mr. Alexander?" The judge seemed unfamiliar with the problem.

"There's no exculpatory information. As you'll see at the bail hearing, the evidence of guilt is overwhelming."

"Mr. Foreman?"

"Well, for example, what if an eyewitness gives a positive identification at trial but said at a show-up earlier that he could not be positive and that was recorded in a police memo? *Brady* would require that memo to be turned over."

"It wouldn't be exculpatory," interjected Alexander, "only impeachment."

"Anything that impeaches evidence of guilt is by definition exculpatory," replied Foreman.

Alexander had no reply at the ready, so he kept mute, eyes squinting, face twitching. Reporters scribbled. Sketch artists fixated on the scene, drawing, as the journals would publish, thin lines to mimic Alexander's squints.

"Here's another thing," added Foreman, "The description they gave of the assassin over the police radio was 165 pounds and about thirty. Lee Oswald weighs 140 pounds and is twenty-four. Descriptions like that have to be turned over to the defense."

"For now, here's the deal," the judge fidgeted and bought time. "Give me some briefs on this *Brady* case before the next hearing. We'll take it up again then. For now, this hearing is over."

Foreman was very good, Bebe thought, just as advertised.

# 10  AGENT JIM HOSTY

"OKAY, JIM," BEGAN ABE LATER THE SAME DAY, "HOW'D YOU GET involved with Oswald?" It turned out that the FBI had indeed known about Oswald and had taken no precautions. Abe wanted to find out why.

"Last year."

Abe saw Elaine begin a new sheet of notes. The three huddled around a makeshift conference table on the newly acquired seventh floor of the Santa Fe Building, the home of the FBI in Dallas.

"Tell us the story."

"Sure," Jim answered, "Oswald had been in the Marines, so we needed to evaluate the extent to which his defection, so to speak, posed a national security risk. One of our Dallas agents, John Fain, did all that work. That was about 1959. I wasn't involved yet. Oswald lived here before going to the U.S.S.R. In 1962, he came back—with a wife from Russia. He wound up in Dallas again. A new question arose whether or not he was a spy. Fain tried to interview Oswald, but he was a smart-ass—just refused to cooperate."

Why, Abe wondered, hadn't the FBI seen him as a potential threat, just as columnist Drew Pearson was already wondering in his nationally syndicated column?

Jim continued, "A few weeks later, though, Fain tried again. This time Oswald was polite, calm—answered everything—a totally different person. He basically said that when he was in Russia, he came to see its flaws, that he'd given up on communism, and that his only goal in life now was to work hard to support his young family. Seemed reasonable. Fain heard what he needed to hear, then retired from the Bureau."

Although the director forbade agents to drink coffee on the job, Abe had put a hotplate in a corner, so he invited Jim to pour himself some anyway, offering a throwaway, thin, white plastic cone wedged into a mud-colored plastic holder. Jim took it.

"So, Jim, how'd you get on the case?"

"When they came back from Russia, and then here, Dallas, I raised the question of whether Marina, his wife, was a sleeper agent. So I opened her file and later on inherited his file."

"How'd Oswald get reopened?"

"We found out that Oswald had a subscription to *The Worker*. This contradicted his statement to Fain that he was no longer a communist. So I proposed to reopen his file. My boss said okay. I went out to find their place several times in Dallas but by then they had moved to New Orleans."

"When was that?"

"Just this last June. They'd moved to New Orleans around the end of April, early May, but I didn't learn that until June. So, under Bureau rules, the Oswalds became the problem of the New Orleans office, not ours. Our files on both got sent to New Orleans."

"Why'd they move?"

Jim took a good swallow of coffee.

"He lost his job in Dallas, my guess, so maybe he thought he'd do better in New Orleans."

"What's the New Orleans story?"

"He stayed there five months. Oswald got a job and flat there but spent most of his time on something called the Fair Play for Cuba Committee. In August, he was handing out propaganda on Canal Street and got into a fistfight. Then near the end of September, a lady with Texas plates, who turned out to be named Ruth Paine, came to pick up Marina and their baby girl. Oswald himself slipped away the next day or so."

"Where'd he go?"

"Mexico City. In late October, someone at INS told me Oswald had been in Mexico City and now was back maybe in Dallas. That was news to me, so I sent an Airtel to Washington and New Orleans, repeating what I'd heard. I asked to reopen our investigation in Dallas."

"Did you get the files back?"

"New Orleans sent me Ruth Paine's address out in Irving but wouldn't send me back the files until I confirmed that the Oswalds were actually back here. So I drove out to her residence in Irving, saw a station wagon at that address with Texas plates, asked a neighbor if Ruth Paine lived there. She said yes, adding that a Russian woman was there too with a little girl.

She said no man lived in the house. So I figured we had located Marina."

"Then what?"

"On Friday, November 1, three weeks before the assassination, I dropped by the Paine residence in Irving. Oswald wasn't there. Marina spoke very little English. Ruth had to translate."

"Did you try again?"

"Yes, on the eighth, the next Friday. Again, Oswald absent. I talked to Ruth for a few minutes. I learned later that on that occasion, Marina had slipped out of the house to write down my license plate number—that's how it wound up in Oswald's address book. I only talked to Ruth that day. Meanwhile, I had to cool it until New Orleans sent the files. I wanted to interview Oswald."

"So, prior to November 22, did you actually talk to Oswald?"

"Only to Marina."

"Why not Lee?"

"I wish I had. Maybe I could've caught it all in time."

Jim fiddled with his empty cup.

"I got that cross to bear," Jim completed his thought. "The director has already written me that my work was 'grossly inadequate.' But, honestly, I viewed Oswald only as an espionage threat, not as a violent threat to the president or anyone else. There was no record of violence. We had no way to know about the guns."

Abe could tell that Jim wanted to help, evidently preferring working on Oswald over everything else on his plate.

"Let's go back to Mexico City," Abe asked, "What specifically happened there?"

"Oswald was trying to get a visa to get into Cuba. That's why he went to the Cuban consulate. You can't get one in our country anymore. We kicked all the Cuban diplomats out."

"And the Soviet Embassy?"

"Maybe he thought they could help with the Cubans."

"Didn't he deny going to Mexico City in his police interviews?" Elaine asked, twirling her hair behind her ear with her left hand, her right poised with pencil.

"Yeah, he denied it," replied Jim, "but we know he did."

Afterwards, Abe called FBI Special Agent in Charge Gordon Shanklin to ask that Jim be assigned full-time to the Oswald case. Shanklin, after a pause, said okay.

# 11  RUTH PAINE

OUT IN IRVING, RUTH PAINE OPENED HER DOOR AND OFFERED a cautious smile, a toddler holding her skirt. Tall with short brown hair, Ruth appeared more care-worn than a woman in her early thirties. Ruth showed them in and offered a plate of cookies. She offered Elaine, Jim, and Abe seats. She'd separated from her husband, she said, but he'd moved back into their home for the duration to give support, though he was then at work. An infant slept in a crib. Marina and her children, she went on, now lived in federal protective custody elsewhere. Almost instantly, Elaine swelled with sympathy for Ruth.

How, Abe asked, had Ruth met the Oswalds?

When the Oswalds arrived from Russia in 1962, Ruth explained, they came to Fort Worth, then Dallas, where she met them in early 1963. A Quaker, Ruth prayed for world peace and understanding. She'd studied Russian and had taken a liking to Marina, who spoke only Russian. Ruth saw Marina as a "way to learn the language and culture." The two became friends. Over time, Ruth didn't much like Lee. She saw him as "surly and unresponsive" to Marina's needs. Marina liked to cook but Lee complained about the food. In turn, Marina complained to him about sex, even his manhood. They "argued a lot." In happier moments, Marina sometimes called him "Alek." In May 1963, when the Oswalds moved to New Orleans, Ruth drove the family there to the shabby flat that Lee had gone and found. She hated leaving Marina with no one who spoke Russian other than Lee. Similarly, when the Oswalds left New Orleans in late September 1963, Ruth picked up a pregnant Marina and young child from the same slum to take them back to live with her in Irving.

To be precise, she added, they packed up her station wagon on Sunday, September 22, then left for Dallas on Monday, the twenty-third, "both simmering, listless, oven-like days in New Orleans." Ruth rejoiced, she said, in rescuing Marina.

By mid-October, she said, Lee had returned to Dallas and re-connected with his family. For Marina's sake, Ruth helped him get a job at the Texas School Book Depository in October 1963. A neighbor of Ruth's, a sister of Buell Wesley Frazier, who already worked there, suggested it to her. So Ruth phoned the superintendent out of the blue and got Lee a job interview—"an act of kindness" she would "forever regret." Oswald found a room in Oak Cliff, she added, but made conjugal visits to Irving almost every weekend from mid-October to early November. Frazier gave Oswald rides to Irving on those Friday afternoons, then returned him to work in Dallas on those Monday mornings.

The infant rustled.

Glancing at the crib, Ruth recalled Jim's investigative visits. "It really scared Marina, your interrogations," Ruth turned to Jim, "like the KGB or something." She asked Jim, "Did that possibly have anything to do with it? The assassination, I mean?"

Elaine had wondered the same thing.

Jim found nothing to say.

Ruth confirmed, as Elaine had read in the reports, that on the afternoon of the twenty-second, they had been following television reports about the assassination when the police came. Marina tried to show them that Lee's rifle remained in the garage. But the blanket in which she thought it was wrapped fell limp. Marina's face drained white in horror, Ruth said.

"Could we see where that happened?" Jim asked.

They went into the garage via the kitchen and threaded through stacks of storage, reorganized since the police seizures. Ruth opened the garage door to let in the light. She showed them the corner by the garage door where Marina had tried to find Lee's rifle. Ruth also pointed out the ceiling lamp in the garage with its switch location. On the night of the twenty-first, she'd gone into the garage to do some artwork to find that someone had left it on.

Elaine now figured Oswald had broken down his rifle in the garage, wrapped its pieces up with paper as a bundle, and, preoccupied with the enormity of what he was planning, accidentally left the light on.

"By the way," Ruth became insistent, "that photograph of him with the guns that the police found here in the garage, I had no idea. I tried to respect their privacy, so I never went through their things. I knew nothing about any guns or photos of guns."

"You mean the photo he says we forged and planted here," smiled Jim.

"Perhaps on one of your visits," Ruth punctuated her sentence with a soft laugh.

They gravitated to the front yard. Ruth pointed out the Frazier house. The interview memos, Elaine knew, said that Oswald had asked Frazier if he could have a ride to Irving that Thursday, the twenty-first, rather than on the usual Friday, and that Frazier had obliged. Oswald had told him he needed to pick up some curtain rods in Irving for his boarding room in Oak Cliff, evidently preparing his explanation to Frazier for the long package he expected to carry to work on Friday. Yes, Ruth confirmed, Oswald showed up unannounced on that Thursday evening, the twenty-first. She'd heard nothing about curtain rods, however.

"One other thing—Marina showed me $170—Lee left it for her, his last morning here."

# 12 THE BAIL HEARING

IN CRIMINAL CASES, BEBE HAD OBSERVED ON HER BEAT, THE traditional way in which an accused learned of the evidence against him was to stand trial, then observe the evidence come in, one item at a time. Each prosecution witness could be confronted through cross-examination, one by one. After the state's evidence, the accused had the option to put on a defense. That, in sum, constituted due process. Slowly, however, the law was creeping, Bebe realized, in the direction of giving defense counsel a peek in advance at the prosecution's case so that defense counsel could better prepare to meet it. To take one important example, police memoranda summarizing witness interviews remained secret unless a testifying witness admitted on the stand to having used one to refresh his or her memory, a rare occurrence. So defense counsel found other ways to steal a peek.

One way, as Bebe had seen before, was a bail hearing. Even in a murder case, a judge could, in theory, grant pretrial release on bail. So, when bail was requested, an investigating agent or assistant prosecutor testified to a summary of the case or at least as much of it as would show a likelihood of conviction and, thus, a high degree of risk of flight or danger to the public were the accused freed on bail. In the Oswald case, moreover, the prosecution, Bebe figured, wanted to publicize the strength of its case, all to show the world that the police in Dallas rated as first-class professionals—all in mitigation of their failure to protect the president. The bail hearing, Bebe would report, amounted to a preview of the case against Oswald.

The judge entered. Assistant District Attorney Bill Alexander took the oath and the stand. Wade examined. Alexander methodically described the evidence, often using "we" or the passive voice to avoid specifying who the exact witnesses would be. For a bail hearing, it was not necessary to call the actual witness. The second-hand report by Alexander sufficed.

Alexander testified to the now familiar points: There were three rifle shots. As the president rode in an open-top car past the Texas School Book Depository, two bullets hit him. He died by 1 p.m. Lee Harvey Oswald, employed at the Depository, had routine access to the sixth floor—indeed, had been seen on the sixth floor shortly before the shooting. Police found a sniper's nest at the window nearest the southeast corner on that floor, the corner nearest Houston at Elm Streets, the lower half of the window partially raised. The sniper had a clear shot at the limousine all the way along Elm to the Triple Underpass except for a few seconds when foliage of an intervening oak interrupted the view. Three spent cartridges lay on the plank floor under the window. Police found the rifle on the sixth floor, stuffed between boxes near the opposite corner, with a live round, loaded in its chamber. The rifle was a bolt-action, clip-fed, 6.5mm Italian Mannlicher-Carcano, not a Mauser as had been reported in the press. The FBI traced it and found that it had been ordered from a mail-order house by an "A. Hidell" in Dallas, then shipped to "A. Hidell" at Dallas Post Office Box 2915, a postal box taken out by Oswald. In Oswald's wallet they found a counterfeit selective service card under the false name Alek James Hidell.

New facts came out too. On the fifth floor, three employees stood immediately below the sniper's nest, at open windows watching the motorcade. They heard and felt the three shots immediately above them, very loud. They even heard the ejected "hulls" dropping to the plank floor.

Bebe's mind played that scene—three young men standing within ten feet of the sniper, directly under him, feeling the force of the blasts through the planks, so close they could hear the spent shells hit the floor lumber over their heads.

In about the length of time, Alexander added, that it would have taken the sniper to move from the nest to the stairwell, then to scramble down it to the second floor, Oswald got stopped on the second floor by an incoming police officer. When the manager said he worked there, the officer let Oswald go. A little later, the manager assembled all building personnel, but Oswald had gone missing, the only one missing.

Meanwhile, a description given by one witness who saw the sniper fire the last shot went out on a police broadcast. Within forty-five minutes, over in Oak Cliff, Officer J. D. Tippit stopped Oswald on a sidewalk. When the officer got out of his car and was walking around its front, Oswald killed Tippit with a pistol. Three eyewitnesses saw Oswald do it. As Oswald hurried off, he emptied four spent cartridges out of the pistol and reloaded. A few minutes later, Oswald ducked in a nearby movie theater but got surrounded by police. When confronted by police, he said, "Well, it's all over now." He tried to pull his pistol on the arresting officers but was wrestled to the floor. His identification read "Lee Harvey Oswald" but other cards in his wallet had the Hidell alias. The Dealey Plaza witness identified Oswald as the sniper at a lineup. So did the witnesses to the Tippit murder.

Wade said they would rest on that. A powerful showing of guilt, Bebe thought, for both murders.

Foreman came forward to cross-examine. Wade receded to the front row to consult briefly with Abe. The slight pause prompted the judge to say, "Mr. Wade, would you like to introduce those two?"

"Of course, Your Honor."

Abe and Elaine rose.

"Here assisting us are Abe Summer, a senior trial counsel from the Department of Justice in Washington, and Elaine Navarro, a federal prosecutor with the United States Attorney's Office here in Dallas. Both will be assisting us on the federal aspects of this case."

"Welcome to you both," said the judge.

They nodded, respectfully, saying, "Thank you, Your Honor."

Bebe's bench mate whispered, "What were their names?"

Bebe felt smug: "Abe Summer and Elaine Navarro."

Foreman began.

"I'll need only a few minutes, Mr. Alexander. You said there were eyewitnesses in Dealey Plaza. How many?"

"I know of three so far."

"Have you released their names to the public yet?"

"No."

"Well, let's just call them A, B, and C. What did A tell you?"

"He told the police that shortly before the motorcade arrived, he saw someone generally matching the defendant's description holding a rifle, standing by a window on the sixth floor of the Depository, at parade rest. He said he thought he was a Secret Service agent, so he didn't report it to any of the police nearby."

"Which window?"

"The southwest corner window overlooking Elm."

"So, *not* the window at the sniper's nest."

"Correct."

"Did he actually see the shots fired?"

"No."

"As for B, did he see any shots fired?"

"Yes, he did. He cannot, however, say the man's race."

"Cannot even identify his race. Could he recall any identification feature?"

"He recalls a bald spot on the front of the sniper's head."

"A bald spot. Well, here's my question. On November 24, Dan Rather was on WCBS radio saying that the police had an eyewitness in protective custody who could identify Oswald as the one who pulled the trigger. Is that true?"

Bebe glanced but didn't see Rather in the room.

"The one you are calling C saw the last shot fired. He got a good look at the shooter, who crouched right at the window where we found the sniper's nest. The witness saw the rifle, the fatal shot itself, then saw the man pull the rifle slowly into the window and then disappear."

"Is he in protective custody?"

"Not yet."

"Your Honor," Foreman turned to the judge, "I would like to ask for the name of this witness."

"No, not now. The press'd be all over him," the judge replied.

"So stipulated," Bebe whispered to Schieffer.

Foreman faced the witness, "Was he the witness who said the sniper was about thirty and weighed 165?"

"He was," said Alexander.

Foreman asked, "Well, then, Mr. Alexander, did Witness C make an identification at a lineup?"

"Yes."

"Was Lee Oswald in the lineup?"

"Yes, with three others."

"What did the witness say?"

"He picked Lee Harvey Oswald."

"Did he say how sure he was?"

"Well . . . yes . . . and no, I suppose . . . He said it was Oswald, but he said he would not, at that time, make a positive identification."

"Would not or could not?"

Alexander hesitated.

"Could not."

Hushed commentary gathered in the gallery.

"Mr. Foreman, are you done?" The judge seemed irritated, as Bebe read him, that Foreman, in his fishing expedition, was actually catching some fish.

"Almost, Your Honor."

Foreman paused over his notes, giving the appearance of being done. Bebe figured this was calculated to encourage the judge to refrain, out of politeness, from ending it or even asking how much more he had to go. Finally, "One last question. Please tell us the timing on the three shots."

"Most witnesses thought the last two were closer together than the first two."

"Meaning there was a pause after the first shot, then two in quick succession? Is that what you mean?"

"That's what I mean."

"Your Honor, I'm done, so the witness may step down with our thanks."

"Bail," said Brown, "will be set at one million dollars."

Of course, Oswald had no way to post a million dollars, but the procedure guaranteed by the Eighth Amendment had been satisfied.

"LET'S NOW TAKE UP the issue of the interviews conducted without counsel," said Judge Brown.

It was a major issue—the admissibility of statements made by Oswald to the police during four interrogation sessions at all hours of the day and night without the benefit of counsel. Working its way through the system in Arizona then was an appeal involving an accused named Ernesto Miranda. His name would soon be famous for the Supreme Court's pronouncement that the Fifth and Sixth Amendments in the Bill of Rights prohibited the use of custodial interrogation statements from an accused uninformed of his right to remain silent and his right to counsel or elicited after a request for counsel. In 1963, Foreman had something equally good. Under Texas statutes, custodial interview statements by a "suspect" who had asked for counsel could not be admitted in evidence. As the reporters were to tell the nation, Foreman seemed to be carrying the day, when the judge took a twenty-minute recess.

During the recess, Elaine suggested to Alexander a distinction between use in the prosecution's main case versus impeachment of Oswald should he decide to testify in his own defense. Alexander waved her off, saying we don't need the statements, let them go. Wade overheard this tête-à-tête.

When the argument resumed, Wade asked the judge if Elaine, as a friend of the Court, could make a point. The judge asked Foreman if he objected.

"Fine," Foreman said.

From her seat with Abe on the front row within the well of the courtroom, Elaine suppressed surprise that she'd been called forward. Nevertheless, she walked to the lectern, collecting her thoughts, being very aware that her words would be reported all over the nation and being aware she'd be the first to speak for the United States.

"Thank you, Your Honor," Elaine began calmly. "The point is simply the difference between use of statements as evidence in the prosecutor's own case versus use of the statements solely for impeachment in the event the defendant elects to testify in his own case. Even if the first is barred by the Texas statute, the second would not necessarily be. To rule otherwise would be tantamount to giving the accused a license to lie. We ask you to keep an open mind on this distinction."

"Very well said, Miss Navarro. A license to lie. A memorable phrase. Any response, Mr. Foreman?"

"Alliteration perhaps," replied Mr. Foreman, "but please note that counsel cited no authority for the distinction."

The judge then ruled from the bench; no statement Oswald made while in police custody could be introduced for any purpose save for the possibility that they might be usable to impeach Oswald in the event he took the stand, a question on which the judge would reserve until after the direct examination of Oswald should he elect to testify.

In the front row by Elaine, Abe leaned to whisper, "You did good."

The judge looked over at them, then said, "Would all counsel, including our federal guests, visit briefly in chambers?"

THE JUDGE HID HIS embarrassment. Pipes, tobacco, matches with ashtrays all covered part of his desk. Newspapers, magazines, nutrient supplements, even comic books littered the rest. Before bringing in the famous Percy Foreman, not to mention those federals, he should have, he realized too late, tidied up his chambers, at least removed the comics. Nevertheless, the judge graciously welcomed all. The judge saw that Elaine and Karen already knew each other. They almost hugged. He wondered about that story.

Percy stood by a framed photo on the wall of a buxom bombshell posing beside the judge. "You and her friends, Judge?"

"That's Candy Barr, perhaps the most famous entertainer, I would guess, certainly the most beautiful entertainer, ever produced in Texas."

"Wasn't she on trial here a while back?" Percy asked.

"On trial here for narcotics possession," Brown continued. "Marijuana, almost an ounce. During her trial, I asked her to come in here for a photo. Right where you are now. It's not often we get celebrities. Fully clothed, as you can see."

"How'd the case come out?" Percy asked.

"Fifteen years."

"No way," Karen said, not quite under her breath. The judge felt himself blush.

He saw Karen blush too.

"Well, yes, it sounds harsh," replied the judge, "but she served only three and got out. I hear Jack Ruby wants her over at his club."

To change the subject, he gestured to sit.

"Where're you staying, Percy?" Brown resumed.

"The Adolphus."

"Our best."

"It is."

"Please smoke if you like," said Brown, handling his pipe. He knew they wouldn't, however. To do so would have presumed upon his time by suggesting a longer meeting than he had in mind.

"And you, Mr. Summer, welcome to Dallas."

"Thank you."

"You're staying where?"

"The Baker Hotel."

"Eleanor Roosevelt's favorite," commented Brown.

All waited for the judge to resume.

"So, what again is your role?" This went to Brown's main purpose.

"Miss Navarro and I are just here," Abe replied, "to coordinate the federal side with Mr. Wade and his office. We'll stay strictly in the background. The district attorney, of course, will try the case, not us."

"Hmmm," said the judge. He cut remnants of burned tobacco out of a pipe bowl, dumped them in a circular metal bin, refilled the bowl, and tamped down the tobacco.

"We're obliged for the help," Wade spoke up, "particularly on the federal pieces of the case."

He lit it.

"Will they be at the trial," he asked, drawing on the stem, "meaning in the courtroom?"

"Most of the time," Wade said.

"At counsel's table?"

"No," answered Wade. "Bill and I will do all the trial work."

The judge could see no problem, but he'd never encountered this circumstance before, so he temporized, drawing on his pipe.

Foreman couldn't resist, "Judge, perhaps they will help turn over the *Brady* materials in the federal files."

All let the comment pass. The judge, however, figured it might be a good point.

Women being present, Brown visited the window briefly, raising it enough to mitigate the smoke. Without his robe, the judge knew he just looked like an ordinary overweight, middle-aged man—with a "wondrously wrinkled face," as one journalist would put it.

"Elaine," asked the judge, "tell me about your experience."

"Well, Barefoot Sanders brought me in as a new prosecutor. I've now done two felony trials."

"Where'd you go to law school?"

"University of Texas."

"Mr. Summer," the judge immediately regretted that, twice, he hadn't used Abe's first name, "have you done murder cases?"

"Homicides have come up in my organized crime cases but, no, I haven't had occasion to try straight murder cases."

"Washington?"

"Yes, sir, I'm based in Washington."

Foreman interjected, "If I may, Judge, Mr. Summer is being modest. As you likely know, he was the lead prosecutor on the Profeta conviction down in New Orleans."

The judge acknowledged the achievement with a tilt of his head. Al Profeta had run the rackets in New Orleans until Abe put him away for sixteen years. The judge had read about the trial and the sentencing.

"How long will the evidence take, Henry?"

"Two to three weeks."

"The defense?"

"Pronto," said Foreman, "much less."

"You know we'll have to sequester the jury."

The judge turned to a wall calendar displaying all twelve months for 1964.

"That means," continued the judge, "we'll have long trial days, six days a week through noon on Saturdays. These jurors will basically be in custody, so we need to move it along—to minimize the hardship on them." He let this sink in.

The judge then raised a plan to desegregate the gallery, at least for this case. With reporters from all over the world, the judge said he was being advised to obviate this public-relations problem. It "looks bad," he continued, that blacks "won't be in the jury pool." At least the audience could be mixed.

"Any objections?"

Alexander shifted his weight but no one spoke.

"Also, you'll notice that we've removed or papered over the Colored and White signs on the restrooms and fountains. All are now open to all. With the world here, we must do it."

He glanced at Alexander.

Again, no one spoke.

"Judge, we hope you still have an open mind on our change-of-venue motion," Percy commented.

"Of course," smiled Brown. "Well, thank you for dropping by. I'll be as fair to both sides as possible."

After they'd gone, the judge toyed with a tin of tobacco. Brown had an uneasy sense that a judge with goddamn comic books and heart tablets on his desk was, as Wade had told him, in over his head on the most important prosecution of the century. He knew that some Texas judges, probably even those on the Texas Court of Criminal Appeals, expected that he'd transfer the trial out of Dallas, a transfer he didn't want to make unless, contrary to normal practice, the new venue would let him come along as the trial judge, but so far none would. Somehow, Brown thought, Abe Summer and Elaine Navarro would be part of his salvation.

# 13 OAK CLIFF

ELAINE FOUND IT—A TROUBLING MYSTERY, THIS ONE LURKING in the summaries of FBI witness interviews. On Friday morning, the 20th of December, she proposed to Abe and Jim that they go re-interview Earlene Roberts, Oswald's housekeeper in Oak Cliff. "The boarding house's in my neighborhood," she said. Jim drove.

They arrived in the cold at 1026 North Beckley, a simple single-floor brick home with a small, neat front yard in a residential neighborhood. A graying woman with a double chin in her early sixties appeared on the other side of the screen door. With wingtip glasses, she wore a loose house dress under a half-buttoned sweater.

"Yes?" she said with apprehension, eyes rounded, magnified by her lenses.

"Good morning, Mrs. Roberts," Jim replied, "we're from the FBI and United States Attorney's Office. May we ask a few questions?"

"Well, I already told 'em everything I know. The police, the Secret Service, the FBI, the newspapers, the lawyers."

"Yes, ma'am, we've read those reports, but could we please take a few more minutes?"

"Oh, all right, I guess you can." The door swung into the right-hand corner of the front room, all arranged as a television-viewing den. As she entered, Elaine saw an orderly place. A small Christmas tree blinked in a corner of the next room. She smelled a hint of natural gas. The space heater ran high. No one else was in evidence.

To their left, soft gray light filtered through three windows along the front wall and fell onto a side table and two chairs. At the far-left end of the front wall, set into the corner, came the television facing into the center of the room. The middle of the adjoining wall held an unlit fireplace followed by a chair in the next corner. Along the wall opposite the front ran a long sofa in an L-shape that curved into the room, all facing the television. An archway rear of the sofa, directly opposite the front door, led to a dining room. Elaine paid attention to these arrangements for the light they shed on the point that troubled her.

Earlene showed them to the sofa. Elaine removed her winter wear and folded them on her lap, there being no offer to hang them. Nor came any offer for coffee or tea. Earlene sat in a chair, silhouetted against the front window. The television remained dark. After a show of credentials, Jim assured her that she faced no trouble with the law. She explained she worked as the housekeeper and was not the owner.

Earlene went back over the story. Last October, a man rented a room from her under the name "O. H. Lee." He signed as "O. H. Lee." The police had already taken the registration book. She rented him a small alcove off the dining room. Eight dollars a week. He came on the fourteenth of October. He brought a zip-up satchel with a few clothes on hangers. That's all. He had very few words, stayed home at night, but was usually gone on Friday, Saturday, and Sunday nights. Once he explained to her, "Now, over weekends, I'll be out of town visiting friends." But one weekend he slept at 1026, the weekend before Friday, November 22. She thought he just didn't like people. But he always paid his rent on time. She liked that part.

She then described the day of the assassination. The police came to ask her about Lee Harvey Oswald. She replied she had no one by that name. But it turned out they meant O. H. Lee. Before the police came, a friend had called her to turn on her television—the president had been shot. She was trying to clear up the picture by adjusting the rabbit-ears antenna—here she motioned to the set in the corner—when Oswald came in, walking unusually fast, around 1:00 p.m. "Oh, you are in a hurry," she declared, continuing to fiddle with the antenna. He went to his room and stayed there three or four minutes, maybe changed clothes, but for sure, put on a zippered jacket. He zipped it up as he hurried out the front door. She was still trying to optimize the antenna position.

Then came the part that worried Elaine.

"While he was in his room," Elaine zeroed in, "did anything unusual happen?"

"Yes, maybe not unusual, but I was standing right there," she pointed to a spot just in front of the television, "I heard a car horn go 'tip-tip' out front so I looked out front. It was a Dallas police car, facing north, to our right. Stopped directly in front of my house. Two uniformed policemen in the car."

From the layout of the room, Elaine could see that Earlene, while standing near the television, could have seen a car stopped on the street through the front window. Elaine could see the street herself even seated on the sofa.

"Where was Oswald then?"

"In his room."

"When he came out, was the car still there?"

"No, it had already gone."

"Can you remember anything else about the police car?"

"Well, the reason I took notice is that a while ago I worked for some policemen. One of them was named Alexander. After that, sometimes they would come by here to tell me something cute, like something their wives wanted me to know, so at first I thought it was them, but when I glanced at the car I knew it was not their car because their car was 170. This car had some other number."

"I think you informed the FBI that it was 270."

"207, 107, seems like, I'm not sure. I know it was not 170. Maybe it was 106."

Elaine saw Abe and Jim exchange looks.

"When was the last time you saw Oswald?" Elaine continued.

"After he ran out the door, I last saw him standing on the curb at the bus stop just to the right out front."

Elaine could see that Earlene could've seen the bus stop too. She thought of the bus transfer found on Oswald and wondered if he'd wanted to use it.

"Was this front room arranged like this on that day?" Elaine asked.

"Yes, the same way. The men like to watch television here."

"Can we see Oswald's room?"

"I guess you can."

They looped around the L-shaped sofa, then through the archway into the dining room. Oswald's "room" was off to the left, just an exterior alcove. It appeared small but airy. Elaine immediately noticed that the window had a curtain with curtain rod already in place. A single bed ran alongside the exterior wall with the window and took up most of the alcove. A small bureau occupied one end. Everything that had belonged to Oswald had been seized by the police. The room had not yet been re-rented.

"Did he ever have visitors?" Abe asked.

She shook her head.

"How about the weekend he stayed here?"

"No, no visitors."

"Anything else you wish to tell us?" Jim evidently wanted to wind it up.

"Well, do you know a Mr. Foreman?"

"Yes, ma'am."

"Well, he was here a couple of days ago. I told him what I told you."

"Including the part about the police car?" asked Elaine.

"I would guess I did, yes."

BACK IN THE CAR, Elaine asked, "What do you two make of the police car stopping in front of her house? I find it most curious, almost conspiratorial."

"Maybe she's confused," Abe replied. "Why would any police be casually dropping by her place when every other cop was running ragged in the chaos? Maybe she's confused over what day she saw them. We ought to track down all those car numbers she guessed about. Find out where they were that day."

Jim said he'd do it.

While they were in the neighborhood, Jim suggested they swing by Tenth Street, only a few blocks away, to see the Tippit murder scene. From the boarding house, they drove south on Beckley (away from downtown).

Naked hardwoods looked wet and dark in winter on this leaden day on the verge of snow. The old residential district showed dreary. Lawns had gone fallow. Christmas lights draped doorways, roof lines too, but barely dented the gray. The assassination had taken the life out of the city. Vim had given way to gloom.

After five blocks on Beckley, they reached Neeley Street and paused. Jim commented, "By the way, here's where the downtown cab driver let Oswald out after he left the Depository." He motioned to the curb on the right by the corner.

A faded bumper sticker on a tired car ahead, Elaine saw, said, "K. O. the Kennedys."

"So, he went right by 1026 in the cab for five blocks, then walked back?" asked Elaine, sitting in the rear passenger seat.

"Yep, but stranger even than that," Jim replied. "When he got out of the cab right about here, he continued on foot *south*—even farther away from the boarding house—until the cab was gone, *then* he turned back for the rooming house."

"Pretty clever," remarked Abe.

They too continued south a few more blocks on Beckley and turned left onto Tenth Street, still in a working-class neighborhood. Jim drove slowly for three blocks, then stopped at Tenth and Patton, looking bleak in the dull light. Jim shifted out of gear to idle, letting the heater run.

"This intersection tells the story," Jim resumed. In the rear, Elaine leaned forward to hear better. "Tippit drove slowly along here on Tenth, just as we've been doing, then crossed this very intersection," nodding at a few feet in front of them. "Then about halfway up the next block he eased up alongside Oswald, who was over there on the sidewalk on our right. He called Oswald over. They talked through the passenger-side vent. Tippit got out and, as he was walking around the front of the car, Oswald stepped out and shot him four times."

"On our immediate left, at this very intersection, a waitress on her way to work was about to cross just in front of where we are now. She saw the whole thing from that corner. Catty-corner from her, just there on our right, a taxi driver sat in his cab parked on Patton, eating his lunch, facing the intersection. He heard the whole thing and saw Oswald run by the right side of his cab."

"The same taxi driver who brought him from downtown?" asked Elaine.

"No, different cab."

"Then what?"

"So, after shooting Tippit, Oswald ran through that yard on the corner, veered south on Patton, running right by the cab."

Jim pointed center-right at the house on the southeast corner. "The woman living there heard the shots, then went to her front door where she saw Oswald cross her front yard from her right to her left. She even saw him emptying shells out of a pistol. The empties turned up in her bushes. Four of them. She also saw the waitress at the opposite corner, pointing at Oswald. So she called the police. As Oswald went by, the cab driver heard him say, 'poor dumb cop' or 'poor damn cop.' He is positive it was one or the other. Oswald then headed down Patton, off to our right."

"Will all of them identify Oswald?" Abe asked.

"Yes, have and will, positively."

Jim turned the wheel and crept right onto Patton. Elaine imagined the scene with Oswald part of it, scurrying along, handling his gun, shaking out the spent shells. Halfway down the block, on the left, she saw a used car lot. The day being cold and dismal, it had no customers.

"At that used car lot," Jim pointed, "the manager heard the shots, then saw Oswald trot by with a pistol. About here, mid-block, Oswald crossed over from our left to the right side of the street."

Patton brought them to a busy cross street. "This is Jefferson Boulevard. Here, Oswald turned right on Jefferson and eventually got caught in the Texas Theater—a few blocks west. We'll go there now." They had only gone a block on Jefferson when Jim slowed, "We think Oswald ducked back of this Texaco Station on the right—they found his jacket back there, the same one the housekeeper saw him leave in—and fled through an alley parallel to the way we're going now."

Elaine knew the Texaco station and bought gas there regularly.

"Now, we're back to Beckley," Jim resumed at the intersection of Jefferson and Beckley. "The boarding house is ten or so blocks to our right, but let's stay on Jefferson to the theater." After a couple of more blocks, just before the Texas Theater, Jim idled. "See this shoe store on the right? Oswald ducked in its recessed entryway when the sirens came by, and the manager, who saw him, got suspicious, went outside when Oswald left, and watched him slip into the theater without buying a ticket. He told the ticket lady and she called the cops. Thanks to them, we got Oswald in the theater."

"So, JIM," ELAINE ASKED as they were cruising back to the Santa Fe Building, "where was Oswald headed? He must have figured that the police were on their way to get him—he did that taxi drive-by so he could see, don't you think, whether the police had already come? Then he rushed in, then out, of the house. He waited at the bus stop a moment, got nervous, and hurried off—but where was he going?"

"Who knows?" Jim answered. "On the run. Possibly he was heading to some other bus stop to use that transfer. Not much of a plan, was it? Kill the president and escape on a city bus. A mystery."

"Add that to the mystery," Elaine replied, "of the two cops out front of 1026 tooting their horn."

"*If* there really were two cops there," cautioned Abe. "If."

"Listen, there's one saving grace that cuts through it all," replied Jim.

"What's that?" Abe asked.

"It was his rifle and his gun."

# 14 SILVIA ODIO

JIM AND ABE WERE CHARMED, ELAINE COULD TELL, BY THE twenty-six-year-old brunette exile named Silvia Odio. In stylish dress, Miss Odio arrived on the seventh floor of the Santa Fe Building.

Born in Havana, Silvia had had some schooling in Pennsylvania, so she spoke good English. Her mother remained under house arrest in Cuba while her father languished as a political prisoner on the Isle of Pines. Silvia supported anti-Castro organizations.

She accepted coffee from Elaine.

Silvia said that one night about nine in late September, two Latino men had come to her Dallas apartment with an American introduced to her as Leon Oswald, who said little. She knew none of them. One, who called himself Leopoldo, was tall with a bald spot in the front of his hair and seemed to be Cuban with knowledge about her imprisoned father. The other called himself something like Angelo, was heavy, and seemed to be Mexican. They used "war names"—anti-Castro exiles avoided using their real names for fear of retaliation against those still in Cuba. Leopoldo did most of the talking. Twice, he called the American "Leon Oswald." They asked Silvia to translate a letter into English to be used to help raise money for the Cuban underground. She begged off. Her younger sister, Annie, heard part of the conversation. Leopoldo apologized for the hour of the visit. They said they had just driven up from New Orleans and were headed on a trip. The three left in a red car, with Leopoldo driving.

The next day or so, Silvia continued, Leopoldo phoned her to ask what she'd thought of Leon Oswald. She replied that she'd had no thought about him. Oswald, he then relayed, had said that President Kennedy should've been assassinated by Cubans after the Bay of Pigs invasion because Kennedy had cancelled the air support for the invasion force. Oswald was, said Leopoldo, an ex-Marine and good marksman. When she did not bite on any of these statements, Leopoldo backtracked, saying that Oswald seemed "loco."

Elaine saw Silvia's face turn anxious when she recounted the telephone talk of assassination.

On November 22, when Silvia learned of the assassination, she immediately thought back to the incident and fainted. This was before hearing the name Lee Harvey Oswald on television. She woke up in a hospital where she soon saw the image of Lee Harvey Oswald, by then in custody, on television. She recognized him as Leon. So did her sister, Annie. They did not come forward out of fear, but Silvia confided to a Dallas volunteer working with Cuban refugees, who did come forward, so the FBI tracked Miss Odio down.

Elaine listened and thought of Ruth Paine and her act of kindness in rescuing Marina and daughter from the hovel on Magazine Street on that hot Monday, September 23. Elaine also knew that Oswald—without doubt—had sat on a bus leaving Houston at 2:35 a.m. on Thursday, the twenty-sixth.

"When did they come?" Elaine asked.

"Thursday, the twenty-sixth, or Friday, the twenty-seventh," answered Miss Odio. "I have been trying to piece it together with my sister."

Elaine knew both dates ruled out Lee as Leon.

"How did you settle on that Thursday or Friday?" Elaine followed up.

"Monday, the thirtieth, was my last day in that apartment. I had to be out by the end of that day. I was moving to Oak Cliff. Annie had come to help me move, to babysit my kids. We are pretty sure she arrived on Thursday, the twenty-sixth, and the three men came on the next day. This possibly is off a day or so. I know it was a workday. They came at night, about nine."

"Different question," Abe said. "Did Leon Oswald himself ever say anything to you about President Kennedy?"

"Oh, no, he said little. He was quiet. Leopoldo did the talking. The part about President Kennedy came up only in the later phone call from Leopoldo."

As she parted, Silvia and Elaine exchanged a few words in Spanish. After she left, Elaine said she'd said that Leopoldo had been trying to impress her, she'd felt, just to get a date.

After the Odio interview, the FBI reconfirmed Oswald's movements as follows: (i) He was in New Orleans until at least the morning of Wednesday, September 25, when his unemployment check was cashed (probably by him), and (ii) without question, Oswald boarded a Continental Trailways bus in Houston bound for Laredo (and thence for Mexico) at 2:35 a.m. in the wee hours of Thursday, the twenty-sixth. Very reliable fellow passengers placed him on that bus. Therefore, Oswald could not have been introduced to Miss Odio on the evening of either the twenty-sixth or the twenty-seventh.

Could Miss Odio be off, the federals wondered, in her reconstruction of the timing such that the three men came earlier—on the evening of the twenty-fifth? If so, there would have been just enough time to drive from New Orleans (after cashing the check) to Dallas, then from Dallas to Houston to make a 2:35 a.m. bus departure on the twenty-sixth. In a follow-up with the FBI, she said maybe it had occurred on the twenty-fifth. That was the most she could say.

Jim confirmed with Miss Odio's psychiatrist, who treated her anxiety, that she'd recounted to him the visit by the three men and had done so in a session *prior* to the assassination, thus giving her recollection greater credibility. So did the fainting, Jim added, for no one is likely to faint over a fabrication.

How could this help the prosecution?

Aside from the serious problem of the date of the visit, the prosecutors all agreed that Miss Odio's story, while sensational, appeared too problematic to use as prosecution evidence. Critically, Leon Oswald himself never said anything about Kennedy to Silvia. That part came from Leopoldo only in the phone call, so it was probably inadmissible hearsay against Oswald. Strategically, even if admitted in evidence, the story would run the risk of leaving the impression with the jury that the prosecution's case somehow depended on proving a conspiracy. The prosecutors didn't need that extra burden. They had other solid proof that both murders were by Oswald. Leave Miss Odio, all the prosecutors concluded, for the Warren Commission.

More generally on the issue of conspiracy, Abe emphasized something else. Militating against any conspiracy was the absence of tracks one would have expected a conspiracy to leave. A telling point, for example, was that Earlene Roberts, Ruth Paine, Roy Truly, Buell Wesley Frazier plus his co-workers, all of them, were certain that Oswald never had visitors or took calls (save for once when Marina and Ruth called him at the boarding house). If there had been a conspiracy, therefore, it left none of the tracks one would have expected to see. The same remained true for New Orleans—with one as yet unexplained exception—the New Orleans landlord reportedly had seen "a Latin man" come to visit Oswald. That man had not yet been identified. Was he Leopoldo or Angelo?

# 15 THE MISSING LINK

"THE MISSING LINK" BECAME WADE'S TERM FOR IT—A CREDIBLE eyewitness who could positively identify Oswald as the man who fired the fatal final shot at the president or, for that matter, any of the Elm Street shots. Howard Brennan came close. He'd seen the sniper fire the third and fatal shot, as Brennan watched the parade from across Elm. But Brennan, a steam fitter, had advised the police, at the lineup, that he couldn't be positive. Plus he'd been off on the sniper's age and weight.

When Elaine and Abe arrived for their next meeting at the district attorney's office in the Records Building next door to the courthouse, Wade was already in conference with a prospect.

"Come on in and please meet Ronald Fischer," Wade said. "We're just starting our interview. Have a seat." They shook hands with a young man wearing an open madras shirt, khaki pants, and an Eisenhower-style windbreaker. Fischer worked in the Records Building for the county auditor. He was twenty-five, married. A Zippo lighter plus a pack of Camels rested in front of him.

"Now, Mr. Fischer," said Wade, "take us back to November 22."

"Okay, our boss said that we could just go on down to watch the parade. Bob Edwards and I went down to Houston and Elm."

"And where were you standing?"

"On Houston, where the curb starts to curve toward Elm."

Everyone realized that this was very near where Howard Brennan had been.

When no one lit up, Fischer asked in a husky voice, "Can I smoke?"

"If you got 'em," said Wade, looking at the lighter and pack.

Up came the Zippo lighter. With a whoosh, a flare and the smell of lighter fluid, Fischer took his first drag. Wade pulled an ashtray over in front of Fischer. Elaine hated it. She never complained, however, about others smoking—for fear it would just be turned into one more weakness against women.

"Now, what'd you see?"

"About ten or fifteen seconds before the first car came off of Main onto Houston, Bob punched me and said, 'Look at that guy there in that window. He looks like he's uncomfortable.' So I looked up to watch him for, oh, I'd say, ten or fifteen seconds. He was leaning forward, looking to his right, down toward the Triple Underpass, not watching for the parade. Just sat there staring."

Fischer took another drag, then exhaled to the side.

"In what window did you see the man?"

"The southeast corner on the fifth or sixth floor of the Texas School Book Depository."

"How much of him could you see?"

"I could see from about the middle of his chest past the top of his head. As you're looking toward that window, he was in the lower right portion of the window. He seemed to be sitting a little forward. He had—he had on an open-neck shirt, but it—uh—could have been a sport shirt or a T-shirt, light in color, probably white, I couldn't tell whether it had long sleeves or short sleeves, but open-neck, light in color. He had a slender face and neck—uh—and he had a light complexion—he was a white man. He looked to be twenty-two or twenty-four years old."

Fischer tapped ashes into the tray. Elaine thought about opening the window.

"Do you remember anything about the color of his hair?"

"His hair seemed to be—uh—neither light nor dark, possibly a light— well, possibly a—well, it was a brown was what it was, but as to whether it was light or dark, I can't say. So, it wasn't dark but it wasn't light. Uh—he didn't have black hair and he didn't have blonde hair. It—uh—must have been a brown but, like I say, there are a lot of different shades of brown— I'm not—I can't—it's hard for me to say just exactly what shade of brown I saw that he had."

"Did he have a thick head of hair or did he have a receding hairline—or couldn't you tell?"

"I couldn't tell. He couldn't have had very long hair because his hair didn't seem to take up much space—of what I could see of his head. His hair must have been short."

"Well, did you see a full view of his face?"

"I could see the tip of his right cheek as he looked to my left straight at the Triple Underpass."

"Could you see his hands?"

"No."

"Could you see any other objects in the window?"

"There were boxes stacked up with space for a man to walk through there between the window and the boxes."

Elaine couldn't help herself. "Well, was he smoking?"

"Didn't see that," Fischer exhaled.

"What then happened?" Wade resumed.

"The motorcade came by—the limousine then made the wide turn onto Elm. I heard a shot. By that point, the limousine was obscured by the crowd. At first I thought it was a firecracker. Everybody got quiet. There was no yelling or shouting or anything. Everything seemed to get real still. And—uh—the second shot rang out, then everybody—from where I was standing—everybody started to scatter. And—uh—then the third shot. At first, I thought there were four, but as I think about it more, there must have been just three."

"Now, you said the first shot you thought was a firecracker? What about the second and third ones?"

"I had heard high-powered rifles before. I knew those were shots. It still didn't dawn on me that anyone would try to shoot at the president, but I knew that somebody was shooting at something."

"Did you look back at that window?" Wade pressed.

"No. I never looked back at the window."

"Where did the shots seem to be coming from?"

"They seemed to be coming from just west of the School Book Depository Building. There was a rail yard in there."

"What'd you do?"

"We ran across Elm toward the sound. There were a man, his wife and two children lying on the ground. Someone was helping them up off the ground. The man said at that time that the president had been shot."

Fischer crushed the butt out in the tray.

"After that, we ran up to the top of the hill there where all the Secret Service men had run, thinking that that's where the bullets had come from since they seemed to be searching that area over there."

"What then?"

"After that, about five minutes after the first shot, we went back up the office, here in the Records Building. Bob and I separated. I listened to the radio to learn exactly what had happened. Then I heard a bunch of sirens, police cars, so I leaned out the window. Police cars were all surrounding the Texas School Book Depository Building. Then, I realized the guy I saw might have been the assassin."

Wade showed him a picture of Oswald. Fischer saw some similarities but the most he could say was that it "could have been" the man in the window.

"Okay. Thank you, sir. We will tell you if we need your testimony. That Commission in Washington may want your testimony too. Let us know, please, if anyone serves a subpoena on you for our trial."

After Fischer left, Wade lit a cigar. "See what we're up against?"

"At least he's honest," Wade drew on his cigar. The end glowed orange. "But he's not our Missing Link."

Elaine hated cigar smoke even more. Sometimes she felt her lungs would seize.

"What he can do," Abe said as he opened the window, "is pin down that someone who generally looked like Oswald was in that southeast window on the sixth floor moments just before the motorcade arrived."

"Thank you," said Wade, referring to the fresh air.

"Alone too," added Elaine. "The man in the window was alone."

"Listen," Abe resumed, "he can help a little on premeditation, namely that the guy was staring intently down toward the Triple Underpass where the fatal shot eventually hit, not toward Houston and Main, where the motorcade would first emerge into view."

"All right. Fair points but the hair thing—you saw how he waffled. He'd get eaten alive on cross. Saw no rifle. Can't identify Oswald. Saw all that but thought the shots came from the rail yard. Okay, enough on him."

Wade looked to the door.

"Will, who's next?"

"A woman named Carolyn Walther. Bring her in?"

"Please."

Fritz guided in a tall nervous woman, then introduced her. She took a seat. She explained that she worked nearby and had watched the motorcade with a friend from work while standing right in front of the Records Building on Houston Street. Just before the motorcade came around the corner from Main (on her left), she looked up (to her right center) at the windows of the Depository where she saw a man in the southeast corner window of the fourth or fifth floor "with another man standing to his right."

Mrs. Walther didn't ask to smoke and quietly pushed away the filthy ashtray.

The first man, she repeated, held a gun, a short one. It "wasn't as long as a rifle." He was holding it pointed down. He was kneeling in the window, or sitting. His arms were on the window. He was holding the gun in a downward position, and he was looking downward. Both his hands were extended across the window ledge. "Possibly it was a machine gun," she added.

Alexander groaned, "Machine gun?"

"Yes, sir. He was holding it in his hands. The barrel was pointing downward. He was looking toward Houston Street. Both his hands were extended across the window ledge."

"And it seemed like I saw, at the same time, a second man standing in the same window to my left of the man with the rifle, meaning to the right of the man with the rifle. This second man was wearing a brown suit coat. I could only see his body from the waist to the shoulders. His head was hidden by part of the closed window."

She added she could not identify as any particular person. She didn't see them well enough for that.

"You said they were on the fourth or fifth floor," Wade tried to clarify. "Possibly, do you mean the fifth or sixth floor instead?"

"No, sir, I still feel it was the fourth or fifth floor."

"Then what happened?"

"The president passed us. The last of the cars went by, then I heard the shot. I thought it was a firecracker. Then I started back to work, along the curb, and then came two shots right together, and then another one. I'm sure there were four shots.

"And then I said, 'It's gunshots.' People started screaming. We got over to the motorcycles in front of the Depository and listened to their radios to learn what had happened. Then I went back to work. Later, I got interviewed by the FBI."

"When you stood by the police motorcycles, did you say to anyone what you'd seen?"

"No, sir. Just later."

Wade thanked and excused her.

"Well?" Wade raised his eyebrows.

"No go," said Alexander, who had ceased taking notes and had drawn out his pocketknife and begun whittling when he heard about the machine gun. "Why would a presidential assassin advertise his whereabouts, I mean, hang out the window with both arms, displaying a machine gun before the victim even arrived, all in time for someone to call him out? Why? It just makes no sense. No go."

"She says fourth or fifth floor," Abe piled on. "But those three Depository workers were at that very corner on the fifth floor. We know that for sure. And the fourth-floor corner windows just below them were closed shut. We know that too."

"Here's what bothers me most," Fritz leaned over his Stetson. "She never said any of this to her friend standing right there with her—even after hearing the shots. She told that story only later. Plus, she stood right by the police motorcycles and said nothing. Don't you think you would, if you saw what she says she saw, run to tell us immediately?"

Elaine responded, "But don't you think she really did see a man with a firearm of some sort and is just confused on the details? Surely she's not making it up?"

"And," Alexander added, sweeping cuttings from whittling into the trash bin, "if you saw a man with a machine gun in a window of a building, would you go stand by its front door and risk being in the line of fire if and when he shot his way out?"

"Bill's right," Wade concluded. "No go. We gotta keep on looking."

# 16   SMELLING A RAT

ANOTHER PERSISTENT WORRY FOR THE PROSECUTION REMAINED the fact that the Secret Service had removed the president's body from the hospital without allowing for the autopsy required under Texas law. In fact, the Texas medical examiner had literally stood in the hospital doorway to block the removal, but the Secret Service had forcibly pushed him aside—with good cause. On November 22, the danger of a wide conspiracy seemed manifest. Getting LBJ and the presidential party out of harm's way, back to Washington, ranked urgent. LBJ, however, would not leave without Jackie, and she would not leave without the body of her husband. The Secret Service, therefore, forced aside the medical examiner, then took the body, Jackie, and LBJ to Air Force One at Love Field. Put simply, it was a murder case under Texas law, but the autopsy required by Texas law for murder cases had gone undone.

Elaine listened as Wade summarized a *modus vivendi* that would eliminate this trouble. Wade had been approached by Foreman with the following offer: The defense would drop its *Brady* motion as well as the issue of the thwarted medical examination and would even not challenge the competency of the Bethesda pathologists (who were mere clinical pathologists, not forensic pathologists) in exchange for the prosecution (i) agreeing not to raise any uncharged bad acts by Oswald and (ii) turning over in advance all interview memoranda for witnesses in the prosecution's case and all interview memoranda of Dealey Plaza and Tenth Street witnesses, plus all memos summarizing the Oswald interviews, all of this to be deemed in full satisfaction of the new *Brady* rule.

On that Wednesday morning, January 15, the windows glistened with ice, the temperature having dropped before dawn to thirteen degrees. Water pipes had burst all over Dallas. Elaine shivered in place, her wool coat still on.

"You know Percy," Wade said. "He'll put the police on trial. The medical examiner snafu would embarrass us, so taking that off the table would be good for us. What do you think, Abe?"

Among the four, no one had yet brought up the idea of the federals joining in as prosecutors at counsel table.

"I like the part about the medical examiner—we all do, of course. Where we may differ is on the *Brady* part," Abe began, standing with his suit jacket still on, a scarf around his neck, holding his hands to the radiator. "I don't feel as strongly against this as you might. On the federal side, we often turn over the entire file, even though not required to. Even before *Brady*. It helps get guilty pleas. Of course, a guilty plea is impossible here—we want an execution. But even when the defendant goes to trial, we live with it—it works out fine."

Elaine wanted to go warm her hands over the radiator too but stayed put.

"Now," Abe continued, "I realize that your Texas law is strong in keeping the interview memos secret unless used to refresh the memory of a witness. Fair enough. But we still have the *Brady* problem, don't we? If the Supreme Court ultimately holds some memo in our file was exculpatory and should have been produced, then you may have to retry the case years later. I think we ought to work a trade."

"But none of the memos are exculpatory," said Alexander, handling his pocketknife, unopened. Elaine supposed it was too cold even to whittle.

"Here's another thing," Abe pushed on as if Alexander had said nothing. "We have to worry, don't we, about the verdict of history. The Warren Commission will eventually publish all the memos anyway with all the evidence, whether we withhold it or not. The public will scour them to find things we didn't see. Somebody'll say, 'Hey, look at this, Oswald didn't get a fair trial.' Aren't we better off just turning all of it over, taking that issue off the table? We've got a strong, strong case and can afford to take a small risk."

"If we turn them over," Alexander resisted, "Foreman'll have a field day tripping up our witnesses."

"Well," Abe left the radiator to take a seat, "that's what historians—and maybe the Supreme Court—will say that Foreman should have been able to do. Aren't we better off going over these memos with our witnesses and working out the kinks before they testify?"

Wade kept his hands wrapped around a mug of coffee. He said he agreed with Alexander. "But your Warren Commission point," Wade acknowledged, "is one I haven't considered." Wade pondered, "Let's at least do this—let's review all of our memos and pick out the worst twelve or so problematic ones, then see how we feel."

Alexander rolled his eyes, like, why bother?

"The dirty dozen," Elaine grinned.

"Yes, the dirty dozen," Wade grinned too.

Elaine said she'd do it.

They turned to the uncharged bad acts.

"What uncharged bad act is Foreman talking about?" Alexander asked.

"I raised that," Wade said. "Foreman just said any and all uncharged bad acts. The only example Foreman gave me was hitting his wife. He wants that out. But Foreman wants any and all uncharged acts of any type excluded. Foreman made clear we could, of course, prove up the Connally part of our case. Also the fistfight on Canal Street. He's okay with those."

"What else we got?" Abe asked.

"Nothing, so far," Wade replied.

"I'd go slow on this, real slow," Alexander slipped his knife into his pocket, "until we figure out what else is out there. Percy wouldn't give up on the medical exam crap unless he was afraid of something Oswald did that we don't know about yet. I smell a rat."

# 17 THE WALKER STORY

THERE WAS INDEED A RAT.

Came next one of the most exemplary chapters of professional work in the entire case, most of it done indoors in the first few weeks of the new year, weeks of bone-chilling cold in Dallas. Elaine had been sifting through all of Oswald's items seized from the boarding house in Oak Cliff and the Paine garage in Irving. One item given short shrift by agents was a photograph of the back of a residence. Although seized from the Paine garage, the photo showed nothing in that neighborhood. Nor was it from any of the Oak Cliff places Oswald had lived. It lingered as a small puzzle lost in the drama of a larger mosaic. "What do you make of this?" she asked Jim one day, who studied it, then shrugged.

Later on, unconnected with the photograph, the Secret Service showed Elaine an undated note, obviously to Marina in Lee's handwriting. It hadn't been seized in the police searches. Rather, Ruth Paine subsequently found a Russian book on her shelf that belonged to Marina. She'd simply turned it over to the Irving police to return to Marina, who remained in Secret Service protective custody. The police gave it to the Secret Service, who checked it and found the note inside. Undated, written in Russian, the note portended some ominous, dramatic act, presumably by Oswald. After being translated, it read as follows:

1. This is the key to the mailbox which is located in the main post office in the city on Ervay Street. This is the same street where the drugstore, in which you always waited, is located. You will find the mailbox in the post office which is located four blocks from the drugstore on that street. I paid for the box last month so don't worry about it.

2. Send the information as to what has happened to me to the Embassy and include newspaper clippings (should there be anything about me in the newspapers). I believe that the Embassy will come quickly to your assistance on learning everything.

3. I paid the house rent on the 2d so don't worry about it.

4. Recently I also paid for water and gas.

5. The money from work will possibly be coming. The money will be sent to our post office box. Go to the bank and cash the check.

6. You can either throw out or give my clothing, etc., away. Do not keep these. However, I prefer that you hold on to my personal papers (military, civil, etc.).

7. Certain of my documents are in the small blue valise.

8. The address book can be found on my table in the study should you need same.

9. We have friends here. The Red Cross also will help you.

10. I left you as much money as I could, $60 on the second of the month. You and the baby can live for another two months using $10 per week.

11. If I am alive and taken prisoner, the city jail is located at the end of the bridge through which we always passed on going to the city (right in the beginning of the city after crossing the bridge).

"Mother Mary," she exclaimed, "Alive and taken prisoner? What had he been up to? And, when?"

Plainly, she thought, Oswald had been planning some criminal act that might land him in the Dallas jail and certainly one where he was leaving behind Marina plus everything he had. He was planning something big enough to hit the papers. Elaine mused over the coincidence that "the main post office on Ervay Street," referenced in the note, was in the same building where she worked. The nearby "drug store" was the one she frequented herself. In the last paragraph, she figured he meant "county" jail, not "city" jail, the very prison in which Oswald now, with irony upon irony, found himself.

Was this about November 22? No, it could not have been, she saw, because the postal authorities had reported that Oswald had use of the post office box on Ervay Street only from October 1962 through May 1963. So the note, though undated, related sometime in the period October 1962 through May 1963.

What was Oswald up to back then? she asked herself. Maybe, she thought, this could explain why he moved to New Orleans that April.

Elaine wanted to talk to Marina to get the answer, but Marina, although in federal protective custody, had her own lawyers. She refused to cooperate in any way against her husband, invoking the marital privilege, both as to the trial and as to the Warren Commission.

Meanwhile, unconnected with the photograph or the note, as early as November 30, the FBI had wondered over a possible connection between the JFK murder and the attempt on General Edwin Walker in Dallas back on April 10, 1963. That night, someone had fired a shot at Walker as he sat at his desk preparing his income tax return. The bullet had barely missed, having been deflected by the window frame, prompting him to say, "That is the closest I have ever been missed in thirty years of military service."

The police recovered the slug, but it was too mutilated to analyze. After the JFK assassination, the FBI examined the slug again. The FBI lab could not reach a firm conclusion but found that it "could have been fired" from the Carcano rifle, the general rifling characteristics of the slug matching a test-fired bullet. But the FBI could not pin it on the specific Oswald rifle.

Did Oswald, Elaine asked, even have the Carcano by that evening? The answer turned out to be yes. He'd received the Carcano just a few weeks before the attempt on Walker.

Elaine tracked down the police detectives who had worked on the Walker case. Their description of the Walker home rang a bell—she retrieved the mystery photograph from the Oswald materials from the Paine garage.

"Hey, I think that's the back of the Walker house," one of the detectives said. He and Elaine drove out to check. The front yard displayed a full-size billboard of the John Birch Society blaring "Impeach Earl Warren," but, sure enough, the backyard matched the photo!

"God, thank you," whispered Elaine.

Oswald had developed the negatives, then printed them, she figured, in the commercial darkroom that had employed him (and fired him) in March 1963, the Jagers company in Dallas. It had been a step in his preparations to kill Walker. The mystery note, although itself undated, had to have been written by Oswald to Marina just before the Walker attempt, for the dates lined up—the Walker attempt was on April 10. April was the last full month for the postal box on Ervay Street.

But more came. The discovery led to a renewed effort to track down all witnesses from that time frame, thus in turn to a telephone interview with George de Mohrenschildt, a former Oswald friend, once a Dallas resident, who had since relocated to Haiti. De Mohrenschildt related to Elaine that shortly after the Walker attempt, which got considerable press, he went to visit the Oswalds in Oak Cliff. After Lee let him in the flat and after he learned (on that very visit) that Oswald had a rifle, he said jokingly, referring to the very recent attempt on Walker, "Lee, how could you have missed?" Lee's face went white, de Mohrenschildt said, then Lee went speechless. But Oswald never specifically admitted to the shooting. Oswald wound up giving him a photo of himself dressed in black with a rifle.

*Wait. A photograph? The photograph?*

Elaine, with Jim on the line too, asked de Mohrenschildt if he still had the photograph or any materials from Oswald. No, he said at first, but he then remembered that they had left some things in storage in Dallas. Could the FBI have access? Yes. De Mohrenschildt wrote a letter giving the FBI access to those items. Out to the storage locker they went.

*Pay dirt!*

Among those stored items was the photograph showing Oswald holding the rifle, wearing the pistol and brandishing copies of *The Militant* and *The Worker*. The backside bore an inscription in Russian: "To my friend George from Lee Oswald" (which analysts soon concluded was Oswald's handwriting) plus "Hunter of Fascists, ha, ha, ha" (which analysts could not say was Oswald's handwriting).

Thus, the very same image that Oswald had branded as an FBI forgery had his own handwriting on the rear of the newly found copy. How could Oswald now say it was a forgery?

Finally, as all this was coming together, Elaine asked Jim if the FBI could examine Oswald's Imperial Reflex camera, seized from the Paine garage, to determine whether it had been the camera used to take the Walker house photograph. The FBI determined that the microscopic edges of the images on the print matched perfectly the microscopic edges of the test film shot in the Imperial camera. The exposure frame in every camera had small imperfections along the edges. Each camera thus left its own "fingerprint" on the film, detectable under a microscope. Fortunately, Oswald had printed the entire negative so that the edges showed in the de Mohrenschildt print.

With Abe, Elaine shared all of this with Wade and Alexander.

"Bill, why didn't you figure this out?" Wade asked, only half teasing.

"Just dumb as dirt," replied Alexander, squinting.

"Miss Navarro," smiled Wade, "We have a job here waiting for you any time you want it."

Alexander had smelled a rat. Elaine had found it.

# 18 A PUFF OF SMOKE

"DAMN IT, WILL, WE GOTTA GET TO THE BOTTOM OF THAT 'PUFF of smoke,'" Henry Wade told Fritz, who then asked Jim to join him. Abe invited himself along.

On the railway bed, Abe felt the crunch of the cinder rock under his soles. They walked with Sam Holland, a signal supervisor for the Union Terminal, taking in the aroma of coal smoke and creosote on a windless, damp, cold noon hour. When they got dead center over Elm Street on the Triple Underpass, cars whining and droning below them in accordance with the Doppler Effect, Holland announced, "Right here."

Holland looked in his fifties, tall, skinny, wore LBJ-style glasses, and had the manner of a railroad man. On the twenty-second, before the motorcade, he'd gone to this very spot on the top of the Triple Underpass to let police know which railroad workers belonged there. So, Holland had been standing right above Elm Street as the motorcade approached.

"Tell us, Sam, what you saw and heard," Fritz asked, talking over the traffic below.

They could already see for themselves a lot of what he'd seen. From the top of the Triple Underpass, they had a view of every important landmark. On their center-right (eastward), the open space of Dealey Plaza occupied the foreground with the Criminal Courts and Jail Building, farthest right, and next door, the County Records Building, all dominating the background. In the center came Elm Street with its shallow S-curve descending toward and under them. On the center-left (northward) lay more parkland, some oaks, a pergola, then, looming in the background, the Depository with its sniper-corner window angling away above the foliage. Closest of all, also on the center-left, sloped a grassy knoll that became steeper as Elm descended. Leftward, from their perspective, it rose up from Elm to a wooden stockade fence along the crest of the knoll running parallel to Elm. Beyond the fence (farther left, partly out of view) lay a rail yard and a crude, unpaved parking area. On the Elm side of the fence, three young trees graced the brow of the knoll.

"The motorcade," Holland answered, aiming his arm from right to left, "went on Houston in front of the Court and Jailhouse, then the Records Building, then turned sharp left onto Elm, heading down toward us. The motorcycle escort made a lot of racket. Lots of cheering too."

Abe strained to hear over the whine of cars cruising beneath them.

Holland's arm aligned with Elm.

"I saw the limousine make the turn on Elm. Two young ladies stood right over there on our right in the plaza with a camera. Mrs. Kennedy waved to them. The president waved to our left. Then I heard a loud report.

Holland dropped his arm and stared at Elm.

"At about that time, the president pulled forward and his right hand just froze momentarily. The car went on a few yards and Governor Connally turned to his right with his hand out and then there was another report. This time the president slumped over. Mrs. Kennedy had been looking at the two girls take a picture but now she turned back to the president because she realized what was happening, I guess. The second shot knocked him completely down on the floor, he just slumped completely over."

"Did you hear a third report?" Abe kept his voice up over the traffic.

"I heard four reports altogether. On the third or fourth, I saw a puff of smoke come out about six or eight feet above the ground right out from under those trees."

He pointed to their center left to the three young trees on the knoll, only forty to fifty yards away.

"A puff of smoke. I can't say it was or wasn't a rifle shot. It was like someone had thrown a firecracker. That sound wasn't as loud as the other reports," Holland continued. "Now, I have no doubt about seeing that puff of smoke come out from under those trees. Also, I have no doubt about four reports but the one with the puff of smoke was not as loud. The others seemed to come from the upper end of Elm." He gestured toward the Depository.

"You saw the governor go down too?" Fritz asked.

"Yes, sir. Now, I'm not sure which shot. Then, two motorcycle police in the motorcade—one of them threw his motorcycle down right in the middle of the street—he ran up towards where I saw a puff of smoke with his gun in his hand. The other one tried to ride up the hill, got halfway, and had to run up the rest on foot."

"When?" Fritz inquired from under his Stetson.

"Right when the shots were fired."

"Did you see anyone by that fence?"

"No."

"You were this close?"

"Right here."

"Let's go over this again. When you saw the puff of smoke, did you yourself see a weapon or see a person or muzzle fire over there?" Fritz drilled down.

"No, sir."

"And it was six to eight feet above the ground, you say, the puff of smoke?"

"Yes, sir."

"What'd you do then?" Jim asked.

"Immediately, a group of us up here ran that way, off to our left, northward, along the track until we got off the overpass and could swing right to check behind the stockade fence, in that parking area."

"Okay. Let's do now what you did then," suggested Fritz.

They retraced their path along the track and cinder rock, back to their left, northward.

"As soon as we got off the overpass, about here, we ducked over to our right, eastward. We ran up along this stockade fence to get up behind the pergola area."

They duplicated the movement without running.

"So, what did you find in here?" Fritz asked, as they walked the stockade fence line.

"Well, nothing. No one. No empty shells. No cars leaving. I saw a lot of footprints in the mud along the fence at one spot, like someone had been standing there. Maybe a hundred footprints. Some mud on a nearby car front fender, like someone had stood on it."

He showed them the approximate place where he'd seen the footprints. Abe thought it was just an ordinary patch of dirt.

Abe halted at the stockade fence, stood on his tip toes, looked over it, then studied Elm Street, the killing zone in plain view. But if, as he thought it through, if a shooter had fired from this spot, there was no way a puff of smoke would have appeared where Holland placed it.

"Mr. Holland, you saw the puff of smoke over in those trees, ten or eleven feet in front of this fence where we are now?" Abe asked.

"Yes, sir. Sounded like a firecracker."

FRITZ REPORTED ON THIS at the next meeting.

"If," Wade grumbled, "there was another shooter up on that knoll, then we owe it to Texas to find and execute him." Turning to Abe, he thumped the table. "Abe, I know you federal people don't like the word 'conspiracy,' but two shooters would mean a conspiracy. Any day of the week. Period."

Elaine had recently read Hoover's report concluding that Oswald had acted alone. She'd noted a number of grammatical errors, even lapses in logic. Maybe Oswald had acted alone, she thought, but we ought to do a better job than that.

Wade resumed, "Right now, we gotta go forward on Oswald and we can go after a second shooter later. But we must get to the bottom of it. If there were two shooters, there were two. So be it. Let's find out."

Wade's blood was up. The federals knew they should proceed with care.

"Of course, you're right," Abe said, "how can we help on this?"

"The puff of smoke," complained Wade. "That's the main thing, isn't it? Plus, some people *did* think the shots came from that area west of the Depository, the knoll. Roy Truly was one."

"Here's the problem on that," answered Fritz, respectfully, slowly, "three shots *did* come from the Depository. We know that. We know for an absolute, positive fact that they came from the sixth floor—those three guys on the fifth floor—they heard—even felt—three rifle blasts right above them. They even heard the hulls drop. We found the three hulls, right there, right above where they were standing. I myself ejected a fourth cartridge, a live one, from the chamber. So, if there was a fourth shot, it had to have come from somewhere else, but three came from the sixth floor—for an absolute, positive fact. Now, the thing is, Roy thought *all* the shots came from west of the building, not just one. We know—positively, absolutely—he was wrong about that. Positively wrong. He was standing out in front of the Depository.

Roy must have been thrown off by sound bouncing off buildings."

Unwrapping a cigar, Wade didn't miss a beat. "You're not coming to grips with one thing, Will. You're right that anyone who thinks *all* the shots came from outside the Depository is wrong, but that's not Sam Holland. He thought three shots came from the Depository end of Elm but *one*—now this is the point—a fourth came from the knoll."

Wade crushed the cigar cellophane into a tight ball and dropped it in the amber ash tray.

"And, with it, he saw a puff of smoke. Are we gonna just ignore this?"

Elaine stayed out of it, watching the cellophane ball trying to unfold itself.

Abe had kept quiet, then said, "May I respond?"

"Sure." Wade held a box of matches at the ready.

"Holland's a good man," Abe noted, "but he didn't see anyone over there and he didn't see any weapon over there—remember, he was pretty close. Some motorcycle officers went up there. They went up almost immediately. They saw nothing—no shooter—no ejected shells, no weapons, no cars leaving, no one running away. Period. Just the police. We know that for a fact. They would've seen them. It's just my opinion, but I think Holland mistook something for a puff of smoke."

"Well, good for you, Abe," Wade interrupted. "Your opinion and a nickel will get you a cup of coffee." Abe held up both hands in a mock surrender. He was used to resentment from locals when the federals came to help.

Wade turned to Fritz, "Will, remind us how many shots other people heard."

"Three," Fritz replied, "out of all the people we have interviewed from the plaza, almost all say three, a few say four, and a tiny number say five or more. Some just heard two. A strong majority, however, heard three and most thought they came from the Depository with some, like Roy, thinking they came from west of the Depository."

"That knoll *is* west, isn't it?" Wade persisted.

"Of course it is," answered Fritz.

Wade lit a match. It stung Elaine's nostrils.

"Could," Wade drew on his cigar, "echoes account for it, Will?"

"Possibly. There're a lot of tall buildings there for reflections. I'm not saying that's what happened. I'm just saying it could have been echoes."

"Let me ask this," Alexander spoke, aligning his pocketknife, blade closed, along the side of his yellow pad, "would a rifle shot even give off a puff of smoke? I mean, no one saw puffs of smoke from Oswald's rifle. We didn't see puffs of smoke in the war."

"Rifle cartridges produce almost no smoke these days," answered Fritz. "Same as with your infantry rifles, to avoid giving away your position."

"Did anyone else see a puff of smoke?" Wade blew a puff of his own.

"Not exactly," Fritz answered. "One guy saw some steam get released. There is, in fact, a steam pipe up there along the tracks by that fence. That wasn't exactly where Holland saw his puff of smoke, but the wind could've blown the steam toward those trees where he saw it."

Wade just stared at Fritz.

"Maybe," Abe tried again, "it was as simple as one of the motorcycles in the escort. One of them could've backfired a puff of smoke."

Wade ignored Abe's explanation.

"Listen, Henry, I keep coming back to this," Fritz continued, "Holland didn't see the puff of smoke at the fence; he saw it well in front of the fence—ten or eleven feet in front of the fence, about six to eight feet above the ground. Now, if somebody had had a rifle right there where he saw a puff of smoke, then the shooter plus his rifle would have been in plain view, and if the shooter was behind the fence, then the puff of smoke was too far away. Something's wrong there."

"And you, young lady," Wade lightened up, "you're being awfully quiet. What are your ruminations?"

Elaine appreciated his courtesy of including her.

"Maybe," Elaine looked to Wade, "it really *was* a firecracker, just like he said. That would've produced a puff of smoke and would've sounded just like he said it sounded. Could it have been a diversion?"

# 19 MARILYN SITZMAN

"OKAY, MARILYN, I'LL MEET YOU THERE IN HALF AN HOUR."

Bebe hung up the pay phone in the foyer of the Depository. She then walked to the pergola. Marilyn Sitzman, for whom she was waiting, served as a receptionist and secretary for Abraham Zapruder.

A young brunette hurried up from the direction of Elm and Houston. In her tailored gray suit, she could have been a fashion model instead of the assistant producer of the most famous home movie in history. Her stylish skirt, expensive wool, just fell below her knees.

"Bebe?"

"Yes, Bebe Boudreaux. So nice to meet you, Marilyn. Thank you for taking the time.

They exchanged obligatory compliments on attire.

"So, Marilyn, let's go over what occurred that day, I mean, from your perspective."

"Well," Marilyn gestured toward the concrete pier, then toward Elm Street beyond, "Mr. Zapruder went home to get his movie camera to film the presidential parade. Our office is just over in the Dal-Tex building, right across Houston from the Depository, fourth and fifth floors. He gets vertigo, so I said I'd stand behind him to hold him while he filmed. We wound up standing right over there, on that concrete pier."

She led Bebe a dozen steps to the concrete pier, jutting out in the general direction of Elm, then placed her hand on its flat top, torso high.

"Right here's where I stood. Mr. Zapruder was just in front of me. I have on the same suit now that I wore that day, if that matters."

"So, tell me what you saw and heard."

"We got up there. I was behind him but could see over his shoulder, just under his hat. I'm as tall as him. You could hear the cheering and it got louder and louder as they got closer. Then came the motorcycle racket. Then more loud cheering, clapping. We could see over everyone's heads into the president's car. As they came down Elm," she swung her arm left to right in an arc along Elm, "I heard three shots. The first two I thought were firecrackers. After the second one, Kennedy raised his arms like he was reacting to the noise. A few moments later, on the third shot, I saw the president's head splatter. Then, of course, we knew they were rifle shots." She pointed to the roadway. "Right there. Through it all, Mr. Zapruder kept filming and I kept holding his shoulders. We were shocked but somehow had the gumption to see it through."

"Three shots?"

"Three."

"Could you tell from where?"

"Seemed like up and to my left. All three. Over there."

She pointed leftward to the Depository.

"Ground level or higher?"

"Higher."

"As high as the sixth floor?"

"Hard to say which floor."

"Now, did you hear any shots from your right?" Here, Bebe had in mind the grassy knoll, just steps away.

"No."

"See anything on your right?"

"No, but I wasn't looking there. I was looking ahead."

Bebe made cryptic notes.

"But," Marilyn continued, "if a shot had been fired from our right or behind us, meaning from anywhere near that stockade fence, like they're saying in the papers, it would have been so close, we would've jumped sky high and our movie would've jumped all over. But we kept filming all the way until the car disappeared through the underpass."

"Did you hear anything over on your right?"

"This much I definitely remember. A young Negro couple was sitting by the pergola having lunch behind us on that park bench, right there," she gestured to an empty bench, "and about the time the president's car disappeared through the underpass, one of them knocked over a glass coke bottle, so it busted with a crashing noise. It wasn't gunfire. I knew it was glass when I heard it, but it shattered; being so close, it was loud." Both stared at the bench, now empty. "Possibly some people mistook it for a shot or something."

"Then what?"

"Well, at the same time, a lot of police and spectators rushed up the grass to look around the fence and pavilion, just over to our right, just here. It didn't look like they found anything. They asked me what'd happened, and I said they'd killed the president. I saw his brains come out. I escorted Mr. Zapruder back to work. We were both upset, but he was very upset."

"Did you see any puff of smoke off to your right or in the vicinity of the fence?"

"Again, I wasn't looking there."

"So, you're saying you heard no shot from your right side?

"Nothing but the smash of the glass bottle. If there was a rifle shot on my right, mind you, I'm not saying there was, it had to have been with one of those silencers."

"All right, thank you, Marilyn. By the way, have you seen the film yet?"

"Yes, the next morning. It's sickening."

"Has anyone else interviewed you?"

"No."

"Not even the police?"

"No, not even them."

A scoop.

Marilyn, Bebe would later write, had witnessed twenty-six seconds of extraordinary history and yet had remained as composed as anyone could've in the perilous circumstances. Her composure had saved the film project. Most would've run for cover. She hadn't. Nor had she bragged or embellished. She'd told it like it was. This, Bebe would report, was a strength of America.

# 20 WHICH BULLETS HIT WHOM?

THE QUESTION OF WHICH RIFLE BULLETS HIT WHOM INCREAS-
ingly vexed the prosecution, presenting a puzzle that could spin out of control,
even confound the jury, one that Foreman might turn into reasonable doubt.
Wade called a meeting to dissect it. He wheeled in a portable blackboard.
Elaine lifted a window in anticipation of smoke to come.

Alexander led off, saying, "Governor Connally and Miz Nellie believe
the first shot hit Kennedy in the neck by his upper back, the second shot hit
Connally, then came the fatal head shot. Seems right to me. At that short
distance, it would've been hard to miss." Alexander drew Elm Street and
the Depository on the blackboard. He chalked three rectangles representing
the car at three progressive positions with circles in them for the occupants.
"Like this—one Kennedy's back, two Connally's back, wrist, and leg, three
Kennedy's head," marking each circle as he went. The chalk squeaked and
clacked against the blackboard.

Abe thought Alexander had done a good job drawing it to approximate
scale. Abe offered, "That's also what Hoover said in his report."

"Thing is," Fritz countered, "we've only recovered what amounts
to two bullets. If all three bullets hit the targets as you say—one, two,
three," Fritz rose to touch the board where Alexander had ticked off the
shots, "then all three bullets should have landed in the car or left a hole
or gash where they ricocheted out. But we've recovered one nearly whole
bullet—that one, we think, worked out of the governor's thigh, finally
coming to rest on a gurney at the hospital. Obviously, that one came
from the car and made all of Connally's wounds. Also from inside the
car, we found a bullet nose, base, and fragments, all adding up to almost
another bullet. So that gives us two bullets in the car. Now, here's the
bugaboo—we can't find any evidence whatsoever of a third bullet. If all
three bullets hit in the car, all three bullets or their fragments or at least
ricochet marks should have been in the car. But there were only two. No
gash. No bullet hole."

Alexander lit a Lucky Strike, blew an upward plume of blue smoke, then squinted: "One of the bullets could've veered out of the car after hitting the president, most likely the head shot."

"Well," answered Fritz, resuming his seat and wiping chalk dust off his fingers with a bandana. "Say that the head shot did just that, veered out without leaving a mark on the car. That'd still mean that the Kennedy back shot stayed in the car, but we can't find any bullet hole or gash in the interior of the car that would match up with that angle or anything close. To say it again, there's no bullet hole or gash at all in the car. There's some tiny cracks from fragments hitting the inside of the windshield with a little dent in the chrome over the windshield. But nothing like what a whole bullet coming out his neck would've caused."

"Then maybe," replied Alexander, "the head shot fragmented and stayed in the car."

"Yeah," replied Fritz, "I think the head shot actually did fragment, so that'd account for the fragments in the car plus the tiny cracks around the windshield, but, again, the back shot hit only soft tissue and exited just below the knot in his tie. It was on a downward path when it left his body. That shot had to have continued on inside the car. Yet, there is no gash, no bullet hole inside the car."

Abe felt vaguely uneasy. For an airtight case, this one had some possible holes.

"Remember Virgie Rachley," Fritz continued, "the bookkeeper for Roy Truly? She said the first shot missed the entire car." Fritz returned to the blackboard to draw an X behind the first rectangle.

Elaine observed, "*That* would explain why only two bullets were found in the car."

Abe spoke, "But then we'd have *two* shots reaching the car, yet *three* sets of wounds to account for."

"Couldn't it be," Fritz continued, drawing two checkmarks inside the rectangle for the limousine at the second shot, "that the second shot hit both men, Kennedy then Connally?"

"No, no, no. That'd mean that Governor Connally and Nellie are wrong," grumbled Alexander. "They were actually there. Shouldn't we place some stock in their recollection?"

"And," added Wade, "it'd mean Hoover was wrong."

"Listen, my friends," Alexander continued, "Oswald just couldn't have missed the entire car at that close range. He was a Marine, for Christ's sake." He stubbed out his cigarette and resumed a whittling project, like he had heard enough.

"Will," summarized Wade, "you're thinking the first shot missed the car, the second shot went clean through Kennedy's back, then wounded Connally and wound up on his gurney, and the third shot shattered Kennedy's head and left those bullet fragments all over the car?"

"That's what I'm thinking."

"We ought to," Wade concluded, "study the hell out of that Zapruder film to see if Will's right."

# 21 THE ZAPRUDER FILM

Of the three home movies made in Dealey Plaza that day, the Zapruder film became far and away the most important. Abraham Zapruder chose a sweeping view of the motorcade route by Dealey Plaza. He stood on a concrete pier, part of a WPA pergola on the Depository side of Elm Street. He was, thus, about sixty feet north of the edge of the roadway itself, halfway between the Depository (on his left) and the Triple Underpass (on his right), near the edge of the grassy knoll (even closer on his right). He held a Bell & Howell 8mm camera with no sound, running color film at 18.3 frames per second, using a zoom lens. His receptionist, Marilyn Sitzman, held him steady from behind.

Zapruder's film ran 26.5 seconds. The FBI made a blowup of each frame, each numbered, a total of 486 frames, Z1 to Z486, as they came to be known. The first scene consumed 132 frames. It simply showed the leading motorcycle escorts as they turned off Houston onto Elm. To save film, Zapruder paused before Z133 and resumed filming moments after the midnight-blue presidential limousine, with its smartly snapping fender flags, completed the same turn. From there, to the end, his filming continued without interruption, panning left to right as the open limousine went by.

Screening it, the prosecutors saw the limousine come onto Elm, with its occupants waving to well-wishers on their respective sides. The president and the governor sat on the right side of the car, the camera side, the president in the back seat, the governor in a jump seat in front of the president, both facing forward. Also in the back seat, just left of the president, the First Lady's pink suit with pillbox hat shone in the sun. In front of Jackie sat the governor's wife, wearing nondescript brown, on a jump seat, to the left of the governor. Onlookers applauded from both sides of Elm. Given Zapruder's elevated position, the camera angled above the near-side crowd to catch all occupants. Soon after the car turned onto Elm, when it was directly in front of the Depository, the governor, in a fast movement, looked very briefly over his left shoulder, then more deliberately over his right shoulder, rearward and upward. For the next few moments, all appeared well. The president and Jackie continued to smile and wave. Then, for almost 25 frames (1.4 seconds), they all went, as seen on the film, behind a traffic sign. When they reappeared, the president's arms were already jerking up with his elbows at shoulder level, his hands grasping toward his lower neck, obviously wounded. A few frames later the governor slumped over onto his wife's lap. Meanwhile, having turned away from the well-wishers on her left, the First Lady placed both hands around the president's shoulders, peering into his neck region. She drew ever closer, leaning within inches of his face when—in an instant of eternal agony—the right front top of his head exploded forward in a froth of red and gray. The president jerked forward, then rearward, then collapsed. Mrs. Kennedy scrambled out onto the rear hood as if to retrieve something. A Secret Service agent leaped from behind onto the rear hood, then moved her back into the seat. The car accelerated forward and out of view.

Upon seeing the president's head explode, Elaine heaved, wanting to vomit. She averted her gaze, closed her eyes, and concentrated on shallow breaths. That she'd shaken the president's hand, even hugged Jackie, in Houston made it all the more palpable. And the indignity—everyone deserves when they die, she felt, to do so with dignity, not in a public spectacle. As awful, no one should have to live through the horror, the helplessness that the First Lady plainly felt.

*Dear Father, Son, and Holy Spirit, accept our president, comfort him, and his loved ones, and forgive us, God, forgive us.*

Not just Elaine. All of them. The film, she could tell, hit all of them like a gut punch. Even Alexander, who disliked Kennedy, looked away at times. They took a recess. They forced themselves, nevertheless, to watch it—over and again—for clues on the sequence of shots and how the murder of the president had occurred.

As they studied the film, they noted its limitations. Remarkable as it was, it had no sound. It could not reveal directly the timing of the first two shots. Nor could it reveal positively whether the first versus the second shot hit the president. The president and the governor remained out of view for critical moments as they were eclipsed by the roadside sign. The film itself was small, only eight millimeters wide, with part of it taken up by sprocket holes.

These became the critical reference points: The president's car first appeared at Z133; passed behind the foliage of an oak tree (as seen from the sixth-floor window) at Z166 and emerged therefrom at Z210 (again, as seen from the sixth-floor window); and passed behind the roadside sign (as seen on the film) at Z200 and emerged therefrom at Z225 (again, as seen on the film). The final shot plainly hit the president's skull at Z313. The car came closest to Zapruder at about Z300.

They studied the film for visible reactions and, in turn, what those reactions might say about the timing of the three shots. As for the first shot, Governor Connally reacted markedly to something at Z149, turning his head briefly to his left, then at Z162 quickly turning his head far more back to his right, upward as well, as if he were looking back over his right shoulder to locate a shooter, as he said he had. Assuming he reacted to the sound of the first report, further assuming a normal reaction time, Abe said the first shot probably came before Z149, *i.e.*, about Z140. That would have been a second and a half before the limousine passed behind the oak tree along Elm, as seen from the sixth floor.

As for the second shot, the president was desperately reaching for his throat at Z225–26 as he emerged from behind the roadside sign. Before disappearing behind the sign at Z200, he'd been waving normally to the crowd. Abe said it clear-cut that, while behind the sign, Kennedy was struck in the upper back (exiting at his throat). Plainly, given the severe way the president moved his arms, he'd been hit by Z225–26, surely some brief moment earlier. As for Governor Connally, he began a slumping reaction seven to eight frames later, less than half a second. They brought in a lip reader who said that between Z242 to Z250, Connally said, "No, no, no, no," the painful expression the governor uttered, according to his own memory, just after he was hit. Exactly when the second shot was fired remained unclear, but Abe thought it had to be a tad before Z225–26, at a time while the victims were hidden by the sign. So, Abe placed the second shot at about Z220, just after the president cleared the tree as seen from the sixth-floor window (Z210) and before he cleared the sign as seen on the film (Z225–26).

As for the final shot, the fatal head shot, Z313–14 captured its hell.

Elaine agreed with Abe. Alexander and Wade weren't sure, except, of course, for the head shot.

Z140 to Z313 covered 173 frames or about nine seconds, translating to three shots in nine seconds. If the first was already in the chamber, as it surely would have been, that would have meant three squeezes of the trigger, separated by two shell ejections, all in nine seconds. A good marksman could easily do that, Abe noted, with time to spare. But if the first shot missed, as seemed evident from the president's subsequent waving and smiling and from the firsthand account of Virgie Rachley, then *both* victims had to have been hit after the first missed shot but before the fatal head shot—indeed, after the car cleared the tree but before the fatal head shot. Not even an expert could have gotten off two separate shots, one hitting the president (in the back) and a different one hitting the governor (also in the back) in so short an interval. Either the second bullet (of three) got them both or there were two shooters (and four shots)—and two shooters (and four shots) would equal a conspiracy. It seemed, however, clear to Abe, based on the separate known fact that only two bullets ever reached inside the limousine, that the second shot at about Z220 had struck both men, Kennedy first (through the neck) and then Connally. Even Elaine, who otherwise entertained suggestions of conspiracy, agreed.

"Let's do a re-enactment," Wade concluded, "to see if Kennedy and Connally ever lined up with the sniper's window."

They puzzled too over something else. Most of the witnesses heard the last two shots bunched together. That is, there had been a gap after the first shot, then two shots in more rapid succession. Shots at Z140, Z220 and Z313 were evenly spaced and contradicted this pattern.

# 22 TOO BIG FOR YOU

IN DEALEY PLAZA ON THAT SAME DAY, A BRISK DAY, WADE WAS out for a noontime stroll. He bumped into Judge Brown with his pipe and a *Superman* issue rolled under his arm. He advised Wade how impressed he'd been with Abe and Elaine. Brown continued, "Henry, you told me that this case was too big for me. Maybe it is. But you know something? I think this case is too big for you and your pal Alexander. You need to find a way to bring in those federals to help you try the case. I mean as trial counsel."

Wade simply smiled, "Maybe you're right, Judge."

Wade meant it. Alexander would resent it but Wade respected Abe and Elaine. They were superb lawyers. On appeal, more importantly, the judges would pause twice before they went against not only a Texas district attorney but also the United States of America.

# 23  ADULT REFRESHMENTS

J<small>UDGE</small> S<small>ARAH</small> H<small>UGHES</small> <small>THRUST DOUBLE SCOTCHES AT</small> A<small>BE AND</small> Elaine, saying, "LBJ-style."

In her chambers, the three settled into luxurious leather reading chairs.

"To the President," the judge raised her glass, and her guests followed.

It was Friday, January 25.

"Listen," she continued, "I can't drink with someone and call them Mister. May I just call you 'Abe'?"

Abe beamed. "Please, of course."

Elaine liked the judge. They were the only women with law degrees in the building, so they commiserated at times. Elaine also liked that the judge took to Abe.

Hughes lapsed into telling LBJ-JFK stories. She explained how she'd first campaigned for Johnson in 1948, then for his Senate races in the 1950s. As a co-chair of the Dallas County Democratic Campaign committee in 1960, she'd ridden with Kennedy and Johnson along a thirty-mile campaign motorcade from Fort Worth to Dallas.

"Was *so* funny! At one traffic stop," Hughes began to laugh, "some woman reached into the open car to try to take Kennedy's handkerchief from his jacket pocket, but he placed one hand over it to keep it and with the other hand reached over to yank Lyndon's from his coat and handed it to the lady."

All three laughed.

"The look on Lyndon's face—Kennedy's, too—I'll never forget it," she started to laugh again. "A little later, Lyndon introduced me to Kennedy, telling him if he ever wanted to appoint a woman to something, here was the woman to appoint, or words like that. So maybe Kennedy felt bad about that handkerchief and I owe my appointment to some woman out there with an LBJ handkerchief."

The judge took a robust drink, then waited for them to do likewise.

"If I'm lying, I'm dying," she ended the tale.

"LBJ, I hear, got you through the Senate in no time," Elaine said.

"Two weeks. There was some resistance, mind you, on account of my being a woman, but Lyndon made some deals for me. He got me through in two weeks."

After refills, Hughes turned to the Oswald case.

"Lyndon called me the other night, late of course, and asked about you. I let him know that you two were tops. Lyndon wants to get this trial over and done with. The convention's right around the corner. He knows Henry Wade and wondered if he should call Wade and tell him to bring you two onto the trial team. Just to get things moving."

Elaine blushed but loved at the idea that her name had sailed into the ear of the president.

"I told him," the judge continued, "by all means."

"Listen, Lyndon owes me. That man kisses me every time I see him."

When the time came to leave, the three shared a moment of sincerity. The judge cautioned them that the Oswald case was "too important to the nation" to be left solely to the locals, "good as they might be," and that it "cried out" for the steady, capable hands of good federal prosecutors. "You two," she concluded, "will be part of American history."

"I'LL COME RIGHT TO the point, Bill," Wade navigated his way through piles of papers on Alexander's office floor in the Records Building, "I think we should bring Abe Summer and his assistant to help to help try the case!"

"No way," Alexander squinted. "We don't need 'em."

"Maybe we don't but Judge Brown thinks we do."

Wade left out that LBJ had called, knowing how Alexander felt about Kennedy and Johnson. Wade remained standing.

"This is state," Alexander pushed back and stood, his jacket off, his holster evident, "they're federal."

"Bill, we got a lot of federal to deal with—Secret Service, FBI, forensics, maybe Mexico City—it was the president, for Christ's sake."

"We can handle it, Henry."

"Like you handled that General Walker mess?" Wade forced a smile, "You saw what Elaine did with it. We can use help like that."

"Whoa, now, Henry, whoa. We're talking a Dallas jury now. You think she'll play to a Dallas jury?"

"Percy's got a young lady on his side."

"Not a Mexican."

Wade resented the way Alexander had barged into the case, assigning himself to the case, taking charge on Tenth Street and at the boarding house even as the police arrived. To be sure, Wade felt at home in a white men's club, but he found Alexander's explicit prejudice uncouth. Wade also disliked the way Alexander wore a gun, even in court.

"Listen, Bill, Elaine's Tejano. As Texas as you or me. Her family signed the Texas Declaration of Independence."

"That dog won't hunt, Henry." Alexander sat back down and began to whittle. "This is my case. Let me handle it."

"Actually, it's not your case, Bill. When you run and get elected district attorney, then they'll all be your cases. Right now, they're all my cases."

Alexander whittled, then said, "How about just Abe?"

"He won't come without her," Wade answered. "I've already asked. Anyway, we need her for Mexico City. She speaks Spanish."

Wade waited for Alexander to say it was okay but all he heard was the shaving of wood.

"Elaine lost her dad at Anzio," Wade ended it. "I think we owe him this—her too. Bill, we're gonna do it."

WADE CALLED ABE AND invited him and Elaine to join the trial team. "We'd be honored," replied Abe. Elaine was with him and saw the news on his face. "May I tell my mom?" she soon asked.

"Of course."

# 24 THE CAROUSEL CLUB

THAT EVENING, BEBE AND PERCY FOLLOWED A CROWD TO THE Carousel Club. Ruby was throwing a benefit for the widow of Officer Tippit with all proceeds for the first ninety minutes to go to the widow. Law enforcement were turning out in force. Abe had declined the invitation so Bebe invited Percy, who accepted on the condition that everything he said would remain off the record.

From the outside, the Carousel Club at 1312-1/2 Commerce Street, across the street from the Adolphus and near the Baker, had a seedy look, not a classy look. It was in a cluster of joints supported mainly by cops and the hotel district, sandwiched in among a deli, a pawn shop, and a parking garage. An exterior display of eight-by-ten black-and-white photos showed strippers with big hair in provocative poses.

"That woman," said Percy, pointing to a photo of Shane, "is famous for her ability to twirl a ten-gallon Stetson on one nipple, then flip it over to the other, still twirling it, while spinning pistols in both hands, sometimes even loaded."

"Her or the guns?"

"That question is what makes it charming."

Customers normally paid a two-dollar cover charge at the top of the stairs, but tonight five dollars cut it, all for the cause. A wall at the top of the stairs displayed a mirror. Someone made a show of waving through it, like it was one way. After entering a large barn-like square room, Bebe saw, on her left, a boomerang-shaped bar that ran the length of the wall. In the center rear stood a stage the size of a boxing ring. Black plastic booths hugged the other walls. Dark-red carpet covered the entire floor, even the lower half of the bar wall. She and Percy snagged good stools at a corner of the bar. Bebe saw gaudy gold plastic on the top of the bar. Gaudy gold-mesh drapes hid the windows on the wall opposite the bar. Gaudy gold crowns dangled from the ceiling. A painting of a stallion, framed in gold, hung on the wall behind the bar. It was gaudy too.

A handsome black kept a tidy, well-run bar.

"Good evening, Mr. Foreman," he said.

"Good evening, Andy."

Ruby came over and gave Percy the cold shoulder but greeted Bebe. She pulled a "Volveremos" bumper sticker from her purse and presented it to Ruby, who jived over it, then asked Andy to give them the "good stuff"—on the house. Bebe remembered, as Percy had advised her to do, to tell Ruby his place had "class," a lie. Ruby answered, "Even more so, now that you're here, Miss Boudreaux." Then, Ruby moved on.

Out of respect for the fallen officer, Ruby's performers, doubling as bar maids before the show started, wore a little more than usual and, to raise money, pushed a little cheaper champagne than usual, the corks popping, with themselves drinking as little as possible. Blue haze choked the room.

"Tell me, Percy, something I don't already know," Bebe leaned in across the bar corner.

"You go first," replied Percy.

"Fair enough." She paused until the barkeep was far enough away, then lowered her voice, leaning in. "Jack Ruby was up to something big time the morning they moved your client over to the county jail. I saw him forced back up a ramp of the basement by a cop just as your client got led through. Then I saw him at the top of the other ramp, the exit ramp, just after they drove him out. Ruby was crying. Crying, no lie. Now, what the hell was he up to?"

Percy glanced down the bar and blew smoke.

"I swear and cross my heart," she added.

"Some people," Percy observed, "just like the cops. They wanna be one. They wanna be with them. Just like right now," his eyes scanned the room.

Percy tapped his cigarette onto an ashtray.

"Your turn," she declared.

Bebe waited.

"We said off the record?"

She nodded.

"Why," he went slowly, "would two guys dressed in police uniforms pull up in a squad car in front of Lee's boarding house soon after the assassination during the exact five minutes he was inside and toot their horn?"

"Did they?"

"So says the housekeeper," Percy continued. "She looked out right at 'em and they took off, pronto. When Lee went out, they were gone."

"Dear me, you're saying that's why he was just wandering around over there—he just missed his ride?"

"You tell me."

On the back of the stage, the drummer practiced a roll.

"I don't believe," Bebe took a swallow, "the cops would've been in on it."

"I don't either. But maybe guys dressed like cops were in on it."

The haze became warm and stuffy. Percy removed his jacket and loosened his tie.

Ruby took the stage. He teared up as he praised J. D. Tippit and exhorted everyone to drink—"all proceeds without deduction for the first ninety minutes will go to the Widow Tippit." Ruby called out the first act, a comedian.

"Hey," the comic said, as the applause faded, "you cops know this is a tough town—tough. A thief steals a calendar and gets twelve months." The room groaned. "Then the judge sends a drunk through an upholstery machine. He's fully recovered." More groans. "A dentist marries a manicurist—they fight tooth and nail."

In the audience, Baby Lou, another star, draped herself over some cops, howling at the lines. She had a raucous laugh that went on too long and too loud. Finally, the comic paused, "Lady, even a train stops."

Little Lynn canvassed the room, taking Polaroids, giving them to guests for free. Bebe disliked hers. The flash made her look too hard.

"Hey," continued the comic, "the papers said Oswald used a German Mauser, but it had to have been Italian because it went, 'wop, wop, wop.'"

When the benefit part ended, a subdued Ruby stood to announce that the Carousel Club would continue to rock out with its normal stars and "class" acts after an intermission. As the intermission drew to a close and patrons settled back into their seats, Ruby, still maudlin over Officer Tippit, retook the stage, this time with Sheba in his left arm.

"My friends," Ruby spoke genially into the mike, "Seeing Oswald's lawyer here tonight—"

A chorus of boos erupted.

A drum roll followed.

"Seeing him reminds me of that Sunday morning. Hey, meet Sheba. She was with me. I got cranked up and went down to get that scum that Sunday."

"Well, what the hell?" gasped Bebe. Percy watched unruffled.

His brow sudoresque, Ruby let the crowd draw down.

"Yeah, you heard right. I was at City Hall that Friday when they showed him off to the press. He grinned like a skunk."

The band waited. Little Lynn stood in the shadows.

"So that Sunday morning, I started down to see the cocksucker go county—with this in my pocket."

Ruby slid his right hand into his suit jacket pocket and brought out his Cobra .38. Bebe clutched Percy's elbow. The room froze.

"Jack, be careful, now," said a voice in the darkness.

"I always carry it. Protection. Perfectly legal."

He slid it back in his pocket.

"I started down there, thinking I'd do something good for the country, that I'd be a Jew with guts. I almost got to him, almost, but a guard—Roy Vaughn—stopped me. Roy, you here tonight?"

"You should've finished him off then and there," a drunk yelled.

"You talk big now, don't you, asshole?" Ruby's face went red.

"Tits and ass," another cop interrupted. "Come on, Jack, start cooking—be a Jew for tits and ass."

Sheba licked his cheek. Ruby slacked. The crowd took up a chant, "tits and ass." The bartender came up to help Ruby ramble off the stage.

The band, at the back of the stage, struck up bump-and-grind music. Soon, Little Lynn, now in her stage costume, danced on. The lights went ultraviolet. The drum beat to the jolt of her pelvis. The crowd went wild.

Percy leaned close, "Bebe, you were on the money."

Another scoop.

# 25 BISCUITS AND BACON

ELAINE REHEARSED THE CALL, DEBATED WHETHER TO MAKE IT, finally dialed the Baker Hotel, and asked for his room. "Abe Summer," he answered.

"It's Elaine, Abe. Why don't you come over here, so I can make you a proper breakfast?"

"Don't you have mass?"

"Went already."

Abe accepted.

"One last thing, Abe. My mother told me never to feed pork to anyone whose name is in the Old Testament. So do you like bacon or not?"

"Bless your mom," Abe replied. "I love it. I was named for the president, not the prophet."

She felt Abe deserved this salute. She liked him. Thanks to him, she'd made the trial team. Still, she didn't want Abe to misinterpret her hospitality for more than it was.

She let him in, the sun behind him, and smiled wide at a bouquet of daffodils. Sizzling bacon and coffee aromas filled her small, warm flat. The front room glowed with pleasant morning light. Her Zenith table-top radio played classical. She led him into a simple kitchen, a floor of alternating black and white, twelve-inch squares of asbestos tiles, a window rearward, a back door, a porcelain sink, an old gas oven under a stovetop, a modern Norge Jet-D-Frost refrigerator, finally a small wooden table for two. She installed Abe at the table, poured him coffee from the Chemex hourglass flask, then continued at the stove, claiming she was almost done. He asked why her coffee tasted so much better than the hotel coffee. She replied he would have to ask the hotel that question, delivering a platter of bacon, covered by a paper towel.

"I hope you like your eggs scrambled because that's the way you're getting them."

"Most excellent."

After a swallow, he rose to help, a gesture she appreciated, so she assigned him to produce real orange juice from orange halves and the electric squeezer.

Elaine had her hair in a ponytail to keep it clear of grease and heat. She wore jeans, a sweater under her apron, with sneakers, looking, she realized, like a college coed.

"Okay, these eggs are ready. Let's eat." With a click, she pulled the handle on the Norge to stow a glass milk bottle. Off came her apron.

At the small wooden table for two, the scrambled eggs fell onto the plates, steaming. Biscuits then emerged from the oven, perfectly tanned. The heat from the open oven felt toasty on the winter morning.

"Bienvenido a Casa Elena."

"Gracias."

They dug in.

"Well, here's to the trial team. I can't believe it's really true," she raised her juice. "I don't know exactly how but I know you got me there, so, Abe, I thank you."

Abe smiled and asked, "How'd you learn to cook like this?"

"On a wood-burning stove in Corsicana."

"Pretty damn impressive, Elaine." He buttered a biscuit.

"Next time we'll add grits."

"Your work's been the best, Elaine. You deserve to be on the team. You've earned it."

She repressed color.

"I asked Wade how we can help," Abe continued. "He wants you to go to Mexico City and me to check out New Orleans. He's worried about our most likely worst-case scenarios, meaning plausible lies that Oswald could just make up, lies hard for us to impeach."

"But Percy never puts his people on the stand—supposedly."

"True, but what if he does? Wade thinks one set of Oswald lies would involve Mexico City and the other New Orleans. I think he's right."

Elaine brimmed with worry too. Still at the top of her list were the cops in front of 1026 North Beckley "tooting their horn at precisely the moment Oswald changed clothes," as she put it to Abe. "Were they confederates waiting for Oswald?"

He replied, "We got Jim working on that, but we got no one working on Mexico City and New Orleans."

Abe had cleaned his plate, so she offered him more warm biscuits, which he sliced open, then slathered with butter and jam, tucking bacon between the halves to make a sandwich.

"I've never seen anyone do that."

"My mom made breakfasts like yours, even during the Depression. As a kid, I started doing this—putting bacon in the biscuits with butter and jam, like a tiny sandwich. I'm embarrassed to do it in the hotel dining room."

"Please, be my guest," she laughed. She felt delight. "Have another one, for luck."

When they adjourned to the front room, Abe paused before a photo of a soldier beside the Zenith tabletop.

"Your dad?"

"Yes."

She settled on a rattan sofa, he in the armchair.

"Tell me about him, would you?"

"That radio," her voice caught a moment, "that radio brought us the news of Pearl Harbor. He'd given it to me for my eighth birthday. I was listening to big band music when they interrupted to say the Japanese were bombing the Hawaiian Islands. I went screaming for mom and dad."

"Where was this?" Abe asked.

"Just north of Dallas. Dad said, 'We're in it now.' He enlisted right away. Mom and I moved in with her family near Corsicana."

She glanced at the photograph.

"That was taken on his last home leave. They were headed overseas. He hugged me and told me to listen for the news of victory."

Abe's daffodils rested by the radio. She felt her throat thicken.

"North Africa, then Italy. Killed at Anzio." Even these short phrases were hard to say.

"I'm sorry." Abe seemed genuinely to understand her angst.

"I don't think you know this, Abe," Elaine moved on, "but I saw the president and Jackie down in Houston the night before they came to Dallas."

Abe cocked his face.

"I drove down to Houston," she continued, "for a Latin League reception. It was only word of mouth that the Kennedys might show—an off-schedule thing—but they did. The Rice Hotel Ballroom. The Kennedys came in the front door and got greeted by one of our soldiers who'd won the Medal of Honor. JFK was gracious. Jackie stole the show—spoke to us in Spanish. That brought the house down. Everyone chanted, 'Viva Kennedy, Viva Kennedy.' A lovely evening. Then, all this."

"Yes, then all this."

"I just keep wondering," Elaine shifted back to business, "whether Castro had anything to do with it. Back in September, you know, he told a reporter that he knew the Kennedy people were trying to kill him, even said if it continued, the Kennedys themselves wouldn't be safe."

She paused. She felt he didn't want to hear any conspiracy theories, so she shifted again, "And, that business with Silvia Odio."

She threw a sleek look, then smiled. Abe did too.

"Keep this to yourself, Elaine, but on the day of the assassination, the attorney general raised that very thought with me and my boss. I've wondered about it too. If Castro had anything to do with anything like that, what Oswald was doing down in Mexico City would be the key," answered Abe. "But that's a big 'if.'"

She used her left hand to slowly twirl her hair around a finger, her right hand poised to write. It helped her think.

"I mean," Abe added, "if you were Castro or anyone else for that matter, would you throw in with a loser like Oswald? A loser and a loner. He tried to kill General Walker all by himself. He's just not the type to throw in with anyone."

She continued to twirl, listening.

"Except for John Wilkes Booth, every presidential assassin acted alone. No one threw in with them." Abe added.

"Maybe no one threw in with Oswald," she answered, "but maybe someone used him, maybe promising a ticket to Cuba. Maybe Oswald bragged about Walker and someone, maybe that Leopoldo guy, put him onto killing Kennedy. I'd love to see Cuba's file on Oswald."

"While we're just speculating," Abe replied, "maybe Leopoldo was actually anti-Castro pretending to be pro-Castro to use Oswald to kill the president expecting it'd get blamed on Castro and lead to an invasion. You see the problem, Elaine. This kind of speculation gets fantastic, too fantastic, too fast. We don't need it to convict Oswald. Going down that rabbit hole would just undermine our case."

When it was time for Abe to go, Elaine insisted on driving him back. Barren hardwoods stood against the winter sky. Dreary winter light made it worse.

She asked if his parents were alive. No, he said, only a sister. She'd seen he wore no ring. Had he ever been married? Engaged? She wondered.

Elaine worked the stick and pedals as she summoned the courage to ask, but he changed the subject.

"Say, how do you know Karen Eisenstadt?"

"The March on Washington last summer."

"You went?"

"In this very car. Almost at the last minute, I decided to drive up. I talked my ex-boyfriend into going. Somehow he knew Karen. So we all drove up."

"How was it?"

"*So* cool. We parked at Arlington Cemetery and walked over the Memorial Bridge, then joined a gigantic crowd near the Lincoln Monument. We stood up near the front."

"What's she like?"

"A true believer. Civil rights. Criminal defense. Funny as hell. It's pure coincidence that we've both showed up in this case."

"And, what'd you think of the March?" Abe asked.

"Going there, we got worried about getting arrested. The radio said thousands of cops. I didn't want to embarrass Sanders or lose my job. But once we got into the crowd, we got swept up by it. There was no trouble at all, thank God. You know, even the weather turned out great, especially for August. Peter, Paul, and Mary did 'Blowin' in the Wind.' I cried. King made his speech. I cried then, too."

Low on the car radio was Russ Knight, the "Weird Beard," curating a program of rock music on KLIF 1190.

"Truth be told," Abe smiled, "most of Main Justice thought the March would do more harm than good, especially if it turned nasty. They had lots of jail space ready. But it turned out fine."

As they crossed the viaduct in the gathering darkness, the Hertz clock on top of the Depository read 5:00 p.m. Abe, she saw, peered down into The Bottoms at the lantern-like glow from shanty windows.

"The other reason I went, Abe, was to visit my dad. He's in Arlington."

# 26 MODUS VIVENDI

ABE KNEW THEY HAD A STRONG CASE, BUT HE ALSO KNEW THEY had to find good answers to nagging problems. At the top of the dirty dozen, he realized, ranked the memo stating that Howard Brennan had refused to make a positive identification at the lineup. While bad for the prosecution, this fact had already come out at the bail hearing. Also curious, if not troublesome, was the memo regarding Oswald's housekeeper. She'd seen two strange policemen toot their car horn out front just as Oswald changed clothes. But Foreman already knew this, according to Earlene Roberts herself. And, what about the "puff of smoke"? If Foreman wanted to say Oswald was part of a conspiracy, then God bless him—all the way to the electric chair. Overall, no interview memo would cripple the prosecution's case.

This led Abe to suggest that Wade cut a deal—the prosecution would turn over all state and federal interview material for any eyewitnesses bearing on the charged murders in exchange for the defense stipulating that the foregoing completely satisfied *Brady*. That was a good deal for the defense. Alexander opposed it on the ground that it would allow Oswald to see the memos in advance to construct a good lie. Everyone else saw this risk too, a genuine downside. Still, the federals took the long view—future generations will condemn us if we withhold this. We should turn it all over. We'll still win the case.

With misgivings, Wade came over, feeling the weight of history. But he insisted on a further condition—that the defense agree to keep the trial in Dallas—no change of venue. That would even it up, a fair trade.

Foreman agreed, pronto.

Defense counsel further agreed to make no reference to the Texas medical examination requirement and to make no objection to the qualification of the Bethesda and Parkland pathologists to explain the cause of death and paths of the bullets through the bodies of Kennedy and Connally. In exchange, the prosecution further agreed to avoid any reference to domestic abuse by Oswald of his wife or family. Before bringing up any other uncharged act before the jury, moreover, the prosecution (having the Walker assassination attempt in mind) further agreed to raise it with the judge to give defense counsel an opportunity, however brief, to move to exclude or restrict its use. Neither side mentioned to the other anything about General Walker.

Trial loomed close enough for Wade to assign witness examinations. The federal witnesses, he said, would be examined by either Abe or Elaine. All other witnesses would be done by Wade and Alexander, with one exception—Oswald himself. The conventional wisdom held that Oswald would not testify. This was anchored in Foreman's reputation for keeping his clients off the stand and trying to put the police on trial. So, they offered the cross-examination of Oswald to Abe. He understood the calculus. He could see a large risk of doing much preparation only to have it go for naught if Oswald elected not to testify. Still, Abe had undertaken this burdensome chore in many cases, a necessary precaution. He said yes, of course, he would accept the assignment.

# 27 NEW ORLEANS

"JIM GARRISON, HE'S SOMEONE YOU OUGHT TO MEET, ABE."

Bebe was calling Abe to say that she'd been in New Orleans for Mardi Gras, and as part of her regular beat, had had lunch with the district attorney, Jim Garrison, who wanted to meet Abe to share some ideas he had about the Kennedy assassination. Abe then offered that he was coming to New Orleans that very Friday for interviews.

"God, that's great!" She continued, "I'll arrange a lunch for you with him, or dinner, as you prefer."

Abe said a lunch would be best, somewhere private so they could talk.

"Call me when you get here," she added. "Maybe on Saturday afternoon we can do something." She gave him her home number. She called again on Thursday to say that a one-on-one lunch would be in Garrison's office.

"LET'S ROLL," ABE DECLARED as he settled into the front passenger seat and lit a cigar. They left Dallas at two in the morning on Friday. Jim's rear view featured, for thirty miles, the giant red Pegasus rotating atop an oil derrick on the Magnolia Building in downtown Dallas. Speeding in the darkness through East Texas, working the floor switch to dim, then brighten, his headlamps, Jim told inside stories about Hoover and the FBI. Hoover had dirt on every president, even Kennedy. Usually it involved women. That's how Hoover stayed in power. Hoover hated Martin Luther King, Jr., thought he was a phony, thought he was a communist, and wiretapped his lines. Hoover, Jim said, had recordings of King with women. Hoover had dirt on Earl Warren, too, but Warren got confirmed anyway as chief justice. Warren despised Hoover for having nosed around in his private life. Hoover didn't want any commission to investigate the assassination, to second-guess the Bureau's own tracking of Oswald. He wanted the FBI's report, the one done in December, to be the definitive report. If there was to be a commission, Jim emphasized, Warren ranked as the last person Hoover wanted to head it up. Hoover had a Napoleon complex—Jim laughed in saying this. His desk rested on a platform so that he would be taller than anyone to whom he granted an audience—"Like the Pope," Jim chortled. Within the Bureau, FBI agents lived in everlasting fear that Hoover would decide they had erred or embarrassed him in some way and would send them off "to Siberia," meaning some place like Mississippi, to snoop on movement workers while pretending to stand up for civil rights. Shanklin, Jim's boss in Dallas with a worry-lined face, remained paralyzed by such nightmares, especially over being blamed for Oswald.

As the first gray streaks of dawn lit the sky, Jim held forth on Judge Brown and his famous stripper case, the one where she posed with Brown in chambers and eventually got fifteen years for marijuana possession. "She didn't deserve fifteen years for Mary Jane," Jim commented, "but maybe she did for trying to shoot her husband in the balls."

By nine, they breezed along the brown and green of the tropical bayous northwest of New Orleans. By ten, they were in the FBI office in the French Quarter. They debriefed Agent Jack Quigley, the New Orleans agent who had spoken with Oswald in jail after the fistfight in August 1963. Abe gathered from the interview that Oswald had been building up a pro-Castro resume to try to get into Cuba, such as the Fair Play for Cuba leafleting on Canal Street, his fight with the well-known exile, Carlos Bringuier, then his debate with Bringuier on WDSU.

Abe and Jim visited the Reily Coffee Company at 640 Magazine Street, in the warehouse district in New Orleans, whose main product was Luzianne coffee. Oswald "sucked" as an employee, reported the manager, "unreliable. Fired his ass." That summed it up. Abe looked at the employment file. Oswald had been paid sixty dollars per week. On his employment application, Oswald had listed as references "Sgt. Robert Hidell" and "Lieut. J. Evans," at least one obviously fictitious name.

"Can we keep this file?" Abe inquired.

"Sure," the manager answered.

"You may need to testify. Are you willing to come to Dallas?"

"You bet," he replied. "I knew that son of a bitch was no good."

From the Reily Coffee Company, they walked one block to the corner of Camp at Lafayette Streets—the Newman Building. At the entrance at 544 Camp, they met Sam Newman, the owner. They showed him a yellow flyer for the Fair Play for Cuba Committee seized from the Paine residence, with an address rubber-stamped on the rear stating 544 Camp Street. Newman replied he hadn't rented any space to Oswald or any "committee." In fact, he hadn't rented space in the building at 544 Camp to anyone since September 1962 (before Oswald had even returned to New Orleans). Jim and Abe concluded that Oswald possibly intended to rent space there, it being close to his workplace, or just pretended to have done so, but never actually did, perhaps explaining why the stamp appeared on only a few of the leaflets. Five Forty-Four Camp Street, they decided, was just another dry hole.

At one, they arrived at the district attorney's office in the French Quarter. Bebe awaited them. She directed Abe into Garrison's chambers, introduced them, and left with Jim for lunch at Brennan's.

In Garrison's commodious chambers, the two started with pleasantries about Bebe. "She's got a genius for being looked at," quipped Garrison. Readers in New Orleans enjoyed her columns on the local court beat,

Garrison said. He admitted, with a wry smile and in a rich Garden District accent, that he tried hard to stay on her good side. "She's never, however, written anything so good about me as she wrote about you in that Profeta case. You got a remarkable verdict, Mr. Summer, and put away that scum. You did New Orleans right."

A secretary announced the arrival of lunch. In came shrimp with salad from Antoine's, served on china with silver and linen napkins. They dined at his desk, with Abe on the opposite side, using its pullout tab. An aroma of American Burley lingered despite an open, tall window and a gently turning seven-blade ceiling fan. A bird chorus performed outside the window on a champagne day in February.

Garrison had been elected in 1961, he went on, and had been in office two years. His main effort so far had been vice busting. He recounted some of his recent prostitution raids in the French Quarter. "Strip clubs are okay. Hell, Jack and Jackie went with Governor Long to the Sho Bar to see Blaze Starr. We couldn't very well arrest them. But whore houses—no, we don't tolerate them anymore," he paused to sip iced tea. "So be careful where you go tonight." He seemed half serious. "Friday is Arrest Night in the Quarter," he added, "and tonight's Friday."

Finally, Garrison got around to the assassination. His main point "zeroed in" on New Orleans. Oswald had been born there and spent most of his youth there. He'd returned to New Orleans in May 1963, then stayed until September, when he left for Mexico City and his family moved back to Texas. What happened, Garrison asked, "in New Orleans or maybe in Mexico City to cause Oswald to take the life of the president?" Garrison listed the leafleting, the fight, and the WDSU debate, all familiar now to Abe. Garrison stressed that Oswald was a "hard-core admirer of Castro."

"Was Oswald connected to organized crime here?" Abe asked, thinking back to the attorney general's worry. Professionals would have been smart enough, Abe felt sure, to steer clear of a loose nut like Oswald.

"No, not that we know."

"Was he connected to the pro-Castro people here?"

"You would think so, wouldn't you?" said Garrison, "but we actually don't see that connection yet. Now, you must remember, Castro's people here all pretend to be anti-Castro. That way they can infiltrate and keep tabs on the opposition. Kinda like double agents. It's hard to know who here is truly pro-Castro."

Garrison lit his American Burley.

"You ever run across," Abe filled the pause, thinking of Miss Odio while watching the curl of the smoke, "two guys with war names of 'Leopoldo' and 'Angelo'—possibly real exiles, maybe pretenders?"

Garrison asked for their descriptions. Abe repeated what Odio had said. Garrison wrote down the names, having trouble with Leopoldo and getting repeats of the spelling, but finally said, "No, never heard of them."

"Well," Abe finally got blunt, "do you have any specific leads we ought to know about?"

"None actually," Garrison replied, drawing on his stem and waving out another match, "except this—the man defected to Russia, defected back, then he angled down here in New Orleans to ingratiate himself with Castro." Garrison swiveled to the side and leaned back, his feet propped on an open desk drawer. "I mean, look, you don't go murder the president of the United States without a getaway plan. John Wilkes Booth, now, he had a good escape plan—not good enough to allow for a broken leg but good in theory. But Oswald—he had thirteen dollars plus a bus transfer in his pocket. I bet he had a lot more on him when he went to Mexico City. So, how in hell did he plan to escape from Dallas, then out of the country? Maybe to Cuba. So he had to have help. But somehow all that help went haywire in the actual event. Help means a conspiracy, and I think the roots of that conspiracy are either here in New Orleans or in Mexico City."

A swarm of blue smoke covered the desk, gently swept by the downwash of the fan. Garrison arrested his speech to pull a grain of tobacco from the tip of his tongue.

Blather like this—general speculation, nothing more—irritated Abe. He was a trial lawyer. He needed witnesses, people who saw or heard something incriminating firsthand—someone who could and would testify in court. Abe figured that Garrison just wanted to meet him and somehow get tied into the case of the century.

"Mr. Garrison, I thank you for your kindness and hospitality. If we turn up something here in New Orleans along the lines you have outlined, we will, of course, phone you."

"Well," said Garrison, "you'd better do the same in Mexico City."

"We are."

"If I can help you with dinner reservations, please call me." He handed Abe a card with his office number printed on the front, his home number inked in on the back. "Good luck to you, Mr. Summer."

Jim and Bebe tittered over New Orleans politics as Abe arrived to join them for dessert. He thanked Bebe for arranging the meeting, even though it had produced nothing of value.

"Now," Bebe replied, "Jim here tells me you'll have time tomorrow afternoon, so let's do our profile interview then. How about Audubon Park?"

JIM AND ABE DROPPED by 4905–4911 Magazine Street, a double shotgun that included Oswald's rental unit. In the left side of the double shotgun, front to back, lived the manager, Jesse Garner with his wife, at 4911. In the rear half of the right side had once lived the Oswalds, at 4905.

Chickens clucked and scattered as Mrs. Garner took them to 4905. Its entry was halfway down a right-side driveway, through a door facing the front on a screen porch stuck on like a sidecar. Although it had an adequate parlor, it was otherwise cramped—and grimy. The Oswalds, she told them in the parlor, had been tenants from May to September 1963. She'd regularly heard the Oswalds fighting, often shouting. She worried for the safety of Marina. She steered them back to the screen porch. "I saw him right here aiming a rifle out toward the street, but he never fired it, thank God." The Oswalds had no telephone. A woman with Texas plates on her station wagon brought Marina and the child to the unit in May, then in September came back to pick them up. Oswald didn't go with them. Also, she remembered him walking back and forth with books in his hand, probably from the neighborhood public library, three blocks away.

For his part, Mr. Garner added that Oswald was sullen and unfriendly. He had heard someone in 4905—Oswald he presumed—on the evening of the day Marina and their daughter left, Monday, September 23, but that was the last he'd heard of Oswald, who left for sure by the twenty-fifth without paying his rent. No one ever came to visit the Oswalds except twice—"a short, heavyset Latin guy, and a white man from WDSU."

"You say he lived in 4905 but some leaflets say 4507," Abe stated, showing him one of Oswald's yellow "Hands Off Cuba" leaflets with the 4507 address stamped on.

"The leaflet's wrong," declared Mr. Garner. "Truth wasn't his strong suit."

Jim and Abe walked the neighborhood, all lower middle class. Trees, budding already in the waning tropical winter, made it look nicer than it really was. They visited the library. Yes, the librarian remembered Oswald. He'd been a model customer, returning his checkouts on time in good condition. He'd said little, acted polite, and preferred books on communism. Yes, she'd compile at least a partial list of his books and would set aside his checkout cards as potential evidence. Ironically, one she remembered off the top was John Kennedy's *Profiles in Courage*.

The next morning, business seemed light at Bringuier's Casa Roca, a clothing store on Decatur in the Quarter. Carlos Bringuier, a slender Cuban lawyer, had immigrated to the United States via Argentina after the revolution. With him, the federals went two doors down to 117 Decatur, the Habana Bar, passing cars with bumper stickers declaring, "Volveremos." Street washmen sprayed, but rank morning-after smells lingered.

At the bar, business also ran light. They called for coffee and huddled about a small table near the open front by a cigarette machine. Over it hung the flag of Cuba. Bringuier reported that Oswald had no real connection to any pro-Castro groups or, for that matter, to any anti-Castro groups. Oswald, he said, was just a misfit, a loner, a loser with illusions of grandeur. Bringuier had first met him when Oswald came to his store and pretended to be *anti*-Castro, a ruse to infiltrate Bringuier's anti-Castro organization. A day or two later, Bringuier discovered the ruse when Oswald was handing out *pro*-Castro FPFC leaflets a few blocks away, a trick that led to their Canal Street confrontation. Oswald had tried to infiltrate Bringuier's anti-Castro group, he surmised, in order to hold himself out to the Fidelistas as a hero who'd risked his neck for the regime. "A nobody pretending to be somebody. He wanted me to find him out, I say this to you, then wanted me to deck him. He dared me to deck him. Would've looked good to Fidel."

Oswald's Fair Play for Cuba Committee in New Orleans, Abe had already concluded, reeked of fraud—a one-man facade dressed up to look bigger. In fact, the only other member was none other than A. J. Hidell, the fake name sometimes used by Oswald. Abe asked if Bringuier knew anything about anyone ever visiting Oswald's place on Magazine. Yeah, he answered, he'd sent someone to visit Oswald there, to check out Oswald—a Latin guy. So, that small mystery—who had visited Oswald at 4905 Magazine Street—was solved. There remained no tracks from any possible conspirators—with the exception of the story told by Silvia Odio. Bringuier had no knowledge of Angelo or Leopoldo or Silvia Odio.

Bringuier admitted that in the WDSU debate Oswald had been outnumbered and ambushed but had remained calm and courteous and held his own.

Had Bringuier heard of any whispers about assassinating the president? No, he said. Kennedy's cancellation of air support at the Bay of Pigs had "stabbed his heart," but of all the world leaders, JFK had still been the most outspoken against Castro, the most supportive of exiles. On balance, Kennedy had still been "Numero Uno" for liberating Cuba.

Abe liked Bringuier.

The bartender came over to say something fast in Spanish to Bringuier. The two walked to the end of the bar by the pay phone, their hands and faces animating a private conversation. Jim and Abe finished their coffees.

Bringuier returned. "The barkeep says, Oswald came in here last August with another guy. About two-thirty in the morning. Both drunk. Oswald ordered a lemonade, in English. The other guy spoke Spanish and ordered a tequila. Oswald had a taste of the tequila, then vomited. The Spanish talker gave the barkeep shit about what a capitalistic bar this was. The barkeep saw Oswald's picture after the assassination. Says he was the lemonade guy who threw up."

"The other guy, the Spanish—what'd he look like?" Abe asked.

Bringuier waved the barkeep back, spoke rapidly with him, then turned to Abe.

"Latin looking, Cuban probably, about twenty-eight, hairy arms, about five foot eight, 155 pounds. Doesn't know his name. Never saw him again."

Jim made notes on a pocket pad.

Another rapid Spanish conversation ensued.

"He says he had a high forehead and his hairline was back in here," indicating no hair in the front.

Jim and Abe exchanged glances.

"The barkeep's name?" Jim asked.

"Evaristo Rodriguez."

# 28 AUDUBON PARK

FOR THE AFTERNOON, BEBE HAD SELECTED AUDUBON PARK, New Orleans' answer to Central Park, both sharing a common landscape architect, Frederick Law Olmsted. John James Audubon, the celebrated painter and naturalist, though born elsewhere, had made New Orleans an important chapter in his career. Bebe met Abe at the main gate, as arranged. "February in New Orleans is glorious," she declared with pride. Indeed, it was. They roamed long enough to find a cypress-slat and wrought-iron bench under spreading live oaks resplendent with hanging moss, away from the drive wending about the park, but in view of moms and nannies with strollers and children. In a clearing, a pair of college-age boys with Tulane caps tossed a baseball. Robins, sparrows, and mockingbirds performed. The grounds shone.

Bebe was writing profiles on all the lawyers and the judge. She congratulated Abe on making the trial team.

"Okay," Bebe flipped a page in a steno pad and said, "Let's begin with your childhood."

"Born 1923. Manhattan. Public schools. One sister. My mom and dad were schoolteachers. They loved American history, particularly Lincoln and the Civil War. Lincoln saved this nation, held it together. They named me in his honor. One or the other always managed to have a job in the

Depression. They drilled home this message—get an education—it's the only ticket to a good life."

What was it about trial work that Abe liked? Abe believed, he answered, in our court and jury system—decisions based on the merits, not politics. The system, though, depended on having advocates skilled enough to examine and to cross-examine witnesses—more than that, to do so in front of a jury. Abe had a gift, he said, for the "trial triangle"—the witness, the lawyer and the jury. The lawyer stood before the witness and beside the jury, a three-cornered dynamic. Unless and until there was an objection, he explained, the judge receded, and the lawyer-witness-jury triangle took over. What happened in that trial triangle usually controlled the verdict. Excellence in witness examination remained paramount. He'd become good at it. This had become how he could "best serve the country."

Bebe loved this answer. In due course, the trial triangle would show up more than once in her "Letters from Dallas." Abe, she felt, was going to put her on the map.

She turned to his service in the war, knowing most veterans rarely talked about it. But he'd won a medal. She wanted to know how.

"I was eighteen in 1941," Abe answered, "when Pearl Harbor hit. I enlisted. Infantry. Training took all of 1942. In 1943 we shipped out. To Scotland, then England, then North Africa. Most of the fighting in North Africa was over by the time we arrived. So they eventually shipped us back to England to train, train, and train for the invasion of Europe. On D-Day, my unit came ashore at Utah Beach, third wave."

He interrupted himself, "You know, it'll be twenty years in June. Hard to believe, isn't it? We can still reach back, still touch it, can't we? I can still feel it, still feel the wet sand under my boots."

Bebe murmured agreeably and jotted.

"Even lose sleep over it," he added, watching the boys toss the baseball.

"Do you mind telling me about D-Day?"

"We were lucky," he resumed. "Omaha Beach turned out to be the hard one, murderous. Our landing on Utah went easier. Still, I was just a kid and sweated every moment. Odd thing, not a shot got fired by our unit that day—the Germans were almost all gone from the beach when we landed.

Their mines, however, remained. Another terrible problem was their long-range artillery, the shells hitting at random. Mines exploded at random. The beach overflowed with our tanks, troops, jeeps, boxes—a colossal traffic jam. Everyone and everything had to get across a causeway over large flooded lowlands behind the beach. You just had to hurry up and wait—until the beach-master sent you across.

Abe let her notes catch up. She liked this about him, subdued thoughtfulness.

"No Luftwaffe, thank God—thanks to our air corps. We would've been sitting ducks. Eventually, they sent us across a causeway, then out to a crossroad to meet up with the airborne, then relieve them. Hold it, they told us. We did. Still that day, no one in our unit had to fire a shot. That was D-Day for me. All our trouble came later."

Abe stopped. Bebe let his silence linger, hoping he'd pick up with more. The most off-limits question, she'd learned the hard way, was to ask a vet about close combat. When he didn't resume, she asked what happened next.

"May I," Abe stalled, "just skip to my happiest memory of the war?"

Bebe obliged.

"About eight weeks later, somewhere on the Cotentin Peninsula, we liberated a village, unharmed. The Germans just fled. Well, that little village went wild. Flags went up—French, American too. So, they celebrated. They brought out wine hidden from the Germans—and barrels of Calvados."

He looked her way.

"Here's the good part. A pretty French girl about my age brought me some Calvados with stew and bread. I could tell she liked me."

"How could you tell?"

"I could just tell."

Bebe smiled sideways, "Men can't ever tell; they only think they can."

Abe pulled out his wallet and held it.

"Calvados?" she resumed.

Some children squealed nearby at play.

"It's a brandy, made from apples." Abe answered.

"We went through a dozen towns during the war," Abe continued. "No children squealing. Those towns all stunk like burning rubber or smoldering wet mattresses—but not this village—it was untouched, clean. Those children celebrated too, squealed just like those kids over there."

Bebe went back to writing.

"Her name was Marie. She was lovely, my age, and spoke broken English. I ate the stew in my mess kit. Delicious. Bread too, so fresh. Her mom and dad stayed close by. I gave them all my cigarettes, gave her all my chocolate.

"So here's the best part. She wanted to give me something. So she reached into the pocket on her skirt. She pulled out a handsewn flag of France, a little item she'd made herself, a small flag made against all the German regulations of occupation. She gave it to me."

Bebe's mind had journeyed to a small village in France in 1944, but her hand was in Audubon Park in 1964, jotting phrases quickly, expecting to fill in the blanks from memory.

"Would you like to see it?"

"Would I? Of course," Bebe replied, not quite realizing what it would be.

Abe opened his wallet. Inside lay a cloth item folded inside a paper. He extracted it and placed it on Bebe's lap. It was a small flag of France, the size of an army patch, its colors fresh, its edgework clean.

"You carry this every day?"

"Every day. Wouldn't you?"

Bebe held the flag in her hand, admitting the care and devotion evident in its elegance.

"I gave her my name and address but never heard from her again. I got her address too, but my letters went unanswered. Nothing happened between us, but it's my best memory of the war."

"You ever marry, Abe?"

She wanted to know.

"Still looking for Marie."

"And what's that folded around the flag?"

"Roosevelt's D-Day Prayer," Abe replied.

"Are you serious? I remember it like yesterday. May I see it? I was thirteen. The newspapers printed it so we could pray along with President Roosevelt on the radio that evening."

"We didn't hear it on the radio, of course. But later, we got this." He handed her an achromatized mimeograph.

Bebe unfolded it to read this much:

Almighty God,

Our sons,

Pride of our Nation,

This day have set upon a mighty endeavor,

A struggle to preserve our Republic,

Our religion, and our civilization,

And to set free a suffering humanity.

Lead them straight and true;

Give strength to their arms,

Stoutness to their hearts,

Steadfastness in their faith.

Bebe stopped there, refolded it. She still could feel the drama of that evening broadcast with her family praying with the president, knowing even as a young teenager that the fate of civilization in Europe hung in the balance and that thousands of Americans had bled that day in Normandy.

She simply remarked, "'Our sons, Pride of our Nation.' So very true."

Abe resumed, slowly, deliberately. "Every time I go into a hard case or a tough assignment, I read this. I say to myself, if we could do that then, I can do this now."

Bebe forgot to ask about the medal.

# 29 A DINNER AT THE COURT

"FOR DINNER TONIGHT," BEBE DECLARED AT THE STREETCAR AS they parted, "we have a table at the Court. Will eight do?"

Abe heard himself say yes. She asked if Jim would join them. He said no. She said too bad but smiled. "The street car'll go right near your hotel.

I'll walk home. It's close. I'll drive in and meet you at the Court. Remember now, eight. Keep your suit on."

"Oh," she added, pulling a clipping out of the back of the steno pad, "here's the piece I wrote about you in the Profeta trial."

On the streetcar, as it lurched along, Abe observed how whites would enter, drop coins in the pay box, then sit in the front half while blacks would enter, drop coins in the pay box, then sit in the rear half, precedence always being given to whites, all done in a routine, every day, curiously mannered way. Audubon Park itself had been all white. Blacks could walk through it, going someplace else, he'd learned, but could not stay to enjoy the park. Restaurants throughout New Orleans, he knew from his time in the Profeta trial, brimmed over with whites. Blacks entered only as musicians or wait staff or kitchen staff. When Abe had asked Bebe why Audubon Park remained white only, she replied, "Well, 'they' have their own parks."

As Abe watched the tree-lined walks along Saint Charles glide by, his mind drifted to Oswald, who'd lived only a few blocks away. Six months earlier, one of those hurrying to catch the car might've been Oswald. On this very seat, Oswald might've sat. The window raised, spring aspiring, Abe felt sweet air, felt it fresh on his face.

From his trial in New Orleans, Abe understood that Bebe had meant the Court of Two Sisters on Royal Street in the Quarter. It stood on Governor's Row, so called for the first governors of Louisiana, who'd lived on the street. In earlier times, two Creole sisters had run a notions business there. When the two died, in a back-to-back way in the late forties, others converted their courtyard into a Creole patio restaurant. It came to be known as the Court of Two Sisters or, locally, "the Court."

Back in his hotel room, Abe shaved, showered, and returned to his suit. He decided to enjoy an hour walking around the Quarter. He left the hotel on a perfect evening—fresh, pleasant, no heat, no humidity. A waxing moon hung over the western horizon—a crescent moon for the Crescent City, he thought, the same moon America aimed to reach. On Bourbon Street, the Sho Bar, made famous by Blaze Starr, was stirring into readiness. Live music wafted through the Quarter. On Toulouse Street, a swaying crowd flowed out of a joint onto the cobblestones. Inside, a man with a guitar sang a catchy tune about someone named Bojangles.

As he turned a corner, a "second line" performed its own music in a makeshift jazz parade in honor of a departed soul, whose body remained elsewhere but whose friends had him well in mind. Men wearing top hats with swallowtail coats and women wearing tropical colors cut quite the figures as they flounced along. All in the procession were black. Nonetheless, out of respect, both races gave wide berth. Some on foot, even whites, removed their hats. Abe watched with wonder. Odd that out in the streets, the races mixed, even extended common courtesies—but inside, white only reigned, rigidly so.

Abe figured that Bebe's interest in him remained business, meaning as a reporter covering a story. By having access to Abe, she'd be a step ahead of the competition. She used her good looks to professional advantage. Abe accepted that. He was not out to get entangled with a woman. He had a case to try. But it was a Saturday night in the French Quarter. It was okay for a single man to have a good dinner with a single woman, pretty or not. Stop worrying, he told himself, as he was led to a table in the spacious courtyard. Abe waited alone, with a scotch under the stars.

Bebe arrived with excuses over parking and sent for scotch with ice. "Now," Bebe announced, "this is a date, not an interview. Nothing will be used against you." She winked, glancing sideways. Her pixie eyes suggested a perpetual smile. Abe thought her striking in her slim sleeveless black dress with decolletage, freckles faint. Her hemline accentuated long legs, even longer in heels, shimmering in black stockings.

Abe admired her professional wiles.

They touched glasses.

"I know what you're thinking. You're worried that that some jerk will learn you're here with a woman. So what? Listen, they love me here. You're under my protection. Relax. We'll be fine."

That, indeed, had been Abe's thought. Irritated with himself, he let it go. Caution was one thing, excess caution another.

"Let's start with a dumb question," Abe asked, "What's the difference between Cajun and Creole?"

"Big difference but both French. Creoles," Bebe replied, in a practiced way, "descend from the French, who first settled New Orleans, and free coloreds, with varying shades of complexion. Some pass for white. Some don't. In this town, complexion matters, a verifiable fact. Creoles don't always pass as white but, nevertheless, view themselves as above slave descendants. They're city folk, sophisticated, most would say. Cajuns, by contrast, are country folk. They're white. They come from the French Acadians who left Canada when the British took over way back when, then came to the swamps of Louisiana. Cajun's short for Acadian. Blue bloods in the Garden District make fun of us Cajuns. Both Cajuns and Creoles, however, make jambalaya and gumbo. Just different versions."

"Boudreaux?"

"Cajun. My dad and mom came from south of here, deep in the bayous. They moved to New Orleans. So, I got raised here. My mom died when I was fifteen. A drunk driver."

"I'm sorry," Abe replied.

"I suppose I shouldn't drink at all, given how she died, but it's in our blood. We can't help it. Alcohol's a way of life here."

She rattled her cubes. A waiter nodded and brought two more scotches.

During the war, she elaborated, was when they'd come to New Orleans. Her dad got a job with Andrew Higgins, who supplied "many thousands of landing craft to the Navy." Higgins had soared as a major wartime industry, big employment in New Orleans. Her dad became a floor manager for Higgins. "He wanted to enlist but the War Department insisted he stay, essential where he was." Between Higgins and speculation in New Orleans real estate, the Boudreaux family had done well, winding up on a quiet lane bordering Audubon Park.

Abe replied that one of her dad's boats had brought him ashore at Utah Beach. "Without Higgins, your dad, New Orleans, and those landing boats," Abe pronounced, "there would've been no D-Day."

Her dad, she said, "looks like a Confederate postage stamp" and "is very conservative. He opposes desegregation. He hates the Kennedys."

"Their attitudes came out of the Civil War," she continued. "His own dad had been six when the Civil War ended. He'd lived through General Butler's occupation of New Orleans. The Yankees stole all the silver plus anything else of value. It's taking a long, long time to get over it. We're not over it yet." He knew she meant General Ben Butler, who had run New Orleans as a federal military district after it fell in 1862.

Abe let Bebe order for him. He wanted authentic. She was authentic. She selected a French red wine—"to remember Marie," she said. Gumbo. Crabmeat. Jambalaya. Authentic.

"You know, Abe, all this supposed corruption down here just goes back to General Butler and the Yankees. The only way to get along was to cut him and his claque in on it. They left, eventually, but the corruption stayed." This she said with enough of a smile to show she only half believed it.

"Speaking of corruption," he complimented her on the Profeta column. Abe said he found it entertaining, well composed. "Way too generous to me," Abe feigned protest. "But I thank you."

"Can I tell you a trade secret?" Bebe leaned in. "A few years back, when I started at the paper, I had no clue about writing, so I got *The New Yorker*. It's so good. I studied and mimicked its style. That's been my post-graduate study—*The New Yorker*. I still do it. It's cheating, isn't it?"

Her lean in seemed calculated.

"I'll say this too, while we're on that subject. An interviewer's gotta study up beforehand, so you won't interrupt with dumb questions. Anybody worth talking to will talk in kind of shorthand. If you make them stop to explain, they'll quit on you. So, do some homework, I say."

"Even on me?"

"Even on you."

Abe changed subjects and asked what she'd thought of President Kennedy.

Terrible on Bay of Pigs, she answered, brilliant on the Cuba missile crisis, but imperiled his re-election with civil rights.

"Shouldn't we have civil rights reform in our country?" Abe asked, feeling safe it wouldn't offend her at least to ask.

"You know," she replied, straightening up, "we were born into a system that's unfair—of course, it ought to be changed, but, meanwhile, it *is* the only system we have. Bad as it is, we still saved the world from Hitler and his pals. It produced Roosevelt and Kennedy. In time, we'll solve the Negro problem and get to where we should be."

She adored Jackie with her continental style, Bebe said, shifting off the race issue. JFK too. Kennedy, Bebe elaborated, had some memorable speeches with some hilarious lines. The one in Berlin: "*Ich bin ein Berliner.*" Yes, those Berliners roared with approval, Bebe noted. "But did you know that what it really meant, as a figure of speech, was 'I'm a jelly roll'? They knew what he meant but loved him for how it came out."

Abe chortled. Even Abe could not maintain his guard beyond the second scotch.

"Yes, yes, it's true," she said.

"A double . . . " Abe fumbled for the right word.

"Double entendre, exactly," she finished his thought. "The Berliners loved the double meaning."

Bebe radiated sensuality. Abe noticed her makeup—a bare minimum, carefully applied, except lipstick, elegantly applied.

"They also loved Jackie," she kept on, leaning in again, this time a little more. "Will she testify at the trial, Abe?"

Abe skewed his face, recognizing that she was working him.

"What do you think, Bebe?"

She smiled.

The waiter poured wine.

"Those Kennedys," Bebe reset, "so athletic, don't you think? Sailing, touch football, and those amazing fifty-mile hikes. Abe, have you done your fifty-mile hike yet?"

"I did all my hiking in Europe."

"I suppose you did."

She sampled the wine. Her face signaled a new line of thought.

"Roosevelt," she began, "had such a gift for phrases, didn't he?"

He looked agreeable, waiting for more.

"Most presidents would've begun that prayer on D-Day with 'Heavenly Father,'" she elaborated, "but Roosevelt went with 'Almighty God.'"

Her hand gently brushed back her hair behind her ear.

"We didn't need a father in heaven on our side—we needed an Almighty God on our side. Roosevelt understood that. But even better was," Bebe braced herself, "'Pride of our Nation.' That simple, earnest phrase perfectly captured how we felt about those boys, *our boys*, from every corner of our nation. Boys like you, Abe. We felt like every one was our brother or son."

She tilted closer to finish her point, both hands on the stem.

"And now, twenty years later, that generation—the Pride of our Nation—is running the nation. If we ever get a real Civil Rights Bill through after a hundred years of trying—and, yes, Abe, I actually do think it's high time—it'll be the war generation, your generation, our generation, that carries the day. Pride of our Nation. War and victory. The torch has passed. Just like Kennedy said."

Abe raised his glass in salute.

At thirty-three, Bebe looked, Abe thought, like the cover of *Vogue*. Part of it was her hair. She'd cut it short, just above her shoulders, gently styled for a professional look. Like Jackie. Expensive hair work, Abe thought. One thing Bebe said she liked about her Dallas gig was Neiman Marcus, America's premier department store for the rich. She'd picked up several suits and dresses there, she'd bragged, including the black dress with slip she had on—as well as her stockings.

He'd already noticed them, the stockings.

After dessert, she extracted a cigarette. A waiter arrived with a match, lit. Abe allowed he was unaware that she smoked. "One per day, usually in the evening; one coffee per day, usually in the morning; otherwise, it stains your teeth and nails. Yes, yes, I know what the surgeon general is saying. But, you know," she said exhaling, looking sideways, "I'm going to consider the jury still out on that."

Bebe continued, "And you?"

"I cut back to two cigars a week. I've already had my two for the week."

"Well," Bebe ruled from the bench, "I hereby enlarge your allowance to three."

"Thank you," Abe acquiesced. He found a cigar in his inner jacket pocket, unwrapped it, worked through a drill, then touched a wooden match from a matchbox left by the waiter. Their table was soon enveloped by blue and gray. The courtyard was open to the stars.

"When Kennedy imposed the trade embargo on Cuba," Abe grinned, "the press knew he liked Cuban cigars, so they insisted on knowing what would become of his stash. The White House said, don't worry, they'd all be destroyed—'one by one.'"

They laughed together.

She gave his wrist a clench. Abe felt a tingle. She had a genuine laugh, the laugh of someone keen on life.

"Abe, tell me this. Why aren't you married?" She asked, the laughter still fresh on her face.

Abe wasn't quite ready to get into it.

"I thought the interview was over."

"Exactly. This is the date part."

"It's too hard to explain to a pretty woman."

"Have you explained it to Elaine?" She wouldn't give up.

"What do you think, Bebe?"

"Here's what I think. I think you're married to your job," shifting her weight and tilting her face.

Abe allowed a faint smile.

"Well," she went on, "I'll tell you why *I'm* not married. I was once. My dad sent me to LSU to find a man. We got married as soon as we graduated. Handsome. Political. But he was no good for me and I was no good for him. So that ended."

They both let that much sink in.

"Then my dad got me this job. Again, to find a man, I'm sure. But no luck."

"Bebe, for me, the answer's simple," Abe answered. "I'm forty. That ship has sailed."

When it was time to go, Bebe offered a ride to his hotel. Her car was near the Jax Brewery over by the river, so they strolled that way.

"I guess now I can only write good things about you, I mean, now that we've dated and all," she deadpanned along the banquette.

"Wouldn't that violate some code of ethics?"

"Honey," came a stage whisper, "this is New Orleans. We don't have those things down here."

At Saint Louis Cathedral, she ushered him through a heavy tall door. "Come on, let's take a peek." Inside, candles glowed while a smattering of parishioners prayed. They paid a moment of quiet respect before they sneaked out.

"I got baptized here," she remarked, back in the lane, "even attended mass here until I became a heathen. But on the night of the assassination, I came here and prayed."

The clock in the tower rang eleven times.

"It was full that night."

As they entered Jackson Square, she took his arm. Abe liked the feel of her close.

"I'm so proud of our square. Older even than your Central Park."

"You know, of course," she remarked, "who had that built?" Andrew Jackson on horseback loomed over them, larger than life. Hearing no answer, she resumed, "Butler the Beast, our *loup-garou*. Hard to read in the dark," she pointed, "but he had it inscribed 'The Union Must and Shall Be Preserved'—right there, see it? He did that just to get under our skin."

Abe answered, "Sounds right to me, the preservation part."

"That inscription," she continued, "became part of a piece I did called 'Why Separate but Equal Failed,' but my editor said 'no way,' so that item sunk without trace."

The moon had set. Stars coruscated the heavens.

"Let me show you something, Abe."

She gently steered him to an empty bench.

From the bench, the statue became a silhouette against the glow of the cathedral, a stunning scene.

"'Jesus Christ and General Jackson' right before our eyes. My dad thinks that old profanity started right on this bench. We'd sit here after mass. Daytime, of course. He liked to see the women go by."

Abe's hands felt clumsy and headed for his knee, but she tugged a sleeve and leaned against him. His arm settled around her shoulder.

"Much better," she said.

Latin rhythms, scented by sweet olive and crepe myrtle, floated out of the Habana Bar or some place like it.

He felt her warmth.

"Brothers or sisters, Bebe?"

"I'm it. After me," she waited a moment, "I guess my mother didn't want more. She worried he'd leave her. She wanted to keep her figure."

She tightened her coat against the cool air.

"Here's something my mother told me."

"What?"

"'Women are like flowers and men are like bushes.'"

"How's that?" Abe laughed.

"Come on. You figure it out."

"You're still full flower, Bebe."

A foghorn sounded down the river.

"Tell me something, Abe. Tell me the story behind the medal."

Abe wanted to tell her, but this war memory provoked anguish. Worse, it brought on guilt and shame, not pride or valor. He'd learned to repress it and his way to do it was to call up a gratifying memory, usually the memory of Marie.

"It was the Bronze Star."

She waited for more.

"You know," he evaded her question, "who else got a Bronze Star?" A rhetorical pause served for effect. "J. D. Tippit, paratrooper, European Theater. For valor."

A couple strolled by. Abe waited for privacy.

"Twenty years later," Abe finished, "he gets gunned down by some low-grade loser."

Together in silence, for a polite moment, they took it in—General Jackson, Saint Louis Cathedral, the heavens, fugitive samba sounds.

She left it there.

# 30 A BOMBSHELL

"ABE, I NEED TO SAY SOMETHING TO YOU." JIM SOUNDED SERIOUS the next morning.

Abe waited for more. They sped toward Shreveport through a land of ploughed fields and wet sloughs.

"Something I never told you, Abe, but you need to know. So here it is. On the day after Armistice Day, almost two weeks before the assassination, Oswald came to the FBI office, asked to see me. The receptionist said I was at lunch. He left a note for me, which I read when I got back from lunch. He was gone by then. The note said something like, 'If you want to know about me, come talk to me directly. Stop bothering my wife. If you don't stop it, I will take appropriate action.' The note was unsigned, but I figured it was him."

Jim had his right hand on the top of the wheel, his left elbow out the window, left hand loose on the side of the wheel. The sun and wind felt tropical.

"What else?"

"Just this. I kept the note in my desk but when Oswald got arrested, Shanklin got it and put it in his 'Do Not File' drawer. I think it's still there. He's petrified that Hoover will can us all."

"What again did it say?"

"If you want to learn about me, ask me directly. Stop bothering my wife. If you don't, I will take appropriate action."

"Anything about violence or Kennedy?"

"No."

"How'd you figure it was from Oswald?"

"Just suspected, based on what the receptionist said."

"Which was?"

"That he asked to see me, became irritated that I wasn't there. He didn't leave his name. She described him and it sounded like Oswald. Mind you, I hadn't met Oswald yet. I never saw him until after the assassination."

They passed a large billboard showing a black-and-white photograph of a black man in a white short-sleeve shirt in a classroom, entitled "Martin Luther King at Communist Training Camp." It flew by without notice, an everyday occurrence, taken in stride.

"So how do you think this fits in, Jim?"

"Possibly, it shows a motive to get even with the government. I already look dumb for not spotting Oswald as a risk. But now, I look dumber."

"I need to see it," Abe insisted.

"Shanklin's got it," Jim answered. "Want me to ask him for it?"

"No, I'll ask him."

"I'll take a lot of heat. I wasn't supposed to tell you. I'm sorry for holding out on you, Abe."

# 31 MEXICO CITY

BACK FROM MEXICO CITY, ELAINE REPORTED THAT ON HIS TRIP there Oswald had gone twice to the Cuban consulate seeking a visa for entry to Cuba. This had been on Friday, September 27, 1963, once in the morning and once in the afternoon. The key witness was Silvia Duran, she said, a Mexican national who worked at the Cuban consulate as a receptionist. Duran admired Castro. Duran had liked Oswald and had genuinely tried to help him obtain a visa, but his application had to go to Havana for approval, which would've taken longer than the duration of Oswald's visitor permit to remain in Mexico. Her consular boss wouldn't make an exception. If, however, Oswald could've gotten a Soviet visa to travel to Russia, then the consulate boss would've issued, on the spot, a transit visa through Cuba. Once in Cuba, Elaine figured, Oswald would've tried to stay (rather than transit on to Russia). This had led to a shuttle by Oswald back and forth between the Soviet and the Cuban embassies. The Russians, though, refused to help.

The bad news, Elaine continued, was that much of what she learned came from CIA camera surveillance and sources that could not be made public or used at trial. Equally bad was that Elaine had never been allowed to interview Duran—she'd only seen secondhand reports of Duran's statements taken by Mexican police. The State Department kept trying to line up an interview but kept saying that the Mexican government couldn't line it up.

Oswald had stayed in Room 18 on the third floor of the Hotel del Comercio on Calle Bernardino de Sahagun, four blocks from the bus station, near downtown. A maid said he hadn't spent much time at the hotel. No one was seen with him. He hadn't used the telephone at the hotel (the only one being in the reception area). He ate several times next door at a cheap café. No drinking. After Oswald struck out on the visa, he remained several days, evidently playing tourist. The guide map of Mexico City seized from Oswald's boarding house room had pencil and ink marks on it. Elaine visited all of the marked places to show a photo of Oswald to storekeepers, students, and others who might have seen him, all to no avail.

"Any evidence or talk about assassination, or Walker, or Kennedy?"

"No, Abe, especially if we believe Senora Duran."

# 32 AS REAL AS IT GETS

In their trial practice sessions, Percy drilled Oswald.

*Never smirk, he instructed; no smiles; no laughter; this is a death prosecution; never appear frantic; if you need to say anything, whisper it to me or maybe Karen, but stay silent—look respectful.*

To Karen, as the day of trial approached, Foreman emphasized the need to move with slowness, deliberateness, and only as necessary.

*Never appear panicked. Move slowly, no pronto. No matter how bad it gets, appear to take it in stride. Don't talk or whisper except as genuinely needed. If the judge chews your ass out, you say, "Thank you, Your Honor." Never laugh.*

*When the judge cracks a joke, smile briefly no matter how dumb it might be, but don't laugh—this is a capital case.*

When nine jurors had been sworn with three to go, Foreman finally said, "Lee, now is the time for you to tell us what happened that day. Are you ready to go over it all?" Oswald said he was. Karen felt her heart pumping in her chest. Foreman went for the meat of the matter—"Let's start with the twenty-second and where you were at noontime that day." Oswald looked toward the ceiling. Foreman interrupted, "No, look at me. Look at me as you tell it. Lean forward, like you want us to understand. No looking away. No looking up." Oswald smirked. Foreman pounded the table, "No smirking either, Lee. I mean it. We're trying to save your goddamn life."

Over two afternoons, Foreman gradually led Oswald through the twenty-second, backwards in time from the twenty-second, back through the two weeks leading up to the twenty-second, eventually all the way back to Mexico City and New Orleans. Sometimes, but not often, Foreman's quizzing caused Oswald to clarify his recollection, sometimes changing a date or adjusting his account in response to a question like, "But how did you realize that back then?"

It had seemed like an airtight prosecution case, but Oswald was now telling them a story of innocence that fit with almost all of the known facts, innocence in the sense that, if accepted, the jury would have to decide that a critical element of guilt was absent. Karen marveled that Oswald had mastered the details of the case against him, thanks, she realized, to Percy's having worked a deal to get the interview memos.

Astounding, she thought.

After Oswald had been taken away, Percy and Karen remained in the interview/interrogation room. That late afternoon, the fourth of March, had brought dark winds over thirty miles per hour, flowing off the northern plains. The windows rattled. Intermittent rain splattered the glass. Through the bars, charcoal smeared a pewter sky.

Foreman paced, then offered in muted tones, "Well, after what we just heard, we need Amos Euins, don't we? We need the bald spot. We need him. Amos is a good kid, don't you think?"

Karen kept quiet, gathering that Foreman was thinking out loud.

"Thing is," he paused before his satchel and fiddled with the handle, "Amos is colored. We got people on that jury that'll think twice before they go against the district attorney on the word of a colored kid."

She didn't like where this was headed.

"I'll do his exam," he continued, "and the jury will see me as old school Texas. That'll help."

He interrupted himself to ask, "We got any white witness who can back Amos up?"

He looked to her for an answer.

Thunder rumbled.

"No, not on the point that matters, the bald spot, but remember, Percy, Amos couldn't even say whether the sniper was white or black," whispered Karen, still unsure the room wasn't bugged. "He'll get creamed on cross."

The lights flickered as the storm heckled the power.

"Yeah, we gotta live with that, but on the bald spot Amos is strong."

He quit stalling. He sat down and leaned in to her.

"Karen, I need to ask you to do something, something you won't like—I don't like it either."

She gave him her full attention, seated straight, still.

"I want you to go visit with the mom and dad to ask them *not* to attend court when Amos testifies. Yeah, I know the judge has desegregated the gallery but if the mom or dad shows up in the public seating while Amos is on the stand, our jury will figure out who they are. Somebody on the jury will resent it—too uppity, just too goddamn uppity is what they'll think. It's wrong but that's what'll happen. There they could be, sitting on the front row surrounded by whites, with someone on the jury seething about it, and Amos and his testimony doing us no good."

Karen felt crushed.

"Percy, you want me to tell 'em *not* to attend court?"

"Yes."

"On account of their race?" She couldn't believe it.

"Only on account of their race," he insisted.

"No way, Percy, I can't do that." She felt tears welling and tried hard to hold back. "That's against everything, everything—That mom and dad have every right to be there."

"Coming from you, Karen, it might work," Percy continued. "You're young. You're female. You can talk to the mom. She's the boss. Listen, I don't like it either, but it could make a difference. I'd hate to lose a holdout over something like this."

She felt a storm inside and tried hard to maintain composure.

"Karen," he dropped to a deliberate whisper while thunder rumbled, "a holdout is our only chance."

"Percy, I just can't do it. It'd be as wrong as wrong can be."

"This is Texas, Karen. We're talking an all-white jury. We're talking the death penalty."

In silence, she sought refuge out the window and the tempest beyond.

He waited, then finally said, irritation and resignation evident in his tone, "Okay, *I'll do it*. I'll drive out to their place, see what I can do."

He rose slowly, then held his trial-worn briefcase on the arm of the chair in front of him, adjusting his raincoat.

"Young lady, let me ask you this—have you ever been to an electrocution?"

Lightning flashed with instant thunder.

"No."

"I have. It's rotten business. You never forget the smell. This isn't some moot court, Karen. This is as real as it gets."

# 33   THE DOORWAY TO IMMORTALITY

In his civilian clothes, Lee Oswald had breakfast in his sixth-floor cell in the Criminal Courts Building overlooking Dealey Plaza. Given a simple bowl of oatmeal with coffee, he skipped the oatmeal, just went with the coffee, staring out the window at the scene of the crime, a scene now catapulted to the apex of worldwide attention, a scene now dusted with snow. He'd soon be taken downstairs to a holding cell serving Judge Brown's courtroom. Now and then his mind hovered over how the story was playing in Cuba. Surely, he imagined, he was a hero there; if he could beat these charges, hosannas would flow in Havana; if not, maybe they'd flow anyway.

"Oswald!" came a shout from the far-right end of the cell block. What they really meant, he knew by now, was "Bring Oswald."

He downed the last of his coffee, then submitted, his back to the bars, thrusting his wrists behind him through the rectangular opening used to slide food trays in and out. From the outside, a deputy cuffed him. He felt the cold nickel-plated steel close around his wrists, then heard the ratchets click. He stepped into the middle of his cell, letting his arms fall slack against his ass. A deputy unlocked the door, then two deputies entered and affixed leg irons with just enough lead for short steps. Resisting was no good, he figured—they'd just beat the shit out of him. All three exited, then proceeded to the end of the cell block. Along the way, an inmate spit hard at him and shrieked, "Fucking asshole!" He instinctively shrank away, then silently reproached himself for cowardice. At the end of the cell block, the supervisor, who'd called his name, unlocked a gate. They passed through.

"Court visit," the supervisor said. "Trial."

As they waited for the secure elevator, he saw his name in the headlines on the supervisor's desk.

"Looks like I'm guilty already," he scowled.

"Your fandango'll come," said the supervisor, "soon enough," then added, "in Huntsville." Oswald knew about Huntsville—the place of electrocutions.

In silence, the three rode down to the second floor in the elevator, where he was steered through another locked door into a windowless holding cell adjacent to the courtroom, then into a small dim cell within the cell. As he leaned forward, resting on the concrete bench, still fully restrained, his nostrils curled at the lingering stench of vomit and bleach. Just take it, he told himself. He was better than them. Show them. His gaze fell on human shit smeared on the cinder block wall. Fuck them. Fuck that fucking fandango shit, too. Through the ventilation ducts, he heard the babel of a crowded courtroom. All of those voices had come, he realized, just for him.

They were the scribes of history. This was history. He was history. He was ready. He was better than them all, smarter than them all.

*Yes, fuck them, they have me now, I'll take this shit now, but my name, not theirs, will live forever.*

Through the vents he heard, "All rise, the District Court in and for Dallas County is now in session, the Honorable Joe B. Brown presiding."

The babel melded into the swoosh of a rising courtroom.

Then silence.

Two quick knocks came loud from the other side of the secure door labeled "Courtroom." Deputies unlocked his cage, then ordered, "Let's go." He walked two steps to the door, a deputy on each side. He waited, he supposed, at the entrance to immortality. The deputy on his left knocked twice. The secure door opened briskly. Brightness flooded past him. As his eyes adjusted, he took in the packed gallery, the walls lined with standees, every eye on him. They entered as fast as his leg irons allowed. He scanned for his family, saw his mother, then Marina on the front row. Their eyes met. She started to cry. Goddamn bitch is sorry now, he thought. The practiced movement of the wrists of the sketch artists, also on the front row, next caught his eye. He got steered left. As they proceeded to the center of the well, he thrust his chin at the artists. They made another left turn, then arrived beside Percy Foreman. He stood before immortality.

# 34   OPENING STATEMENTS

"On behalf of the People of the State of Texas," the judge began, "District Attorney Henry Wade will now make his opening statement."

Wade rose, placed notes on the lectern, adjusted the microphone, nodded to the judge, then Foreman, then slowly looked across the jury box.

He took his time, letting this moment of silence linger. On an easel, a blowup of the backyard photo projected just the message Wade wanted—a smug Oswald brandishing the murder weapons, an image an ocean away from the clean-cut collegiate look of the Oswald seated at the defense table.

Reporters were still taking in Oswald in civilian dress—what a change! Bebe would tell readers he looked like a cross between a Sunday school teacher and actor Tony Perkins (as Norman Bates) in *Psycho*.

"May it please the Court. Ladies and gentlemen of the jury—this man, Lee Harvey Oswald," Wade pointed to the photograph, "is accused by the People of Texas of murdering President John Fitzgerald Kennedy and Officer J. D. Tippit last November 22, here in Dallas. We have the burden to prove this beyond a reasonable doubt. You must hold us to our burden of proof. We will meet it."

Wade then introduced the other prosecutors, all seated at the table closest to the jury box. He explained that Abe and Elaine, though federal prosecutors, were specially admitted by the judge to co-represent the State of Texas, so that they would be full participants at counsel table. They intimated only a hint of a smile. A capital trial over two murders, the room understood, was not an occasion for charm.

Using diagrams and maps on easels in the well, and proceeding at a deliberate pace, all to better underscore what was at stake, Wade then traced the evidence—the motorcade, Dealey Plaza, the Depository, the sixth-floor layout, the sniper's nest, the three shots, the three spent cartridges, the Mannlicher-Carcano rifle with scope, which he held with one hand above his shoulder for the jury to see, its hiding place, its purchase history, the Alek J. Hidell alias, the elevators plus stairs in the Depository, the lunchroom on the second floor, the escape route of Oswald, the boarding house, the four shots at the Tippit murder, the .38, which he held upward for all to see, the four spent cartridges, then the Texas Theater where Oswald pulled his revolver, tried to fire it, was captured saying, "Well, it's all over now."

On another easel rested a blowup of the fake draft card with the name of Alek James Hidell complete with Oswald's photograph. "This card," Wade told the jury, "came from this wallet," holding up an ordinary brown wallet, "taken from this man upon his arrest." Wade pointed to Oswald.

Wade then surveyed the ballistics, the fingerprints and other forensic evidence, including the pathology. He summarized the eyewitnesses and previewed the Zapruder film.

He told the jury they'd get a firsthand view of several scenes, Dealey Plaza, the Depository, the scene of the Tippit murder, and the boarding house.

Wade took care to explain that one bullet, the second bullet, wounded *both* the president and the governor. He explained that a single bullet could do so because it went straight through the president, hitting only soft tissue, then struck Governor Connally, leaving the three wounds suffered by him, that is, entering his back, exiting his chest, completely through his wrist, then lodging in his thigh. This was possible, easily so, Wade said, because of the straight-line arrangement of the two victims with the rifle at the time of that shot. Wade used a diagram to show this.

All three shots were fired, he said, holding up three fingers, from the sixth-floor sniper's nest. "The evidence will prove beyond a reasonable doubt," he said, "that Oswald fired all three." Wade made no mention of Cuba, Russia, Mexico City, New Orleans, or conspiracy. He emphasized that motive was not an element of the crime, so that the prosecution did not need to prove why Oswald did it—only that he did it on purpose.

Fronting the eyewitness problem, Wade remarked, "Unlike the Tippit part of the case, there were not as many eyewitnesses to Oswald killing the president. When the president and First Lady came by, most eyes locked on them, so almost everyone missed seeing Oswald pull the trigger. Oswald had hidden himself in a sniper's nest. He was not out in the open as in the case of Tippit. We will, however, present one witness in Dealey Plaza who saw Oswald fire the last, fatal shot. Our case as to the president's murder does not depend on any eyewitnesses. The physical evidence alone is entirely sufficient to show that the man who killed President Kennedy was Lee Harvey Oswald. That is also why we will not need to put our former First Lady on the stand to relive the horror, or, for that matter, Mrs. Connally or Mrs. Tippit."

Wade ended by asking the jury to be fair to both sides and to hold the prosecution to its burden of proof. If they did so, he ended, they would find Oswald guilty as charged.

The judge waited while Wade found his seat and then paused a moment longer, a judge's way, Bebe understood, to compliment a well-done performance. From Bebe's seat, the jury box lay along the right wall up front. Leftward, on the wall opposite the jury box, she admired an old mechanical wall clock with Roman numerals. Beside it hung large red-and-black-on-white monthly calendars for March and April 1964. Under the calendars waited a home movie screen, a film projector cart, plus Wade's blackboard on wheels. It seemed a place where the death penalty might be imposed.

"Mr. Foreman, do you wish to make your opening now or to reserve?"

In his tailored navy-blue wool suit, white shirt, blue tie, with gold cufflinks, Percy Foreman rose. Of all counsel, Bebe found him the most imposing, not merely the most famous. He paused a moment before the box, letting the jurors take in his full frame, erasing Wade's image. By pre-arrangement, the backyard blowup of Oswald disappeared, as did the blowup of the Hidell card.

Outside, snow accumulated in the windowsills.

"May it please the Court. Ladies and gentlemen of the jury, I'll be brief. In this trial, it's my privilege to represent Lee Harvey Oswald. He's accused of murdering our president and murdering a dedicated police officer in Dallas. If he's guilty, he ought to die in the death chamber. If he's not, he should be set free, so we can turn to finding who really did it. The accused is presumed innocent—and what the evidence is going to show you is that he is in fact innocent.

Marina, Marguerite, and Robert Oswald—the wife, mother, and brother of the accused—sat in the front row a dozen feet from the defense table. On the first bench behind the prosecution table (and thus closest to the jury box) were the Widow Tippit and Senator Edward Kennedy, recently elected to his first term. Somber determination creased his young face. Thin, young, with sandy brown hair, he'd announced that he would give no interviews and make no comment on the trial. Robert Kennedy, Bebe would report, had considered attending but, as the attorney general, he'd concluded, for ethical reasons, he should pass. Mrs. Kennedy declined to attend.

"Most of what you just heard from my friend, Henry Wade, we accept and will not challenge because it's true. So very often in this trial, you are going to hear me say, 'No questions,' meaning I have no cross-examination or quarrel with that particular witness. For example, we're not going to contest that three shots were fired from that window or that one of them, maybe two, killed the president. We will not contest that the rifle belonged to Lee. Many other things won't be in dispute. This'll become clear to you as the evidence proceeds. Now and then, I'll have some questions, sometimes just to clarify a point. You'll eventually see, however, that there *are* certain issues that'll be the key to deciding what happened. Here are those issues:

"*One,* how could a marksman good enough to hit the president so precisely in two shots in a row have *missed* the entire car on his first shot, the closest shot of all? Missed the entire car? What accounts for that absurdity?

"*Two,* why was there a pause between the first shot and the last two shots? What was going on with the rifle during this pause? The timing of the shots, please pay attention to this evidence as it comes in, for it is part of the key to the case.

"*Three,* you'll learn that two men wearing police uniforms drove a squad car up to the front of the accused's rooming house and honked their horn thirty minutes after the assassination at a time when every police car in Dallas was busy with the national emergency. They did this precisely when Lee was in his room changing clothes, as if on cue. They waited a bit, but when the housekeeper looked out at them, they drove off before he came out. Who were they waiting for? Were these two really police officers and what were their true roles in this case?

"*Four,* was Officer Tippit shot based on a reasonable apprehension of death or great bodily harm? Based on what you have heard so far, this may sound far-fetched, but I ask you to wait until you hear all the evidence. It won't be far-fetched then.

Foreman introduced Oswald and Karen, both of whom kept respectful faces. Some of the jurors, Bebe noted, looked away rather than exchange glances with the accused.

"I want to make something very clear. We don't contend the accused is insane. He is innocent. Innocent. I repeat it: innocent." One by one, Foreman locked eyes with the jurors, especially those who had refused to look at Oswald.

"Finally, you must keep an open mind. The prosecution has the burden of proof, so they get to go first. You'll just be hearing their side of the case. There'll be weeks of testimony. Be fair, please, to both sides, so wait until you hear both sides before making up your mind. I've tried many cases in almost every county in Texas—sometimes the most important thing we hear is the last thing we hear.

# 35  SCROGGINS AND MARKHAM

"Brilliant" would be the way Bebe would eventually describe the prosecutor's selection of opening witnesses, but her initial reaction inclined toward puzzlement. Why jump ahead to the Tippit story, she wondered, rather than begin with the assassination? The first prosecution witness was William Scroggins, forty-eight, paunchy, with a flat-top, wide-brim taxi cap with medallion, stained with years of sweat and hair oil. His cap came to rest on the witness bench.

On the twenty-second, he testified, he'd parked his cab at the corner on Patton facing Tenth and facing north, in a working-class neighborhood in Oak Cliff. Wade displayed a poster map showing it was perhaps ten blocks south of the boarding house. Several jurors leaned forward to study the map. Scroggins told the jury that he'd noticed a police car drive by, crossing left to right in front of him, proceeding slowly, eastbound on Tenth, while Scroggins, alone in his cab, enjoyed a sandwich and coke for lunch. Wade continued:

"What time was this?"

"Around 1:20 in the afternoon."

"Then what'd you see?"

"The police car stopped about 150 feet east of me on Tenth. To my right. I looked to see why he was stopping, and I saw this man with a light-colored jacket on, facing west on my side of Tenth. My vision of him got cut off by a bush as he stepped toward the police car."

"Did you see the police officer do anything?"

"I saw him get out of the police car. Then he took approximately one or two steps, and I went back to my eating, and about that time I heard the shots."

"How many shots did you hear?"

"Three or four. They was fast."

"Then what?"

"Then I saw the policeman falling, grab his stomach and fall. I was excited when I heard them shots. I started to get out. I must've seen him fall as I was getting out of my cab. In the process of getting out, I seen this guy coming around, so I got outta sight. I crouched behind the side of the cab."

"Did you see the man?"

The witness ran a finger along the brim of the cap.

"I saw the man coming kind of toward me as he cut through the corner yard, and he never did look at me. He looked back over his left shoulder as he went by. It seemed like I could see his face, his features, everything, plain."

"Was he walking or running or trotting?"

"Kind of loping, trotting."

"Did you hear him say anything?"

"I heard him mutter 'poor damn cop' or 'poor dumb cop.' He said that twice. I don't know whether the word was 'damn' or 'dumb,' but anyway, he quoted that twice."

"Did he have a gun?"

"A pistol."

"Do you see the man now, here in the courtroom, who ran by your cab with the pistol after the officer was shot?"

Scroggins zeroed in on the defense table.

Foreman had plainly anticipated this. He'd prearranged with Oswald to stand and face his accuser. This move, Bebe thought, was brilliant too—to take away the usual sting of a witness pointing the finger at someone in a chair who might appear to be sinking under the table in shame. Instead, Foreman reversed the image. It said, "Here I am—go ahead and accuse me." Foreman stood with him.

"Right there, the one by the lawyer."

Also at that murder scene had been Helen Markham, forty-seven, with shoulder-length, dark-but-graying hair. She testified next, nervously. A waitress on her way to work at the Eatwell Cafe, she stood on the northwest corner (diagonally across from the taxi driver), waiting to cross Tenth to catch a bus a few blocks away.

Off to her left, on the other side of Tenth, going away from her, heading east, a police car "eased up alongside" a man walking on the sidewalk opposite her side. One officer was in the car. The car stopped. The man on the sidewalk leaned toward the passenger side window, appearing to talk through the window. The man then drew back. The policeman opened the door, calmly "crawled out," then walked around toward the front of the car. He got even with the wheel on the front driver's side when she heard multiple shots.

Bebe could see the hands of the witness tremble until, out of evident embarrassment, she placed them on her lap, out of sight beneath the witness bench.

Wade continued:

"What'd the policeman do?"

"He fell to the ground. His cap went a little ways out on the street."

"What'd the man do?"

"The man, he just walked away calmly, fooling with his gun."

"Toward what direction did he walk?"

"Come back towards Patton."

"Toward Patton?"

"Yes, sir, towards Patton. He didn't run. When he saw me, he looked at me, stared at me. I put my hands over my face like this, closed my eyes. I gradually opened my fingers like this, then I opened my eyes. He started off in kind of a little trot, going away from me on Patton."

She put her hands with fingers closed over her face, then flared her fingers to look through them. They still trembled.

"Which way?"

"On Patton towards Jefferson, away from me."

"What'd you do?"

"He began to trot off, so then I ran to help the policeman."

"Before you put your hands over your eyes, did you see the man walk towards the corner?"

"Yes, sir."

"What'd he do?"

"He stared at me."

"What'd you do?"

"I didn't do anything. I couldn't."

"Didn't you say something?"

"I couldn't. I could not say nothing. He looked wild. I was afraid he was fixing to kill me."

"Fixing to kill you? How far away from the shooting do you think you were?"

"Maybe three houses away."

"Where was he when he looked at you?"

"Catty-corner from me."

"In what hand did he have his gun, do you know, when he fired the shots?"

"Sir, I believe it was his right. I'm not positive because I was scared."

Some jurors glanced at Oswald and saw he was taking notes with his right hand.

"Do you see that man here in the courtroom today?"

She became visibly frightened. Pausing, she looked down, then at the judge.

"Do you see him, Miss Markham?" asked the judge.

"Over . . ."

Her voice cracked. The judge leaned forward as if he were going to intervene, but she collected herself in a tight, quick voice, "Over there, the young one."

Foreman said, "We stipulate that the witness pointed to Lee Oswald."

"That'll do. No more questions. Thank you, Miss Markham."

Foreman passed on cross-examination of both witnesses.

# 36 GOVERNOR JOHN CONNALLY

WADE ANNOUNCED, "THE PEOPLE CALL GOVERNOR JOHN CON-nally." The doors in the back of the courtroom swung open. In came Governor John Connally escorted front and rear by Texas Rangers, provoking murmur in the gallery. Tall, handsome with silver hair, he wore a tailored dark gray suit, carried a light gray Stetson, and walked in hand-tooled, well-polished, brown cowboy boots. He looked the part of a Texas governor. His familiar strong stride absent, he walked pointedly, still recovering from his wounds. The judge smiled, then welcomed him. He was sworn, repeating, "So help me, God." Connally placed his Stetson on the witness table, the same Stetson he'd held in his lap on the twenty-second. Bebe Boudreaux plus a hundred other journalists sensed the weight of history. Pens and pencils hovered over steno pads.

Henry Wade went to work.

"Please tell us your current position."

"I am now Governor of the state of Texas."

The voice of the witness needed no amplification but with the microphone it filled the courtroom.

"Did you have any occasion to be in the automobile that carried President John F. Kennedy through Dallas back on November 22?"

"Yes, sir."

"Please tell us the circumstances."

"Going back to 1962, the president said he ought to visit Texas. The trip kept getting delayed. Finally, in November 1963, he was able to do it. The first stop was San Antonio on the twenty-first, then to Houston for a reception for Congressman Henry Gonzales and a dinner for Congressman Albert Thomas that night at about eight o'clock. That same night, we flew to Fort Worth, spent the night at the Texas Hotel, had a breakfast meeting there the next morning, that is, the morning of the twenty-second, then left at 10:30 a.m. for the short flight over to Dallas at Love Field."

"What time did you land?"

"About noon, shortly before."

"Describe the ceremony there."

"The president had a receiving line at the airfield. I conducted Mrs. Kennedy through the receiving line and introduced her to the official welcoming committee."

"Then what?"

"We got into the car. Mrs. Connally and I sat on the jump seats. The President and Mrs. Kennedy were in the main car seat."

"Please explain the jump seats."

"The jump seats were those little seats that fold away when not in use. In this case, they were a little lower and little more toward the center than the president and First Lady. Their backseat was about six inches higher than the jump seats. The president was in the rearmost seat on the right. Mrs. Kennedy was beside him on his left. I was in front of the president. Mrs. Connally was on my left."

"Who else was in the car?"

"Roy Kellerman was in the right front. Bill Greer was driving. Both Secret Service."

"Please describe the motorcade."

"We left Love Field. As we got closer to downtown, we saw groups of well-wishers. Some applauded. As we approached downtown, going down Main Street, the crowds stacked from the curb—even outside the curb into the streets, back up against the walls of the buildings, a huge crowd. I would say just in downtown there were 250,000 people. The farther we went the more enthusiastic they became. It was tremendous. Just before we turned on Houston Street, right in front of this courthouse, Mrs. Connally remarked, 'Well, Mr. President, you can't say there aren't some people in Dallas who love you.' The president replied, 'That is very obvious.' It was the best reception in all of the four cities."

"Did the limousine stop at any time?"

"Yes, sir, it did. There was one little girl with a sign saying, 'Mr. President, will you please stop and shake hands with me?' He told the driver to stop. So he shook hands with that little girl. He also stopped to speak with a Catholic nun and students from her school."

A woman on the jury, a mother of three, lifted a Kleenex to wipe her eye.

"As the automobile turned onto Elm Street from Houston Street, what then occurred?"

"As we were heading down Elm Street to pick up the freeway out to the lunch at the Trade Mart, the main crowd had thinned out. We were maybe 150 feet onto Elm Street, still going slow because there were still some well-wishers in Dealey Plaza. There on Elm Street, I heard what I thought was a shot. I immediately took it to be a rifle shot. I instinctively turned to my right because the sound seemed to come from over my right shoulder, so I turned to look back over my right shoulder. I saw nothing unusual, but it crossed my mind that this was an assassination attempt. To my right, I could not see the president, so I turned to my left, to look over my other, my left shoulder, but I never got that far in my turn because something hit me in the back."

"How quickly did that occur after the shot you heard?"

"Very brief span of time. I looked down. I was covered with blood. I wondered if it was an automatic rifle. Because of the amount of blood, I could tell the bullet had passed through my chest. I assumed it was fatal for me."

Two jurors looked away. Bebe saw no jurors making notes, all too taken with the story unfolding before them. Reporters, however, wrote, and sketch artists drew—with fury.

"What wounds did you sustain?"

"The chest wound, a fractured right wrist and a wound in the left thigh, just above the knee. The thigh wound measured about an inch or more deep, a third of an inch wide."

"All of this on one shot?"

"Yes."

"What'd you do?"

"I doubled up. Mrs. Connally pulled me onto her lap. My head was in her lap. I remained conscious. Then I heard the third shot. I heard it hit. It was a very loud noise, audible, very clear. Immediately, I could see on my clothes and the interior of the car, brain tissue. One chunk of brain tissue the size of my thumbnail landed on my trousers. I faced away so I did not see the president, but I could tell he had been hit."

In the jury box, a veteran of Iwo Jima clenched his right fist, its vessels bulging. For a brief moment, Bebe closed her eyes.

"Did you say anything?"

"I said, 'Oh, no, no, no. My God, they are going to kill us all.' Nellie pulled me over more on her lap to say, 'Don't worry. Be quiet. You are going to be all right.' She just kept telling me I was going to be all right."

"Then what?"

"After the third shot, I heard Roy Kellerman tell the driver, 'Bill, get out of here. Get us to a hospital quick.' We pulled out of the cavalcade. Then I lost consciousness."

"What was your impression of where the shots came from?"

"Behind us, over my right shoulder and at an elevation."

At this, several jurors glanced at large blowup photographs of the Dealey Plaza topography on an easel. The sixth-floor window fit the governor's testimony perfectly.

"Did the Kennedys say anything?"

"Mrs. Kennedy said, after the final shot, 'They have killed my husband.'"

"Anything else?"

"Yes, she said, 'I have got his brains in my hand.'"

Every member of the jury fixated on the testimony, but when they heard that the First Lady had the president's brains in her hand, the chest of the juror who had teared began to heave. She turned away. Wade paused, stepped to the jury box, then handed her a clean handkerchief, folded neatly. Some of the jurors glared at Oswald. He kept a respectful face. Ted Kennedy's face turned ashen, Bebe noticed. He stared at the floor, seeming to count the grain lines in the wood, to maintain his composure.

"When did you regain consciousness?"

"In the hospital on the next day."

"Which shot hit you, Governor?"

"It just couldn't have been the first one because I heard that one. I heard the first shot yet still had time to turn to my right, then to my left before I felt anything. It was only then that I felt the blow. I never heard the second shot, but it must have been the one that hit me. I didn't hear it, I am sure, because of the blow itself and the fact that the bullet traveled faster than the sound and I was already wounded by the time the sound came from the second shot. I did hear the last shot. I was already wounded, so the second shot got me. The entire thing from first to last shot lasted ten to twelve seconds."

"No further questions. Thank you, Governor."

Oswald passed a note to Percy. Foreman, however, simply rose to say, "Governor, we are all glad that you are able to be with us today. I have no questions beyond those already asked by Mr. Wade."

The governor looked at his Stetson while Foreman spoke. In fact, Bebe noticed he'd never looked at Oswald or the defense table during his entire time in court.

"Governor," said the judge. "You may please step down. You are discharged from any subpoena. Thank you for giving us your time."

The governor stepped down. Holding his Stetson, he walked out as carefully as he'd walked in. As Connally reached the front row, he nodded with compassion to Senator Kennedy and the Widow Tippit. Before Oswald could smirk, Bebe saw, Foreman placed his hand on Oswald's forearm.

# 37 HOWARD BRENNAN

OUT OF RESPECT AND FRIENDSHIP, WADE REMAINED ERECT AS Connally moved through and out of the courtroom, then announced, "The People call Howard Brennan." Wade showed no worry.

A man in work clothes came through the heavy public doors, down the aisle, through the swinging doors between the well and the gallery. After the oath, he took the witness chair. Howard Brennan testified that he was forty-five, lived in Dallas, was married with two children, had been a steamfitter since 1943, and carried a union card.

Wade then turned to the key facts.

"Where were you at the time of President Kennedy's assassination?"

"In Dealey Plaza. I was seated on the low ornamental wall that curves around the lagoon. This wall runs along the west side of Houston Street. I was at the end by Elm Street facing directly toward the main entrance to the Depository."

"How good is your vision?"

"I'm farsighted, good vision at distances."

"Before the president came by, who, if anybody, did you see in the Depository?"

"I saw three black fellows leaning out the windows on the fifth floor. Above them on the sixth floor I saw a white man by himself who sat sideways on the low windowsill. All of this was on the southeast corner of the building."

"How far were you from the man on the sixth floor?"

"Perhaps 120 feet."

"On the sixth floor, how many people did you see?"

"On the sixth floor, I saw only the one man."

"Did you hear the first shot?"

"As the president passed by me, I heard a crack that I positively thought was a backfire of a motorcycle."

"Then what?"

"Then I thought maybe someone had thrown a firecracker from the Texas Book Store from one of those open windows, so I glanced up. This man I saw before was aiming for his last shot, the man in the sixth-story window."

"Describe in detail what you saw."

"He appeared to be standing up, resting against the ledge of the window-sill with the gun shouldered to his right shoulder, holding the gun with his left hand and taking positive aim. He fired his last shot. He drew the gun back from the window as though he was drawing it back to his side, pausing as though to assure himself that he hit his mark, then he disappeared. At that same moment, I was diving off that firewall and to the right for bullet protection from this stone wall that is a little higher on the Houston side."

Foreman made eye contact, Bebe noticed, with the court reporter and pointed his index finger at her machine. She acknowledged with a nod, while continuing to work her steno keys. At the next pause, she made a slight tear in the edge of the paper tape to mark the record location.

"What kind of gun did you see?"

"It looked like a high-powered rifle."

"Scope?"

"I don't know if it had one or not."

"How many shots did you hear?"

"Two. Possibly I heard another, but I just was aware of the first and last. The first was the one I thought was a firecracker. Then I heard the last shot.

"How much of the man's body could you see?"

"I saw from his belt up."

"How much of the gun did you see?"

"I calculate 70 to 85 percent."

"What direction was it pointing?"

"About thirty degrees downward, aiming down Elm Street toward the railroad overpasses."

"How was the weather?"

"Fine. Sunny. Not at all like today."

He glanced at the white-on-gray windows.

"Describe the man you saw fire the rifle."

"To my best description, he was a man in his early thirties, fair complexion, slender but neat, possibly five foot ten inches, about 160 to 170 pounds, white. I don't remember his hair color."

Members of the jury stole glances at Oswald to vet the description. It was a loose fit at best.

"Clothes?"

"He had on light-colored clothes, like a khaki color."

"What'd you do next?"

"After the shooting stopped, I came out from behind the wall. I ran over to an officer and told him they were searching in the wrong direction, meaning they were searching over by the rail yards, but the shots had come from one window down from the top of the building."

"Did you eventually go to a lineup?"

"That night, they took me to the police station for a lineup. I said one man in the lineup had the closest resemblance to the man in the window. I told them, however, I could not make a positive identification."

"Was it true that you couldn't make a positive identification?"

"No, sir, it wasn't true. I was very positive. I hedged because I was afraid for my family and myself."

"Why?"

"I feared that maybe a communist attack on our government was underway. I didn't want us harmed."

"Are you able today to make an honest and positive identification?"

"Yes, sir."

"Were you then?"

"Yes, sir."

"Mr. Brennan, do you see the man you saw shoot that rifle anywhere in the courtroom today?"

"Yes, sir."

"Please point him out."

As before, Foreman and Oswald stood. The witness said, "The man standing there at counsel table, not the lawyer, the other one."

"No further questions."

"Cross-examination?" asked the judge.

Foreman said he wanted to consult the court reporter briefly, so he asked the judge if it would be possible to proceed to the lunch break. The judge said fine.

After the break, Foreman's cross came right to the point.

"At the lineup on the night of the assassination, you told the police you could *not* make a positive identification, didn't you?"

"That's true."

"And that was how soon after the last shot was fired?

"About ten hours."

"Same day?"

"Correct."

"So the first time you were asked to make a positive identification, ten hours after the event, you said you couldn't do it, true?"

"That's correct."

"And from that night until you came in here today, you've never made a positive identification, have you?"

The witness fidgeted.

"No, sir, I haven't."

"So, today, right here, is the first time you have ever, in all this time, given a positive identification?"

The witness glanced down.

"Yes, sir, that's true."

"As the last shot was fired, you say you were ducking for cover at the same time, true?"

"I'm not sure. Did I say that?"

"During the break, Mr. Brennan, I asked our excellent court reporter to read me back your answer so that I could copy it down exactly. Now, in answer to the question, 'Describe in detail what you saw,' you told us about the gun being shouldered to the right shoulder and his taking positive aim, and his drawing back the gun to his side and pausing. Then you said—I quote exactly from the reporter—'At that same moment, I was diving off that firewall and to the right for bullet protection . . .' Recall that?"

"Yes, sir."

Bebe admired this mark of experience. To have taken the time to copy down the exact wording from the court reporter headed off any sideshow over whether Foreman had misquoted the witness.

"So, at that same moment, meaning the last shot, you were actually diving for cover?"

"Yes, sir, at the last shot."

"Fearing for your safety, were you?"

"Sure."

"And you were moving?"

"I must have been."

"Fast, would you say?"

"Pretty fast."

"As you were ducking for cover and moving pretty fast and fearing for your safety, you were also looking down at where you were going to land, weren't you?"

"I suppose so."

"So, while you were diving, and looking down and fearing for your safety, you weren't looking up at the sixth floor, were you?"

He fidgeted again. Sweat showed on his shirt under his arms.

"Not the entire time."

"Not the entire time. Now, before you went to the lineup, you'd seen a picture of Lee Oswald on television?"

"Yes, sir."

"The news said he'd been arrested for killing the president, and the television showed his picture, right?"

"True."

"Did you tell the police at the lineup that you'd seen that?"

"I did, yes, sir."

"What else did you say to the police about that?"

"I said possibly seeing him on television had 'messed me up' in my ability to identify the man I saw in the window."

"'Messed me up.' You used that phrase with them?"

"Yes, sir."

"And then later on, on January 7 of this year, you were interviewed again, this time by the FBI, true?"

"Early January."

Foreman made a small show of consulting an interview summary as he examined the witness.

"And, on January 7, just about two months ago, you told the FBI agent that you had viewed a lineup on the night of November 22?"

"Okay, I did say that."

"You also told the FBI agent that before going to the lineup you had observed Lee Oswald's picture on television, true?"

"I believe so, yes."

"And you told the FBI agent that"—here Foreman's voice went into quote mode—"seeing his picture on television had not helped you retain the original impression of the man you saw in the window, didn't you?"

The witness paused, then looked at Wade, who kept a dour poker face.

"I said something like that."

"Which was another way of saying it 'messed you up'?"

"Yes, sir, I suppose so."

"And you told the FBI agent that of the four people in the lineup, you felt Oswald 'most resembled' the man in the window."

"Well, I identified Oswald."

"No, I am asking did you use the phrase 'most resembled'?"

"When?"

"When you talked to the FBI agent"—Foreman held up and glanced between Brennan and the interview memo—"Didn't you tell the agent that you felt that Oswald 'most resembled' the man whom you had seen in the window?"

Brennan paused. The room was silent save for the wall clock.

"Yes, sir. I said that."

"So out of four people in the lineup, the most you could say was that my client 'most resembled' the man who made the last shot, true?"

"I said that, yes."

"You said earlier today you thought a communist conspiracy against our government might be underway and that was why you declined to make a positive identification on the twenty-second."

"That is correct."

"Seven weeks later on January 7 of this year, when you were speaking with the FBI, were you still afraid a communist conspiracy might be underway?"

"No, not really."

"Thank you, Mr. Brennan. Nothing more."

Foreman, Bebe felt, had hurt Brennan.

Wade rose. "Mr. Foreman brought out that you were diving for cover at the third shot. Now, Mr. Brennan, was the third shot the first time you saw the man in the window?"

"No, sir, I'd seen him a few minutes earlier before the motorcade arrived."

"Same man?"

"Yes, sir."

"Were you diving for cover then?"

"No, sir."

"Got good look at him?"

"Yes, sir."

"And who was it?"

"Him, the defendant, Lee Harvey Oswald."

"Your Honor, the witness may now be excused," Wade said, presuming against any re-cross.

Bebe now saw the shrewdness in having first called the rock-solid eye-witnesses to the officer's murder. Foreman hurt Brennan on cross, but he'd had nothing to shake Scroggins and Markham. Right off the bat, with the first two witnesses, Oswald got tagged as a murderer.

# 38  ROY TRULY

IF WADE FUMED INSIDE OVER BRENNAN, HE DIDN'T SHOW IT, Bebe would report, as he called Roy Sansom Truly, his fifth witness. Through the hallway doors Bebe saw a tall man with a crew cut and glasses enter to take the stand. Truly was fifty-three, he told the jury. He'd worked for the Texas School Book Depository, a private firm, since 1934 and was now the superintendent.

"Mr. Truly," Wade asked, "when did you first hear of Lee Harvey Oswald?"

"I heard the name last October 15, give or take.

"And from whom did you hear the name?"

"I received a phone call from a lady in Irving named Paine."

"What'd Mrs. Paine say and what'd you say?"

"She said, 'Mr. Truly, I am just wondering if you can use another man.' She said, 'I have a fine young man living here with his wife and baby. His wife is expecting another baby in a few days. He needs work desperately.' I told Mrs. Paine that—to send him down. So he came in, introduced himself to me as Lee Oswald, so I took him in my office and interviewed him. He seemed to be quiet and well mannered. I gave him an application to fill out, which he did."

"Did he fill it out in front of you, or not?"

"Yes, he did. He said he'd just served his term in the Marine Corps and had received an honorable discharge. He listed some things of an office nature that he had learned to do in the Marines. He used the word 'sir,' you know, which a lot of them don't do these days. So I told him he could come to work on the next morning which was the beginning of a new pay period."

Truly explained that Oswald began work the next morning. His hours were 8:00 to 4:45 with a forty-five-minute lunch break. No one punched a clock. Oswald proved a good worker. He seemed to catch on and learn the location of the stock. The main publisher handled by Oswald was Scott, Foresman & Company, most of whose books rested on the sixth floor. Orders came in to the first floor where order fillers, like Oswald, would take order forms and then go fetch the books. Oswald was paid $1.25 an hour. He never missed a day of work.

"Did you ever see," Wade continued, "whether or not he seemed to strike up any friendship or acquaintanceship with the other employees?"

"No, I never noticed that anywheres."

"When the motorcade came, where were you?"

"From the front door of the Depository, we crossed the Elm Street Extension, then reached the closest curb that runs along the new part of Elm Street. The president was to come toward us on Houston, then turn left onto Elm Street. We stood at the curb to see him."

"Tell us what you saw."

"A block away, we saw the motorcycle escort come off of Main, then turn right onto Houston Street coming toward us. The president's car followed close behind at an average speed of ten or fifteen miles an hour. After one block, they turned left off Houston onto Elm Street, close to where we were. The driver of the presidential car swung out too far to the right, and he came almost within an inch of running into an abutment on Elm. Not being familiar with the sharp left, he came too far out when he made his turn, coming very close to us. So he slowed down perceptibly, then pulled back to the left to get over into the middle lane of the parkway."

"What time was that?"

"12:30."

"Then what happened?"

"I heard an explosion, which I thought was a toy cannon or a loud firecracker from west of the building, to my right. Nothing happened at this first explosion. Everything was frozen. Immediately after, two more explosions, which I then realized was a gun, a rifle of some kind. I saw the president's car swerve to the left and stop. That's the last I saw of his car. When the third shot rang out, people began screaming, falling to the ground. The people in front of us surged back in panic. The crowd just practically bore me back to the first step on the entrance of our building."

"Then what?"

"I saw a young motorcycle policeman—Marrion Baker his name I know now—run up to the building, up the steps to the entrance of our building. I ran up and caught up with him. It occurred to me that this officer wanted on top of the building. He doesn't know the plan of the floor. That just popped in my mind, so I ran in with him. As we got in the lobby, this policeman asked me where the stairway is. I said, 'This way.' We ran diagonally across to the northwest corner of the building where the stairs and elevators are."

"Once you got there, then what happened?"

"The call elevator would not descend to us because someone had left the safety gate open. The other elevator could only be boarded where it was left last, which in this case was one of the higher floors. So both elevators were useless for us."

"Then what?"

"I went up on a run up the stairway. This officer stayed right behind me. I started to continue on up the stairway to the third floor. I went up two or three steps, then I realized the officer was no longer following me."

"What happened then?"

"I came back to the second-floor landing. I heard some voices, or a voice, coming from the area of the lunchroom on the second floor. I opened the door to the lunchroom."

"What'd you see?"

"I saw Officer Baker facing Lee Oswald. The officer had his gun pointing at him. The officer asked, 'This man work here?' I said, 'Yes.'"

"Then?"

"Then we left Oswald immediately to continue to run up the stairway until we reached the fifth floor. From there we took an elevator to the seventh floor. Then we ran up a little stairway to the roof."

"Did the officer say to you why he wanted to go up to the roof?"

"The officer soon told me as we walked onto the seventh floor, 'Be careful, this man will blow your head off.' I told the officer that I didn't feel like the shots came from the building. I said, 'I think we are wasting our time up here.' After we reached the roof, the officer looked down over the boxcars, the railroad tracks, and the crowd below. Then he looked around the roof for any evidence of anybody being there."

"Where'd you think the shots came from?"

"I thought the shots came from west of our building."

Bebe understood him to be referring to the knoll by the rail yard.

"Now, did you next go down to the sixth floor with Officer Baker?"

"Yes, sir. He glanced over the sixth floor quickly."

"Could you see the southeast corner of the sixth floor from where you were?

"No, sir. Too many boxes."

"Then what?"

"Then we continued on down. We saw officers on the fourth floor."

"Then you got down eventually to the first floor?"

"When I got back to the first floor, at first I didn't see anything except officers and reporters running around. It was a regular madhouse."

Truly added that he eventually gathered up the staff, then noticed that Oswald had gone missing—the only worker out of fifteen to go missing. He reported that fact to Captain Fritz, who had come on the scene. Fritz said he would take care of it. Truly gave him Oswald's address in Irving.

Wade ended with showing that Oswald had had no visitors and had made no calls.

Foreman rose and waited for the judge to nod, then said, "Mr. Truly, you said the place was a 'regular madhouse.' Did I hear that correctly?"

"A regular madhouse, yes, after we came down from the roof."

"And you said there were reporters there as part of that madhouse. Did I hear you right?"

"Yes. Many reporters."

"And by reporters, do you include news photographers?"

"Yes, of course."

"And was there any effort then being made to make the reporters leave the premises?"

"No, not that I could see."

"So, they mingled in with the police and everyone else in the Depository?"

"Yes, sir."

"Including the sixth floor?"

"Yes, sir."

"And when you saw Lee in the lunchroom, did you yourself know yet whether or not the president actually had been hit?"

"I heard that later."

"Finally, did your business keep any private security guards inside?"

"No guards."

"Or maintain a sign-in desk for members of the public?"

"No."

"Thank you, Mr. Truly."


THE FIRST DAY OF testimony ended. The jury left first, escorted out by the bailiff, returning to their sequestration floor higher in the building. The judge then asked counsel if there was any further immediate business. The lawyers said no, so the judge called recess. Re-secured, Oswald was escorted by deputies to the holding cell.

Reporters fled. They had pockets and purses full of change for the pay-phones, three per floor, or had made arrangements with nearby merchants to use their lines, or hurried back to their hotel phones. Hours later, when all their reporting was done, they wound up in small groups in bars to drink, smoke, compare notes, and size it up. Dallas, they figured, was ground zero of the most consequential story of their lifetimes.

At the Dallas Press Club that evening, Bebe and her new friends laughed over drinks at a small table. The assembled reporters gave her a gag award as Scoop Master. Bob Schieffer produced a small lead winged horse painted red and green, like the giant one atop the Magnolia Building. The "Pegasus Scoop Master Award," he grinned.

"You got a scoop on Marilyn Sitzman and a scoop on Jack Ruby," intoned Schieffer, touching his glass to hers. "You have put us all to shame, but we love it."

"Well," she played along, "I have a long list of people to thank." All laughed. "But I'll settle for saying how good it feels to have edged out the great Jim Lehrer, who out-scooped me, on Little Lynn fainting in the hallway during jury selection."

"A distant second," beamed Lehrer.

"You know," continued Lehrer, "I stood right by Jack Ruby in the back of the room that Friday night when the police brought Oswald out to show him off to the press. Who would've thought that thirty-six hours later he'd try to kill Oswald? My God. A scoop was standing right beside me, and I missed it."

"What a different trial," Bebe replied, "that would've been."

They then turned to the main event. "Which leads us to the question before the house," Lehrer asked, "What can we make of the first day of trial? Bebe, what say our Scoop Master?"

"I'm stuck on Percy's opening," Bebe answered. "He conceded that Oswald killed Officer Tippit. He says it was self-defense, but it could not possibly have been self-defense. You heard that cab driver and waitress. Cold-blooded murder. Wade was masterful to call them first right after Percy had laid the idea of self-defense before the jury. That, to me, is the big story. That alone means the electric chair."

"You have a point, Bebe," Schieffer responded, "but Foreman's so good, I suspect he wouldn't have said that unless he'll pull a rabbit out of the hat. To me, Foreman's cross-examination of the steamfitter became the highlight. The witness went from straightforward in-court identification to a wishy-washy 'I think so, maybe.'"

Lehrer offered a different take: "The mystery of the two cops tooting their horn out front of the boarding house while Oswald was changing clothes will somehow explain away why Oswald killed the officer a few minutes later, which in turn means that Oswald's going to have no choice but to testify. Then we'll see the rabbit out of the hat."

# 39   THEY HEARD THE HULLS DROP

NEXT MORNING CAME THREE OF OSWALD'S COWORKERS WHO had been one floor down at the time of the shooting, immediately below the sniper's nest.

First up came Bonnie Ray Williams. He testified that he was twenty, married, lived in Dallas, and had finished high school. He got his job at the Depository on September 8, only a few weeks before Oswald. Williams started as a wrapper, then moved to checker. Business got to be slow, he said, so they moved him to cut lumber and lay new wood over the fifth floor, afterward on the sixth floor. They had just started laying the sixth floor on November 22. To set up for that work, they had already moved some book cartons on the sixth floor from the west side to the east side, so cartons piled high on the east side (the sniper side).

Alexander examined.

"On the morning of November 22, what time did you go to work?"

"Eight."

"Do you know Lee Harvey Oswald?"

"Not personally but I'd seen him working. He never said much. I never said anything to him. Sometimes I saw him go out for lunch. Sometimes I saw him in the domino room reading the paper; that was on the first floor."

The domino room on the first floor served as a lunchroom for blacks but whites could sit or eat there too. The Dr Pepper machine was in the domino room. The second-floor lunchroom, with the Coca-Cola machine, remained white only.

"On the twenty-second, did you see him?"

"Little after eight. He had a clipboard in his hands. This was on the first floor. Maybe I also saw him between about 11:30 and 11:50 on the sixth floor. I'm not sure about that one."

"Where'd you work that day?"

"On the sixth floor. Five of us. We were working on the west side. Laying floor and moving stock."

"What'd an order filler like Oswald do?"

"Take books down to the first floor."

"Do you recognize Mr. Oswald here in court?"

"Yes, sir."

"Please point him out."

Again, Oswald rose with Mr. Foreman.

"That's him. The shorter one."

"When'd you break for lunch?"

"Five to ten minutes before noon. We wanted to wash up for lunch to see the president."

"Did you hear Oswald on your way down to wash your hands?"

"Yes, sir. I was in the elevator. He was on either the fifth or sixth floor. He said we should close the gate on the elevator when we got down so he could call it up to the floor he was on."

"So you washed your hands. Then what?"

"I got a Dr Pepper from the machine on the first floor. I took my lunch from home back up to the sixth floor where I thought all of us were going to have lunch and watch the motorcade, but no one joined me there, so I ate my lunch on the sixth floor, at the third or fourth set of windows, facing Elm, then I left to go find the others."

"Could you see over to the southeast corner of the sixth floor?"

"No, sir, there was too many boxes."

Bebe imagined Oswald hidden behind the boxes, recalculating his plan to account for Williams.

"Which end were you closest to?"

"About the middle."

"How long were you there?"

"Five to ten to twelve minutes. I finished my lunch. I left the lunch sack and empty Dr Pepper bottle there."

"What time did you leave?"

"Approximately 12:20, maybe."

"Are you sure?"

"No. It might have been earlier."

"Where'd you go?"

"To the fifth floor."

"How?"

"By the east elevator. The one with the hand pedal and gate."

"How does the other one, the west one, work?"

"Push button. You have two gates to pull. You can call that one to your floor by call button so long as the gates are pulled shut."

"What happened on the fifth floor?"

"I found Harold Norman and James Jarman there on the fifth floor facing the Elm Street side at the southeast corner."

"So did you get there before the president's car arrived?"

"Even before any of the motorcade made the turn off of Main Street."

"What happened as the president's car passed your window?"

"There was a loud shot, like a salute or motorcycle backfire. There're three shots. The second and third shots were closer together than the first and second. It shook the building. Cement fell on my head from the ceiling."

"You say cement fell on your head?"

"Cement, gravel, dirt, or something from the old building because the shot shook the windows and everything. Harold Norman said it came from right above our heads. If you want my exact words, I could tell you."

The witness had the only black face in the courtroom except for two reporters in the now desegregated gallery. He seemed reluctant to volunteer the words used for fear of being perceived as disrespectful to the whites present.

"Tell us."

"My exact words were, 'No bullshit.' We jumped up."

A suppressed ripple of comic relief swept the gallery. Without smiling, the witness continued, "Norman also said, 'I can even hear the shells being ejected from the gun hitting the floor.'"

"Heard the shells hit the floor. What else was said?"

"Junior Jarman said, 'Man, somebody is shooting at the president.' I said again, 'No bullshit.' Then Norman said, 'You got something on your head,' and Jarman said, 'Man, don't you brush it out,' meaning it was evidence, save it, but I forgot and brushed it out anyway downstairs. We saw police and a crowd run to the west, so we ran over to look out the windows on the west to see whatever it was they were running to. Then Jarman said maybe we should get out. We were frightened."

"What'd you do?"

"We ran down the stairwell. We saw policemen on the first floor who took our names. Then we went out the front door."

"No further questions."

Foreman rose and said he'd be brief.

"How many shots did you hear fired?"

"Three."

"And, again, what was the timing?"

"There was a pause after the first one. Then there was two real quick."

"You say you sometimes saw Lee go out for lunch—did I hear that correctly?"

"Yes, sir."

"Out of the building, you mean?"

"Yes, sir."

"No more questions, thank you."

Next came Harold Norman. He testified much the same as Williams, saying that on the fifth floor, he could hear the shell hulls hitting the floor, even hear the ejecting of the rifle. He heard three shots. He had told the other two at the time, "I believe it came from up above us." He saw the ceiling dust fall on the hair of Bonnie Ray Williams.

Norman was followed by Junior Jarman, who testified to the same story as Norman and Williams except he was also asked, "On that day, did you have lunch with Lee Harvey Oswald?"

"No, sir."

Foreman waved off cross-examination of Norman and Jarman.

The night before, Bebe would eventually report, Wade and Alexander had gone over to see if it was possible to hear hulls falling as these witnesses testified. Alexander listened while Wade, a floor above in the sniper's nest, dropped three empty shells. Alexander heard all three.

# 40   SECRET SERVICE

BUTTERFLIES FILLED HER. ON THIS SECOND DAY OF WITNESSES, Elaine would perform in the trial of the century. She'd marched with Abe through the courthouse doors on Main Street that morning. A photographer for the *Dallas Morning News had* snapped their picture. She seemed calm but was, in truth, all nerves.

To a packed house she rose to say, "We call Agent Roy Kellerman." A man well over six feet with movie-star looks came forward, took the oath, and found his place in the witness box. This being the first exam by a federal, Barefoot Sanders came to lend moral support. Her mother sat by Sanders.

After his background, Elaine turned to November 22.

"What were your specific duties back on November 22, 1963?"

"I was in charge of the Secret Service detail for this trip of President Kennedy, for the trip to Texas in those two days."

"Please summarize what led up to the motorcade."

"On November 22, the activities started at around 8:25 in the morning when the president, accompanied by then Vice President Johnson and a few congressional leaders, walked out the front door of the hotel in Fort Worth. Across this street was a parking lot. The president made a short speech there. It was a light drizzle at the time. From there we returned to the hotel. He attended a breakfast given by the chamber of commerce and a citizen's group. After breakfast, the president returned to his suite. The weather was then changing. It had quit raining, even looked like it was going to break out to be a real beautiful day. In the neighborhood of ten o'clock in the morning I received a call from Special Agent Lawson, who had the advance from Dallas."

"Agent Lawson is with the Secret Service, is he?"

"Yes, ma'am, he is. He asked me to determine whether the president's bubbletop car should have the top down or up."

"What is it made of?"

"It is composed of plastic, clear plastic substance. Its use would be for a weather matter whereby the president or his occupants can see out."

"Is it bulletproof?"

"It is not bulletproof. Nor bullet resistant."

"Why didn't you use the bubbletop on the twenty-second?"

"As I said, the weather cleared in Fort Worth, a nice day. I asked Mr. Kenneth O'Donnell, who was President Kennedy's appointment secretary, 'Mr. O'Donnell,' I said, 'the weather, it is slightly raining in Dallas, predictions of clearing up. Do you desire to have the bubbletop on or off?' His instructions to me were, 'If the weather is clear, have that bubbletop off.' That is exactly what I relayed to Mr. Lawson."

Elaine had the witness describe the makes of vehicles in the motorcade—lead car, president's limousine, Secret Service car, vice president's car, and so on.

"Why weren't Secret Service agents on the running board of the president's car, like they were on the car just behind?"

"President Kennedy instructed us not to stand there. He wanted to have the people feel close to him and the First Lady."

"What time did you turn onto Elm?"

"12:30."

"After you turned onto Elm, what happened?"

"As we turned off Houston onto Elm, we were away from buildings. We were out in the open, and there was a report like a firecracker. I turned my head to the right because whatever this noise was, I was sure that it came from the right, perhaps into the rear. I was in the right front seat. As I turned my head to the right to view whatever it was or see whatever it was, I heard a voice from the back seat. I firmly believe it was the president's 'My God, I am hit,' and I turned around and he had his hands up here, like this, in the collar section."

"As you are positioning yourself in the witness chair, your right hand is up with the fingers at the ear level as if about to clutch the head. Would that be an accurate description of the position you demonstrated there?"

"Yes, ma'am. There was enough for me to verify that the man was hit. So, in the same motion I said to the driver, 'Let's get out of here; we are hit' and I grabbed the mike and I said, 'Lawson, this is Kellerman,'—Lawson is in the front car. 'We are hit; get us to the hospital immediately.' I then looked back. This time Agent Clint Hill, who was riding on the left front bumper of our follow-up car, had run forward and was on the back trunk of our car. The president was down sideways into the back seat."

"Indicating on his left side."

"Correct, yes. Governor Connally by that time is lying flat backwards into her lap—Mrs. Connally—she was lying flat over him."

Elaine took him through the number of shots. Kellerman said that he actually heard three shots, thinking that the first one had been a firecracker. Because, however, he thought Kennedy had four wounds and Connally three, Kellerman had earlier come to the opinion that after the first shot, a "flurry" of shots must have come into the car. Nevertheless, he confirmed that he'd actually heard only three shots. Negotiating this clarification before an overflowing courtroom gave Elaine anxious moments, yet outwardly she projected professional confidence.

"Now, did President Kennedy say anything besides, 'My God, I am hit'?"

"Those are the last words he said."

"What happened as you arrived at the hospital?"

"As we arrived at the hospital I immediately got out of the car. Our follow-up car is in back of us. I yelled to the agents, 'Go get us two stretchers on wheels.' I turned right around to the back door and opened it. By this time Mrs. Connally had sat back up so that the Governor could lie in her lap, face up. His eyes are open and he is looking at me, and I am fairly sure he is alive. By this time I noticed the two stretchers coming out of the emergency room. I said, 'Governor, don't worry; everything is going to be all right.' He nodded his head, which fairly convinced me that man was alive. By this time the stretcher is there. I get inside on one side of him, Special Agent Hill on the other. Somebody is holding his feet, and we remove the governor to put him on the stretcher. They take him in. We then get in to help Mrs. Connally out. Our next move is to get Mrs. Kennedy off from the seat, which was a little difficult, but she was removed. Then Agent Hill removed his coat and laid it over the president's face and shoulder. We lifted up the president and put him on a stretcher and followed him right into the emergency room."

Kellerman gave additional information about actions in the emergency room and described the moment when doctors declared the president dead. He remained remarkably composed the whole time.

"What time did the plane arrive back at the Washington area?"

Kellerman consulted his report, then stated that 5:58 p.m. was when they landed and 7:00 p.m. the body arrived at the Naval Hospital in Bethesda.

"And about what time, then, did they complete their autopsy work?"

"They were all through at 3:30 a.m."

One last thing. Did you scan the Dallas newspaper coverage to see if the paper had published the parade route?"

"The exact route was published at least twice by Wednesday, November 20. The news said that the motorcade would travel slowly so that the public would have a good view."

"And did it travel slowly?"

"Yes, about ten miles an hour in an open convertible limousine."

Again, the defense had no questions.

# 41  AN URGE TO RETCH

AFTER A RECESS, THE ROOM RECONVENED TO SEE THE FILM projector in the center of the well, aimed at a screen. Senator Ted Kennedy's seat was now empty.

Abraham Zapruder worked as a dress manufacturer in the Dal-Tex Building on Elm catty-cornered from Dealey Plaza. At almost the last minute on the twenty-second, he'd run home to get his Bell & Howell 8mm home movie camera to film the motorcade. He and his receptionist, Marilyn Sitzman, then stood on a concrete abutment on the west end of the pergola, a WPA project, on the north side of Elm between the Depository and the Triple Underpass. She was behind him, hands on his shoulders, to hold him steady.

Wade decided to call Sitzman rather than Zapruder to get the film in evidence. In their preparation interviews, Zapruder had repeatedly broken down in tears, becoming at times incoherent. In the actual event on the twenty-second, he'd become distraught. His ability to remember accurately had been compromised. Sitzman, on the other hand, had remained composed.

Wade called Sitzman to the stand and took her through the run-up to the filming, their location, her holding Zapruder steady, her watching over his shoulder, the three shots, all from the direction of the Depository, then the devastating moment of the splattering of the president's head on the third shot. As for the grassy knoll that rose to meet the stockade fence, Wade asked if she'd heard any gunfire from that direction.

"No," Sitzman answered, "and if we had, it would have been so close and so loud that we would have lost our gumption and have been unable to continue steady as we did." This prompted her recollection of the young couple on the bench and how their coke bottle had fallen and exploded just to her right as the couple scrambled for cover in the terror of the rifle shots.

The film can and reel were then shown to the witness, authenticated, and moved into evidence. Wade then asked for permission to show the film to the jury. The judge approved.

Wade slipped the reel onto the top spindle of the movie projector. He threaded the film through the lens box and rollers to the down spindle, then snapped the lens box in place. The screen stood in the far front corner opposite the jury, turned at an angle so that the gallery could see it as well as the jury. The judge left the bench to stand by the jury box so he could see better.

"Could we please dim the lights and pull the shades?" asked Wade. The judge signaled to the bailiffs. Soon the room dimmed. Deputies seemed to pay close attention to Oswald. In fact, with the film coming, Wade had added yet another deputy.

Wade turned the play knob. The projector cast the Zapruder film onto the screen. Sketch artists had another memorable scene. Their wrists quickened to the darkened scene. The sprocket works stuttered with their familiar rhythm.

The color film began with the first three of five lead motorcycles turning left off Houston onto Elm and, after a few seconds of that scenario, jumped forward to show the president's midnight-blue convertible having made the same turn, flags flying on the front fenders. Then, almost immediately, Connally looked back over his shoulder as if he'd heard the first shot. The motorcade proceeded from screen's left to right, so the film panned from left to right to keep them, more or less, in the center of the image. In bright sunshine, the president and the governor, on the right side of the car, were nearest the camera, but the First Lady's bright pink hat and suit outshone them all. She sat in the left rear, by her husband. They smiled and waved to well-wishers on their respective sides. They proceeded down Elm, grass plus crowd in the foreground. The car passed behind a traffic sign. As they emerged (moving left to right) from behind the sign, Kennedy (immediately), then Connally (moments later) reacted, but both still upright. Elbows out horizontally, Kennedy's hands jerked for his neck. Mrs. Kennedy reached for and looked quizzically, ever closer, at her husband. Connally began gradually slumping onto Nellie, on his left, in the jump seat in front of Jackie.

Just as the First Lady had her forearms close about her husband and peered at his upper chest, the front right top of the president's head exploded forward and upwards, blood and brain matter visibly filling the air about his head. This happened within inches of her face.

The president's body jerked forward, then backward, and finally slumped down.

As if to retrieve something, Mrs. Kennedy crawled onto the rear trunk hood with only her calves and feet remaining in the passenger compartment. Meanwhile, Agent Clint Hill, who had run up from the trailing car, leaped onto the rear hood of the moving car, then pushed her back into the seat.

The car then raced off.

Several jurors looked away. One, her chest heaving, forced a lace handkerchief to her mouth. Marina Oswald sobbed through the film. At Frame 313 she groaned uncontrollably. Robert Oswald escorted her into the hall. Even through the closed door, her shrieks could be heard as she was led away. The accused watched without emotion.

The lights came up. The judge asked if anyone in the jury needed a cup of water. The lady with the lace handkerchief raised her hand and Wade walked one over to her. Finally, Marina was no longer heard.

Wade had the witness authenticate an eight-by-ten still of Frame 313, then passed it among the jurors. While it passed through, the only sound was the ticking of the old wall clock. Because it all had gone by so quickly, the judge allowed the film to be shown again, lights re-dimmed. While some jurors looked away, others leaned forward intent on learning how the shots hit. Seeing the juror interest, Wade asked to show it yet again, but the judge said, "No, twice is enough for now."

A noon recess was then called.

The gallery emptied quickly. The Zapruder film had never been shown in public. It was a sensational, horrific event, showing as it did, a brutal murder, all the more so because it showed the murder of a president.

Bebe sat stunned by what she'd just witnessed, as did everyone around her. They had just witnessed a film of the president's head exploding in the most gruesome and cruel way imaginable.

She felt ill and went out for air, then walked around the block, collecting herself. She eventually crossed to Dealey Plaza and wound up on the same bench used by the couple whose coke bottle had burst, the one Marilyn had pointed out. She needed her one cigarette for the day. As she smoked, she realized she was looking straight at the place on Elm where the fatal head shot had occurred, where the First Lady had crawled out onto the rear hood. She sat very near where Zapruder and Sitzman had stood. Bebe turned slightly east—to the sixth floor window. It remained just as it had been on November 22. With a glance, she saw where Brennan had sat. A confluence of horrors, she would write, while the echoes still seemed to ring—but, in truth, for her, it was so sickening, so palpable that, like the juror, she felt the urge to retch.

Jim Lehrer had also gone out for air. He walked up, slowly.

"May I?"

Bebe gestured politely and brushed ash from her lap.

Lehrer remained standing, not presuming further on her. He held a pipe, unlit, giving his hand something to do.

"I've never seen anything so gut-wrenching," she said.

"It was good the senator wasn't there," observed Lehrer.

"The only good thing about it."

After a pause, Lehrer continued, slowly. "This world has some awful things, doesn't it—the way we imprison the insane, the way children live over there in the river slums, the way we execute the condemned, the murders we must relive in trials. If we dwelt on it all, we would fall apart. Thank God we have happy memories, too."

Traffic swept by. Pigeons pecked the grass. The Hertz sign blinked out the time. A mother and young son pointed to a locomotive at rest on the overpass.

"Well said, Mr. Lehrer." Her throat was thick. "Don't wait for me, Jim. I'll be along."

# 42 ROBERT HUGHES

THE AFTERNOON SESSION BEGAN.

While the projector still rested in the well of the courtroom, Wade called another home-movie maker to the stand, Robert Hughes, an appraiser for the United States Customs. He had stood at the northwest corner of Main and Houston with his 8mm Bell & Howell filming the motorcade while it turned off Main, glided up Houston, then made the turn onto Elm. He stopped filming one or two breaths before the first rifle shot. He authenticated the film. With permission of the judge, Wade screened it for the courtroom, again color without sound.

As the lights dimmed, Wade interjected, "Your Honor, may we ask everyone to pay particular attention to the part of the film where the sixth floor of the Depository is briefly shown."

Unlike the elevated perch Zapruder had selected, Hughes had filmed at street level. The limousine came within a dozen feet of the lens as it made the turn off Main, Jackie and the president easily visible in their last happy moments, Jackie the closer of the two. The car then receded northward (toward the Depository), soon turning left onto Elm, well-wishers in great abundance. The screen captured the bottom few floors of the Depository rising behind the heads of spectators. As the limousine turned onto Elm, the camera panned leftward and, more importantly, for almost half a second, upward enough to catch the sixth floor. As that momentary scene flickered by, a human form appeared to occupy the middle of the sniper's window, the southeast-most window on the sixth floor. Wade replayed the short clip. Several jurors leaned in with manifest interest to catch whatever was in the window.

Wade asked for the lights to come up.

"Mr. Hughes," Wade asked, "showing you eight still photographs, please tell us, if you know, what they are?"

"These are blowups of eight of the frames from the film."

"Which eight?"

"Where the camera pans past the sixth-floor window of the Depository, as the car completes a turn onto Elm."

Wade moved them into evidence and displayed them briefly to the jury.

"Mr. Hughes, what can you see in the rightmost window on sixth floor of the Depository?"

"The rightmost window is raised open but not as far open as the windows on the floor below. Maybe half as much. It looks like a man is seated behind the rightmost window. Possibly a woman. But a person, for sure. Sitting still. Possibly kneeling. Wearing a white or light-colored shirt."

"Can you make out any features or make out any identification?"

"No, the image is too blurry for that."

Wade passed the clearest of the fuzzy images among the jury.

Wade tendered the witness to the defense.

Foreman waited until the jury had examined the image, retrieved it, then returned it to the witness. Foreman stood just left of the witness, facing the jury, looking over the shoulder of the witness.

"Now, Mr. Hughes," Foreman pointed, "look at that next set of windows on the sixth floor, the set of windows just to our left of the person in the open window."

Hughes removed his glasses. For a few seconds, he studied the image up close, glanced left at Foreman, then said, "Okay."

"Now, Mr. Hughes, both windows in that set are closed, am I correct?"

"Yes, sir."

"And they look a bit dirty too, right?"

"Yes, sir."

"Nevertheless, standing right behind one of those closed windows, the one on the right, as we look at them, is a *second* person, right?"

He paused to look again.

"It's too hard to tell."

"Well, isn't that light spot right there the head and this part here the body?" Foreman hovered a pencil over the supposed form of a second person.

The witness again studied the image.

"You could be right, Mr. Foreman, but I just cannot tell."

"Thank you, Mr. Hughes."

On redirect, Wade rose but remained at counsel table.

"Sir, isn't that speck just dirt on the window?"

"Could easily be, Mr. Wade, it is just too hard to tell."

"But the corner window, how about that one?"

"One person for sure in that window."

"How many?"

"One."

The witness was excused.

To accommodate the press, Judge Brown decided to break early that afternoon so that reporters could have more time to report details on the Zapruder and Hughes films. He finished the day with the jury by informing them of the "view" that was to be conducted on the next court day, a jury view of the Depository and Dealey Plaza.

After the jury was gone for the day, by prearrangement, the judge allowed stills of some key frames to be distributed to the press. Bebe collected her copies. She sent her paper an item summarizing the Zapruder film. Deep within her, she sensed something more profound, but she had not yet worked it out, a realization that more was at stake than a news story—blood, bone, flesh, incalculable pain, the miracle of life, the finality of death, and their meaning pressed on her. That wonderful young family with its sacrifice for the nation—so cruelly rewarded. She went to her hotel room, called her dad—he didn't answer; she had a drink, then another, then fell asleep on her couch.

# 43 THE FIRST VIEW

BEBE'S PHONE WOKE HER THE NEXT MORNING. IT WAS JUDGE Brown. He couldn't allow all reporters to attend the view, he said, but he wanted to select two to do so on the condition that they share their notes and stories with all other correspondents. Would she?

"Why, sure, of course, Your Honor, but why me?"

"I think most other reporters would approve. I consulted Jim."

Bebe met the judge and the other selectee in his chambers moments before they left for the view.

The view occurred without convening in the courtroom. The jurors walked with their bailiff from their quarters to a corner opposite the Depository. The judge, the two reporters, counsel, deputies, and Oswald met them there. No one could say anything to the jury except that Wade, by stipulation, pointed out the location where Brennan had been. They proceeded to where Zapruder had filmed. By stipulation, Wade placed his hand on the spot on the concrete pier. Next, they gathered on the first floor of the Depository, observing all entrances, after which they took the freight elevators to the sixth floor. There, Wade pointed out the southeast and southwest corners. From the southeast window, each juror got to look down Elm to imagine the scene as the sniper fired and to take note of the angles obscured by the oak. Bebe saw the Iwo Jima vets stare at the scene then stare grim-faced a moment at Oswald, who stood away a respectable distance. By agreement, Wade further pointed out where the rifle had been found on that floor (nearer the elevators). As the jury gathered up in that direction, Bebe saw Oswald step to the window to note the scene immediately below. Next, they walked via the stairway to the second floor, out via the lunchroom, next through an interior hall, down the main front stairs, and finally out the front entrance.

Most of the proceedings occurred in silence with only short instructions to the jury as to where to proceed or stand and the short non-argumentative statements by Wade of what was being seen. Foreman, Bebe would report, had previewed and approved all of Wade's comments. The view took the entire morning. The jurors returned to their courthouse suite for lunch.

DURING THEIR USUAL LUNCH in the conference room that day, Elaine saw a frown on Wade's face as he reported that Sam Holland had phoned to say that he'd been subpoenaed to testify in the defense case.

"What's Percy want him for?" Alexander asked.

Alexander sliced an apple with his pocketknife, then offered Elaine a slice. She appreciated his gesture. She took it and ate it. Maybe, she thought, he was warming to her.

"The goddamn puff of smoke," Wade replied, "What else?"

Elaine's mind replayed Abe on how it would do Oswald no good to prove a conspiracy, for he would still be guilty of murder, even if by conspiracy.

"Bill, you were right—we should've never turned over all our interview memos. Look at how Brennan got tripped up. Now, we gotta deal with the goddamn puff of smoke." Wade looked first to Alexander, then to Abe, and finally shook his head.

"Listen," Abe took it with grace, "you can blame me all you want. But you know it was right."

Over at Melendorf's with Jim Lehrer, Bebe listened, transfixed, as Lehrer's colleague at the Dallas *Times-Herald*, Bob Jackson, a young photographer, described having seen the rifle being drawn back through the window even as echoes of the third shot reverberated. Bob had been in an open convertible with other photographers, the eighth car back, and had just tossed a roll of film to a runner at Main and Houston to get it developed for the afternoon paper when he heard the three shots, the last two closer together. "As I told the police, I saw some fellows on the fifth floor straining out the window and looking upward toward the sixth floor." He followed their line of sight to the corner window above them just in time to see a rifle being slowly drawn back into the shadows. He couldn't see the sniper. "A photograph of that rifle might've won a Pulitzer Prize," he lifted his coke, "if only I'd still had film."

A few tables away, wishing he had a drink in hand, Foreman remarked to his young assistant, "One bad thing about sequestration. The jurors become close friends. By the time they get the case, it'll be hard for anyone to dissent, to vote not guilty, to hold out. I'm goddamn sure, at this very moment, they are in the jury room together solving a jigsaw puzzle—an old judge's trick. Almost never does a sequestered jury hang up. My young friend, that's what we're up against."

# 44 SEARCH OF THE SIXTH FLOOR

THEY RESUMED IN THE COURTROOM FOR THE AFTERNOON SESsion.

Luke Mooney had served four years in the Army. He had been a deputy sheriff since 1958. On direct examination by Alexander, he testified that he had been in front of "this very courthouse" on Main Street when the motorcade approached. "When the president came by, I took my hat off." The motorcade passed, then turned onto Houston (and thereafter turned onto Elm). He heard the shots. Following a crowd, he ran up the knoll toward the railroad yards, finding nothing. He then entered the Depository via a back entrance, took the elevator to the second floor, then proceeded by the staircase to the sixth floor. "And how come I get off the sixth floor, I don't know yet."

"You were alone?" Wade asked.

"I was alone at that time."

"Were there other officers on the floor?"

"I didn't see any. I began crisscrossing the floor, looking through boxes, looking at open windows—some of them were open on the south side by

Elm. They had started laying floor up there. I was checking the fire escapes. Then I said I would go up to the seventh floor. Three of us did. It was dark up there. We had to wait for flood lights to come up, so I went back to the sixth floor."

"What happened next?"

"At that time, some news reporter, I don't know who, was coming up with a camera. He wasn't taking pictures. He was just looking."

Foreman caught the attention of the court reporter, pointing his index finger, so she tore the edge of her paper tape to mark the passage. Bebe scrawled "camera."

"Tell us about the sixth floor."

"On the sixth floor, I went straight across to the southeast corner and saw all these high boxes. Stacked all the way around. I squeezed between. The minute I squeezed between these two stacks of boxes, I had to turn myself sideways to get in there—that is when I saw the expended shells and the boxes that were stacked up as a rest for the weapon. There was a slight crease in the top box, whether the recoil made the crease or it was placed there before the shots were fired, I don't know. But anyway, there was a very slight crease in the box, where the rifle could have lain—at the same angle that the shots were fired from."

"Did you disturb the scene?"

"No, at that time, I didn't lay my hands on anything because I wanted to save every piece of evidence for fingerprints. So I leaned out the window, the same window from which the shots were fired, looked down, where I saw Sheriff Bill Decker and Captain Will Fritz on the street in front of the Depository. So I hollered to get the crime lab officers on route, that I had the location spotted."

"What happened next?"

"I stood guard to see that no one disturbed anything until Captain Fritz came up with Deputy Boone and some others."

The witness vouched for the three spent shells as well as photographs of the sniper's nest with the three spent cartridges in place. They came into evidence. Wade displayed the three spent shells in his hand and walked the length of the jury box, then said, "Your witness."

On cross-examination, Foreman asked about press photographers and timing of the shots.

"You said when you got to the sixth floor, you saw a news photographer. Did I get that right?"

"Yes, sir. He had a camera."

"How do you know he was a newsman?"

"He had a camera."

"What was his name?"

"I don't know."

"Did you ever see him again?"

"Not to remember it."

"What'd he look like?"

"I don't recall—just he had a camera."

Bebe underlined the word "camera."

"How many press photographers were up there?"

"Eventually, there were a number of photographers up there. I assumed they were the press. They had cameras. Some were shooting pictures."

"How long were they there?"

"They were there when all these officers and everybody was up there."

"Did you hear all three shots?"

"Yes."

"What was the timing between them?"

"I can still hear them distinctly. The last two shots were pretty close together, but there was a short time lapse between the first and second shot. Why, I don't know."

EUGENE BOONE WAS ALSO a deputy sheriff, age twenty-six. Alexander examined. On the twenty-second, he'd been viewing the parade with Deputy Mooney on Main Street near Houston. When they heard the shots, they ran to the rail yard but found nothing. The control man in the rail yard tower, a Mr. Lee Bowers, said he hadn't heard the shots and hadn't seen anybody moving around out in the yard. Boone went to the sixth floor.

"What'd you do after you got up to the sixth floor?"

"Well, I proceeded to the east end of the building. Mooney, I learned, had already found the shells. We started working our way across the building to the west wall, looking in, under and around all the boxes and pallets and what have you that were on the floor. Looking for the weapon. As I got to the west wall, there were windows there, with a slight space between some boxes and the wall. I squeezed through them. I had my light in my hand. I was slinging it around on the floor, and I caught a glimpse of the rifle, stuffed down between two rows of boxes with another box or so pulled over the top of it. So I hollered that the rifle was here near the stairwell in the northwest corner."

"What happened then?"

"Some of the officers came over to look at it. I told them to stand back, not to get around close, they might want to take prints of some of the boxes, but not touch the rifle. At that time, Captain Fritz and a lab man came over. They came over to photograph the weapon as it lay. Then Captain Fritz picked it up by the strap to remove it."

The witness then identified the actual Mannlicher-Carcano as the rifle he had seen. It was moved into evidence. Alexander walked it slowly in front of the jury box, pointing upward, bolt open, so that all jurors could see it.

Foreman had no cross.

WILL FRITZ CAME NEXT, examined by Wade. Fritz had come to the Dallas Police Department in 1921, he told the jury, and was now the captain of the homicide-robbery bureau. After the assassination, he was ordered by his boss to go to the hospital, but once there, he let him go to the scene of the crime, arriving there at 12:58. He drew his gun because the police thought that the shooter was still in the building. Fritz ordered the building sealed, then took charge of the search in progress. It wasn't long before a deputy shouted out his find of the three empty cartridges on the sixth floor at the corner window, so Fritz went there. Fritz told them not to touch anything until the crime lab could take pictures and dust for fingerprints. A few minutes later, another deputy found the rifle on the same floor near the back stairway. Again, he told them not to touch anything until photographs and prints were taken. Also in the corner in the same sniper's nest, Fritz found the wrapping paper evidently used to wrap the rifle.

Wade continued:

"Did you find any more shells?"

"After the pictures had been made and the rifle dusted for prints, I then ejected a live shell, a live cartridge from the rifle. Oswald's prints were on the boxes by the window, but all exterior surfaces of the rifle had been wiped clean. Shells too."

Superintendent Truly soon told him, Fritz continued, that one of his employees had gone missing from the building, someone named Lee Harvey Oswald. Truly gave Fritz an address in Irving. Before heading out to Irving, Fritz first went to the police headquarters to see if Oswald had a criminal record. While at the police headquarters, he learned that Officer Tippit had meanwhile been killed and a suspect arrested—someone named Lee Harvey Oswald. He sent some officers to Irving anyway to search the Paine residence for evidence.

After he learned of the boarding house, he sent others to search it. Fritz stayed at the headquarters to interview Oswald. When Oswald got booked, a bus transfer was found on his person as well as four bullets of the brand used in the revolver. No empty casings or other weapons were found on him, in the Depository, or in Dealey Plaza.

Fritz next explained that, based on a simple field test, the travel time to reach the second-floor lunchroom from where Officer Marrion Baker heard the shots was the same as the travel time from the sniper nest to the lunchroom via the stairs, both about seventy-five seconds, according to two tests done after the fact via the stairs for each starting place.

Foreman had three questions. He asked what most witnesses thought was the number and the timing of the shots.

"Three shots . . . The second and third shots were bunched together, most people thought, with a pause after the first."

"Do police reports always set forth everything the reporting officer did or observed?"

"No, sir. The main points, usually, but things sometimes get omitted."

"So, does the absence of a fact in a police report mean the officer didn't observe it?"

"No." Foreman knew that any other answer would get Fritz in trouble in other cases and maybe even in this case, for police officers frequently needed to embellish on what was in a report.

Finally, he asked Fritz to repeat the description sent out by police dispatchers on the assassin.

"White male, approximately thirty, slender build, height five feet ten inches, weight 165 pounds."

"And this came from Mr. Brennan?"

"I believe so."

"Captain Fritz, you know that Lee Oswald weighs 140 pounds and is twenty-four years of age, true?"

"Maybe 145 but yes, sir, that's true."

# 45 ERNEST SEWARD COX

AT THE DALLAS PRESS CLUB THAT EVENING, BEBE AND LEHRER speculated on how Oswald could possibly squirm out from under the evidence.

"Tell me something, Jim. Why is Dallas such a right-wing mecca, the City of Hate?"

"Easy—the *Dallas Morning News*," he answered. "It has relentlessly gone after the Kennedys, painting them in with communists and one-worlders. The *Morning News*, you know, is run by Ted Dealey. Yeah, Dealey Plaza's named for his dad. Sure, his dad was a decent guy—he ran the Klan out of Dallas in the 1930s—but Ted, the son, is a different story. He's a hardcore racist, so he runs a racist paper. Hates the Kennedys. That's just the start of it."

"What's the rest of it?"

"We got General Edwin Walker, the man who thinks he'll be our next president. General Walker even says—are you ready for this?—*Mad* magazine is a subversive influence on kids. No lie. You'll love this too—the general now has on his front lawn a full-sized billboard put up by the John Birch

Society saying, 'Impeach Earl Warren.' Full-sized billboard. Front yard."

Lehrer saw her eyes tracking someone behind him.

"Hey, isn't that Ernest Seward Cox?" Bebe whispered excitedly, nodding at a large man across the room.

"Well," Lehrer turned to see, "yes, would you like to meet him?"

"Of course."

Lehrer walked over and brought back the storied legal reporter from New York and sometimes contributor to *The New Yorker*, Ernest Seward Cox. "Ernie, please meet Bebe Boudreaux of the *Times-Picayune*."

"Miss Boudreaux," Cox pulled over a seat. He'd won a Pulitzer Prize in the mid-1950s, still reputed to have influence with the committee. Cox plainly liked to eat and drink. He wore a rumpled suit with expensive brown leather shoes, well scuffed. His tie hung slack.

"We were just contemplating the 'City of Hate.'"

Cox seemed unimpressed. He took a hasty drink and said nothing. His face displayed splotches of red.

"I've admired your items, Mr. Cox," added Bebe. "In fact, I kept that one you did on the Berlin Wall in *The New Yorker* as a model to inspire me."

"Thank you. You're the woman from Louisiana?" He flashed his eyes on her briefly.

"Indeed, I am."

"The one who got to do the jury view?"

"Yes, a lucky break."

"I've been wondering how you, being from Louisiana and all, are holding up now that the judge has desegregated the gallery and restrooms. Drinking fountains too, I suppose. Quite a change for you, no?"

"I'm making it just fine, Mr. Cox."

"Your pieces on the trial, Miss Boudreaux, have gotten some notice. One was reprinted in the *Washington Post*, the one about the so-called trial triangle. I read it myself. I said to myself, I wonder where she got that notion, trial triangle."

"Thank you, Mr. Cox." Bebe put on a smile.

Cox took another swallow. Lehrer worried Cox had had enough.

"I wish, Jim, that the papers in Louisiana and Mississippi would be as brilliant in reporting on racial injustice as they are in reporting on trial triangles."

Bebe's smile fled.

"When this assignment is over, Mr. Cox, I'd be pleased to have you join me in New Orleans. Perhaps we could do that project together."

"Boudreaux is Cajun, isn't it?"

With her best bayou accent, she replied, "Why, yes, Mr. Cox, it certainly is. Perhaps you know how our people have been treated?"

"Miss Boudreaux, I must ask this: Where *did* you get that trial triangle idea?" He turned squarely toward Bebe.

"A trial lawyer told me. A good one. It was his idea."

"So I thought." Cox signaled a waiter to bring another round. "It was too original an idea to have come from your paper."

Lehrer was sure now.

Bebe rose, her eyes dilated with holy indignation. "I am sorry, Mr. Cox, to have confused you so. We're really pretty simple where I'm from, never pretending to be anything more than we really are. Now, you must forgive and excuse me, but it is a workday tomorrow and dullards like me need their sleep."

She left without extending her hand.

There was a long silence while Cox drained his glass. Another arrived.

"I was rude again, wasn't I, Jim?"

"Yes, Ernie, you were."


# 46 IRVING

ON THURSDAY MORNING, RUTH PAINE ARRIVED AT THE STAND. She was tall with short brown hair and angular features. She testified to the familiar history with Marina and how she helped get Lee a job at the Depository.

On most Fridays, Oswald caught a ride with Frazier to Irving where he stayed at her home with Marina until Monday morning, when he rode with Frazier back to work at the Depository. On weekdays, he stayed in Dallas. On the weekend before the assassination, he didn't come out to Irving, but he did on Thursday, the twenty-first, a day earlier than normal. Later that night, Ruth went into the garage to discover that someone had left its light on. She didn't know about the rifle until after the assassination. When the police came on the twenty-second, Marina tried to show them that the rifle was still in storage in the garage, but when she picked up its wrapper, it felt limp. She confirmed that the pro-Cuba leaflets, communist literature, camera, and photographs seized by police from her garage weren't hers and must have belonged to Oswald.

Wade ended with, "Oh, by the way, did you ever hear Marina call Oswald by any nickname?"

"Yes."

"What name?"

"Alek."

BUELL WESLEY FRAZIER CAME next. He testified that he worked at the Depository and helped get Oswald a job there in early October. After reciting the usual commute routine, Frazier testified that on Thursday, the twenty-first, a day earlier than usual, Oswald came to him at work on the first floor, sometime between eight and ten, to ask for a ride to Irving that afternoon so that, Oswald said, he could "pick up some curtain rods for his room at the boarding house." On the morning of Friday, the twenty-second, Oswald carried a package wrapped in brown packing paper to work in Frazier's car. It looked about forty inches long. Oswald placed it in the rear seat. Again, he said it was curtain rods. Oswald also had a small lunch bag. After they parked, Oswald took the package and, oddly, hurried on ahead of Frazier, reaching the rear entrance well before Frazier. The witness was shown the torn-up packaging found on the sixth floor. He said it seemed like the remnants of what Oswald had brought to work.

On cross, Foreman brought out that there were no locked gates inside the Depository. On a workday, anyone could walk most anywhere in the building without any necessity for a key. He further brought out that on the twenty-second, so many employees went to watch the motorcade, anybody might have walked through any part of the facility with little likelihood of being noticed.

DETECTIVE GUY ROSE STARTED with the department in 1954. He testified that on the twenty-second, he and others went to the Paine residence. She allowed a search without a warrant. He asked Mrs. Paine to ask Marina if Oswald had a rifle. Marina said yes, he did. She led them to the garage and pointed to a blanket whose shape resembled a wrapped rifle. Rose picked it up. The blanket fell limp, empty. Marina's face went white. In addition to pro-Cuba leaflets seized there, he authenticated one of the photographs of Oswald holding the rifle and communist literature as well as the negatives, also seized there. So too did he identify the camera, an Imperial Reflex 620 Duo Lens, a cheap Rolleiflex knockoff. All were received in evidence without objection.

Received in evidence via another detective was the Oswald pocket address book, seized from the boarding house pursuant to a warrant.

# 47 OWNERSHIP OF THE CARCANO

TO TRACE OWNERSHIP OF THE RIFLE, ELAINE CALLED TO THE stand a series of quick witnesses from the Post Office, the Treasury Department, and Klein's Sporting Goods Company in Chicago. The essence of their testimony was straightforward and methodical.

The Mannlicher-Carcano bore a serial number C2766. A unit bearing that number was shipped by Klein's Sporting Goods Company of Chicago to one "A. Hidell, Post Office Box 2915, Dallas, Texas" on March 20, 1963, according to its business records. Klein's received the handwritten order on March 13 on a coupon clipped from the *American Rifleman* magazine.

The envelope containing the coupon order had the same name and address. A document examiner from the Department of the Treasury testified that the handwriting belonged to Oswald, based on known samples of his handwriting. Also enclosed was a Dallas postal money order for $21.45. Printed in the "From" box was "A. Hidell, P. O. Box 2915, Dallas, Texas," also determined to be in Oswald's handwriting. The price included a four-power scope. The rifle with scope shipped, via parcel post, to "A. Hidell, P. O Box 2915, Dallas, Texas" on March 20, 1963.

Postal Inspector Harry D. Holmes of the Dallas Post Office testified that the postal records revealed that "Lee H. Oswald" rented Post Office Box 2915 from October 9, 1962, to May 14, 1963. The handwriting expert opined that the handwriting on the application was by Oswald. Pursuant to postal regulations, the post office had discarded the part of the form that listed all recipients entitled to receive mail at the box. Thus, at trial, it could not be determined directly whether the application had listed Hidell as an authorized recipient for Box 2915. When Oswald closed the box rental, he filled out a change-of-address card dated May 12, 1963, by which Oswald requested that mail addressed to that box be forwarded to him in New Orleans. A postal inspector from New Orleans testified that Lee Harvey Oswald rented Box 30061. Contrary to regulations, that office had retained the list of additional recipients. That list included Marina Oswald and A. J. Hidell. The handwriting expert confirmed that the handwriting on the New Orleans form belonged to Oswald.

# 48 HUNTER OF FASCISTS

THE AFTERNOON SESSION BEGAN WITH GEORGE DE MOHRENschildt, a character, flamboyant, even charismatic. The main point in calling him was to present the backyard photograph showing Oswald brandishing the firearms used in the murders.

De Mohrenschildt was born in 1911 in czarist Russia. After the revolution, he escaped to Poland with his parents. He came to the United States in 1938 after attending university in Belgium. He became acquainted with the Bouvier family and met Jackie Bouvier (Kennedy) as a child. He was tanned, had an accent, and suggested the grandest of hotel manners. Lehrer whispered to Bebe that de Mohrenschildt belonged in a novel rather than a trial and imagined he had some connection to the CIA.

In 1962, de Mohrenschildt and his wife had lived in 1962 in Dallas where they'd met the Oswalds through the local Russian community. They socialized. They visited the Oswalds' small flat in Oak Cliff.

De Mohrenschildt was shown the backyard photograph found in his Dallas storage locker of Oswald holding the rifle and magazines. He testified that Oswald gave the photo to him. The handwriting on the back was Oswald's, except that the "Hunter of Fascists" line was his own, not Oswald's. He testified he and his wife learned Lee had a rifle in his and Marina's apartment as of April 1963. The photograph was moved into evidence without objection.

Foreman's cross, in key part, was:

"Sir, in your social conversations with Lee, did the subject of the Kennedy family come up?"

"Indeed. He liked the Kennedy family."

"Specifically, did Oswald express any opinions on the politics of President Kennedy?"

"He said he approved of the policy of the president to promote civil rights for Negroes in this country."

De Mohrenschildt further testified on cross-examination that he and Oswald had engaged in a fair amount of good-humored teasing such that when Oswald gave him the photograph, de Mohrenschildt took it as good-natured teasing over his own obsessive hostility to fascists.

"You see, I lived in Europe when the fascists took over. I know how bad they were."

IN WADE'S CONFERENCE ROOM during a break, Alexander whittled and made small talk.

"That guy de Mohrenschildt," he said, studying a woodwork in progress, "makes you wonder. Why would a communist kill the most liberal president in history?"

"Bill," deadpanned Wade, "I understood you thought FDR was the most liberal?"

"JFK plus his Civil Rights Bill go FDR one step more."

"I think I know why," said Elaine, watching him whittle.

"Clue us in," replied Alexander.

"Oswald's hero is Fidel," Elaine explained, "as in rhymes with Hidell. Yes, Kennedy was a liberal, but Kennedy was out to get Castro. So, the single biggest threat to Oswald's hero was Kennedy. Killing the president first would have guaranteed Oswald a place in Cuba's history book"

# 49 LAB TESTS

[*The Times-Picayune*, March 14, 1964]

## LETTERS FROM DALLAS
### By Bebe Boudreaux

The drama that began our first week of trial has given way to science, all drawn out of the laboratory—fingerprints and ballistics. Federal prosecutor Abe Summer, on loan to help the state, has conducted the examinations. He has masterfully presented the science. Starting late Thursday, the twelfth, and over the next several sessions, he presented an impressive array of lab results based on the physical evidence. The methodical task of proving expert credentials, explaining the steps used to conduct lab tests, and explaining the results consumed many hours. Defense Attorney Percy Foreman had very little cross-examination.

In brief, FBI fingerprint expert Sebastian Latona testified that Oswald's right index fingerprint and both palm prints remained on book cartons in the sixth-floor sniper's nest. Dallas Lieutenant J. C. Day of the Dallas police crime lab testified that he lifted a palm print from the rifle barrel, the part covered by the wooden stock. The FBI identified it as belonging to Oswald. Otherwise, the rifle was wiped clean.

Robert Frazier, a renowned FBI firearms expert, next testified, also examined by Attorney Summer. As to the bullets themselves, he explained ballistics methodology. Guns were originally smooth bore. Starting in France in the mid-1800s, rifling was introduced, spiral grooves cut into the inside of the barrel. The spiral shape puts a spin on the bullet as it races through the barrel. The spiral spin gives stability in flight, just like a spiral gives stability in flight to a football, improving distance and accuracy. Importantly, however, rifling impresses groove marks onto the bullet. Rifling grooves are unique to each rifle barrel, just like a fingerprint. By comparing a test bullet with a subject bullet, side by side under a comparison microscope, the lab can tell whether the two came from the same barrel.

A nearly pristine bullet, recovered from a gurney used by Governor Connally at the hospital, matched rifling on test bullets fired from the Mannlicher-Carcano found on the sixth floor. Inside the limousine, bullet fragments, including a nose and base, together add up to almost another whole bullet. Their rifling marks also match the Carcano. No further bullet has been recovered. Thus, all bullets recovered match the rifle, which even the defense agrees belongs to Oswald.

Frazier further testified that the three cartridges found by the sixth-floor window, based upon so-called toolmarks, had been ejected from the Carcano to the exclusion of all other rifles. It was possible, he said, to fire three shots from the Carcano in less than five seconds with reasonable accuracy, although the three shots actually fired were spread out over a longer period. The Carcano was a "very accurate weapon."

Within fourteen hours of the event, Frazier conducted a search of the limousine and found the bullet fragments but found no holes or dents other than one small dent in the chrome plating above the windshield plus tiny marks on the inside of the windshield, nothing consistent with the force of a nearly whole bullet. For example, if a nearly whole bullet had passed through the president's neck and hit the windshield, it would have left a hole three-eighths to one inch with radiating shatter cracks. Nothing of the sort was found—anywhere in the car. Likewise, if a nearly whole bullet had hit the chrome, it would have severely damaged it, not just dented it. This raises the question of what happened to the other bullet.

The holes in the jacket and shirt worn by President Kennedy were made by a bullet consistent with a 6.5mm caliber. The fibers on the shirt front pushed outward, indicating that the bullet had exited his throat, then passed through the shirt.

This technical but fascinating testimony took hours to present. Still, the jury paid close attention. At noon on Saturday, Frazier's direct testimony was still underway. Interrupting, the judge said, "That's enough for our first week. We'll continue with Agent Frazier on Monday," adding, as he usually does, "The jury may return to their quarters. Please, no talking about the case." After a brief conference with counsel, the judge suggested they all take a little time off to rest. The trial would resume at 8:30 on Monday morning.

# 50  TOTAL EXHAUSTION

THAT SATURDAY, BREVITY MARKED THE AFTER-COURT CONFER-ence among the prosecutors. Used up, they craved rest. A good first week, all agreed.

As they left, Elaine invited Abe over for another Sunday breakfast. He said he'd come. Then Abe walked alone back to the Baker, got his messages from the front desk, scanned them in the elevator, then decided they could all wait until after a nap.

Exhaustion. Total exhaustion.

Abe closed his eyes and slept.

Two hours later, the phone woke him.

"What a great week for the prosecution," began Bebe. "Congratulations."

"Thank you, Bebe," Abe began slowly, finding his bearings, "but please, please save all that until the end. Meanwhile, I see you snagged a good seat."

"Indeed, with lovely bench companions. Listen, Abe, why don't you come over here and have supper with me? I could really use the company right now."

By now, Abe had learned that "supper" was Southern for dinner, "dinner" meant Sunday lunch, "the show" meant a movie, and "coke" covered any brand of soft drink.

Tired, Abe felt unsure of what to say.

He heard her turn away from her handset to use a Kleenex.

"I know," she continued, "what you're thinking. Someone'll see you with me. Don't worry. It'll be fine."

Abe needed sleep.

"Bebe, I am worn out. My plan is to hit the sack soon. You must forgive me, but I'd be a bad companion tonight."

She seemed to accept the rejection.

After the call, he tried to resume his nap but, instead, lay awake staring out the window at the rotating neon-red Pegasus atop the Magnolia Building, mounted on an oil derrick, then worrying about the trial. In a day and a half, it'd be show time again. His gut told him they were overlooking some point of important detail.

The phone rang. It was Bebe again. Her voice betrayed angst.

"Abe, I am having a little crisis. I'm sorry, but I really need to talk. Please come for just a while. You don't need to stay long."

Her voice pleaded.

"Sure," he replied. He got her room number at the Adolphus.

She had a large room with a sitting area, even his-and-her bathrooms. Still dressed in her court clothes, shoeless in stockings, her face anxious, she wore a forced smile.

"Thanks for coming, Abe. You gotta be totally pooped. But I need to talk."

With dark-ringed eyes, she had a drink going. As he took a seat on the wraparound sofa in the sitting area of her small suite, he heard the squeak of a cork.

"No ice?"

"No ice, thanks." Actually, he wanted no alcohol either. He was not there to drink. He had to work the next day. He'd go slow.

She handed him the glass then sat down across from him and started in.

"When you showed that film of the assassination, the one by Zapruder, and we saw the head of the president explode, right in the face of Jackie, I wanted to vomit. So much blood. His brain splattered all over. Connally even had a thumb-size piece on his trousers. She had his brains in her hand. Oh, God, a repulsive, sickening scene."

She took a hard swallow. The ashtray told of heavy use. Smoke stenched the air. Crumpled Kleenex tissues littered the couch.

"How," she continued, "can she possibly stop reliving that everlasting nightmare?"

Circling her rim with her finger, she announced, "That son of a bitch will fry."

Abe, unready for this, stayed quiet, waiting 'til she was done, collecting his reply.

"The other night," she veered off, "I had a horrid time with that asshole Ernie Cox. He said my item on the trial triangle was too good to have come from me or my paper. He said I should be back home fighting for racial justice. It was unreal. Right in front of Jim Lehrer. Horrendous put-down. I came back, all worked up. I'm still not over it."

"He's a jerk sent from below," Abe spoke up. "Once he took me to task for putting communists in jail."

"But here's the thing," Bebe stepped on Abe's point, "and why I need to talk. Maybe he's right. Here was our president making that brutal sacrifice, our First Lady, another brutal sacrifice, for the country. So, now I'm asking myself, asking what sacrifice have I ever made? Zero. Nothing. What *have* I ever done for the country? Fucking nothing. All I write about are ideas you and others give me. I've never had an original idea. Cox is right. I'm a tinhorn reporter for a tinhorn paper. Swamp trash, in over my head. My dad got me this job. I didn't deserve it then and don't deserve it now."

Her voice quaked, then quit. She looked away, out her window.

Out her window, Abe could see the giant Pegasus slowly turning, brighter now in the night, casting its hue on Bebe. He could see her eyes flood.

Abe found the best words he could.

"Bebe, you're a woman in a man's racket but your stories are every bit as good. Usually better. Cox's just jealous. Let it be."

On the windowsill he noticed a small metal souvenir copy of the Pegasus painted red and green. Still she stared away.

"Yeah, Brenda Starr, rich little girl cub reporter." She gave him another empty smile. "And here's another thing—I drink too much." Her voice quivered. "I drink too much because, deep down, I know I'm in way over my head."

Drinking too much was true, Abe thought, but let it pass. Abe hated being in this spot. He'd never been any good, he felt, in saying the right thing to a woman. But he liked Bebe and felt for her and wanted to find the right thing.

"I'm sorry," she managed, wiping her cheeks.

"You are doing, Bebe, what good reporters are supposed to do—describe, report on the ideas or doings of others. If it was your own idea, you should move to the editorial page. You shine right where you are."

Shine was a good word, he thought.

"You know, Bebe, anybody in the heat of anything worthwhile will always be in over their head but somehow we put it through. We learned that in the war.

There was a pause.

"What's that thing you say, Abe, about the D-Day Prayer?"

"If we could do that then . . ."

"Exactly," she cut him off. "If we could do that then, I ought to sweat this shit now, but I just can't, Abe. Jim said something nice to me this week. I don't know why I can't fix on that, but Cox got me so upset—that's all I fix on. Listen, I'm sorry."

Her face was a mess but an attractive mess.

"Tell me," Abe shifted, "how are the profiles coming?"

Her eyes glistened, she finished the glass, then leaned it against her leg on the couch.

"You see the one on Percy?"

"I did."

"Percy's been generous with his time. What'd you think of it?"

"I learned something. Contrary to local lore, every now and then, Percy puts his client on the stand."

"Better be ready."

Abe continued, "Who's next?"

"Wade and Alexander. Tomorrow. Already did the judge. Last will be Abe and Elaine. The best for last."

"When this is over, Bebe, no other reporter will have done what you've done—a set, an anthology, of profiles. The lawyers will treasure them. You'll be how history remembers them. Nothing Cox has done on this trial will be worth saving."

Anthology was another choice word, he thought.

"You know, Abe, you really did have a good week. Your case seems very strong. The Zapruder film's so powerful, so moving. The jury was ready to convict then and there." She daubed her pixie corners. "How do you think it is going?"

Abe gathered his thoughts.

At his pause, she protested, "Oh, Abe, please, stop it—quit worrying. All this is just between us."

"Bebe, that's not it," Abe replied, embarrassed to be called out again for worrying. "I hesitate because our case is going in too well. Percy's up to something, asking so few questions. That tells me he has a defense he'll spring on us after it's too late to adjust."

"You worry so goddamn much."

She folded herself over a sofa pillow, then yawned.

"Listen, Abe, I haven't slept since the Cox thing. I'm ready to drop. I think I can sleep now. Bless you. Just one more thing."

"Okay." Abe set down his glass, still half full.

"About Elaine—I interviewed her for the profile. She's doing something remarkable for her country. Truth is, she's got good cause to resent the way her people have been treated but she loves this country anyway. Oh, she told me, by the way, about those little bacon sandwiches you make. You should know, Abe, that she's had you over to her place because she's afraid some racist asshole will make a scene if you go out together. It broke my heart to hear that."

# 51 GRITS

ELAINE'S FACE LIT UP AT ABE'S BOUQUET. SHE TUCKED THEM IN a vase, placed by the radio. "Come on," went her familiar lilt, "help me make breakfast." Rain was on the way. Storm light brightened the flat.

"We're having grits too, this time," drying her hands on an apron. Abe went to work on the juicer. Cracked open, venting heat, the oven warmed biscuits. Fried bacon rested on a paper towel.

"I've been meaning to say—I have a washing machine here and clothesline. You're more than welcome to use it or give me a pile of clothes to wash. Don't be shy. I'm not afraid of cooties. I mean it. Hotel life must be hard."

Restored by a night's rest, the clarity, even wholesomeness, of the moment gratified him. Life was a perfect invention.

After they adjourned to the front room, they turned to the single-bullet theory, puzzling over why Foreman accepted it.

"It necessarily means," Abe observed, "that Percy admits the first bullet missed."

"Missed the entire car?"

"Exactly," he replied.

"A Marine missed the entire car?"

"Exactly," he repeated.

"Maybe," she mused, "he'll say he meant to miss?"

Elaine had a way of slouching comfortably in her chair, holding her left hand behind her left ear to twirl her hair, her right poised to write. It was casual, relaxing, and helped her think.

"Don't you think Oswald's going to testify?" she asked. "I mean, he can't concede so much, then just stand mute?"

Abe closed his lids for a moment. It was true.

"How can I help you, Abe, get ready for his cross?"

Abe felt obliged to concentrate fully on the most important assignment of his life.

"That's on me, I'm afraid."

Wind blew rain against the front window.

"There's something we're missing, Elaine, possibly staring us in the face."

"Like what?"

"That's the question," he worried with a pen, "but I've got a hunch it's got something to do with the timing of the shots. We never have been able to account for the gap after the first shot."

She took it in, poised to write, twirling her hair in thought.

Time came to drive Abe back into town. Rain now swept the landscape. They made a dash for the Volkswagen bug. Soon, its wipers slapped simple time. Elaine studied the roadway as sheets of rain swept by.

"All this conspiracy talk in the newspapers," Abe broke her concentration, "is based on a refusal to accept coincidence for what it is."

"There's a world of difference," he continued, "between random coincidence versus cause and effect. Take you and Karen—both of you are friends and on this case. But it's just a coincidence. One didn't cause the other."

They drove over the Houston Street viaduct toward downtown. The Hertz clock on top of the Depository glowed through the mist.

"A better example," he developed a rhythm. "Oswald's on the *sixth* floor of the jail. Wade's on the *sixth* floor of the Records Building next door. The sniper's nest was on the *sixth* floor of the building catty corner to Wade. A conspiracy of sixes, right?" All three buildings loomed before them.

She laughed.

"No," Abe answered himself in a quiet voice. "No. Six thousand times, no. It's just a coincidence. Just coincidence. Elaine, there are two types of people. One type accepts coincidence for what it is. The other sees it as evidence of something ominous, usually conspiracy."

Rainwater poured out of Dealey Plaza. The scene of the crime was drenched, but the little car blew big heat.

"There will always be," he continued, "people who insist on Biblical certitude as the standard of proof, usually the conspiracy types. On Oswald, the proof is overwhelming. Ninety-five out of a hundred will say fry the bastard but five will see in the very same evidence the hand of mastermind conspiracists and say he was just a patsy. No amount of proof short of Biblical certitude will satisfy them. They're willing ears for any conspiracy theory."

Elaine pressed her lips. "Thing is," she replied, "Percy only needs one holdout for a hung jury. Does five out of a hundred boil down to one out of twelve?"

"Not if we picked our jury right," he said with confidence, "and I think we did."

"I like that phrase," she teased. "Biblical certitude."

"Almost as good as a license to lie. Hey, drop me at the office," he asked. "I've got to meet my witness."

She veered up North Ervay to stop in front of the Post Office and Federal Building. He opened the door. Rain blew in.

"You're the best, Elaine. We're in this together. I'm glad we are." He pulled his hat and stepped out. "When we're done, I'm taking you to the best goddamn place in town."

# 52 EUREKA!

THE WITNESS WAS ROBERT FRAZIER, WHOSE TESTIMONY HAD begun on Saturday. Abe wanted to study the sniper's nest with him before his testimony resumed. He'd already arranged with Fritz and Truly to meet them on the sixth floor. Abe wanted to see if they had overlooked something.

On the sixth floor, the tapering storm glowed silver-gray through the large windows. Boxes still rose in stacks, casting cold shadows. They started at the southwest corner and studied Dealey Plaza, now puddled. They then walked along the seven sets of double windows to the southeast corner, the sniper's nest, then opened the window halfway, inviting a wet breeze.

On Elm after the turn, they saw that a sniper would've had a clear shot, save for two possible obstructions. The main one was the well-noted oak tree, on their right. Its foliage veiled a couple of seconds of travel time along Elm. But even before the tree, rose another, if lesser, obstruction—a traffic extension arm angling horizontally off a mast on the Depository side of Elm, dangling a signal light over the center lane of Elm. The sniper window faced directly over the Elm-Houston five-way intersection (counting the Elm Street Extension). The mast for the traffic light corresponded to the midpoint between the third and fourth sets of double windows (out of seven sets) counting from the sniper's corner.

Abe replayed the familiar scene. When he got to the turn onto Elm, he stopped.

"Mr. Truly," Abe asked, "what was it you said about the car turning too wide?"

Truly joined them at the window.

"The driver swung too wide. See how Elm takes an extra sharp left. He didn't turn left sharply enough. He swung wide and almost hit the curb where I was standing." Truly swung an arc with his finger.

That the president's car had just corrected from an unexpectedly wide turn might have thrown off the sniper, Frazier noted. The sniper's sweep from left to right, he said, would have been swiftest at the time of the first shot. Putting all of that together, the sniper would have been tracking moderately fast from left to right, likely surprised by the unexpected swerve of the car and confronted by two obstacles, first the extension arm, then the tree. The first shot, though the closest, was not so straightforward after all.

Abe nodded.

"Wait a minute. Something just occurred to me," Frazier interrupted himself. "May I see those binoculars?" He took the glasses and aimed toward the extension arm and traffic light. "This could be important," he said, still peering through the glasses.

"What do you see?" Abe moved closer and looked into the twilight.

"You know how most eyewitnesses said there was the first shot, then a gap, then two quick shots?" Frazier lowered the glasses. "But our Zapruder film workup has the shots evenly spaced. Doesn't square up. Always bothered me. If what I'm seeing proves out, then those eyewitnesses were right, and we were wrong."

He pointed to the traffic signal. "On the back plate of that signal light, lower right corner, there's a small hole—look carefully, hard to see with your naked eye. Maybe that hole is just part of the plate but maybe, just maybe, it's a bullet hole. If it's a bullet hole, then, *eureka, that's* why he missed the closest shot of all. It got deflected by that back plate. But it'd also solve another mystery, the gap mystery. Based on when Connally turned his head in the film, we've been placing the first shot at about Z140, but a bullet hole right there would've put the first shot about two seconds sooner, thus accounting for the gap. The car would've been at an earlier spot."

He handed the glasses to Abe. Sure enough, Abe could make out the pencil-sized hole.

"So," Abe surmised, "deflection saved Walker and deflection almost saved Kennedy."

"At least on the first shot," Frazier noted, "if this proves out."

Abe handed the glasses to Fritz and said, "It would also explain what Virgie Rachley saw, the sparks on the pavement. Where was she standing?"

"Right by me," answered Truly. "She was on Elm straight in front of the main door to the Depository, directly out front of us now."

"A ricochet fragment off the traffic sign could've hit the pavement where she was looking," Frazier continued. "Another fragment might've splattered the curb on Main Street down by the underpass, like the police reports say."

Abe felt amazement. In one fell swoop, Frazier had suggested a single unifying theory that could explain four of the nagging curiosities in the case.

It got even better.

"Mr. Truly," Frazier resumed, "it might also explain yet another mystery, namely why you and those near you, like Virgie, thought the shots came from the west, which happened to be the direction of the traffic light from your location. The bullet impact on the plate would've made a sharp whack sound. Since the bullet itself traveled faster than the speed of sound, the two sounds would've reached you at almost exactly the same time, and the noise from the light may have tricked your ears into thinking all of it came from that direction. It might also explain why the governor looked back over both shoulders, his left and then his right, leftward for the ricochet report and rightward for the original report."

"Can you," Abe asked, "be ready to testify on this tomorrow?"

"No way. I'd need to study that hole up close, do a metallurgy test, then do some measurements, some math, plus study the witness statements, then see whether our re-enactment has the president lined up with that traffic light. It's just a theory now. Of course, I can explain tomorrow why it wasn't such an easy shot, but I can't be ready on any deflection theory. After my testimony tomorrow, I'll get on it and try to be ready for rebuttal testimony."

# 53 SINGLE-BULLET TESTIMONY

"Welcome back, Agent Frazier," Abe resumed his examination. "Please tell the jury what, if any, investigation you conducted to determine the alignment of the sniper's nest on the sixth floor with the positions of President Kennedy and Governor Connally?"

"While seated at the sixth-floor window in question a few weeks ago, I looked through the telescopic scope on the actual Mannlicher-Carcano in question while a re-enactment of the motorcade took place so as to determine whether or not the president and the governor lined up at the same time with the scope. The answer is that yes, they did line up."

"And why, Agent Frazier, did you undertake this test?"

"We wanted to determine whether or not it was possible for a single bullet to have wounded both men. We determined that yes, it was entirely possible."

"Now, Agent Frazier, what prompted your investigation?"

"Of the three shots, only two bullets actually hit inside the car, yet two bullets hit the president and one hit the governor, for three sets of wounds. Two does not equal three, of course. So, this suggests that maybe one bullet hit both of them. We wanted to see if this had been physically possible."

"And, what'd you do to determine the answer?"

Frazier went through the details of the re-enactment, the stand-ins, the chalked circles on their backs, tying into key positions to the Zapruder film.

"At Frames 207 to 210, when the two victims emerged from under the oak foliage, again, what was the alignment of the two as seen from the sniper's window?"

"They were perfectly aligned at that point. A shot at Frame 210 could have wounded both. They continued to be aligned, more or less, for several frames thereafter up to about Z225."

"What was the angle of declination of the rifle at that point, meaning Z225?"

"We had a surveyor measure it. It was about twenty-one degrees, downward."

"How did that compare to the angle between the chalk circles indicating bullet entries on the stand-ins in the re-enactment?"

"That angle was about eighteen degrees, downward. But remember, Elm was descending at that point at an angle too. That angle was close to three degrees. Taking that into account, as you must, the actual angle relative to flat ground was twenty-one degrees."

"The same as the rifle barrel?"

"Yes, the same as the rifle barrel."

"Could one bullet have wounded both men?"

"Yes, just as a single bullet passed clean through the governor's chest, then clean through his wrist and then into his thigh, it could have passed first clean through the president's neck and upper back since all of that was soft tissue, not bone. We must remember that the muzzle velocity of the Carcano was almost twice the speed of sound."

"Was the bullet metal jacketed?"

"Yes, a copper alloy."

"What difference would that have made?"

"Upon impact with flesh, the metal jacket would keep the bullet from mashing up. If it hit bone matter, it would fragment but if it hit only soft tissue, then it would very likely stay intact."

"How many times did you do the test on Elm Street?"

"Twice with my eye. Then we filmed it. So three times."

The film came into evidence.

Then the projector came out. The lights dimmed. The soundless movie flashed onto the screen. More than half of the jury box, including the Iwo Jima veteran, leaned forward with intense interest. They watched in black and white, very nearly what the murderer saw in the last seconds of the president's life. Sure enough, after emerging from the other side of the tree, for almost two seconds, the torsos of the two stand-ins overlapped.

The lights came up.

"Agent Frazier, new subject: Have you also considered the question of the extent to which the first shot from the sixth-floor window was an easy versus hard shot?"

"I have."

"What have you done to study that question?"

"I stood at the window in question, partially opened as it was that day. I considered how the sniper would have to crouch or stand to get an angle on the limousine. I considered obstructions and the movement of the car, including the unexpected swerve that I understand Mr. Roy Truly testified to."

"What assumptions did you make about the first shot?"

"I assumed it was after the turn onto Elm, yet before the tree."

"What'd you conclude, if anything?"

"The first shot was the closest shot but there were complications." Frazier turned to the jury and held up a blowup of the view from the sniper's window. "*First*, the driver did not make a clean turn, based on Mr. Truly's testimony, but misjudged how sharply left he needed to turn, so the car swerved closer to the curb, meaning nearer the Depository than it should have. The driver soon self-corrected, but this would have been an unexpected swerve. This might have thrown off a sniper." The witness indicated a swerve with a mechanical pencil. "*Second*, two obstacles posed problems. A traffic light with its extension arm came off a tall pole by the curb on the Depository side of Elm. The car went right under it, as seen from the window. This obstruction occurred soon after the car made the turn onto Elm." The witness's pencil pointed to the lower right corner of the traffic signal. "A moment or two later came the next obstruction, the oak tree whose leaves and limbs would have obliterated a clear view of the car. So the sniper had to time the shot to avoid these obstructions. The unexpected swerve may have upset his timing. *Third*, the sniper had the left-to-right sweep problem. Precisely because it was the closest shot and because the car moved left to right, the sniper and rifle would have had to track left to right more swiftly compared to the later shots."

"How did the second and third shots compare to the first?"

"Most importantly," the witness held up a blowup of the view toward the underpass, "there was almost no left-to-right tracking problem for the second and third shots because, for those shots, the car moved directly away from the sniper. The down slope of the roadway partially compensated for the outbound travel, so the car and the president were nearly a steady fixed target. There was no swerve. There were no obstructions. There was no severe down angle. The sniper could use the boxes set up by the window or lean against the wall to steady his aim. The second and third shots were easier by comparison to the first."

"Thank you. Perhaps Mr. Foreman has questions."

Foreman stood at the lectern, silently peering at his notes, then looked up.

"To sum it up, Agent Frazier, would this be consistent with your findings—that the first shot missed the car altogether, the second shot wounded first the president, then the governor sometime during the moments they lined up, and the third shot hit the president's head?"

"Yes. I think that's the most likely scenario."

Abe found it slightly unsettling that Foreman was emphasizing the very sequence advanced by the prosecution itself.

"Was the first shot a tough shot?"

"It was harder, as I said, in the sense that the tracking angle swept faster from left to right than for the last two shots where the declination of the rifle moved only slightly downward as the car moved away."

"But to answer my question, was it a difficult shot?"

"Depends on the skill of the shooter, but a good marksman would probably have hit the target or very close to it."

"Very close to it. It would have been easy for a United States Marine to at least have hit the car, don't you think?"

"Of course, unless an obstruction got in the way."

NEXT CAME THE BETHESDA pathologist and Parkland doctors. Their testimony boiled down to this: The cause of the president's death was the head shot. It entered from the rear (making a small clean hole in the skull), then exploded out the right front of his head. As to the apparent backward jerk of the president's head upon the head shot, a close frame-by-frame look of the Zapruder film revealed that, immediately before the jerk back, the president's head had actually moved *forward*. Such a move forward was likely caused by the forward momentum of the bullet. The follow-on backward jerk was likely caused by a neuromuscular reaction.

The president would likely have survived the back-to-neck wound. That bullet entered his upper back, then exited the neck just below the knot in his necktie. The exit became mutilated by the Parkland doctors when they used it to attempt a tracheotomy. This mutilation later confused the Bethesda pathologist, who at first regarded the exit as an entry but later corrected the error. The trajectory of both bullets was slightly downward. A single bullet did all of the damage to Governor Connally.

# 54 OSWALD'S FLIGHT

TUESDAY MORNING BEGAN WITH MARY E. BLEDSOE. A PASSENGER, she'd seen Oswald board the Marsalis-Munger bus about 12:40 p.m. Curiously, he boarded on Elm six to seven blocks east of the Depository. That is, even though there was a stop close by the Depository, Oswald went several blocks farther from the Depository to board at an earlier stop. The bus route would have gone right by the Depository, then to Oak Cliff across the Houston Street Viaduct. She also happened to have been, as fate would have it, the housekeeper at Oswald's earlier boarding house just before he moved to 1026 North Beckley. She'd disliked Oswald so much that she made him leave her boarding house, also in Oak Cliff, so she was positive it was Oswald who boarded the bus. Wade continued:

"All right, now. Tell us what happened."

"Oswald gets on. He looks like a maniac. His sleeve was undone and unraveled, had a hole in it, he was dirty. I didn't want him to know I even seen him, so I just looked off, and then about that time the motorman said the president had been shot."

"How close did he pass to you as he boarded the bus?"

"Just in front of me."

"How far did he go before he got off?"

"About three or four blocks."

Oswald exited, she said, when the bus got caught up in the exploding turmoil of traffic near the Depository.

Foreman had no cross.

The cream-and-olive bus had been driven by Cecil McWatters, a long-time bus operator for the Dallas Transit Company. He testified that on the twenty-second at about 12:40 p.m., he was driving Bus Number 433 on the Marsalis-Munger route. It normally ran west on Elm, past the Depository, then over the river into Oak Cliff. Seven blocks east of the Depository, a man banged on the door, so McWatters let him in. The man paid the twenty-three-cent fare and took the second seat back. Three blocks later, closer to the Depository, the traffic came to a stop, a complete snarl. Sirens screamed. A man in the street told McWatters that the president had been shot. The man in the second seat asked for and got a bus transfer, then exited. McWatters was shown the transfer found in Oswald's pocket and said, yes, it looked like the transfer. McWatters identified Oswald as the man.

Witness by witness, the prosecution was tracing Oswald's movements after he left the Depository. The prosecutors used a red marker to draw the locations in on a large poster-sized street map as the witnesses described them. The street map displayed downtown Dallas plus the Oak Cliff section. A few miles southwest of the Depository, across the river, stood 1026 North Beckley, Oswald's boarding house. Only a few blocks southeast of there lay Tenth and Patton, where Officer Tippit died. All of this fit neatly on the poster map.

Next came a cab ride to Oak Cliff. The name of the taxi driver was William Wayne Whaley. Wade questioned:

"About 12:30 that day, where were you?"

"At the cabstand at the Greyhound bus station."

The poster map showed the Greyhound station was three blocks south from where Oswald left the bus.

"Were you at the cabstand long?"

"No, sir, I started to get out to buy cigarettes but then I saw this passenger coming, so I waited for him."

Whaley explained, based on his log, that the time of the trip started between 12:30 and 12:45 p.m. Whaley continued:

"He said, 'May I have the cab?' I said, 'You sure can. Get in.' Instead of opening the back door he opened the front door, which is allowable, and got in. He said, '500 North Beckley.' Well, I started up, I started to that address. The police cars, the sirens were going, running, crisscrossing everywhere, just a big uproar in that end of town, so I said, 'What the hell, I wonder what the hell is the uproar?' But he never said anything. So I figured he was one of these people that don't like to talk so I never said any more to him. But when I got pretty close to the 500 block, he said, 'This will do fine,' and I pulled over to the curb right there. The trip was ninety-five cents. He gave me a dollar bill, didn't say anything, just got out and closed the door and walked around the front of the cab over to the other side of the street, then he kept going south. I put it in gear and moved on. That is the last I saw of him."

Wade pointed to the blowup map, then placed a circle on the 500 block of North Beckley."

"Sir, do you see 1026 North Beckley on this map?"

The witness pointed to the address and Wade circled it.

"Did you drive him right by 1026?"

"Yes, sir, we drove right by it and continued towards the 500 block."

Cunningly, Bebe saw, Oswald had directed the cab to a destination several blocks past the boarding house, which had given him an opportunity to observe it as they drove by to see whether the police were already there.

"Do you see the man here in the courtroom?"

"Yes, sir. The man standing up wearing the sweater. Right there." He pointed.

"You say this man walked south when he got out of your cab, *away from* 1026?"

"Yes, sir."

As cunningly, Bebe realized, Oswald had, when he exited the cab, walked in the direction away from 1026 so that the driver, if questioned by police, would send them the wrong way.

Next came the problematic housekeeper at 1026, Earlene Roberts, examined by Alexander. On direct, she retraced the same familiar ground. In October, a man registered as "O. H. Lee," and she didn't know, until the police came, that he was really Lee Harvey Oswald. She authenticated the registration book with the signature O. H. Lee. She gave the jury her recollection of Oswald rushing in and rushing out about 1:00 p.m. on the twenty-second, spending only three minutes or so in his room, all as she was trying to adjust her television picture in the front room. She said he zipped up a jacket as he left. Alexander tendered the witness.

This time, Foreman cross-examined.

"Mrs. Roberts, while Lee was in his room, did anything unusual happen?"

"Yes, sir, while I was fixing the antenna, trying to get the news about the shooting of the president, right direct in front of my house, there was a police car, stopped and honked. I had worked for some policemen and sometimes they would come by and tell me something, like maybe something their wives wanted me to know. I thought maybe it was them, so I just glanced out to see the car number, then I said, 'Oh, that's not their car,' for I knew their car number."

"Where was it parked?"

"In front of my house. I saw them through the window. Then they just eased on Beckley toward Zangs and downtown."

"Which way was the car facing?"

"To my right, north."

"Did this police car stop directly in front of your house?"

"Yes. It stopped directly in front of my house. It just went 'tip-tip' with the horn, just the way Officers Alexander and Burnley would do when they stopped, so I went to the door and looked but saw it wasn't their number."

Looking into the faces of the jury, Foreman asked her, slowly and deliberately, "Stopped directly in front of your house and just went 'tip-tip' with the horn—did we hear that correctly?"

"Yes, sir."

"And, again, where was Lee when this happened?"

"In his room."

"And, you say that there were two men in police uniforms in the car?"

"Yes, a standard black car. Had the number on the side."

"But were there two men *in uniform* in the car?"

"Oh, yes."

"When Lee came out, did you tell him about the car?"

"No, why would I do that?"

"Thank you, Mrs. Roberts," Foreman ended, radiating success without quite smiling.

"Did Oswald say or do anything," Alexander began, "that indicated he was expecting anyone to pull up out front?"

"No."

"Did the officers look in your direction?"

"I can't say as I noticed. I just looked for the car number."

"Now, Mrs. Roberts, when you and I talked on the twenty-second, you made no mention of any police in a car out front, did you?"

"If you asked me about it, I'm sure I did, but I have been interviewed so many times, it is hard to say now what you asked."

"You know Hugh Aynesworth?"

"The newspaper man?"

"Yes, ma'am, he works for the *Dallas Morning News*. You were also interviewed by him on the twenty-second, weren't you?"

"I believe I was."

"You didn't tell him anything about a police car out front, did you?"

"I just don't remember. Again, I have been interviewed so many times. The third degree. My mind was a whirl."

"I represent to you, Mrs. Roberts, that he will testify later today that you never said anything about a police car out front. Does that help you in remembering whether or not you actually saw a police car out front on the twenty-second?"

"Sir, all I can say is I remember a police car."

"On Friday, the twenty-ninth, a week later, the FBI came by, so you gave them an interview."

"Yes, sir, that sounds right."

"And that, a full week later, was the *first* time you ever told anyone from law enforcement or the news about the police car, true?"

"If you say so."

"Mrs. Roberts, I am reading from their report. It says, 'Mrs. Roberts advised after Oswald had entered his room at about 1:00 p.m., saw police car No. 207 with two uniformed policemen in the car, which slowed up and stopped in front of the residence at 1026 Beckley, and one of the officers blew the horn on the car and then drove slowly on Beckley toward Zangs Boulevard.' Isn't that what you told them?"

"Yes, sir, I will say 'yes.'"

She appeared mildly flustered.

"And," Alexander continued, "you said the reason you recalled the number of the car was because you had worked for two policemen who drove squad car 170, 'and she looked to see if these two were the two officers she knew parked in front of the residence.' Didn't you tell them that too?"

"Okay, that sounds right."

"So, on the twenty-ninth, you said it was Car Number 207 and you specifically remembered the car number."

"That's what you read."

"And now you know, I suspect, that Car 207 was somewhere else at 1:00 p.m."

"Well, that's what they are saying."

"Now Mrs. Roberts," as Alexander changed tone, "what was the first name of the Officer Alexander who came by from time to time?"

"I'm no good on names. Lloyd?"

"How about Floyd J. Alexander Sr.?"

"Thank you. That's it."

"And what work had you done for him?"

"Housekeeping."

"How often did he swing by 1026 North Beckley to see you?"

"Perhaps once or twice a year."

"And when was the last time before November 22 that Officer Alexander came by your place at 1026 North Beckley?"

"Maybe a year ago?"

"And you say he was always in car 170 with Officer Burnley?"

"Yes."

"So, you are telling us that Officer Alexander drove by your place once or twice in 1962?"

"Yes, about that."

"Now, Mrs. Roberts, we are going to bring Floyd S. Alexander in here to testify today but want to give you a fair chance to refresh your memory. He will say that he once hired you as a housekeeper back in the early 1950s and that he resigned from the force in 1957, six years before November 22, 1963. Did you know that he'd resigned in 1957?"

"No, sir, I didn't."

"Can you explain how he was driving by your place in a police car and in uniform and talking to you all those years when he wasn't even on the force?"

"It doesn't make sense. Something must be wrong with your information."

"Finally, Mrs. Roberts, my last name also happens to be Alexander, you know that?"

"Okay."

"And when I came out to see you on the twenty-second, I introduced myself to you."

"I suppose you did."

"So my last name—Alexander—came up on the twenty-second when we talked, didn't it?"

"Okay."

"And Alexander also happens to be the last name of the officer you knew in Car 170."

"Okay, same last name."

"And on the twenty-second, you say your mind was in a whirl?"

"I guess it was."

"So when my name, Alexander, came up on the twenty-second in that whirl of events that day, do you think it may have whirled up a memory of Officer Alexander in his car?"

"But you say Officer Alexander and the car didn't come up 'til later?"

"Well, that's my point. Do you think that after you heard my name on the twenty-second, your mind, while it was whirling about, began to dredge up memories of Officer Alexander?"

"Are you saying I brainwashed myself?"

A ripple of laughter swept the gallery, suppressed only by the gravity of the case.

"I am just asking if maybe your mind played a trick, meaning my name 'Bill Alexander' went into the whirl on the twenty-second and somehow got spun out a week later as Floyd Alexander?"

"Well, every mind has been known to play a trick or two."

Alexander thanked her.

On re-cross, Foreman asked, "Mrs. Roberts, how sure are you that a police car stopped on the twenty-second while Lee was in his room and honked its horn?"

"How sure? Maybe I brainwashed myself, but I remember it clearly. I would swear to it on a Bible."

Mrs. Roberts was excused.

In short order, Alexander presented an FBI agent who told the jury that on November 29, Mrs. Roberts had recalled the police car out front, said it was Car 207, specifically saying she remembered the number. Officer James Valentine next told the jury that on the twenty-second, he drove Car 207 from City Hall to the Depository, arriving there at 12:55 p.m. He authenticated TV news footage showing him pulling up on the Elm Street Extension at 12:55 p.m. He gave the keys to Sargent J. M. Putnam, who retained them all afternoon and testified he never moved the car—so Number 207 could not have been in Oak Cliff at 1:00 p.m. Floyd J. Alexander Sr. next testified that he'd employed Earlene Roberts as a housekeeper in the early 1950s, resigned from the Dallas police in 1957, and thus was not in front of 1026 in any police car thereafter. Officer Burnley testified that he'd never met or employed Mrs. Roberts. Hugh Aynesworth, a reporter for the *Dallas Morning News*, explained that on the afternoon of the twenty-second, he interviewed Earlene Roberts at 1026 but she made no mention of any police car out front.

AT THE TUESDAY LUNCH break, the prosecution team gathered in a conference room in the Records Building next door. Sandwiches with cold, wet, pale-green, thick glass bottles of Coca-Cola awaited them.

"Bill," asked Wade, "where'd you get that brainwashing idea?"

"Now remember," he replied, "brainwashing was her word, not mine." He offered Elaine a slice of apple and she took it.

"She herself," Alexander continued, "said her mind was in a whirl. The name Alexander went into the whirl on that Friday and spun out a few days later as a different Alexander."

"You thought of that on your own, Bill?" Wade raised his brows, his face poised to smile.

"Just dumb as dirt again."

The best point on this curiosity, however, was yet to come.

# 55 J. D. TIPPIT

ROBERT OSWALD SETTLED BACK WITH OSWALD'S WIFE AND mother on the front row. With shame mounting by the day, Robert thought the evidence against his brother was overwhelming. Why didn't Foreman attack every single witness? When Foreman did cross-examine, he scored points—but why so seldom?

Wade had led off the trial evidence with two strong witnesses to the killing of Officer Tippit (Cabbie Scroggins and Waitress Markham). Now he continued with two more.

The afternoon session began with John Ray Tatum. Twenty-five, employed by Baylor University, he'd run personal errands on the twenty-second. Driving westbound on Tenth (opposite of Tippit's direction), he saw, to his left in the oncoming lane, an officer in a stopped patrol car leaning over to talk to a pedestrian on the sidewalk. He passed them. A few seconds later, he heard the shots. He braked, looked back to see the officer down. The man fired yet another shot at the officer's head. The man headed in Tatum's direction. To get out of harm's way, Tatum drove off, but he got a good look at the shooter. Oswald, he said, was the man.

Barbara Jeanette Davis came next. She testified that she lived at the southeast corner of Tenth and Patton (diagonally opposite from where waitress Markham had stood and adjacent to the curb on Patton where the cab driver parked). On the twenty-second, she heard gunshots, rose from her nap, got out of bed, and opened the front screen door. She saw Markham frozen at the catty corner while a man trotted right to left across her front yard. He had the gun in his hand. As he came through her yard, he emptied it, shaking out shells. She identified Oswald as the man. She called the police to say an officer had been shot. Later, she found spent casings in their yard, which she turned over to the police.

The first officer to respond to the scene testified that Patrolman J. D. Tippit was already dead when he arrived. He further testified that two other spent casings turned up beyond those found by Davis. Tool-mark examiners would show that all four came from Oswald's revolver.

Because Foreman waved off so much cross-examination, the prosecution ran out of witnesses early and had to ask the judge to adjourn early. He did so since Wade promised the judge that they were well ahead of schedule. Robert worried that Foreman himself had given up hope.

FLOWING OUT ONTO THE sidewalk on Main in front of the courthouse, Bebe found herself in the crowd beside Ernest Seward Cox. He motioned her aside.

"Miss Boudreaux, I wish to apologize for my remark the other night. You took offense and rightly so. I am sorry."

On a stage in her mind, Bebe had rehearsed this scene a dozen times.

"Would you please, Mr. Cox," she said after forcing herself to pause, "walk with me back toward the hotel?"

"Of course."

They made an odd couple, he in his rumpled suit, much overweight, she in a designer suit, slim and fit. He trundled. She glided.

When they had cleared the throng, she said, "May I ask you something, Mr. Cox?"

"By all means," he replied as they made their first block.

"Do you believe that all whites from the South are bigots?"

"May I be honest?"

"Please."

"Then, I will say, not all, but almost all. It's not their fault. It's the system they were born into."

"So, the other night, you just assumed, automatically, that I was in the 'almost all' category and would be upset over the desegregation of the courthouse?"

"That's why, Miss Boudreaux, I'm apologizing. I should've given you the benefit of the doubt."

"And, in New York, do you believe most whites there are bigots?"

"I must say most there are too, perhaps in more subtle ways."

"So, when you said I should be out reporting on racial injustice in Louisiana and Mississippi, I could've said as easily that you should be doing the same thing in New York?"

"I suppose you could have. And, if you will permit me to, I will say on occasion I have."

"And, Mr. Cox, do you know whether I've tried to do the same, in New Orleans?"

"That's why I have apologized. I don't know."

"You do know, of course, that you work for a paper that likes those kinds of stories. Do you have any idea how hard we have to work to get such stories past our editors down here?"

"I can only imagine."

"Turner Catledge," she continued.

"Yes."

"Your managing editor at *The Times*.

"A good one, too."

"Know where he's from?"

"Yes, somewhere down here."

"He's from Mississippi. Grew up there. Went to the A&M school, Mississippi State College. Would you say he's a bigot?"

"No, I wouldn't."

"And Lyndon Johnson?"

"He seems perfectly fine to me also, Miss Boudreaux."

"Name a white man from New York who has ever tried to do as much for civil rights as that white man from Texas."

"Your point's well taken, Miss Boudreaux."

They reached Lamar and Main. Bebe glanced toward Sanger's Department Store.

"Please excuse me here, Mr. Cox, I need to run an errand over there. But one last thing, before you go. I think you owe my paper an apology too for the nasty thing you said about it."

"You are right, Miss Boudreaux. I apologize on both counts."

The light changed. As she left him alone standing at Main and Lamar, Bebe gave her verdict, "Your apologies, Mr. Cox, are accepted."

# 56 THE TEXAS THEATER

SINCE IT APPEARED THAT FOREMAN WAS CONCEDING THE KILL-ing of Tippit, Wade decided to pass over some witnesses who could have traced Oswald's flight block by block, alley by alley. Instead, he skipped to the moments leading to Oswald's arrest, nine or so blocks from the Tippit murder.

On Wednesday morning of the second week, Wade began with Johnny C. Brewer, the manager of Hardy's Shoe Store on Jefferson Boulevard, a few doors down from the theater. Brewer told the jury that on the twenty-second he'd heard multiple police sirens. He stood alone looking out his store window and saw a young man on the sidewalk dart into his recessed entryway leading from the sidewalk to the front door of his store. The man acted furtively, keeping his back to the street despite all the sirens. The man breathed heavily. After the sirens had gone by, the man stepped back onto the sidewalk, then headed away from the sirens. Brewer stepped out to watch him. The man slipped into the Texas Theater, a few doors down, without buying a ticket. Brewer hurried over to the ticket seller. She confirmed that no ticket had been purchased and called the police, who soon surrounded the theater. They then brought up the lights on a sparce midday audience. Using Brewer, the police isolated the man and closed in.

Brewer identified Oswald as the man.

A photograph of the outside of the theater from the twenty-second, placed in evidence, showed *War Is Hell* with *Cry of Battle* on the marquis.

Officer M. N. Nick McDonald testified that he had been the first to reach Oswald. As the lights came up in the theater and officers blocked all means of escape, a man who turned out to be Oswald stood up to change his seat from the fifth seat in to the third seat in, all on the third row from the rear. Brewer pointed out Oswald to McDonald, who told him to "get on your feet." Oswald stood, saying, "Well, it's all over now."

Suddenly, however, Oswald cocked his fist and hit McDonald between the eyes, knocking him backward into the next row. A struggle ensued. Another officer put a neck hold on Oswald, who pulled a revolver out of his waistband. Back on his feet, McDonald grabbed the cylinder of Oswald's revolver, a way to keep it from revolving into a firing position. Another officer slammed the butt of a shotgun against Oswald's head and neck. Just before McDonald yanked the revolver free, McDonald heard the snap of the hammer and felt a sting to the web between his thumb and forefinger. Oswald cried, "Don't hit me anymore. I am not resisting arrest. I want to complain of police brutality."

At this, Bebe noticed one juror roll his eyes.

They forcibly escorted Oswald, McDonald went on, out of the theater, through a mob that had gathered after word spread that the cop killer was hiding in the theater, into a patrol car, then to police headquarters.

McDonald identified the accused as the man.

Thus, the president was murdered at 12:30 p.m., and within ninety minutes Oswald was in custody.

Detective Paul Bentley testified that inside the Texas Theater, he saw Oswald fighting with Patrolman McDonald and saw Oswald pull a pistol from his shirt, "so I went to Patrolman McDonald's aid immediately," grabbing the suspect by the neck. Other officers assisted. They subdued then cuffed him. Bentley identified a photo of the police pushing their way out of the theater with Oswald. Bentley was the one, he said, in a suit with a cigar jutting from the left side of his mouth. Bentley got in the back seat on the left side of the suspect. Oswald remained mute when asked who he was. "On the way to City Hall, I removed the suspect's wallet and obtained his name, Lee Harvey Oswald. I eventually turned the identification over to Lieutenant T. L. Baker." Another officer had the .38 pistol, which Bentley had initialed for chain of custody. Both the wallet and the pistol came into evidence after being identified by the witness as taken from Oswald that afternoon. Bentley identified Oswald.

Bentley then went through the contents of the wallet and described them for the jury. Items in the name of Lee Harvey Oswald were (i) a Social Security card; (ii) a selective service local board card; (iii) a Department of Defense Identification Card (expiration date December 7, 1962) showing date of birth October 18, 1939, height 5'11", weight 145 pounds, brown hair, gray eyes; (iv) a Dallas Public Library card (expiration date December 7, 1965); (v) a U.S. Forces, Japan Identification Card issued May 8, 1958; (vi) a Certificate of Service in Armed Forces of United States for U.S. Marine Corps, October 24, 1956–September 11, 1959; (vii) a Fair Play for Cuba Committee card, issued May 23, 1963; and (viii) a Selective Service Notice of Classification dated February 2, 1960, from Local Board 114, Fort Worth, Texas.

Items in the name of Alek James Hidell were (i) a Selective Service Notice of Classification with reverse side signature of "Alek J. Hidell" and front side photo of Oswald (the blowup by Wade in his opening statement) and (ii) a Fair Play for Cuba card, New Orleans Chapter, issued to L. H. Oswald, signed by A. J. Hidell, chapter president. Other items included (i) a photo of Marina, (ii) a photo of an infant, and (iii) thirteen dollars in currency.

On cross-examination, Foreman asked Bentley to repeat how much money Oswald had on him.

"Thirteen dollars plus change," said Bentley.

"And did he have a driver's license?"

"No."

"So, how did you expect he was planning to get away?"

An objection was sustained but the witness nevertheless said, "Beats me."

Sargent Gerald L. Hill next testified that he also assisted in the arrest. Hill drove the car with Oswald in the rear to City Hall. He took possession of the .38, fully loaded. One of the unfired shells had a hammer mark on the primer, indicating a misfire.

"What happened at City Hall?"

"When we got to City Hall, I learned that Captain Fritz was about to go to Irving to find Lee Harvey Oswald, an employee missing from the Depository. I said, "Captain, we'll save you a trip, because there he sits.""

# 57 THE SECOND VIEW

AFTER THE LUNCH BREAK CAME THE JURY'S CHANCE TO VIEW scenes in Oak Cliff. They were herded aboard a bus with an admonition to speak with no one about the case, the judge and the bailiff their chaperones. The bus drove past Dealey Plaza, over the river into the working-class streets of Oak Cliff, showing itself well in the early spring season. The first stop was 1026 North Beckley, where the jurors viewed Oswald's room plus the view of the street from the front room.

As the main party squeezed into the rooming house, Elaine, Jim, and Karen stayed out front, making small talk, facing the street. A line of automobile traffic developed, waiting for the light at the intersection of Beckley and Zangs to go green. When the light changed and the line waited a bit too long, a car in line—directly in front of 1026—went "tip-tip" to signal the drivers ahead to move. Elaine and Karen exchanged looks of wonderment, each whispering "My God," Elaine with a smile and Karen with a gasp. Jim shook his head. Sometimes, the right answer is the simplest, he later said, so simple it escapes detection.

Next the jury tour stopped at Tenth and Patton. By stipulation, Wade pointed out where waitress Markham had stood, where cabbie Whaley had parked, where Officer Tippit had stopped his cruiser, and where the empty shells fell. Then they reboarded the bus to continue down Patton to Jefferson, thence right a few blocks to the Texas Theater. *War Is Hell* and *Cry of Battle* had gone elsewhere. In fact, the theater had closed for the day to allow the view. Management turned on all lights. The jury viewed the front entry, the rear entries used by some of the officers, then the seats in which Oswald had sat, the fifth and third seats in from the right (facing the screen), three rows from the back.

# 58 THE SIMPLEST ANSWER

THE NEXT MORNING, ELAINE CALLED JIM HOSTY TO THE STAND and briefly covered his credentials. By this point in the trial, she was well past any stage fright. All had become a forensic, professional exercise.

"Agent Hosty, yesterday during the jury view at 1026 North Beckley, where were you?"

"Standing out in the front yard with you and Miss Eisenstadt." He turned slightly left to face the jury. "There wasn't enough room for all of us inside."

"Did anything unusual occur?"

"As we waited outside with the jury inside, a line of cars built up along Beckley, waiting for the light to turn green at the intersection of Beckley and Zangs. When the light went green, a car in line, right in front of 1026, went, 'tip-tip' with his horn to alert drivers ahead to get moving."

"How many cars were in that line?"

"Maybe six to eight."

"Remind us how those streets work?"

"A couple of doors up from 1026, to the right as you face the street from the house, Beckley intersects Zangs, at a forty-five-degree angle. So when you ease off Beckley going right onto Zangs, the turn is really just a shallow slide onto Zangs, where you head toward downtown. There's a red light at that intersection."

"How far is 1026 from that red light?"

"It is the second or third house down from the intersection, depending on whether you count the house on the corner."

"When the light is red for Beckley cars, would it be unusual for waiting traffic to back up as far as 1026?"

"It backed up that far when we were there."

"And would it be unusual for any such car to wait in front of 1026?"

"It did when we were there."

"Who else was present?"

"As I said, you and Karen Eisenstadt."

Elaine saw Karen blush. Despite their friendship, Elaine felt obliged to bring this out, that the other side's lawyer had witnessed it too.

"So, Agent Hosty, would there have been anything unusual about a car waiting in a line of northbound traffic in front of 1026 on November 22 at 1:00 pm?"

"Not really."

"Or, in tooting its horn when the light changed?"

"No, not unusual. Also, remember at 1:00 p.m. that day many people were fiddling with radios trying to get the news about the assassination. They may have missed the light going green, so a rearward car might well have beeped its horn to get traffic moving."

"Could the rearward car have been a police car?"

"Speculation," said Foreman finally, and the judge said, "Sustained."

But the point was made.


FOREMAN THEN ROSE TO say he had no questions about North Beckley but asked the judge for permission to examine Hosty on a subject outside the scope of the direct, promising to be brief. The judge looked to Elaine, who, having gotten away with a little herself, said, "Fine."

"How far back has the FBI been keeping tabs on Lee Oswald?"

"Since his return from Russia in 1962."

"In early November 1963, did you visit Marina Oswald out in Irving?"

"Yes."

"Please explain the circumstances."

"The Bureau had a file on Lee Harvey Oswald, due to his time in the Soviet Union and his subsequent return. When we learned that he was back in our district, we were, as a routine matter, supposed to make contact. I went out on November 1 of last year to Irving and had a brief meeting with Mrs. Oswald and Mrs. Paine, with whom she was living. Mr. Oswald wasn't home."

"And then was there a second meeting?"

"Yes. A week later. Also brief."

"Was Lee Harvey Oswald present?"

"No, sir."

"Did he subsequently try to see you at your office here in Dallas?"

"Yes, sir, I think so. He just left an unsigned note. I was out but eventually I got the note."

"Where is the note now?"

Foreman expected a stall or objection, but Jim answered straight away.

"At counsel table, I believe."

Meanwhile, Abe walked the note over to Foreman, who paused, read it silently to himself, handed it to Hosty, then asked:

"This it?"

"Yes, sir."

"Please read it to the jury."

"'If you have questions about my activities, ask me directly. If you don't leave my wife alone, I will take action against you.'"

"Was it signed?"

"Was not."

"Did you perceive this as a threat?"

"Did not."

"What kind of action did you understand he meant?"

"Some kind of legal complaint."

"That would have been perfectly lawful."

"Yes, of course."

"What day was the note left?"

"The day after Armistice Day."

"November 12?"

"Yes, sir, November 12."

"On or before November 22, did you ever say to the Secret Service that you thought Lee Oswald was a threat to the president?"

"No, sir."

"Did you say anyone else was?"

"Yes, sir, someone unrelated to this case, not Lee Harvey Oswald."

"Different question. Has the FBI been able to track Lee Oswald's whereabouts in late September?"

"Just that he boarded a bus in Houston for Laredo and thence to Mexico City on September 26 at 2:35 a.m. Before that, we aren't sure."

"Your witness."

Elaine stood. "Thank you. Everything has been covered. No questions."

# 59 THE PROSECUTION RESTS

THE END LOOMED NEAR FOR THE PROSECUTION'S CASE—ALL could feel it and felt it had been proven in spades. The remaining evidence sailed in matter-of-factly. First came three witnesses to establish Oswald's purchase of the revolver—a representative of the gun dealer, one from the shipping carrier, then a handwriting expert, Alwyn Cole of the Treasury Department. In sum, they established that the .38 Special Smith & Wesson revolver was purchased through Seaport Traders, Inc., in Los Angeles. Seaport Traders placed mail order coupon ads in various magazines. Such a coupon was used to purchase the weapon in question. The coupon showed the name of "A. J. Hidell" with an address of "P. O. Box 2915" in Dallas. The handwriting was, according to the handwriting expert, that of Oswald. A partial payment accompanied the form. Seaport shipped the gun C.O.D. via Railway Express Agency with instructions to collect $19.95 (plus a shipping charge) on pickup in Dallas. It shipped on March 20, 1963. The amount due got paid by "Hidell" in Dallas.

As to ballistics, the ammunition used to kill Tippit was slightly under-sized, thus too narrow to pick up full rifling from the barrel. So the bullets recovered from Officer Tippit—except for one slug—could not be traced to the revolver. The one exception had sufficient rifling marks to make a match with a test bullet fired from Oswald's revolver. A different tool-mark issue concerned the ejected cartridges. The earlier tool-mark expert returned to tell the jury that while the rifle had left tool marks, the .38 special shells had no ejection marks because it was a revolver (from which shells had to be removed by hand). Nonetheless, the spent shells found in Mrs. Davis's yard had breech fire marks, plus firing pin marks matching those of a shell test-fired in the Oswald .38. The unfired bullets found on Oswald, moreover, matched the two brands and caliber of the spent cartridges found near the murder scene.

The final prosecution witness, examined by Wade, was the Texas medical examiner who had studied Officer Tippit's body. He testified that the cause of death was the series of four gunshot wounds. He described the trajectory of each bullet for the jury, using a diagram with gruesome death photographs. This proved the location and angle of each bullet entry, shown by dowels pushed into the wounds. The angle on the head could only have been made after the victim lay on the pavement, said the examiner. The Widow Tippit's seat lay vacant.

Foreman had no questions for any of these witnesses.

Without fanfare came the last of the prosecution's case, a stipulation that in the Marines, Oswald qualified once as a "marksman," once as a "sharpshooter," but never at the highest level "expert."

"The prosecution rests," declared Wade.

A look of relief swept the jury box and gallery. The case had "gone in" in only two weeks. The judge declared a lunch recess. Reporters poured out the exit.

# 60  A TOAST AND A FAVOR

THAT EVENING AT THE DALLAS PRESS CLUB, BEBE PROPOSED A toast.

"To Jerrie Mock—Godspeed."

All responded, "Hear, hear," surprised that she had not toasted the end of the prosecution's case.

Jerrie Mock, age thirty-eight, a recreational flyer, took off that morning from Ohio to do what Amelia Earhart had almost done. Pilot Mock was destined to become the first woman pilot to circumnavigate the globe. At that moment, as they raised their glasses, Pilot Mock bounced in a simple single-engine plane over the vast, dark Atlantic, alone.

"Bless her," Bebe meant it, "She's a woman. No longer a man's racket."

AT THE SAME TIME, Percy Foreman dealt with his Euins problem, namely trying to head off his parents from attending court while their son testified and thus "integrating" the courtroom and, in doing so, maybe aggravating one or more members of the all-white jury. Foreman deplored what he intended to ask.

Foreman took a seat in the front room of the Euins home, a small, well-maintained, single-family residence in the better black part of Dallas. Amos and his parents, Foreman guessed, wondered why the great lawyer had come to visit. Amos with his mom had already seen him for an interview. All three Euins surely regretted, Foreman worried, any circumstance in which Amos would testify for the man charged with killing President Kennedy. On their side table, Percy observed the December issue of *Life* with JFK's portrait.

"I'm here just to answer your questions," Percy began, cradling the coffee offered by Mrs. Euins in his lap. "I suspect this'll be a new experience for Amos."

"Yes, it will," she replied. "We were wondering—what should he wear?"

"His church clothes."

"And on what day?"

"In a couple of days, Saturday morning."

"Should he bring anything?"

"No," answered Foreman.

"A Bible?"

"You mean to take the oath on?"

"No, no, his personal scriptures, to see him through."

"Why, yes, that would be fine."

Foreman liked the image. The Bible held by the witness—instant credibility.

"Amos, you know where the courthouse is?"

"Just about the scene of the crime, yes, sir."

"You'll need to be there at eight. We'll call you to the stand as soon as we can."

"Yes, sir."

"I want to be very clear, Amos. All we want is for you to be as honest as you can be about what you saw. Please don't think we want you to do us any favors or to stretch a point. Just listen carefully to each question, then tell the truth."

"Yes, sir."

"Will either of you two be attending?" Percy looked to the parents, approaching his real purpose.

"We heard," Mrs. Euins began, "that there were no seats—unless you stood in line all night. His father has to work but I'd like to be there when Amos testifies. Should I stand in line or could you please help me get a seat?"

The truth was Percy could.

Percy leaned in. He was about to explain that she should stay home. But he could not bring himself to say the words.

"Maybe. I'll call you."

He could eventually, he calculated, just tell her no seat could be found.

Percy finished his coffee and took his leave. But as the door closed behind him, a feeling overcame him—he was unexpectedly gripped by an appreciation of the toil and tribulation that had led this family to this decent home and to a life that black families in Percy's own youth would have thought impossible. An unexpected feeling of respect welled in Percy, respect for their faith, their civic pride, but mainly, for what this family had done for themselves despite monumental obstacles. He dwelt on it on the drive back.

At the Adolphus, he took a whiskey in his room, then phoned Robert.

"Robert, I need a favor. Would you give up your seat for an hour, probably less, so the mother of a young man we need as a witness can sit there?"

"Fine, just tell me when."

When he hung up, he called Mrs. Euins to say he'd gotten her a seat. In a voice that betrayed surprise, she thanked him.

Karen was right, reflected Percy, alone in his room. There are some goddam things a lawyer need not do for a client. Maybe, as he sipped and thought, doing the mom a favor might somehow help in some as-yet unknown way. Anyway, his client, Lee Oswald, embraced integration. On this one, he told himself, reaching for more whiskey, we'll somehow muddle through.

# 61 THE FIRST SHOT MISSED

"For our first two witnesses," Foreman announced after the lunch recess on Friday, March 20, "Miss Karen Eisenstadt will conduct the examinations." He affected a beaming face with only the slightest hint of a smile.

Karen stood to declare, "We call Virgie Rachley."

A nervous young woman was guided forward and sworn. She testified that she was a bookkeeper at the Texas School Book Depository. On November 22, she'd been standing at the curb where the Elm Street Parkway began to curve down toward the Triple Underpass. The president came very close to her. Karen zeroed in:

"When the president's car passed by you, did you hear any of the shots?"

"Yes, ma'am, I thought it was fireworks because I saw a shot or something hit the street immediately after the first noise."

"What'd you see?"

"I saw the bullet hit the street, Elm Street. I saw sparks. That's why I thought it was a firecracker."

"How far into the street?"

"About the middle lane."

"How close was it to the president's car?"

"Behind it."

"How many shots did you hear?"

"Three."

"When did you realize they were shots?"

"With the second one."

"So which one of the three did you see hit the street?"

"The first one."

"Thank you, Virgie. We tender the witness."

The prosecution had no questions.

Karen continued, "The defense calls James Thomas Tague." A bailiff brought Tague in from the hallway.

James Tague testified that he was twenty-seven, lived in Euless, and sold cars in Dallas. On the twenty-second, he headed downtown to pick up his girlfriend, whom he had since married, to take her to lunch when he got caught up in traffic for the motorcade. He'd been unaware of the parade before that. When other cars ahead stopped, he likewise stopped his car on Commerce Street just after passing through the Triple Underpass. He got out to watch whatever was happening and saw the president's car on Houston, then Elm. He heard what sounded like a firecracker. Then came another, so he realized it was gun fire. He ducked for cover. Because he was ducking, he did not see the president get hit. Karen actually asked this twice so as to reinforce an argument, Bebe figured, against the testimony of Howard Brennan, who had also been ducking for cover but nevertheless claimed to have seen the shooter while doing so. About three minutes later, Tague continued, a patrolman who had been on the overpass came up to say he (the officer) had seen something fly off the street near where Tague had been standing.

"Did the officer point anything out to you about your face?"

"He said I had blood on my cheek. I reached up and, yes, there was a couple of drops of blood."

"What happened next?"

"He asked where I had been standing. So I said, 'Right down here.' We walked to where I had been standing. I said that something stung me on the face while I had been standing there. On the curb we saw a fresh mark that looked like a bullet had hit it."

"Exactly where were you standing when you felt the sting?"

"I was standing on the edge of Main Street. That's the middle one through the underpass."

"Where was the mark?"

"On the top edge of the round of the curb, about twelve to fifteen feet uphill from where I had been standing."

"Could you tell for sure which shot caused the splatter that hit you?"

"Not for sure."

"How many shots did you hear?"

"Three."

"Did any of them come from the overpass?"

"No."

Two good, short examinations, Bebe thought. From these two witnesses, she gathered, the point was that the first bullet missed the car altogether, harmlessly hit the pavement, then ricocheted, in whole or in part, over to the curb near Mr. Tague, splattered the concrete such that a piece of the concrete or lead cut his cheek. Tague too left without any cross.

# 62 SILVIA ODIO AND THE BALD SPOT

FOREMAN CALLED SILVIA ODIO TO THE STAND.

"Miss Odio, have you ever met my client, Lee Oswald, before?"

Oswald stood, respectfully.

"Yes, but he was introduced to me as Leon Oswald."

Oswald resumed his seat.

Foreman took Silvia Odio through the lead-up to her sensational story, testifying that she had been born in Havana in 1937, had gone to school in Philadelphia for three years, returned home, then left Cuba in 1960, after Fidel Castro took power. Silvia belonged to an exile organization called Junta Revolutionary, known for short as JURE.

"Tell us, please, the circumstances of meeting him."

"It was in the last days of last September, six months ago, here in Dallas at the Crestview Apartments. In the evening, I was getting dressed to go out. My sister Annie had come to babysit. She answered the doorbell. She came back and said, 'Silvia, there are three men at the door.' So I put on a housecoat to go to the door."

"Outside the door, one said, 'We are members of JURE.' They were leaning against the outside staircase. Their faces did not seem familiar, and I asked them for their names. The one who talked the most said his name was Leopoldo, his war name. In all this underground, everybody with family in Cuba has a *nom de guerre*—for safety in Cuba. The other one was something like Angelo."

"Describe them, please."

"Let me tell you, they both looked very greasy, like the kind of low Cubans, not educated at all. Angelo was on the heavier side with black hair. The other one had glasses, if I remember, and was the tall one and called himself 'Leopoldo.' The American was in the middle."

"Leopoldo did most of the talking?"

"He did the talking. The other one kept quiet. The American said just a few little words in Spanish, trying to be cute, but very few, like 'Hola,' like that in Spanish."

"Did you have a chain on the door, or was the door completely opened?"

"No, I unfastened the chain after a little while when they told me they were members of JURE. They were trying to have me let them come into the vestibule. One of them said, 'We are very good friends of your father.' This struck me as odd because I didn't think my father could have such friends, unless he knew them from anti-Castro activities. But he gave me many details about my father.

"Then what?"

"After he mentioned my father, he said, 'You are working for the underground.' I said, 'No, I am sorry to say I am not working in the underground.' He said, 'We wanted you to meet this American. His name is Leon Oswald.' He repeated it twice. We shook hands. Then my sister Annie by that time was standing near the door. She had come back to the door to see what was going on. They introduced Leon Oswald—your client, Counselor—as an American who was very much interested in the Cuban cause."

"What'd they want?"

"This heavier man, Angelo I think, took out a letter written in Spanish, saying something like we represent the revolutionary council. We are making a big movement to buy arms for Cuba and to help overthrow the dictator Castro. They wanted me to translate this letter to English and send a whole lot of them to different industries to see if we can raise money. But this same petition had been asked of me by one of the leaders of JURE, here in Dallas. I had told him no, too. I was very busy. I asked who they knew in JURE. They didn't know the people I knew in JURE. So, I asked, 'Well, is this on your own?'"

"And Leopoldo said," the witness continued, "'We have just come from New Orleans where we have been trying to get this movement organized so this is on our own, but we think we could do some good work.' This was all said very fast, not as slow as I am saying it now. You know how fast Cubans talk."

Silvia was talking pretty fast herself.

"Then what?"

"Then I asked something to the American, trying to be nice, 'Have you ever been to Cuba?' And he said, 'No, I have never been to Cuba.'"

"So I said, 'Are you interested in our movement?' And he said, 'Yes.'"

"Anything else?"

"I said, 'If you will excuse me, I have to leave. But I am going to write to my father to tell him you have come.'

"To which Leopoldo said, 'Is he still in the Isle of Pines?' I think that was the extent of the conversation. They left. I saw them through the window leaving in a car. I wanted to make sure they left."

"Do you know which one of the men was driving?"

"The tall one, Leopoldo. Yes. Oh, excuse me, I forgot something very important," Silvia interjected, speeding up again. "They kept mentioning that they had come to visit me at such a time of night, it was almost nine o'clock, because they were leaving for a trip. Two or three times they said the same thing. Please excuse us for the hour.' He mentioned two or three times they were leaving for a trip."

"Describe them."

"Angelo had a hard complexion, a mark on his face, had been in the sun, about forty years old. Mexican looking, short with lots of thick hair. About 170 pounds. Shorter than Oswald. Leopoldo was the tall one, about six feet, the younger of the two, about thirty-four, maybe 165 pounds. Wore glasses but took them on and off, not sunglasses but normal spectacles. No mustache. His hair was pulled back on the side, but he had a bald spot on top."

"Did you say Leopoldo was about thirty-four, maybe 165 pounds?"

"Yes, sir."

"A bald spot, did you say?"

"Yes, a bald spot."

"On Leopoldo?"

"Yes."

"So, Leopoldo was about thirty-four, weighed maybe 165 pounds, and had a bald spot on his head?"

"Is true."

"Let me ask you about Leon Oswald. Was this man right here," laying a hand on Oswald's shoulder, "Leon Oswald?"

"*El mismo*. One and the same."

"Now, Miss Odio, was there ever any mention of President Kennedy or assassination in the presence of my client while you were with him?

"No, that came up separately with Leopoldo."

"Explain that."

"A day or two after they all left, Leopoldo called me and asked what I'd thought of Leon Oswald. I said I'd no thought of Leon. Leopoldo then said that Leon said the Cubans should have assassinated President Kennedy after the Bay of Pigs and that Cubans were gutless. I wasn't interested in hearing such talk, so Leopoldo just said Leon was loco."

"Was my client involved in that phone call?"

"No. It was just Leopoldo."

"When Leopoldo called, did you in any way bring up my client or President Kennedy or assassination?"

"No, that came out of the blue from Leopoldo."

"And at any time while my client was with you, was there any such talk by anybody?"

"None."

Wade rose for the cross.

"Miss Odio, you were interviewed by the FBI, yes?"

"The FBI, yes."

"You were asked when the visit by the three men occurred, weren't you?"

"When? Yes."

"You said Thursday, September 26, was the most probable date?"

"Yes."

"And that was the first date you gave, true?"

"Yes, or Friday, the twenty-seventh."

"You had worked out these dates with your sister Annie because she had come to stay with you and had arrived on Thursday, September 26?"

"Yes, but we were not certain of those dates."

"She was there to help you move from that apartment to another one in Oak Cliff because you had to be out on or before Monday, September 30?"

"That's correct."

"But after thinking it through with your sister, your best judgment was either Thursday or Friday, September 26 or 27, true?"

"Yes, true."

"And that was what you told the FBI?"

"Yes."

"And that is still your best judgment, right?"

Silvia paused, then said it was right.

Wade decided to leave it there—Oswald was certainly on a bus to Mexico City by the twenty-sixth. The jury seemed favorably disposed to her.

"Thank you, Miss Odio."

Foreman had a short redirect.

"Did you give the FBI any other possible dates?"

"I later said possibly it could've been Wednesday, the twenty-fifth."

"Again, Miss Odio, how sure are you now, still under oath, that this man, Lee Oswald, showed up as Leon Oswald at your apartment in Dallas at the end of September with Leopoldo, the man with a bald spot?"

"I have no doubt."

# 63 AMOS EUINS AND THE BALD SPOT

ON SATURDAY MORNING, FOREMAN CALLED AMOS LEE EUINS forward as the lead-off witness, an apprehensive, young, black, skinny teenager. With his Sunday best suit on, a bit oversized, Bebe judged, to allow for growth, he looked even skinnier. He carried his Bible with him. His mom sat in the front row (in Robert's place) in a sea of almost all white spectators. Bebe wondered if some bigot would make a scene. No one seemed to object, though Bebe noticed two jurors glance at the mom. Euins was sixteen and a ninth grader attending Franklin D. Roosevelt School in Dallas. After the preliminaries, Foreman came to the main point:

"All right. Going back to November 22 last year, Amos, do you recall what you were doing early on that morning?"

"Yes, sir. When I first got up, I went to school. Then about 11:30, well, the teachers called us and told us the ones that wanted to go downtown to see the president, come down to the office, get an excuse, and they could go. So I went down to the office. I got an excuse, so I went downtown."

Through Foreman's use of diagrams, Euins made clear that, as the motorcade went by, he stood across the street from the Records Building on Houston. It was plain that this spot was only a few feet from where Brennan had been.

"Tell us what you saw as the motorcade went by."

"I stood on the corner. Then the president came. I was waving, because there wasn't hardly no one on the corner right there but me. He looked my way and waved back at me. Then I seen a pipe, you know, up there in the window, I thought it was a pipe, like a water pipe."

"A pipe? When?"

"Right as he turned the corner onto Elm."

Foreman handed him the photograph of the Depository.

"Now, show the jury exactly where you saw that thing you have described as a pipe come from? Take a good look now before you tell us where it was."

"Right here."

Euins held up a photo, then pointed to the southeast window on the sixth floor, the sniper's window.

"Tell us what happened, Amos."

"They turned the corner onto Elm Street, I was facing, looking dead at the building. So I seen this pipe thing sticking out the window. I wasn't paying too much attention to it. Then when the first shot was fired, I started looking around, thinking it was a motorcycle backfire. Everybody else started looking around. Then I looked up at the window, and he shot again. There is a little fountain right here. I got behind this little fountain, then he shot again. So after he shot again, he just started looking down this way, you know."

"Who started looking down that way?"

"The man in the window. I could see his hand on the trigger and his other hand along the barrel."

"Now, the third shot, Amos, where were you looking then?"

"I was looking up at the building."

"What'd you see?"

"I seen a bald spot on this man's head, trying to look out the window. He had a bald spot on his head. I was looking at the bald spot. I could see his hand, you know, the rifle laying across in his hand. I could see his hand sticking out on the trigger part. After he got through, he just pulled it back in the window."

"A bald spot, did you say?" Foreman looked across the jury box as he asked it.

"Yes, sir."

"Now, describe as fully as you can for us what you saw on the third shot, Amos."

"Well, when he stuck it out, you know—after the president had come on down the street further, you know he kind of stuck it out more."

"How far was it sticking out of the window would you say then, Amos?"

"I would say it was about something like that." He indicated about two feet. "You know—the trigger housing and stock were out the window."

"Now, what direction was the rifle pointing?"

"Down Elm."

"Was it pointing in the direction of the president?"

"Yes, sir."

"Now, could you see anything else on the gun?"

"No, sir, I could not."

"For example, could you see whether or not there was a telescopic lens on the gun?"

"No, sir."

"Son, you mentioned a bald spot on his head. Explain that please."

"All I got to see was the man with a spot in his head, because he had his head something like this."

"Indicating his face down, looking down the rifle?"

"Yes, sir, and I could see the spot on his head."

"How would you describe that man for us?"

"I wouldn't know how to describe him because all I could see was the bald spot and his hand holding the rifle."

"Was he slender or was he fat?"

"I didn't get to see him."

Tall or short?"

"No."

"Of what race was he, Amos?"

"At first, I thought he was colored but, really, I couldn't tell."

"Color of hair?"

"No, sir."

"How far back did the bald spot on his head go?"

"I would say about right along in here." The witness pointed to his own head.

"Indicating about two-and-a-half inches above where your hairline is. Is that about what you are saying?"

"Yes, sir."

Bebe whispered, "The bald spot—Leopoldo."

Foreman might well have stopped there—but his gut, Bebe later ventured, told him to take a gamble, so he did: "Tell us, Amos, does my client, Lee Harvey Oswald, have the type of bald spot you saw?"

Euins paused, looked over to his mom, who remained impassive, then looked over to Oswald sitting at counsel table. Every breath in the courtroom awaited the answer.

"Can I see him a little better?"

"Your Honor, may I ask the defendant to stand and bow toward the witness stand?"

"Yes, proceed."

Oswald stood, expressionless.

Foreman said, "Lee, please lean forward for the witness and jury."

Slowly, Oswald bowed deeply, then maintained the position until Foreman said, "Thank you, Lee, please resume your seat."

"Amos, what do you say?"

Amos gripped his Bible.

"Well, I can't say it's the bald spot that I saw."

A wave of murmurs swept the gallery. Some jurors looked at Wade.

"Thank you, Amos. Nothing further."

WADE FELT HE HAD the ridiculous problem of dealing with the bald spot issue from a witness who could remember no other identification whatsoever, not even the race, only a bald spot. Wade had little to lose on Euins, Foreman having milked him for as much as he had to give. Wade began slowly.

"Son, you were down on the ground?"

"Yes, sir."

"And the man in the window was six floors up, true?"

"Yes, sir."

"And he was looking down Elm Street toward the Triple Underpass, correct?"

"Looking along Elm Street."

Wade figured out where he was headed and picked up the pace.

"So, you also saw him from the side, true?"

"That's true."

"His left or right side?"

The witness thought a moment, then said, "His left side."

"So you saw his left side and you saw him from six floors down."

"Yes, sir."

"From all the way across Elm Street?"

"Yes, sir."

"And he was staring down at an angle?"

"I believe so."

"Your Honor, may we ask the defendant to stand again?"

"Please stand, Mr. Oswald."

Oswald stood. So did Foreman.

"Now, the left side of the defendant is which side?"

"That side," said Euins, pointing.

"Would the defendant turn so that his left side is facing the witness?"

Oswald did so.

"Now, would you say the defendant's hair is receding on the side facing you?"

"What do you mean by receding?"

"Would you agree that the defendant is partly bald, on the side?"

"Yes, sir, some."

"Now, if you were way down on the ground, but he was way up six floors aiming down toward the underpass, you'd see this partly bald spot, wouldn't you?" asked Wade, pointing.

"I reckon so, yes, sir."

"From way down on the ground, looking up six floors, wouldn't this appear to be a bald spot?"

"Objection. Calls for speculation."

"Overruled. Mr. Foreman, you opened the door to this. The witness will please answer."

"Sure might," Euins said, "That's the most I can say."

Wade left it there. Foreman had no redirect. Oswald sat down. The witness left with his mom and Bible.

APROPOS OF THE BALD spot, Evaristo Rodriguez next told the jury, via an interpreter, that the prior August he had been bartending at the Habana Bar in New Orleans when, near closing time, a man he identified as Oswald ordered a lemonade and his companion ordered a tequila, tequila that Oswald sampled and then threw up. Oswald's companion was "Latin looking, Cuban probably, about twenty-eight, hairy arms, about five foot eight, 155 pounds with a high forehead and a hairline in front back to here," indicating a bald spot in front. There was no cross.

# 64 ANOTHER MAN, POSSIBLY LATINO

ARNOLD ROWLAND CAME NEXT. HE WAS EIGHTEEN, A HIGH school student on November 22. He now worked odd jobs like a shipping clerk, he told the jury, plus a pizza maker, but was "fixing to go to college." He'd stood with his wife in Dealey Plaza and heard all three shots. A few minutes before the motorcade came by, he saw two men standing on the sixth floor, one with a high-power rifle. Foreman interrupted to ask if he'd said *two* men. Rowland replied, "Yes, sir, two." He'd assumed, he continued, that they were Secret Service. They were at the southwest corner window above Elm (*not* the southeast corner window, the sniper's nest). Just moments before, he and his wife had been discussing the ugly treatment Ambassador Adlai Stevenson had received in October in Dallas, so security was on his mind. When he asked his wife to look, she did, but both men were gone by then. He could only give a general description and could not identify anyone. He said they were both white, or maybe one was a "light-skinned Latin." The one with the rifle held it at the military position of port arms.

Foreman pressed on to ask for his recollection of the timing between the shots. Rowland answered, "The actual time between the reports I would say now, after having had time to consider, was six seconds between the first and second report and two seconds between the second and third, very fast for a bolt-loading rifle."

"Your witness."

TWO MEN?

The prosecution had decided against calling Rowland because he couldn't identify Oswald. In all prior interviews, the memos said, he had only referred to *one* man, one with a rifle.

Alexander did the cross-examination.

"You were interviewed half a dozen times by Secret Service, FBI, true?"

"Yes, sir."

"You told them about seeing *a* man with a rifle at the southwest corner, didn't you?"

"Yes, sir."

"You never told them about seeing a second man, white or otherwise, did you?

"It seems like I told an officer about two."

"Would it help to see the memos of your interviews?"

"I've read them. You're right that there was no mention in the memos of a second man."

"At least six memos."

"Yes, sir."

"Mr. Rowland, you know that we contend that the shots were fired from the southeast window?"

"I do."

"Did you see anyone there?"

"Yes, I did."

This was another shocker. Previously, according to the memos, the witness had only seen someone at the southwest window.

"Really? Who?"

"An elderly Negro man."

"Now, sir, let's be clear, we're now talking about the sixth floor and the *southeast* window, the one closest to Houston Street?"

"Yes, sir, an elderly Negro man."

"How long before the shots?"

"A few minutes."

"So, just a few minutes before the assassination, you saw *three* people on the *sixth* floor near the windows. Is that your testimony?"

Alexander stressed the words "three" and "sixth."

"All true."

"Would you say, Arnold, that you're sometimes prone to exaggerate?"

"Not really."

"Doesn't your wife accuse you of that?"

"Well, yes. Doesn't yours?"

This was said so innocently that there was considerable laughter in the gallery. Rowland blushed. Alexander kept a bulldog face. A slight narrowing of the slits of his eyes, all but closing, became his only sign of humor.

"Now, son, you've already acknowledged that all of those interview memos have you referring only to having seen one man, true?"

"Correct."

"But you say you told an officer about a second man and it just didn't get written down, right?"

"Yes, sir."

"But even you admit you never before told anyone about a third man on the sixth floor, right?"

"Correct."

# 65 A MAN RAN DOWN THE HILL

QUICKLY TO SHOW UP THE BULLDOG CROSS BY ALEXANDER, Foreman called Deputy Roger D. Craig, to show that Arnold had, indeed, said there were two men. Craig testified that he was twenty-seven, had served in the Army for two years, then with the Dallas County Sheriff's Office since October 1959. In 1960, he had been named the Dallas County Sheriff's Department "Officer of the Year" by the Dallas Traffic Commission. He had received four promotions within the Sheriff's department. Craig had strong features, dark hair, and celebrity-style good looks, resembling Rod Steiger, Bebe would report. On the twenty-second, he was standing on Main Street in front of the Sheriff's Office to observe the motorcade. He heard all three shots.

"Where'd you think the shots came from?"

"I didn't know. Where I was standing on Main Street, I was hearing echoes."

"What was the spacing and timing of the shots?"

"There was quite a pause between the first and second but not more than two seconds between the second and third."

"What'd you do?"

"I ran to Houston and across Elm up to the railroad yard when people began to travel up that way."

"Did you find anything in the railroad yard?"

"No."

"Just after that, did you have occasion to speak with someone named Arnold Rowland?"

"I did."

"Please relate that conversation."

"He said that before the president arrived, he'd seen two men on the sixth floor of the Depository walking back and forth. They were at the west end of the side that faces Elm, the second window from the west end. I asked him were they white or colored and he said white. He said that he looked back a few minutes later, still all before the president arrived, and there was just one man, a man with a rifle. He said the man had the rifle down by his side and was looking straight out the window, to the south. About fifteen minutes later, he said, the three shots were fired."

"Rowland said he had seen how many men at that window?"

"Two."

"Two, did you say?"

"Yes, sir, two."

Foreman looked across the jury box. "What happened next?"

"About ten or twelve minutes after the assassination, I turned Mr. Rowland and his wife over to another officer for questioning."

Foreman had now achieved his main point—to show that Rowland had seen two men on the sixth floor, not just one, as Alexander insisted. There was nothing to be done about any third man on the sixth floor. Foreman continued with a new point:

"Then what'd you do?

"As we were searching for a possible ricochet, I heard someone whistle."

"When?"

"Fourteen or fifteen minutes after the assassination."

"All right. You heard someone whistle?"

"Yes. So I turned and saw a man near the southwest corner of the Depository and he ran down the hill on the north side of Elm Street, running down toward Elm Street."

"And then what'd you see happen?"

"I saw a light-colored Nash-Rambler station wagon, driving real slow, coming west on Elm Street from Houston. Actually, it was nearly in line with him. The driver, a dark-complected man, was leaning to his right, looking up the hill at the man running down."

"Uh-huh."

"The station wagon stopped almost directly across from me. The man continued down the hill and got in the station wagon. I attempted to cross the street. I wanted to talk to both of them. But the traffic was so heavy I couldn't get across the street. They were gone before I could—"

"Describe the man you saw running down toward the Nash-Rambler station wagon?"

"Oh, he was a white man in his twenties, five nine, five eight, something like that. About 140 to 150, had kind of medium-brown, sandy hair—you know, it was all wild looking—had on blue trousers, light-tan shirt—in an awful hurry. To be honest, I think it was your client, Lee Harvey Oswald."

"Deputy, if Lee Oswald was in a cab headed across the river at that point after the assassination, wouldn't it have to have been someone else?"

"If so, then it was someone just like him."

"Exactly. Thank you, Deputy."

Wade rose as Foreman sat.

Wade asked, "Did Arnold Rowland say whether there was a third man on the sixth floor?"

"I asked him whether there was anyone else on the floor, but he said, 'No, just the two of them.'"

THE NEXT TWO WITNESSES, examined by Karen, were called to buttress the Nash-Rambler story. Marvin C. Robinson, who was driving west on Elm when a "light-colored Nash station wagon" stopped in front of him while a white male ran down the grassy incline, jumped in, and the car headed west in the direction of Oak Cliff. Even briefer was Roy Cooper, who testified that he was following Robinson, his boss, when he saw a white male between twenty to thirty years of age wave at a Nash Rambler station wagon, light colored, as it pulled out "real fast" in front of the Cadillac driven by his boss. Neither could give a better description. Again, there was no cross.

Next, Foreman called Carolyn Walther, who gave her account of seeing a man with a short machine gun hanging out a Depository window on the fourth or fifth floor and, importantly for the defense, also seeing a second man standing beside him. Foreman held up the Carcano and asked, "Mrs. Walther, is this a machine gun?" She answered, "How would I know?" On cross, Alexander brought out how her subsequent conduct seemed inconsistent with just having seen the assassin, including her failure to tell anyone what she had seen, even her sidewalk companion or any officer until hours later.

On redirect, Foreman asked, "Why didn't you tell anyone sooner?"

"I thought," she replied, "they were just part of the security."

DURING A BREAK, THE prosecutors peeked into the future and wondered where Foreman was headed.

Wade put in, "It means Oswald will testify."

"How so?" asked Elaine.

"He's setting up corroboration for some screwball story. We've seen this before. It lends an appearance of legitimacy to his tale if it seems to be corroborated."

This time, Abe shifted his weight. He, too, saw it coming.

# 66 A MAN RAN OUT THE BACK

FOREMAN NEXT PRESENTED A WITNESS WHO SAW A MAN RUN OUT the back of the Depository soon after the assassination.

James Richard Worrell Jr. testified that he was twenty and lived in Dallas with his parents. On November 22, he was a high school dropout, unemployed. He wanted to see the president. Worrell stood about four to five feet from the front of the Depository itself with his back to the building, near Houston Street. The president passed within sixty feet. As the president's car was a little past him (going down Elm), he heard a series of four shots. Foreman continued:

"Did you observe anything at about that time?"

"Yes, sir. I looked up, straight above me, and saw the rifle, about six inches of it."

"And where'd you see the rifle?"

"Either in the fifth or the sixth floor on the east corner of the Depository. I heard the first shot. I knew it was too loud to be a firecracker, I knew that, because there was quite a big boom. Just out of nowhere, I looked up like that, just straight up."

"Indicating you looked straight back over your head, raising your head to look above your body at a ninety-degree angle?"

"Correct."

"Did you see a rifle between the first and the second shot?"

"Yes, sir, and I saw the firing on the second but then before the third—I took in everything but especially the car, the president's car, and saw the president slumping. I looked up again, turned around, started running, and saw it fire a third time. I did it all in one motion. I looked up, turned around and ran, pivoted. I never saw the shooter."

"Where'd you run?"

"I ran down Houston Street, going north, toward the rear of the building. I ran alongside the building then crossed Houston Street. I was standing over there to catch my breath about a block behind the Depository when I saw this man come bustling out one of the back doors of the Depository."

"What is your best estimate as to his weight?"

"155 to 165."

"What is your best estimate as to his height?"

"Five seven, five ten."

"Your best estimate as to his age."

"Well, the way he was running, I would say he was in his late twenties or middle—I mean early thirties. Because he was fast moving on. His coat was open, kind of flapping back in the breeze as he ran along the side of the Depository building and went on farther toward the front of the building. Last I saw of him."

Worrell then testified the man was white and wore a dark sports coat with light-colored slacks. His hair was "brunette."

"Did he have a full head of hair, a partial head of hair, or what?"

"I just saw the back of his head—it was full in the back."

There was no cross.

To meet any claim that the rear had been sealed off by police, Foreman next called Special Agent in Charge (in Dallas) Forrest Sorrels of the Secret Service. He testified that he had been in the motorcade, went to Parkland Hospital but returned to the Depository twenty minutes after the shooting. He went to the rear door where he was able to enter without identifying himself. In fact, he found no police officers at the back door at all. The prosecution said, "No questions."

# 67 THE DIVERSION

"WE CALL SAM HOLLAND," FOREMAN ANNOUNCED. THE TALL, lanky signal supervisor with the LBJ-style glasses came forward, was sworn, and took the stand. He told the jury how he had stood on the top of the Triple Underpass above Elm and watched the oncoming limousine as the shots rang out. The shots, he said, seemed to come from the far end of Elm, meaning up by the Depository, with one exception—a fourth noise like a firecracker.

Referring to the trees in front of the stockade-style fence on the grassy knoll near the overpass, he said, "There was a shot, a report, I don't know whether it was a shot. I can't say that. Anyway, a puff of smoke came out about six to eight feet above the ground right out from under the trees between the pergola and the Triple Underpass. And, at just about where I was standing, you could see that puff of smoke about ten or eleven feet in front of the fence, like someone had thrown out a firecracker or something, and that is just about the way it sounded. It wasn't as loud as the previous reports or shots."

Bebe's mind flashed on Marilyn Sitzman and her memory of the Negro couple on the grassy knoll and the crash of their coke bottle.

Foreman turned to face the jury.

"Like a firecracker, did you say?"

"Yes, sir."

"And a puff of smoke like a firecracker?"

"Yes, sir."

Wade's cross was short.

"Sam, you yourself say it didn't sound like a shot, right?"

"True."

"And, for all you know, it was just a cloud of exhaust from a motorcycle backfire."

"I can't say."

THE TIME ON THE clock was 11:45. Some judges would have called it a week, but Judge Brown had said he wanted a verdict before Easter and Passover. He had already told everyone to be prepared to go until one o'clock in the afternoon. He said to Foreman, "Your next witness, please."

"May I have a moment, Your Honor?"

"Of course."

Foreman huddled with Oswald.

Seeing this, Bebe figured that the defense was down to one more witness—Oswald himself, and that Foreman needed a moment to confirm that Oswald really did (or did not) want to testify and to tell his story, a time-honored moment in criminal trials. Oswald kept nodding as if to say yes. Hushed speculation gathered in the gallery.

Bebe leaned to her bench mate. "He's going to testify."

Abe, she knew, had drawn the card to cross-examine him.

Now came the moment all of America anticipated. Foreman stood to turn confidently—regally would not be too strong a word. The room held its collective breath. Exuding elan, Foreman announced, "The defense calls Lee Oswald." The wall clock showed 11:52. It was Saturday, March 21, 1964, the first day of spring.

# 68 OSWALD'S STORY

ABE STUDIED HIM AS OSWALD WALKED FORWARD, DRESSED NEATLY in sweater and slacks, shoes polished, hair combed with face clean shaven. He didn't smirk or slouch. He looked fresh, collegiate, someone incapable of two horrendous murders. This image had been reinforced by two weeks of respectable conduct in court in view of the jury. He raised his right hand, took the oath, seated himself, leaned forward in earnest, and stated his name for the record. He sent a fragile acknowledgment in the direction of his family.

Foreman made for his key point straight away.

"Lee, when the president's motorcade turned onto Elm Street, were you at that southeast corner window on the sixth floor of the Depository?"

"Yes, sir, I was."

"Did you, Lee, fire that rifle?"

"Yes, sir, I fired one shot."

"At the president?"

"No, sir, I aimed behind the car, to miss on purpose. It was meant to make a point."

"What point?"

"To demonstrate the point that if our government was going to make attempts on the life of Fidel Castro, then the other side, meaning Prime Minister Castro, could just as easily do the same to our own leaders. The objective was to have both sides think better of such attempts—to live and let live."

"Who fired the other shots?"

"I gave the rifle to the second man on the sixth floor with me. The second man was the one Mr. Rowland and Mrs. Walther saw up there with me. He was supposed to hide the rifle while I left the building. That was the plan. Instead, as I hurried to the stairwell, he fired two more shots. That was not part of the plan. I heard those two shots as I headed for the stairwell."

"Who was this person?"

"A man I met in New Orleans. His name was Leopoldo. The man described by Miss Odio. The man with the bald spot."

"Lee, were you ever part of a conspiracy to kill the president or anyone else?"

"No, sir, I was not. No one was supposed to get hurt. We were, I thought, simply out to show that the other side could, if they wanted, do the same thing to our country that our president was trying to do to them."

Clever, Abe thought. More than that, astounding.

"Lee, now let's go back to the beginning. Tell us about your childhood."

"I was born and raised in New Orleans. I have a brother plus a half brother. My dad died before I was born. Mother—sitting over there in the front row—raised us. At seventeen, I joined the Marines, like my brother Robert."

He indicated in the direction of Robert.

"Where'd you serve?"

"California, Japan, the Philippines."

What'd you do after the Marines?"

"I received an honorable discharge, came home, then decided to go see what Russia was like. In the Marines, I learned Russian. It seemed like an interesting country. I got myself into Russia. They allowed me to stay."

"When was that?"

"1959."

"Did you get married there?"

"To Marina."

Marina's and Lee's eyes met.

"Why and when did you come back?"

"1962. I got fed up with Russia. I had a job and a decent apartment there, but I could see that their system was bad. Oppressive. I wanted to come back."

"Children?"

"Yes, sir, then just one but now two."

"Let's go back. In the Marines, were you a good shot?"

"Yes, sir, I qualified as a marksman once, another time as a sharpshooter."

"When you came back to Texas, where'd you go?"

"Fort Worth. We lived with Robert until we could find our own place."

"Did you find work?"

"I had several jobs. My best job was as a photo darkroom worker for the Jaggars-Chiles-Stovall Company. I got that job in October 1962. That was in Dallas."

"While you were working there, did you make a counterfeit draft card?"

"Yes, sir—kind of my own on-the-job-training, learning to use the equipment. I made up the name Alek J. Hidell."

"Why'd you do that?"

"After I returned home, the FBI was constantly following us and asking questions. Made it hard for me to keep a job. The FBI was asking questions of Marina—like she was a spy. She was afraid of being sent back. I didn't want to draw attention to us. So I invented Alek J. Hidell as a way to do things."

"Like what?"

"I ordered the rifle and the pistol under the Hidell name. I had never committed a crime and had every right to have a firearm, but the FBI traced my movements, so it was just easier to use an alias."

"Why'd you want the firearm?"

"The same reason as anyone else. Protection. Hunting. Target practice. I had a rifle as a kid. I wanted to pick that up again. I had no criminal record. It was legal for me to have a rifle, just like everyone else."

"What'd you do with it?"

"Just target practice. Most of the time it was just in storage. I wanted to go hunting someday but never did."

Abe jotted "target practice" and circled it in his notes. Oswald, he thought, had just opened the door to the Walker story.

"Target practice. Now, that picture of you with the rifle, the pistol, and the communist newspapers. What was that about?"

"Just a gag. Our friend George de Mohrenschildt was always complaining about fascists here or fascists there—how they should all be eliminated. He was just joking. But he liked to rag on about fascists. He was from Europe before the war, so he hated fascism. I posed for that picture just to give it to George as a gag, me as the enemy of the fascists. Marina took the picture. I made the print at work."

"Did you give it to George?"

"Yes, sir. Somebody wrote on the back, 'Hunter of Fascists.' Both of us laughed it off as a gag."

"Are you a communist?"

"I believe in Marxism."

"Do you believe in America?"

"America's system is better than the Russian system. That's why I came back. Still, I believe America is unfair to millions, especially the poor. Marxism would help the poor."

"By the way, how old are you, Lee, and how much do you weigh?"

"Twenty-four. A little over 140 pounds."

"Did there come a point where you and your family moved to New Orleans?"

"At the end of last April."

"Why'd you move to New Orleans?"

"Jaggers laid me off. I thought there would be better job opportunities in New Orleans. I had a family to support."

"Did you get a job there?"

"At the Reily Coffee Company on Magazine Street."

"A place to live?"

"A little place, also on Magazine Street."

"Lee, what was the Fair Play for Cuba Committee?"

"A nationwide group out of New York that advocates for more peaceful policies toward Cuba."

"What was your connection?"

"I was trying to get a chapter going in New Orleans, so I handed out leaflets on the street. I got jumped and fought back, so they put me in jail for a few days. After that, WDSU broadcast a radio debate between me and an anti-Castro exile named Carlos Bringuier. That was last August."

"Why'd you go to Mexico City?"

"I wanted a visa to visit Cuba."

"When did you leave New Orleans?"

"My family left on September 23. Ruth Paine was good enough to take them back to Irving in her station wagon along with all our stuff. By the way, that included the rifle and the pistol. I left on the twenty-fifth."

"Where'd you go?"

"To Dallas with Leopoldo and his friend, Angelo."

"Who was Leopoldo?"

"He was from Cuba. We met through leafleting in New Orleans. After we got to know each other, he told me he'd been sent here by the Castro government to keep tabs on exiles. He pretended to be an exile. He'd hang out in exile joints. Once, I tagged along with him to the Habana Bar."

"How'd you happen to go to Dallas with him?"

"Leo—he went by Leo for short—knew I was headed for Mexico City, then Cuba. My original plan was to take the bus from New Orleans to Houston and from there take buses to Mexico City. Leo said he'd give me a ride to Houston if I'd go by way of Dallas to check out one of the Odio sisters. I didn't know anything about any Odio sisters, but I went along for the ride to save the bus fare to Houston. So, as soon as I cashed my unemployment check on the morning of the twenty-fifth of September, a Wednesday, we drove to Dallas, met with Silvia Odio at her apartment that night. Then Leo drove me to the bus station in Houston."

"Lee, what was your role with Miss Odio?"

"Nothing. I just tagged along. Leo was trying to keep tabs on her exile organization by pretending to hate Castro."

"Did you make your bus connection in Houston?"

"Yes, just barely."

"What was your route to Mexico City?"

"Houston to Laredo and, after a bus change, Laredo to Mexico City."

"What day did you leave Houston?"

"Early in the morning on Thursday, the twenty-sixth, around two thirty in the morning."

Abe had to admire the deft way in which Oswald had fit the Odio story so neatly into the mystery gap in time on September 25 and 26 during which the FBI had been unable to account for Oswald's whereabouts.

"Why did you want to go to Cuba?"

"The revolution in Cuba was so fresh, they hadn't yet had time to get corrupted."

"In Mexico City, did you go to the Cuba consulate?"

"Yes, sir, I did."

"Why?"

"In the United States, you can't get visas for Cuba. You have to go through Mexico."

"Lee, what happened?"

"A very nice woman named Silvia Duran was at the Cuba consulate. She tried to help me, but the head man said all visas had to be approved in Havana, so he wouldn't give me one on the spot. The problem, however, was that it would take too long to send the application to Havana, have them consider it, and so on. I had a total of only fifteen days to stay in Mexico on my visitor permit. I kept explaining that, but he kept saying no. So I struck out at the Cuba consulate."

"Did you tell the consulate about your support of the Castro government?"

"Yes, of course. I explained about the leafleting, the fistfight, the committee, and the debate on radio—even gone to jail for the new Cuba. I showed them a folder of news clippings plus leaflets and correspondence. Did no good. The consulate man was very stubborn."

"What else did you do?"

"I went to the Russian embassy in Mexico City to ask for their help with the Cubans, but they wouldn't help."

"Anything else?"

"I went back to the Cuban consulate to talk with Silvia Duran. She suggested that I go see a professor at the local university. Maybe he would give a letter of recommendation, she said, to help get a visa. So I went out there and tried to find him but couldn't locate him. I did talk to some students. One of them put in a call to the consulate to try to help me but he struck out too."

"What was the name of the university?"

"National Autonomous University of Mexico."

His accent was passable.

"So you struck out everywhere?"

"Struck out. I was allowed only fifteen days in Mexico, so eventually it was time for me to return to Texas."

"Did anything else happen?"

"I went to a bullfight. Bought a bracelet for Marina. Walked around to see the city. Worked on my Spanish."

"Let's go back to Leo. Did the subject of your rifle ever come up?"

"We got to talking about hunting, so I told him about my Carcano. This was in the car on the way to Dallas to see Miss Odio."

"What else on that subject?"

"He asked if I was a good shot, so I told him about the Marines."

"Was there any discussion about President Kennedy?"

"He brought up the fact that President Kennedy had been making attempts on Castro's life. He warned me that, from Havana's viewpoint, they would worry that I was just trying to get into Cuba as part of yet another CIA attempt on Castro. That's the only way President Kennedy came up."

"And what'd you think about that?"

"In New Orleans, the *Times-Picayune* had already run stories on that—on Kennedy calling for the elimination of Castro. The paper also said Castro gave a speech saying that these attempts were a very bad precedent. Yeah, I knew about that."

Abe knew this part was true.

"So, Lee, did you go back home?"

"When the fifteen days ran out, I returned back to Dallas. This was in the middle of October."

"What'd you do then?"

"I eventually got back with my family. They were with Ruth Paine. Like she said, she helped me get a job at the Depository. I got a room in a boarding house to be near work but, on every weekend but one, went out to Ruth's house to see my family."

"Did the FBI contact you?"

"In early November, Agent Hosty and another federal agent came out to Irving to question Marina—scared her very badly. Being Russian, she thought they were like the KGB. They came out twice. That really scared her. I was at work both times."

"What, if anything, did you do about it?"

"On the day after Armistice Day, I went to the FBI building in Dallas to see Agent Hosty. This was during my lunch break. I wanted to give him a chance to ask me what he needed to know so that he would stop scaring my wife. But he was out. I left a note for him with the receptionist. The note asked him to stop harassing my wife."

"Did they stop?"

"There were no more visits by the FBI."

"What else, if anything, happened?"

"As I was walking back to work, I ran into Leo on the sidewalk on Commerce Street."

"Again, when was that?"

"November 12, the day after Armistice Day, about ten days before the president was killed."

"Tell us what happened there on the sidewalk."

"I was headed back to work at the Depository. Someone called my name. I looked around. It was Leo. I was surprised to see him. He seemed surprised to see me too. He then walked with me as far as Dealey Plaza. I pointed out where I worked. He said he happened to be back in Dallas for a few days and that it was just blind luck that he'd run into me on the sidewalk. I told him how I'd struck out in Mexico City. At some point, he said he had an idea on how I could get into Cuba. He asked me to meet him on Saturday to explain it. We agreed to meet in Dealey Plaza on that Saturday at noon."

"Did you?"

"Yes, we met there but mainly rode around in his car. He asked if I still wanted to get into Cuba and I said yes."

"What was his plan?"

"Well, the subject of assassination attempts on Castro came up again. He complained that the Kennedys were trying to kill Castro just like they had already killed Trujillo in the Dominican Republic and Diem in South Vietnam. I'd read about all that."

"What did you say?"

"Just that it was wrong to try to assassinate the leader of a country, unless you're at war, because if one country can do it, then any country can do it."

"Did you discuss President Kennedy?"

"Yes, sir. He said someone should show President Kennedy how easy it would be to do the same thing to him, so that maybe both sides would think better of it."

"How specific did he get?"

"Just someone should fire a shot in the vicinity of the president but miss on purpose so everyone would know that next time it could work both ways. Like a demonstration."

"An intentional miss?"

"Correct."

"What else?"

"He also said he was here because the president was coming the next week. He was here to scope out a plan."

"What'd you say?"

"I just played along and asked questions. Like, how'd he get away? Even shooting to miss had to mean hard time. Would he give himself up or would he try to get away? Leo said someone would toss a firecracker. That would divert everyone long enough to clear out. He said guys dressed as cops in a fake patrol car would run him out to Red Bird Field where a light plane would take him out of the country."

Elaine whispered to Abe that Red Bird Field was a small light aviation field southwest of Oak Cliff.

"Did he say who'd toss the firecracker?"

"I just assumed a dummy cop."

"What else was said?"

"He asked if I wanted in—he said it would be a sure ticket into Cuba for me. I asked what my part would be, and he said my part would be to use my Carcano and to shoot to miss, then go to Cuba with him. I said I'd think about it. He then dropped me off near the boarding house."

"How again did he know about your Carcano?"

"It came up driving to see Miss Odio."

"How?"

"Just talk about hunting."

"But now you were talking about shooting at the motorcade?"

"No, sir, shooting behind the president's car to make the point that it could work both ways."

"So, Lee, did you think about it?"

"I did think about it, yes, sir. In fact, later on that very weekend I read that President Kennedy had just that Friday given another speech against Castro to the exiles in Miami. He said that Castro should be assassinated— that was my interpretation anyway. It was in the *Dallas Times Herald*. It said President Kennedy had 'all but invited the Cuban people today to overthrow Fidel Castro's communist regime, even promised prompt U.S. aid if they do.' To me, this reinforced what Leo had been saying."

Oswald leaned forward, his arms resting on the witness bench, appearing as if he wanted to help the jury understand.

"What'd Leo look like?"

"He was a light-skinned Latin, along the lines described by Mr. Rowland.

Tall, slender, thirties, sometimes wore glasses, with a bald spot above his forehead. Talked fast. He looked Cuban, all just like Miss Odio and the bartender said."

"Did you meet again?"

"There was no point in me getting involved until we knew the parade route. We agreed to meet on Thursday, figuring the route would be in the papers by then."

"Did you meet that Thursday?"

"Yes, sir. I got breakfast at the Dobb's House, near my boarding house. He met me out front and gave me a ride into work. The motorcade route had just been published. I thought it was too good to be true, meaning the parade would go right by my work. We were both fired up over the route. It was an opportunity and I wanted to take advantage of it. But I told him there were some problems."

"What problems?"

"I was worried that someone would get hurt by a ricochet off the pavement. I also told him my Carcano was at Ruth's out in Irving and I didn't know if I even had any ammo. Leo said, no sweat, he'd get the ammunition if I'd get the Carcano."

"What'd he say about the ricochet problem?"

"He said the trick was to aim so that the bounce would hit up onto the underside of the car, so aim just behind it. No one would get hurt. Again, he said it'd be a sure ticket to Cuba. We'd both be in Havana by Saturday. I said okay, I'd try to get out to Ruth's that evening and bring the Carcano to work on Friday."

"What specifically was the plan?"

"On Friday, I'd bring the Carcano to work. He'd meet me up there on the sixth floor, dressed like he was a press photographer. Sports jacket. Camera. He said the place would be crawling with cops and press within minutes so he'd fit right in as a photographer. He'd bring the ammo. He'd also stand with me to watch for someone coming onto the floor. After I took the shot, he'd take the rifle and hide it while I hurried away. He'd hang around taking pictures, blending in with all the news people, then slip out. Dummy cops in dummy police cars would take us to the airfield. No one was supposed to get hurt. It was just supposed to be a demonstration. I told him I'd try to get my Carcano."

"How'd you get it?"

"On that Thursday morning, I found Buell and asked for a ride out to Irving. That night at Ruth's, I took the rifle out of storage, broke it down, and packaged it up. The clip was empty. The next morning, Friday, the twenty-second, I caught a ride back in with Buell."

"What'd you tell him was in the package?"

"Curtain rods."

"Was that a lie?"

"He asked and, obviously, I couldn't tell him I was taking a rifle to work."

"Did you leave anything for Marina?"

"Early Friday, while she was still asleep, I left her $170 and my wedding ring. I kept only pocket money, thinking the Cubans would take care of me."

"What'd you do next?"

"When I was alone at work, I assembled the rifle. It took only a minute. I hid it on the sixth floor, then went about my normal work duties. I gave a hand signal out the window to Leo to let him know it was all set up."

"Around lunchtime, how'd you manage to clear the sixth floor of other employees?"

"It just happened that way. Bonnie Ray Williams ate his lunch on the sixth floor but left just in time to go elsewhere. Maybe he was the one Mr. Rowland mistook for an elderly Negro gentleman. Somebody else came up to retrieve something but left. If there had been any others there, then we'd have called it off. It just worked out to be clear at the right time. That too, I thought, was providential."

"When did Leo arrive?"

"He arrived a little after 12:15, just after Bonnie Ray left. He just happened to arrive when everyone was off the sixth floor but me. He looked like a press photographer—had a camera, sports jacket."

"Had you told him how to get up there?"

"Yes, up the stairs. We figured no one would notice with the motorcade and all the excitement. If anyone stopped him, which didn't happen, he was just going to say he was a press guy looking for a good overhead angle."

"Once he arrived, what'd he do?"

"He walked around the room to look for the best spot."

"And?"

"He said the southeast corner was best to ricochet a shot under the car."

"Had you already built a cubicle of boxes around the southeast window?"

"No, sir. That was mostly already just stacked up that way. Boxes were shoved on that side to make way for the re-flooring project."

"How were you going to get credit in Cuba if the rifle was in the name of Alek Hidell?"

"I raised that, too. I told him that when they found the rifle it'd be traced to an Alek Hidell, not to me. He said not to worry. He'd vouch for what happened. But to be sure, I kept the Alek Hidell cards on me."

"Another question, why did Leo need to be there at all?"

"He brought the ammo. Also, I needed someone to stand with me to watch the stairwell and elevators so we could call it off if someone came onto the floor. If that had happened, we'd have pretended to be watching the parade. It was, you know, just supposed to be a demonstration. Plus, he was to hide the rifle while I got away. That jacket and camera bought him some extra time to stash the rifle. This allowed me to watch on the street while he watched the room."

"Why were there four cartridges rather than just one?"

"He just brought four and said leaving some behind in the clip would show our intent really had been to shoot to miss."

"Who loaded the bullets?"

"I did."

"Then what happened?"

"We got in place. I crouched down by the window. Leo stood just to my right behind the closed window. Then the parade turned off Main onto Houston."

"Why didn't you shoot to miss while they were on Houston Street?"

"Too packed with people. Farther away. Not safe. We needed for them to be on Elm under us, so that there would be room to safely miss, so the ricochet would just bounce up under the car."

"As they turned onto Elm, in your own mind at that moment, what were you thinking?"

"I was to take one shot just behind the president's car. Make our point. Hand off the rifle. Hurry downstairs. Find the dummy officer and get to Redbird. If for some reason we didn't connect downtown, they were supposed to look for me at the boarding house, which was on the way to the airfield anyway."

"What plan, if any, was there to meet up with the dummy officers?"

"They'd seen me in the window and knew what I had on. After our demonstration, I was to walk along Houston by Dealey Plaza and the dummy officers were to see me, ask my identification. I was to identify myself as Lee Oswald and they'd take me to the dummy squad car. Leo would meet up with a separate car."

"What went wrong, Lee?

"I did my part. I took the shot and missed. Shot just behind the president's car. I handed over the rifle and took off. He was supposed to hide it, then linger on pretending to be a news photographer and then he'd slip out. I was halfway to the stairwell when I heard another shot and then, by the time I was at the stairs, another one. There weren't supposed to be any more shots. Then, I was scared I'd been set up. I was hoping, maybe, that Leo had just shot to miss too."

"What'd you do?"

"I ran downstairs. At the second floor, I heard someone coming up the stairs, so I veered off for the lunchroom and acted like I was getting a coke. Mr. Truly and the officer came in. They let me go. I continued on through the second floor, then down the front stairs, and out the main door."

"What were you thinking as you left the building?"

"I was beside myself—did Leo shoot to miss? Was I a patsy? I didn't know."

"Where'd you go?"

"Well, at that point, there was no way I was going to trust the dummy cops, so I took Elm instead of Houston. I hurried several blocks to catch the bus to go to the rooming house—to get my .38. On the bus, I heard that President Kennedy was hit. Then I knew for sure I'd been set up. All kinds of panic went through my mind. Now I saw why they had taken me to Miss

Odio—maybe even why they had denied me the visa. I'd been tricked into taking the fall for the assassination of President Kennedy. It was my rifle."

"How about your own safety?"

"Well, I figured I was next. That's why I went back for my revolver. They'd told me I wouldn't need money or the handgun. So I had left almost all of my money with Marina and the revolver at the boarding house. I got off the bus, took a cab to Oak Cliff, quickly changed clothes, and got my revolver and extra bullets."

"How'd you avoid the two men dressed as cops at the boarding house?"

"You heard Mrs. Robert's testimony. They came and went while I was in my room. That was a close call."

"Then what?"

"I got away from the boarding house, trying to think. After a few blocks, I was thinking the best thing to do was to call Robert, my brother—maybe he could help me turn myself in to explain—I was headed to a pay phone when Officer Tippit stopped me."

"Lee, what happened with Officer Tippit?"

"That was a huge mistake on my part." Oswald paused, verging, it seemed, on a breakdown. "Leo's men knew what I looked like. I was sure he was a dummy cop. He asked for my name and I said Lee Oswald, then he said he wanted me to get in the car. I thought if I got in, I'd never get out."

"Then what?"

Oswald spoke haltingly, appearing to hold back emotion.

"When he tried to get me in the car, I shot him."

He paused.

"I'm so sorry."

Oswald paused, stared down, giving every appearance of being heartsick. Abe knew it was an act.

"When the police came in the theater, Lee, did you think that they were real police officers?"

"Yes, sir, given how many there were."

"And, did you say, 'Well, it's all over now'?"

"I did. I was in a terrible mess—my ordeal was over."

Oswald wiped the corner of his eye.

"Did you pull your gun?"

"Just to surrender but they thought I was going to shoot. They yanked the gun away from me as they took me down. They roughed me up pretty bad and I tried to cover myself with my hands, but I wasn't trying to shoot anyone."

"Finally, Lee, on that day, did you ever intend to murder anyone?"

"No, sir, never."

"Your Honor, we tender the witness."

# 69 THE CROSS-EXAMINATION OF OSWALD

ABE BELIEVED HARDLY A WORD OF THE STORY. IT WAS A LIE, HE knew, fabulous in scale—yet, a well-constructed lie. As to the president, Oswald's story eliminated a necessary element of the offense, namely intent to kill. As to Officer Tippit, it raised the excuse of mistaken self-defense. Both were slick moves because Leo, no doubt, couldn't be found to be cross-examined. More, it was tied in cleverly to independent verification, like the two mystery "cops" who tooted their horn in front of the boarding house, the fact that the first shot missed the car altogether, the delay between the first shot and the last two, the puff of smoke with the firecracker sound on the grassy knoll, young Rowland's having seen at least two men at the sixth floor window, the news photographer seen on the sixth floor by police, a man running out the back and then running down the slope to jump in a car, and the prominent bald spot seen by Odio and Euins—so the story enjoyed an aura of corroboration.

Trouble was, if it was a monstrous lie, the jury would expect the prosecution to cream Oswald on cross-examination. Could Abe do it? Abe felt the weight of that burden, the weight of history, the craving of an entire nation for vindication.

Foreman and Oswald had given a consummate performance. It was 12:40 on Saturday. The judge, Abe figured, would have called it quits for the weekend in order to give Abe more time to construct his cross-examination. Abe, however, wanted to take advantage of the twenty minutes left on the clock to nail down some Leopoldo points before the recess.

"I am ready, Your Honor."

The judge nodded, "You may cross-examine."

Oswald remained expressionless, leaning forward with his arms on the witness bench, as if in earnest.

"Whose rifle," Abe began, "was used to kill the president?"

"Mine."

"Who loaded the bullets into the clip?"

"I did."

"How many?"

"Four."

"Not just one?"

"Four."

"And whose pistol was used to shoot Officer Tippit?"

"Mine."

"And who loaded that gun?"

"I did."

"And who pulled that trigger?"

"Me."

"How many times?"

"Four."

"Four? Did you miss?"

"No. All four hit him."

"In fact, you fired three in a row, then walked around to fire one into his head after he was already on the ground, true?"

"I don't remember that. I do believe it was four, though. All four hit him. I'm very sorry."

"After the first three, he was helpless, down on the street?"

"Maybe. I don't remember. I was crazed with fear and anger over having been duped."

"With three wounds and bleeding on the pavement, did you still think he was going to kidnap you?"

"I'm sorry, I said."

"Sorry now isn't sorry then. How you felt then is what counts. So, with three wounds and bleeding on the pavement, was Officer Tippit going to kidnap you and take you away?"

"I'm sorry. How many times do I have to say it?"

"Answer the question," Abe insisted.

"I don't remember what I thought."

"Okay, what do you think now?"

"I think he was badly wounded, yes."

"So, you shot him a fourth time, meaning you walked right over and shot him in the head, right?"

"It's now a blur. I can't recall."

"You remember every detail about what Leo did and said, but you can't remember killing Officer Tippit, is that it?

"I'm sorry, I tell you."

"You knew good and well that he was a real cop, didn't you?"

"I thought he was a dummy cop."

"As you ran off, you referred to him as a "dumb cop or damn cop," didn't you?"

"No, I said 'damn dummy cop.'"

Clever again.

Abe shifted.

"Now, where could we find this Leo guy, so that we could subpoena him to check out your testimony?"

"Probably in Cuba."

Abe swept the jury box with a look of sincere disbelief.

"Cuba. Sir, do you think our subpoenas go there?"

"Objection."

"Sustained."

"Let's put it differently. Did Leo ever come to the door of the boarding house to ask for you such that Mrs. Earlene Roberts could come in here to say, yes, a man like that came and asked for you?"

"You saw how good her memory was."

"Sir, answer the question."

"No, he never went there."

"Did he ever phone there?"

"Not that I know."

"Did he ever call or go out to Ruth Paine's?"

"What do you think?"

"Answer the question."

"No."

"How about the Depository?"

"No."

"Anyone at work ever see the two of you in Dealey Plaza?"

"Bonnie Ray said he saw me go out for lunch."

"Did he see you with Leo?"

"You'll have to ask him."

"Sir, in all your meetings with Leo near the Depository, didn't *you* happen to see a single one of your friends from work?"

"Not that I recall."

"Well, where'd Leo stay in Dallas?"

"I don't know."

"Was Leopoldo his true name?"

"No, it was his war name."

"Did you put his name in your address book?" Abe held up the book.

"No."

"You did write in Silvia Duran from the Cuban consulate?"

"Yes."

"You did write in Jim Hosty?"

"Yes."

"Even his license plate number?"

"Yes."

"But not your pal Leo."

"No."

"You spent all that time with Leo, but never wrote in his name or number or address, true?"

"Correct."

"The man was going to get you into Cuba, but you never wrote his name or number in your little book, did you?"

"No."

"Now, on the date Miss Odio said was most likely when the three men came to her door, namely September 26, you were already on a bus going from Houston to Laredo since 2:30 a.m. True?"

"Yes, but she said September 25 was maybe a possibility, and that, in fact, is when it was."

The judge looked at the clock, then interrupted. "We will recess now until nine o'clock on Monday. Counsel must be here at 8:30 a.m. The jury will please remember not to discuss the case." By now, the jury knew the drill. They departed to their quarters upstairs via a back door while all but the judge stood. Then the judge asked if there was any further business.

Abe said, "Your Honor, if you please, counsel need to see you in chambers." The judge said, "Okay. In five minutes." The deputies escorted Oswald back to the holding cell while the rest of the courtroom broke up in frenzy.

In chambers, Abe wasted no time.

"Judge, under our agreement, we must first clear with you an item of evidence involving another crime by Oswald, namely his attempted assassination of Retired General Edwin Walker last April 10."

Karen gasped.

"What?" answered Foreman with his whole body, though Abe was sure it was just another good act.

"We have very strong proof," Abe continued, "that Oswald was the sniper who tried to kill General Walker a year ago. In his direct testimony today, Oswald told the jury he had only used the rifle for target practice. That was a lie. I have that part written out exactly from the court reporter if you wish to see it. He wants the jury to think he is just an ordinary Texan doing what ordinary Texans do with their firearms. No way, Judge. He used that rifle to try to kill General Walker but missed by a quarter inch and only because the bullet grazed the woodwork between the panes in the window."

"Can you trace the Walker bullet to this rifle?" asked the judge.

"No. The slug was too damaged for that, but its general rifling characteristics are consistent with Oswald's rifle."

"Judge," said Foreman, on the apparent verge of agitation, "that should be the end of it."

"No, Judge," replied Abe, "we have other, strong proof. We wouldn't use this if it were weak. It's strong."

"What is your specific proof?" inquired Brown.

"Judge," said Abe, "this is cross-examination. If I lay it out, the defendant will have the rest of the weekend to cook up a story. It's strong proof. I promise."

"If it's so strong, they should lay it out now," said Foreman. "Judge, we'll need a continuance to meet the evidence. We will, for example, want to test the slug for ourselves. This is sandbagging, Your Honor. Completely out of the blue."

"Oswald's the one," Abe replied, "who said he'd used it only for target practice. If we are denied this, Oswald will have been given a license to lie," using Elaine's choice phrase, a phrase that had worked before. "He's opened the door."

The judge sat in silence. He reached for an empty pipe, evidently to give his hands something to do. Comics showed in the jumble on his desk. All pretended not to notice. Abe looked straight at the lines of worry ploughed in the judge's face. Abe believed the judge had come to respect him as a straight shooter. Now was the time to cash his credits.

To maintain momentum, Abe resumed, "We will now give counsel a photostat copy of the police file on the Walker case. I want to be clear we have more proof than this file, but, being cross-examination, we shouldn't be required to hand it over on a silver platter."

Abe handed the police file to Karen. She held it, looking to Foreman for guidance. Foreman glared out the window, giving no sign.

The judge kept quiet, evidently stunned, until finally he said, "I don't know. It's a close call. I want to bring it all to an end, Easter and all, but I also don't want to give anyone a license to lie."

"I'll have an answer for you on Monday," said Judge Brown, "before we start."

As the bar was closing that night, Karen found the courage to raise it.

"If we don't believe his story, Percy, should we have put him on the stand? I mean, ethically?"

"You don't believe it?"

"Well, I doubt it now. That Walker thing stung me."

He downed the last of his whisky. "Is his story inconsistent with something we know is positively true?"

"No." She finished hers.

"Then why do you doubt it?"

"Mainly, it's him. He's told a lot of lies. Maybe this is just another one. He's had the benefit of all those interview memos."

He placed his empty glass on the table.

"Here is the thing, my young friend. *We* aren't the ones who'll go to into the death chamber. *He* is the one. He has the right, if he wants, to tell his story to the jury and to take his chances. We must tell him our opinion on whether or not he should. But he can still say to us, 'Thanks, but I want to tell the jury my side of the story.' If he chooses to tell his side of the story, then we must help him present it to the jury, subject only to one thing—if we *know* it's perjury, then no way. If we only worry it may be perjury but for all we know it's true, then we do our duty."

# 70 CROSS RESUMED

As he gathered his notes in his hotel room, Abe felt this day would always and forever be the toughest witness examination of his life. All of his years in court, he now believed, had been but preparation for a single contest. He took out Roosevelt's D-Day Prayer and got as far as "Pride of our Nation." He closed his eyes and paused. If we could do that then, Abe told himself, he could do this now.

His CHAMBERS REMAINED A mess, but this time a half dozen law books lay open to pages on point, the volumes piled together, the comics gone. The judge began, "Counsel, I am going to let the prosecution use the interview statements of the accused for impeachment. Otherwise, he would have a license to lie." He let that sink in. "On the General Walker evidence, however, I am still of two minds."

Foreman leaned forward on the edge of his chair and pleaded, "Judge, I can accept your ruling on the interviews, but I just can't accept having to defend against a new charge on attempted murder of General Walker—that's a whole new crime. We've been working night and day since December to defend on Kennedy and Tippit. No way we can also defend a whole new crime on Walker in two days. We just aren't ready and can't be. We would need a substantial continuance."

The judge looked to Abe.

"He brought it on himself," Abe reiterated, "by telling the jury he used the rifle only for target practice—a monumental lie."

"Judge," resumed Foreman, "I won't use that in my closing. I give you my word. You can strike that line of testimony if you want."

"Time's short. We're keeping the jury waiting," said the judge, looking at the door. "I don't know. I just don't know. Look, I'll do this—I'll listen to the rest of the cross-examination and then decide on the Walker story. Meanwhile, make no reference to it before the jury."

OSWALD RETOOK THE STAND. The jury returned. Abe waited at the lectern for the jury to settle in. They faced him, poised for his first question. Abe, Oswald, the jury—the trial triangle—as genuine, as decisive as it gets. Bebe felt it. Even Ernest Seward Cox, seated directly behind Senator Kennedy, wore a face of grave apprehension. Abe scanned the jury to acknowledge them.

"Mr. Summer," said the judge, "you may resume."

"Is it your testimony, sir, that you were innocent and double-crossed by this man Leopoldo?"

"Yes, sir, Mr. Summer. That's true."

"If you were innocent and double crossed, did it occur to you to go to an officer to tell him what you knew?"

"I was surprised, shocked, so I really needed some time to think on what to do. They had set me up to take the fall."

"When they stopped you at the coke machine, did you think Mr. Truly was with a real cop or a fake cop?"

"Real, I guess."

"You could've come clean right then and helped the officer catch Leo while he was still in the building, right?"

"I could have and wished now I had but I was hoping maybe Leo had also shot to miss and that the original plan would still work out."

"So when did you learn President Kennedy was shot?"

"On the bus."

"Then you got off the bus, right?"

"Yes, sir."

"Weren't there police officers right there?"

"I suppose but, sir, I was stunned and didn't yet know what to do."

"When the bus got caught in traffic, you got off, went two blocks to catch a cab?"

"True."

"You went to the bus station?"

"True."

"So you were able to think through that move—leaving the bus, then finding a cab two blocks away?"

"That was obvious."

"Well, sir, wasn't it also obvious that if you were the patsy and just an innocent chump, you should have found an officer and told them what had happened while time was left to catch Leo?"

"I was in too much trouble."

"You asked the cabbie to take you to the 500 block of North Beckley, didn't you?"

"Yes, sir."

"That way, he'd drive right past 1026?"

"True."

"Right by your boarding house?"

"Yes, sir."

"So you could see if any police were already there?"

"Or fake police."

"All the better. The point is that you had the presence of mind to direct him so that you'd get a safe look at 1026 as you went by, didn't you?"

"I was trying to protect myself."

"You weren't too stunned to pull off that move, were you?"

"Like I said, I was trying to protect myself."

"Your housekeeper said you seemed in a big hurry. Were you?"

"Yes, I was."

"So when no police car was there at the boarding house, you could've said to the driver, 'Stop right here, I'll get out right here,' couldn't you?"

"I suppose."

"That would've saved you some time, true?"

"I suppose."

"But if you had done that, the taxi driver could have led the police to your door once he realized who you were?"

"I didn't think that far."

"But, sir, you *did* think that far—that's why you let him keep going, right?"

"It was just easier to stick with where I told him." Oswald sneered.

"And, when you got out of the cab and while the cab turned around, you walked south, *away from* the boarding house."

"Correct."

"And only after the cabbie left, did you do an about-face and hurry back to the boarding house."

"Okay."

"So, you were in a big hurry, but you let him drive five blocks past where you really wanted to go, and then, while the cab was still nearby, you acted like you were heading the opposite way you really planned to go. All true?"

"Yeah."

"And all that was an intentional deception on your part—to throw off the driver from being able to tell anyone which way you actually went."

"I got out a little before the block I had given him, so it made sense to just act like I was still going there."

"Why did you care what he thought?"

"I didn't." Another sneer formed.

"Come on, admit it. You didn't want the cabbie to be able to show anyone where you'd gone."

"I wasn't trying to fool anyone."

"Were any cops at 1026 when you got back there?"

"No."

"So, there at 1026, what'd you do?"

"I changed clothes, got my revolver and bullets."

"At the boarding house, you could've called up the police to say you wanted to come in to clear up what had happened?"

"I had to hurry."

"To answer my question, you could've called the police. She had a phone."

"Yes."

"At that point, this guy Leopoldo would have still been in Texas, right? You could've helped the police find him before he escaped, true?"

"Would anyone have believed me?"

"Well, sir, I suppose that's what we're here to find out," Abe paused. "Now, when you left the boarding house, where were you headed?"

"I needed time to think. Leo and his men knew I lived there. So I got out of there fast to buy time to come up with a plan."

"Did you come up with a plan?"

"I decided to call my brother, Robert, so he could call the police to help me surrender."

"You could've simply surrendered to Officer Tippit, no?"

"I thought he was one of Leo's men."

"Did he say he was?"

"No."

"Let's see. Leopoldo was Cuban, right?"

"Yes, sir."

"A light-skinned Latin, right?"

"Yes."

"And Angelo looked Mexican, remember?"

"Okay, yes."

"Did Officer Tippit look Latin in any way?"

Abe held up a photograph of the patrolman.

"No."

"Did he speak Spanish to you?"

"No."

"Have an accent?"

"No."

"Had you ever seen him with Leo?"

"No."

"Did his car look fake?"

"No."

"Did his uniform look fake?"

"No."

"Did his badge look fake?"

Abe held aloft a silver polished badge, Tippit's.

Oswald frowned.

"Would you like to hold Officer Tippit's badge for yourself and see if it feels fake?"

"I see it—it looks real enough."

"So, you thought that this white Texas boy in a normal police uniform with a normal badge in a normal police car was somehow tied in with Leo and Castro?"

"I knew they'd be looking for me. Fake cops."

"When the cops closed in on you in the Texas Theater, did you think they were real or fake?"

"Real."

"You could've just said, 'Thank God, you're here. I'm innocent. Let me tell you what happened. Let me help find the real killers. Let's stop them before they leave the country.' You could have done that, right?"

"In hindsight I should have."

"But you didn't, did you?"

"No."

"Instead, you said, 'It's all over now,' didn't you?"

"Yes."

"In fact, you hit the first officer with your fist and knocked him down."

"He shoved me."

"Then you pulled out your gun."

"I was going to give it up."

"They wrestled it from you, didn't they?"

"They misunderstood. They thought I meant to shoot."

"You had your finger on the trigger, didn't you?"

"If the trigger got squeezed, it was just part of the tussle."

"You heard the witnesses at this trial. The trigger went off and the hammer snapped on the web of the officer's hand. Do you deny it?"

"It was not on purpose."

"It was your finger on the trigger, wasn't it?"

"Yes, sir, but I didn't pull it on purpose."

"Is that the way to surrender a pistol? With your finger on the trigger?"

"It was part of the shoving."

"In the theater, you complained about police brutality."

"They roughed me up, yes, of course, I complained."

"You complained about that—but said nothing, absolutely nothing, about Leo, true?"

"They wouldn't have believed me."

"Actually, you hadn't even thought up this story about Leo yet. That's the real reason, isn't it?"

"Leo was real, sir." Oswald slouched.

"After they put you in the car, how long did it take to reach police headquarters?"

"Maybe twenty minutes."

"What'd you say during that twenty-minute ride?"

"Nothing."

"Were you thinking about Leo?"

"Yeah."

"So Leo was on your mind?"

"Yeah."

"And the fake cops?"

"Yeah, them too." Another sneer formed.

"With these people on your mind, did it occur to you to tell the car full of real cops about Leopoldo and his gang and how they might be fixing to flee the country?"

"By that point, I figured they were already in the air."

"So twenty minutes of radio silence from you with a carload of officers while you fumed about Leo and his gang?"

"They had roughed me up. They wouldn't have believed me."

"But your plan, you said, was to turn yourself in and explain, right?"

"Right, but with my brother or at least a lawyer. Listen, at that point I was oozing blood."

"Those cops turned you over to Captain Fritz?"

"Shackled and hurting."

"When you were in Chief Fritz's office, did you think he was fake?"

"It was hard to think."

"You could have come clean with Captain Fritz, right?"

"By then, Leo and his men were already flying to Cuba. I wanted to talk to my brother. I wanted a lawyer but they kept after me. All hours. Midnight even. Four times. It hurt to talk to them but they kept after me. It wasn't fair."

"Did you ever tell your brother about Leo?"

"Not enough time."

"Not even your own brother?"

"I told my lawyer."

"Didn't you want to turn yourself in and come clean?"

"I told them I was a patsy."

"You never said a word to the police about Leo or fake cops, did you?"

"They weren't fair to me."

"To answer my question, you never once mentioned Leopoldo to them, did you?"

"No."

"Four times over two days you were questioned but you never once mentioned Leo, true?"

"True."

"The president of the Dallas bar association came to see you in jail, true?"

"Yes."

"And he offered to get you a Dallas lawyer to represent you free of charge if need be, true?

"Yes."

"And you turned him down, didn't you?"

"I told him I wanted someone else."

"Was he fair to you, the man from the bar association?"

"Yes, sir."

"So, did you tell him about Leopoldo and the double-cross?"

"No."

"Late that night, they brought you in front of a room full of news reporters, true?"

"Around midnight."

"A lot of them are here right now?"

Abe gestured to the gallery.

"Probably."

"They're fair people, right?"

"They think so."

"Did you shout out anything about Leopoldo to those reporters?"

"I said I was a patsy."

"Now, the police let you answer the questions you wanted to answer and let you keep silent on others, right?

"It didn't seem that way then."

"Some questions you just said you didn't want to answer, right?"

"True."

"And they were good with that, true?"

"Ask them," he sneered.

"Again, you were interviewed four times?"

"Yes."

"Sometimes by police?"

"Over and over."

"Sometimes by the FBI?"

"You bet."

"Sometimes by the Secret Service?"

"Them too."

"Let's be doubly clear, never once, not once, did you mention Leopoldo or the double-cross, did you?"

"No, I didn't."

"So the first time you have *ever*, *ever* uttered a word to law enforcement, state or federal, about Leopoldo and the double-cross was right here in court, on Saturday, true?"

Oswald sat silently, then leaned forward, as if in earnest, then said, "True."

To let it all sink in and to signal a shift in questions, Abe paused a few seconds, then slowed his pace.

"In those four interviews, you told one lie after another."

"Some lies, yes."

"You were asked in Captain Fritz's office if you had gone to Mexico City, right?"

"Ask them."

"I'm asking you."

"I think they did."

"What was your answer?"

"I said I hadn't been there."

"That was a lie?"

"Yes, a lie."

"In Captain Fritz's office, they asked you if you owned a rifle and you denied it, didn't you?"

"Yes, I did deny it."

"That was a lie too, wasn't it?"

"If they were going to railroad me, I wanted to make it as hard for them as I could."

"This is cross-examination, sir. You don't get to make speeches. You must answer my question. That was a lie, wasn't it?"

"Yes."

"That would have been the perfect time to come clean about shooting to miss, wouldn't it?"

"In hindsight, maybe." Oswald showed a scowl.

"When you were in Captain Fritz's office, you denied being on the sixth floor at the time of the shooting, didn't you?"

"That's right."

"That was a lie too, wasn't it?"

"I was protecting myself."

"They asked you if you shot the rifle, didn't they?"

"Yes."

"Another perfect moment to have come clean about shooting to miss, right?"

"Yes, sir, in hindsight."

"You denied shooting the rifle altogether, didn't you?"

"I did deny it."

"That was a lie."

"Yes, sir, I lied to protect myself."

"Instead, you told the police you were down having lunch with Junior Jarman, remember that?"

"Turns out it was a different day." He slouched.

"And, you denied shooting Officer Tippit, didn't you?"

"Yes."

"Another lie?"

"Yes."

"That would have been the perfect time to tell them about the fake cops, right?"

"Maybe."

"You could have told them how awful you felt about it. Instead, you denied it altogether, didn't you?"

"It was a mistake. It was tragic."

"You didn't tell 'em that, did you?"

"I hurt too much."

"You didn't tell Captain Fritz you were sorry, did you?"

"Listen, I said I'm sorry."

"Sir, answer the question."

"No, I didn't."

"You lied and said you didn't shoot him."

"Yeah, you're right, I should've come clean."

Abe turned and faced the jury, as he asked his next question.

"In fact, Mr. Oswald, your life has been nothing but lies, hasn't it?"

"Objection. Argumentative."

"Sustained."

Oswald sat up, then leaned forward when the objection was made.

"Let's take an everyday example. When you applied for a job at the William Reily Coffee Company in New Orleans last year, you filled out an employment application, didn't you?"

"I'm sure I did."

"And on that application, you listed references, didn't you?"

"I'm sure I did."

"And those references were phony, weren't they?"

"I don't remember."

"Well, let's look. Is this document your application?"

Abe approached and stood over the shoulder of Oswald and faced the far corner of the jury box.

"I don't know."

"Isn't that your signature?"

Abe pointed with his finger.

"Looks like it."

"Well, up at the top, doesn't it say employment application?"

Again, Abe pointed.

"Yes."

"And doesn't it say it's for the William Reily Coffee Company?"

"Yes, it appears to."

"Isn't that your handwriting?"

"Yes, sir."

"So isn't this your employment application for the William Reily Coffee Company?"

"Okay, appears to be."

Abe held it up for the jury and those nearest leaned in to see.

"On that application, who'd you write in as references?"

Abe handed it back to the witness.

"Sargent Robert Hidell and Lieutenant J. Evans."

"Hidell. Hmmm. Hidell. We have heard that name before." Abe shrugged at the jury with an expression that suggested, "Can you believe this?"

"Sir, did those people even exist?"

"Not really."

"Not really? They didn't exist, period, did they?"

"No, they didn't exist."

"They were lies, weren't they?"

"It was just a blank to fill in."

Abe handed Oswald another single-page employment application.

"And this page is your application for the Depository?"

"Okay."

"The handwriting, all yours?"

"Yes, sir."

"Filled out just a few months ago, wasn't it?"

"I guess."

"Signed by you—that's your signature, right?"

"Yes, sir."

"You gave it to Mr. Truly, right?"

"Okay."

"One question was 'Where did you last work?' and you wrote 'USMC,' meaning the Marines, right?"

"Correct."

"That was a lie, wasn't it?"

"Not a lie. I had been in the Marines."

Abe returned to the lectern. "Actually, your last job had been with the Reily Coffee Company on Magazine Street down in New Orleans, right?"

"That didn't count."

"You got fired by the coffee company, right?"

"Ask them."

"We're asking you."

"Yeah, they fired me."

"So you lied."

"A white lie."

"And you told Mr. Truly that you had an honorable discharge, didn't you?"

"I did and it was true."

"Actually, that was a lie too, wasn't it? Your discharge had been officially changed from 'honorable' to 'undesirable,' right?"

"They changed it after I went to Russia."

"In the Marines, you got court-martialed twice, demoted once, even served time in the brig, right?"

"A little time, yeah."

"Doesn't that sound undesirable?"

"That's not the full story."

"You didn't like the Service, did you?"

"At first I did."

"You asked for an early discharge, right?"

"I did."

"You told them your mother needed care, so you asked for an early discharge to go care for her, right?" Abe read from a document.

"Something like that."

"And they granted you an early discharge, right?"

"Yes."

"But almost immediately after your discharge, the very next month, you defected to the Soviet Union, leaving your mom behind, right?"

"It turned out that she didn't need me after all."

"Didn't need you after all. Okay. Alek J. Hidell was an alias, right?"

"Right."

"That was a lie too, right?"

"Just an alias."

"Was that your real name?"

"No."

"That selective service card—that was counterfeit, wasn't it?"

"Yes."

"You forged it?"

"Yes."

"That was a lie, wasn't it?"

"In a way."

"And, when you ordered the rifle by mail, you again said your name was Hidell?"

"Yes."

"That too was a lie, wasn't it?"

"Yes. I explained that."

"You put down Hidell as someone who could receive mail at your post office box, true?"

"Yes."

"For both Dallas and New Orleans?"

"Yes."

"When you received the rifle, you had to show your identification, right?"

"Yes."

"And you showed that forged card?"

"I had to."

"And you pretended to be Alek Hidell, true?"

"I did."

"That was a lie, wasn't it?"

"Just protecting myself from the FBI."

"Now, Captain Fritz asked you about Hidell, didn't he?"

"Yes, sir."

"And you said you didn't know any Hidell, didn't you?"

"That was true—I didn't know any Hidell."

Oswald developed a faint grin. Abe let this slick answer and expression sink in. Abe read the jury.

"Let's see if we have this right. You knew Hidell didn't really exist, so you thought it was honest to tell the police you didn't know anything about any Hidell?"

"Yes."

This artifice, Abe thought, deserved a pause for emphasis.

"When you ordered the pistol," Abe resumed, "you said your name was Hidell, true?"

"True."

"But you told Captain Fritz you got the pistol in Fort Worth, didn't you?"

"I think so."

"That was a lie, wasn't it?"

"They weren't fair."

"You told Captain Fritz that in the turmoil after the assassination you had just left work and decided to go to the show, right?"

"Same thing."

"What was the name of the movie you wanted to see?"

"I forget."

"Another lie, right?"

"Yes."

"And when he asked why you needed a gun at the show, you said, 'Well, you know how boys are.'"

"Yeah, something like that."

"That was the best you could come up with? 'Well, you know how boys are'?"

"That was just a little joke in a bad situation."

"So you could come up with little jokes with Captain Fritz but you couldn't come clean with him—do we have that right?"

"It's not the same."

"Just before you left New Orleans in September, you told your landlord your family was leaving but you were staying, right?"

"Something like that."

"Then the next day, you skipped out without paying your rent."

"I needed the money."

"And when you checked into the boarding house on North Beckley, you gave a false name, didn't you?"

"I used O. H. Lee."

"That was a false name, wasn't it?"

"I did it to keep the FBI off my back."

"But was it a lie?"

"Just an alias."

"But you denied to Captain Fritz that you had registered at the rooming house as O. H. Lee."

"You tell me."

"You told Captain Fritz the landlady misunderstood your name."

"Okay, maybe I did."

"All lies, right?"

"The FBI was on my back."

All notetaking in the jury box, Abe saw, had ceased.

"You formed a chapter in New Orleans of the Fair Play for Cuba Committee?"

"Yes, sir."

"You were its only real member, weren't you?"

"No, there were others."

"The only other member was A. J. Hidell, right?"

"Among others."

"Who were the others?"

"I can't remember them."

"There weren't any others, were there?"

"Seems like we had more."

Striding to the stand to hand a single-page letter to Oswald, Abe said, "You wrote this letter, didn't you?"

"Appears I did."

Abe again stood over the witness's left shoulder.

"It was to the Fair Play for Cuba Committee in New York, right?"

"Yes, sir."

"In the letter you said that you—and let's quote it—you were the *only* member of the New Orleans branch of the committee and that you had used A. J. Hidell as one of your aliases."

"Okay—I did use the alias. I admit that."

"That's what you wrote?"

"Yes, sir."

"So, you *were* the *only* member of the New Orleans branch?"

"Okay, maybe I was the only one."

"Now, this photograph," Abe held up the famous backyard photograph showing Oswald with both weapons and the communist magazines. "This photograph was authentic, wasn't it?"

"Yes, sir."

"Who took it?"

"Marina."

"At your request?"

"Yes, sir."

"With your camera?"

"Yes, sir."

"This Imperial Reflex camera?"

Abe held up the Imperial Reflex camera.

"Yes."

"And you printed it in the darkroom at your work from the negative, right?"

"I did."

"And that is you holding all those weapons, right?"

"Correct."

"Where was it taken?"

"Our backyard where we lived in March last year."

"When again?"

"March last year."

"And that's the rifle and gun that killed President Kennedy and Officer Tippit?"

"Yes, sir."

"So, you now admit this photograph is authentic?"

"It's authentic."

"But you told Captain Fritz that the photograph was a forgery, didn't you?"

"Maybe I said it was a forgery."

"By whom?"

"The FBI."

"That was a lie, wasn't it?"

"Yeah. I was tired, beaten up, afraid."

"On the back it says that you were the 'Hunter of Fascists.' Was that a lie?"

"That was a joke." He offered a weak grin.

Abe paused as he drew out his last packet of notes and impeachment materials.

"Your Honor," Abe said in open court, "we have reached the point where the Court wanted to have a sidebar."

"Of course, please approach."

They huddled so close to the side of the bench that Abe could smell cigarette smoke on Foreman's suit and pipe tobacco on the judge's breath.

The judge wasted no time and leaned over to whisper, "Mr. Summer, you've made your point. You don't need the Walker evidence. The Walker story is out. Don't use it."

The lawyers nodded.

Abe tendered the witness.

Foreman's redirect went to one issue.

"Lee, when you were interrogated by the police, did you have a lawyer present?"

"No, sir."

"Did you ask to have one present?"

"Yes, sir."

"More than once?"

"Yes, sir."

"After you asked for a lawyer, how many interrogations were there?"

"A total of four. I asked for a lawyer at the first one."

"What time of day were the sessions?"

"At all hours. Many hours at a time. One of them was around midnight. They got me up after only an hour or so of sleep."

"Did you ever get a full night's sleep?"

"Never."

"Who was present?"

"Police. FBI. Hosty. Secret Service. Sorrels. Other federal agents. Usually, there were seven or eight present."

"How did the questioning proceed?"

"Captain Fritz would ask questions. Agent Hosty would ask questions. Others would ask questions. Rapid fire."

"Was there anyone at all on your side to assist you, like your brother, for example?"

"No, sir."

"So, it was just you, without a lawyer, without anyone to help you, against as many as seven or eight men asking rapid-fire questions?"

"Exactly."

"Were you handcuffed?"

"Yes. Behind my back too. Much later, they moved the handcuffs to my front because it hurt so badly."

"What other injuries, if any, did you have?"

"At the theater, I got a bad black eye and bad cut by my eye. Someone slammed a shotgun against my neck, so I was sore there too. My head and face hurt real bad. Blood was oozing. I needed a doctor."

"Did they give you any medical help?"

"An aspirin."

"An aspirin. So, Lee, in the four interrogations, why did you tell those lies?"

"They weren't being fair with me, so I wasn't gonna be fair with them."

"Were you under oath then?"

"No."

"Lee, now you are under oath. Have you told us the truth in this trial?"

"Yes, sir, I have told the truth in this trial."

"The defense rests."

WADE'S TEAM, LIKE MOST prosecutors, preferred to present no rebuttal witnesses at all, feeling the atmospherics were better. A rebuttal case implied that the defense case had scored some points. No rebuttal case implied the opposite. If you were winning, moreover, just get the case to the jury for decision and avoid the risk of a rebuttal witness going haywire. Wade leaned into Abe for a final call on whether to call Frazier or anyone else. The metallurgy lab had not yet completed the lab work for Frazier. As problematic, the FBI remained of two minds whether the president, the traffic signal, and the sixth-floor window had ever lined up. Frazier wasn't ready. Abe paused, then shook his head no.

Wade stood to announce, "No rebuttal case, Your Honor."

The judge turned to the jury and said, "We have reached a milestone. You have now heard all of the evidence. The case will go to you tomorrow for your decision after the closing arguments and instructions of law."

As the courtroom emptied, Wade asked Abe to give the rebuttal portion of the closing argument, a sign of respect for a job well done.

# 71 THIS IS HISTORY

AFTER THE CLUB HAD CLOSED FOR THE NIGHT, THE TWO UN-wound in Ruby's small backstage cinder-block office. In a sweet plea, Little Lynn proposed, "Jack, let's just stay up, go over, and get in line to see the closing arguments. If we go soon, we'll get a couple of those seats set aside for the public. We can sleep later. This is history." She still wore her stage costume, a robe loose around her shoulders.

"Fuck history."

"Come on, Jack, no crapola, do this for me. I'm not gonna stand out in the dark by myself."

"There's nothing to see. He'll fry."

"Listen, Jack, I want to tell my grandkids I was there. It's just a short walk. We're already up. Let's go get in line."

He fumbled to light a cigarette.

"Come on, asshole, do this for me." She hugged him from the rear and pushed her chest against his back.

He said nothing, exhaling smoke. She knew this meant he was giving in.

"And, of course," squeezing harder, "you'll have to leave your gun."

"Fuck that noise."

"They'd get it at the door anyway. You, for sure. Just leave it. I'll leave mine too. Maybe you'll run into the beautiful Bebe Boudreaux."

She gyrated gently on his back while he stared through the one-way mirror.

"Change your clothes," he said.

# 72 SUMMATION

IN A PACKED COURTROOM WITH STANDEES ALONG THE WALLS, Judge Brown nodded to Wade, then said, "Now, on behalf of the People of the State of Texas, District Attorney Henry Wade will address the jury in summation." Bebe's pencil hovered over her steno pad, a spare inside the spiral.

Wade began by thanking the jurors for their sacrifice, their service, and reminded them that they were honor-bound to hold the prosecution to its burden of proof—proof beyond a reasonable doubt—"not beyond all doubt but proof beyond reasonable doubt."

The lights then dimmed. He turned the knob on the projector and the Zapruder film held center stage. Reverential silence filled the room, broken only by the sprocket works of the projector, and the faint tick of the wall clock. The last 26 seconds of the president's life flickered by. This time, Bebe noted, Marina kept quiet, trance-like. Senator Kennedy concentrated on the floor. Bebe wanted to avert her gaze too but, out of professional duty, studied the courtroom's reaction. She saw Jack Ruby's chest quake and saw him close his fist. Little Lynn grasped his knuckles. When the lights came up, the cheeks of two members of the jury showed streaks.

"In your deliberations, never forget this—it was his rifle and his gun."

Wade gestured to an easel with a blow-up of the backyard photo of Oswald. Wade held up "the most notorious rifle in history," as Wade put it to the jury. Then he displayed Oswald's pistol, "as despicable as the Derringer fired by John Wilkes Booth." The same weapons as in the photograph, a photograph, he stressed, holding them alongside the blow-up. The photo was made just after Oswald got the weapons, acquiring them under the false name Hidell. The photograph, he explained with irony, had been made almost exactly a year earlier. As his closing progressed, Wade gestured to the blow-up when he referred to Oswald, not to the clean-cut collegiate-looking kid at the defense table.

Wade traced the physical evidence on the sixth floor: the three spent cartridges by the southeast, open window, the sniper's nest, the wrapping paper, the ride to work with Frazier, the rifle's hiding place, the fingerprints, the palm print, the bullet ballistics, the purchase order in the name of "A. Hidell," the shipping record to Box 2915 in Dallas, Oswald's box. He held up the wallet with the draft card in Hidell's name, displaying again the blow-up. Another easel presented a blowup photograph of the sniper's nest with the ejected hulls on the plank floor. Wade then traced the physical evidence on Tenth Street: four discarded hulls that matched Oswald's gun, and the shipping records for the pistol, again to A. J. Hidell. Here he made a long pause to again hold the weapons alongside the blow-up of Oswald wielding both.

"It was, I repeat, his rifle and his gun."

On another easel stood the poster map with Oswald's escape route indicated in red.

"In the same length of time it would have taken the shooter to hide the rifle, then hurry down the stairs to the second floor, a patrolman and the building manager coming up the other way, encountered Oswald on the second floor. He managed to fool them. They let him go. Then, Oswald immediately went missing from the Depository, the only employee to do so. He boarded the bus at a strange location on Elm. He was a man in a hurry. Most everyone else at work was *outside* when the president came by, then went *inside* when the president was shot. Oswald did the opposite—he was *inside* when the president was shot, then went *outside* as far, as fast away as he could. When his bus got snarled in traffic, he jumped off, then snagged a cab. Yes, he was in a hurry. But, he told the cab to go past the boarding house by five blocks—even though he was in a hurry. Why? So that he could see if the police were already there. So that the driver could not lead anyone back to him once he figured out who his fare had been. When Oswald exited the cab, he even kept up the charade by heading away from the boarding house, going south, until the cab disappeared. Then he reversed field and hurried back. He rushed in and out of the boarding house. His landlady said, 'My, you are in a hurry.' He was in a hurry—he was on the run.

"He was next seen ten blocks away, walking alone, walking to where? To the show? No, the show was a different way. And, why did he have a gun? Do you need a gun at the show? No, he was on the run, so he needed a gun. The police had broadcast a description of the assassin. Officer Tippit saw Oswald on Tenth and called him over. After a few words, Tippit got out of the car, possibly to arrest him, possibly to check his identification. We'll never know for sure now. For all Oswald knew, his name was all over the radio, having gone AWOL from the Depository. The last thing he wanted the officer to see was this wallet with his name in it."

Wade held up the wallet and pulled the identification out. "So, Oswald shot him four times, including once in the head as he lay helpless in the street. That we know for sure."

The Widow Tippit, Bebe saw, wept silently. Senator Kennedy leaned in to her. He offered his hand and she took it.

Wade continued, "He shook the shells out of his revolver, then reloaded. He scurried like a rat, scurried several blocks and alleys, finally to duck into the darkness of the Texas Theater. The police surrounded him. Even then, he pulled his gun and tried to shoot. He got taken down and said, "Well, it's all over now."

"Let's talk about eyewitnesses. We have several on the Tippit murder but really only one, Howard Brennan, on the president's murder. I want to be frank about this. In many cases, of course, there are no eyewitnesses at all, because the eyewitnesses get killed. That's why physical evidence is so important. When the president of the United States is coming by, all eyes will be on him and his pretty wife, not gazing up at windows. Oswald could count on that for the president, but when he was out on Tenth Street, he could no longer shrink into the shadows. He had to kill Tippit out in the open. He had killed the president. He was on the run. Oswald had to kill Tippit to stay on the run, witnesses or not.

"It was his rifle and his gun.

"By his own admission, three times Oswald pulled triggers of loaded firearms that day—the rifle on the sixth floor, the gun on Tenth Street, then the gun in the theater. Is it even remotely believable that in handling so many weapons, pulling in so many triggers, so many times, in so short a time, that he had any kind of innocent intent? No, not even remotely believable. Can you think, in all of our history, where an innocent man pulled so many triggers in so short a time, leaving two people dead and one wounded, for some innocent purpose? I defy even the renowned Percy Foreman to name such a case.

"The accused took the stand and blamed it all on someone named Leopoldo. The accused now says the plan was to take just one shot and miss, but remember, he put *four* bullets in the rifle. We've had some pretty good cross-examinations in this trial, including by counsel for the defense, but none was better than the cross-examination of the accused. Our colleague, Abe Summer, tore that story about Leopoldo to shreds. Oswald has lived a life of lies. In all of its critical parts, Oswald's story about Leopoldo depends entirely on one witness—himself, a dealer of deceit, a library of lies. This jury has seen and heard too much real evidence to believe a word of it."

Wade ended by asking the jury to return verdicts of guilty on both counts and to set the punishment at death by execution. He returned to his chair, settled in. After a respectful moment, the judge called a twenty-minute break.

"WHEN WE HAD OUR opening statements," Foreman began, "I said that most of the evidence presented by our friends at the prosecution table would not be contested. We've been true to that. I also asked you to consider some key issues as the evidence unfolded, and laid them out for you—the paradox of how someone good enough to squarely hit the president with those last two shots could, if he really intended to kill anyone, miss the entire car on the first and closest shot. I also asked you to consider the spacing of the three shots, including what accounted for the gap between the first shot and the others, then too the mystery of the two police officers tooting their horn in front of the boarding house while Lee was in his room, thirty minutes after the assassination. We've tried to develop answers to these questions. I want to go through it with you now.

"Let's begin, first, by concentrating on that window on the sixth floor, that southeast corner window. Let's freeze on that moment in history when the sniper leans out to set himself for that last fatal shot. Frame that moment in your minds, a moment that will haunt America forever. In that moment, sixteen-year-old Amos Euins, down alongside Houston Street, looks right up at the sniper. In that moment, Amos Euins fixes on one important thing. He sees a prominent bald spot on the man with the rifle as he leaned out the window. The bald spot is so prominent that he zeroes in on it and it alone as the thing to remember. A bald spot in the *front* of his hairline. That bald spot is a key to this case.

"Now, ladies and gentlemen, *who* in this case had such a bald spot? Was it Lee? We asked Amos that question. Lee stood, got inspected. Lee's hair was different. Receding on his side, yes; bald spot in the front, no.

"So, *who* did have such a bald spot?

"Silvia Odio gave us the answer: Leopoldo. Silvia told us Leopoldo had a bald spot. Thick slick hair on the sides but in front, a bald spot. Now *she* first used the term, 'bald spot.' No lawyer put that phrase on her lips. She put it there herself. Same with Amos. He used that term. No lawyer put it on his lips either. They both, independently, described it. Both, on their own, came up with the same eye-catching feature—a 'bald spot' in front.

"Now, Silvia also told us Leopoldo was 34 and weighed 165 pounds, just like the description of the sniper sent out over the police radio—about thirty and 165 pounds. That deserves repeating. Leopoldo, not Lee, had the same description as the one sent out over the police radio.

"Now, a few minutes before that terrible moment, *two* men were up there together on the sixth floor. Just minutes before the shots rang out, Arnold Rowland saw two men on the sixth floor, one with a rifle, the other a light-skinned Latin. Light-skinned Latin. Remember that? Of course, the prosecutors ridiculed Arnold. They had to. They called him an exaggerator, a liar, telling you he really only saw one man, one man with the rifle. They had to re-arrange the facts to fit their theory of the case.

"But Arnold stuck to his memory, a memory that was confirmed by Deputy Roger Craig, the Dallas 'officer of the year,' an officer promoted four times, a man whose credibility shines in this case. He came in and confirmed that minutes after the assassination, he interviewed Arnold right there in Dealey Plaza before anyone could have possibly cooked up a story, and Arnold said he'd seen *two* men together at a sixth-floor window, not just one.

"I submit to you the light-skinned Latin up there with Lee was Leopoldo, the Cuban, the man with a bald spot in front. Arnold saw them both, Lee with Leopoldo, right there on the sixth floor, minutes before the motorcade arrived. So did Mrs. Walter. Even if she was wrong about which floor, she was right about seeing two men, one with a firearm. Remember this too—someone looking like a news photographer was on the sixth floor even as the first police arrived—you'll remember Deputy Mooney testified specifically to that. That was Leopoldo, disguised as a news photographer, all as planned.

"And I submit to you the light-skinned Latin was the one who wiped his own fingerprints off the rifle, knowing that Lee's prints were everywhere else.

"And, a little after the assassination, we have a man running from the rear exit of the Depository. James Worrel told us all about it. A man in a sports jacket ran out the back, then along the side toward the front of the Depository. This back-door escape was possible because the building hadn't been sealed off yet. Even Chief Secret Service Agent Forrest Sorrels admitted that. He confirmed for us that no one had sealed off the back exit by the time he himself came all the way from the Trade Mart.

"Then Deputy Craig saw a man run down the hill from the direction of the back of the Depository to jump into a Nash-Rambler station wagon on Elm Street then go west. Marvin Robinson plus his workman Roy Cooper saw the same thing. So, a man did run out of the Depository, and then down the slope to the car. But who was it? We know it wasn't Lee. Lee was on the bus or in a taxi going to Oak Cliff. We also know it wasn't someone who worked there because Mr. Truly took roll. That man running down the slope was Leopoldo, making his escape.

"So, we have a second man, a light-skinned Latin, on the sixth floor with Lee just before the shots. We have a sniper with a bald spot. We have someone looking like a news photographer with a camera on the sixth floor. We have a man hurrying out a rear exit, someone who doesn't work there, then running down the grassy hillside, then hopping in a Nash-Rambler stopped on the Elm Parkway leading to Oak Cliff or the freeway. It adds up. Leopoldo was making his escape.

"A signal supervisor for the Union Terminal, Sam Holland, came in to tell us about the puff of smoke that sounded like a firecracker over by that grassy knoll between the WPA pergola and the Triple Underpass—right under the tree about six to eight feet above the ground. Many witnesses ran over there looking for a sniper. They found no shells, but I submit to you nothing was found precisely because it *was* a firecracker, just as he testified. Sam Holland said it sounded like a firecracker. He was exactly right—it *was* a firecracker, a diversion. There *was* a puff of smoke, just like a firecracker makes.

"Note, my friends, that none of this depends on Lee's testimony, absolutely none. Let me repeat—none of this comes from Lee. All of it comes from Arnold Rowland, Agent Sorrels, Deputy Craig, Deputy Mooney, and Witnesses Worrell, Robinson, Cooper and Holland. No one can question their honesty. Or, would our prosecutors call them liars too?

"Actually, they do call Arnold a liar, or more politely, an exaggerator. He's the young man who saw the 'light skinned Latin' with a man with a rifle and, separately, the "elderly Negro gentleman" on the sixth floor just before the motorcade. They took him to task because the police—not Arnold—failed to note the second man in their reports. But Deputy Craig confirmed Arnold did, in fact, report a second man up there with Lee. Then, they ridiculed Arnold over his seeing a third man too—an "elderly Negro gentleman' at a separate window. But, as you know, the fact is that there was indeed a Negro gentleman on the sixth floor by a window in the moments everyone waited for the motorcade—and that was Bonnie Ray Williams. He wasn't elderly but he was Negro, he was a man, he was on the sixth floor, he was there when Arnold said he was, namely before the motorcade arrived, and he was by a nearby window, even if not the window on the corner. That's pretty close. How exactly precise do ordinary civilian witnesses have to be before they are credited by my friends at the prosecution table? Isn't his memory at least as good as their star witness, Harold Brennan, the steam fitter?"

Bebe was so drawn into Foreman's narrative that she stopped taking notes.

"Please ask yourself this, if the man who jumped into that light-colored Nash-Rambler was simply someone else, some innocent bystander or a newsman, why hasn't he or the driver come forward, after all this notice and attention, to say wait a minute, not so fast, that was just me? I submit to you that there's a reason that no one has come forward—they got something to hide—the man who leaped into that car was Leopoldo. The same's true for the puff of smoke. Why hasn't whoever threw that firecracker come forward? Ask this too—if the man with that bald spot who came to see Silvia Odio was really an anti-Castro patriot and was really innocent, don't you think he would've come forward to explain? There is a reason, isn't there, that these people haven't come forward?

"Now, let's turn to the shots themselves. We all agree there were three shots. We all agree that the first shot missed the car altogether. We all agree that a gap separated the first shot from the others plus the last two came together quick.

"Remember Virgie Rachley—the accountant from the Depository? She saw the sparks fly off the pavement behind the president's car. The first shot. It missed the car. Hit behind it. That part is certain. Now, the next part is not quite as certain, but doesn't it seem right that a fragment from that first shot was what splattered the curb over where James Tague was standing, drawing blood on his cheek? And we also know the first shot missed for another reason—because only two bullets or parts of two bullets were found in the car. There were no ricochet gashes or dents. One of those three shots had to have missed the car entirely.

"I ask you this again: How could a marksman good enough to have hit the president square on in the last two back-to-back shots have missed the entire car on the first shot, the closest shot of all? The entire car? On the closest shot? Going only eleven miles an hour? It makes no sense. It makes sense only if the shooter *intended* to miss that first shot, especially if the shooter was a Marine."

Foreman dropped his voice to a whisper, standing inches from the jury box.

"A surgical miss.

"Now, does any of this depend on Lee's testimony? No, all of this was established *before* Lee ever took the stand—three shots, the first one missed, then there was a delay, then the last two hit the president in fast sequence. None of this depends on Lee's testimony."

He let that sink in while he walked over to the poster map with the red circles. His full voice resumed.

"Now, let's go to Mrs. Earlene Roberts and the boarding house," he pointed to the red circle at 1026. "She is the kind of work-a-day lady who makes America run. Suddenly, she's caught up in the case of the century. She testified that at the very time Lee changed clothes in his room at one o'clock, thirty minutes after the assassination, a police cruiser pulled up with two men who looked like officers in uniform. They stopped in front and tooted their horn. 'Tit-tit,' she said. Now, let's think about that. Thirty minutes earlier, the assassination of our president shocked the world. Dallas police immediately swung into action. Police cars raced left and right. Siren upon siren. All hands on deck. All points bulletins. Is it really plausible that any *real*—I stress *real*—police officers would be in a *real* police car casually stopping by 1026 North Beckley to toot their horn? Not likely, is it? I submit to you those men were not, I repeat not, *real* police officers. They just dressed like them. Was that even a real squad car? No, of course not. It was just made up to look like one, a clever trick, a way to whisk away someone without being stopped. When Lee didn't come out on cue, when Mrs. Roberts peered out at them, they eased away. Who *were* those men? Don't you think that if they were real cops the prosecution would have brought them forward to explain? That silence speaks volumes, doesn't it? That silence is important. If those had been real cops, my friends Henry Wade and Bill Alexander, two of the best lawyers in Texas, would have brought them in here to explain. Those men, I submit to you, were dummy cops.

"I want you to appreciate that still, none of this depends on the word of Lee Oswald. All of this was proven before he took the stand."

Bebe admired Foreman's work. He was right. Independent witnesses backed up a large part of Oswald's story. Only one witness—Howard Brennan—directly contradicted Oswald's story.

"Okay. Now let's turn to the word of Lee Oswald. Although my friends at the prosecution table have relentlessly attacked him, I ask you to remember how much of his word has been proven by their own witnesses.

"Before coming here to testify under oath, Lee Oswald has told a lot of lies but they were not under oath. Most of them were under terrifying circumstances. Let's be clear about that. We admit he lied. To be fair, let's also ask ourselves why he lied. Many of the lies revolve around his use of an alias, Alek J. Hidell. He explained that. He invented that name because the federal government tracked his every move, so he needed a way to do things the rest of us take for granted. It was perfectly legal for him to have a gun and a rifle. He had no criminal record. Yet, the federal government had him under surveillance. He used the alias to do what every citizen of Texas takes for granted. So that's the alias.

"A more serious set of lies came when he was arrested, beaten up, locked in handcuffs, sometimes painfully behind his back, but always in handcuffs, and interrogated at all hours by a room full of police without the benefit of sleep, medical care, counsel or even a family member. Sure, he denied going to Mexico City. Sure, he denied owning the rifle. He asked for a lawyer, he said he was a patsy, he was trying to get through an ordeal. They kept on interrogating him even though he begged for counsel, begged for rest, begged for medical help. Repeatedly, they dragged him out of his cell, kept him cuffed to bombard him with questions. They wanted to force a confession out of him but that's one thing they couldn't get. Instead, they forced lies out of him, lies he told to protect himself in terrifying circumstances.

"Always remember this—Lee's on trial for murder, not for lying. My friends at the prosecution table have to prove murder. It's not enough to prove lies.

"Maybe you wouldn't believe a word Lee said if it wasn't corroborated -- but it is corroborated. Doesn't that make a difference?

"Now, let's consider Lee's testimony, the only account he's ever given under oath. Let's ask ourselves if it's supported by the rest of the evidence and, just as important, whether any evidence at all contradicts it. Lee admits he brought the rifle to work and fired that first shot that missed the car altogether. The prosecution agrees. Lee testified that he then handed the rifle off to Leopoldo and began his exit, which is what accounts for the gap after the first shot. This, the prosecution disputes. But is there any positive evidence that contradicts it? No, none. This is worth repeating—no evidence contradicts Lee's account of what really happened.

"The closest they come is with our steam-fitter witness, Howard Brennan. He saw a man fire the third shot and said here in court it was Lee. But on the night in question, at the lineup, when it mattered most, he said that he could not be positive. More than that, he had seen Lee's arrest photo on television. He admitted that may have 'messed up' his memory. A very good point, Mr. Brennan. He even repeated it to the FBI in January. And, he also said he was leaping for cover at the time of the third shot. Well, if he was leaping for cover, where do you think he was really looking? Remember Mr. Tague, the man driving into town to have lunch with his girl—he flat-out said that he didn't see the third shot because he, too, was diving for cover.

"Brennan gave a description of the sniper—about age thirty and weight 165, almost exactly how Silvia Odio described Leopoldo. Exactly.

"There is simply no positive identification of Lee firing that fatal shot. None at all. Again, there is no positive evidence that contradicts what Lee told us happened on the sixth floor.

"So, go back with me to Amos Euins and that moment that will forever haunt this great nation—let's focus on that last shot. Amos was the teenager in his Sunday best suit and Bible whose mother sat right with us in the front row. A good kid with a good family. He did see the fatal shot. He did see the shooter. He was positive about one thing—the shooter had a bald spot in the front of his head. When he was first asked about it, we had Lee stand up. Amos Euins looked him over. No bald spot in front. Henry Wade tried to undo that testimony, but you remember the way it came out. This, my friends, is the case of the missing bald spot.

"We all know—you know, I know, they know, Silvia Odio knows—who in this case had that bald spot—Leopoldo. We all know who was about thirty and weighed 165—Leopoldo, the same man who phoned Miss Odio after Lee was long gone, and planted the idea, out of the blue, that Lee had been talking about assassination."

Foreman paused a moment, looked earnestly left to right through the jury, then resumed.

"Yes, Lee's a Marxist, but it's a long way from there to saying he killed the president. Not so long ago, Russia remained our ally against the Nazis. These days, we hate communists. I hate them. You hate them. But Lee is not on trial for being a communist.

"His support of Fidel Castro, nevertheless, explains something important in this case—Lee disapproved of efforts by our government to kill Castro. President Kennedy himself warned of killing Castro, just a week before his death. Lee simply wanted to protest against those efforts and to do so *without anyone getting hurt*. It was just a demonstration. Almost everyone these days, it seems like, gets into a demonstration. That's all

Lee intended—a simple demonstration. He expected that his demonstration might lead us to reconsider. This, Lee thought, was in the interest of peace. Live and let live. Peace. Bring them to their senses. That's how the communist angle fits in this case. Lee thought he was doing something to save lives, not to end them.

"As to Officer Tippit, Lee admits to his terrible mistake—but that's what it was, a mistaken belief that Officer Tippit was one of the dummy cops. Lee acted in self-defense, or what he thought was self-defense.

"The burden's on the prosecution to prove every element of the murder beyond a reasonable doubt. We have no burden. We have no duty to raise reasonable doubt. It's their burden to eliminate all reasonable doubt. But I submit this to you—we have raised reasonable doubt. The prosecution has not answered it.

"You have a duty to your oath, in this case, a duty to history, and most of all, a duty to the president who lost his life. Your verdict will reverberate down the annals of time long after all of us in this room are gone. You owe it to history, this great nation, and that great president, to hold the prosecution to their burden of proof, regardless of your politics, regardless of your like or dislike of communism, regardless of your like or dislike of Lee.

"The fact is that they have not met their burden. There *is* reasonable doubt. It is your duty to acquit."

FOREMAN HAD LIVED UP to his billing. The defense, Bebe sensed, now had hope. They needed only one vote to win a hung jury, a hold out. Then Foreman might work a deal for life in prison.

The judge waited until Foreman settled in his seat, then told the jury that the rebuttal would be by Abe Summer.

Abe stood, then made a long look across the jury box.

"Ladies and gentlemen, I too thank you for your service. You've remained most attentive throughout, most respectful to all counsel, including me, a guest from out of state. Thank you for that. It's been a rare opportunity for someone like me to appear before you and His Honor Judge Brown. It's been very special to serve as counsel with my colleagues, as well as to appear with Percy Foreman plus his young and able assistant.

"Because we have the burden of proof, we are allowed the last word. District Attorney Henry Wade has given me that privilege.

"This story you have heard about Leopoldo is a lie, a well-constructed lie—but a lie—dressed up with some true facts but thoroughly false at its core.

"It is easy to construct a lie when the liar goes last—after all the other evidence is laid out. That way, the liar can adjust his story to navigate around inconvenient truths and to exploit those minor and curious circumstances that emerge in almost every trial. More than that, it is even easier when the other side—meaning us, the prosecution—shares in advance its evidence and witness statements. In this trial, for example, you've seen how all of the counsel, including defense counsel, have held up FBI memos of interviews and read from them. How'd they get these? Before trial, a large number of these memos were turned over to the defense. And, of course, just like us, the other side could always go out to interview witnesses on their own, just like we did. So, going into this trial, the accused was in a position to know the evidence against him. The accused was in a perfect position to concoct a lie, a rubberized story stretchable to say whatever he needed to say.

"To be clear, I am in no way suggesting that Percy Foreman or his colleague have done anything wrong. To the contrary, they have been superb advocates. What I am saying is that they represent a man who has concocted a monstrous lie.

"Let's go back over some of the lies told by Oswald.

"He used a false name to buy the rifle.

"He used a false name to buy the pistol.

"He told Captain Fritz that he had no rifle.

"He told Captain Fritz he bought the pistol in Fort Worth.

"He told Captain Fritz that he hadn't been on the sixth floor at the time of the assassination, claiming he had been having lunch with Junior Jarman instead.

"He told Captain Fritz he hadn't gone to Mexico City.

"He gave false references on his job applications.

"He registered at the boarding house under a false name.

"He told Captain Fritz he 'didn't know' any Hidell.

"He told Buell Frazier the package was curtain rods.

"He told Captain Fritz that the backyard firearms photograph was a forgery.

"There's more but you see the point.

"All lies, bald-faced lies.

"So, now, this pathological liar wants you to accept the story that, yes, *his* rifle killed the president but, no, it was someone else who pulled the trigger?

"This pathological liar wants you to believe that he thought Officer Tippit"—Abe held up the officer's photograph—"was somehow tied in with Castro, so he killed him, execution style.

"These preposterous propositions depend on the say-so of one man, Lee Harvey Oswald, a pathological and relentless liar. His word is worth nothing.

"Now, isn't that the end of it right there? Once we see that the story about Leopoldo pulling the trigger is just another lie, isn't it all over, just like he said in the theater when he was finally surrounded by police?

"Once we see the lie, we don't have to fool around with the miscellaneous curiosities out on the fringes. For example, once we reject Oswald's story about Leopoldo, we don't need to solve the curiosity of who Earlene Roberts saw in front of the boarding house in that patrol car. It's probably as simple as this—a police car happened simply to be waiting in a line of traffic for the light to change and when it did, they beeped their horn to get the line moving so they could swing into action in the aftermath of the assassination. The car wasn't waiting for anyone inside the house. The car was just waiting for the line to move and its place in line simply fell in front of the house.

"Another curiosity—young Arnold's testimony that he saw a second man on the sixth floor despite half a dozen interview statements where he only said he saw one. To top it off, now he claims to have seen a *third* man, some elderly black gentleman, seated right smack dab in the sniper's nest, an impossibility. Does any of that make sense? No, of course not. What makes sense is that Arnold's memory has played tricks.

"A clever liar will dress up his lie with as much truth as convenient, trying to fool us into believing the whole thing. He'll weave some true facts in with the false facts in hopes it will all look right.

"Let's see how that played out in this trial. Yes, the accused went to the

FBI and left a note for Agent Jim Hosty. So stipulated. How does this put Leopoldo on the sixth floor ten days later? Of course it doesn't.

"Yes, someone who looked like the accused visited Silvia Odio, but it could not have been the accused since he was on the bus headed to Mexico City when she was most sure the visit had occurred.

"Yes, the first shot missed. True. But how does this prove anything other than Oswald, due to the car's unexpected swerve or just out of nerves, missed what was not such an easy shot after all?

"Yes, young Amos Euins saw a bald spot. But he couldn't identify even the race of the shooter. From six floors down and across the street in the drama of the moment, the receding hairline of the accused on his left side would've seemed like a bald spot. The witness admitted as much. Howard Brennan, the steam fitter, gave the description of the killer that went out over the police bands. That description was not exactly right but it was close enough.

"The Leopoldo story doesn't make sense anyway, does it? It's a double-cross story. Leopoldo double-crossed the accused by taking two more shots, killing our president, then hiding the rifle.

"Ask yourself this, wouldn't an innocent patsy who found himself the victim of any such double-cross have wanted to tell the police, right away, what he knew and wanted to help the police catch the double-crosser?

"Less than two minutes after the shooting, the accused ran into the officer and Mr. Truly in the lunch room. That would have been the perfect time, if the story were true, to say—'Officer, I can help—the sniper is up there on the sixth floor. He's dressed like a photographer and calls himself Leopoldo. I'll help you find him right now.' Instead, the accused pretended he was just buying a coke.

"A few minutes later, he heard on the bus that the president had been shot. The whole area was full of police. Wouldn't that have also been another perfect time, if the story were genuine, to run to a policeman to say, 'I know what happened. Here's a description of the killer. I'll help you.' But instead of running to a policeman, he ran to a cab to get away from the police as fast as he could.

"When Officer Tippit stopped him, that was yet another perfect moment to tell what he knew, to help the police catch Leopoldo and his gang—instead, now, he's trying to fool us all into believing he mistakenly mistook this white Texas boy for one of Castro's Cubans, then shot him four times, the fourth shot execution-style to the head as the man lay dying.

"When he was surrounded by officers in the theater, as well as in the squad car going downtown, as well as the station house, wouldn't those have been another good times, if his story were really true, to say, 'Hey, I got double-crossed. Let me help you catch the real killer before he gets away'? Instead, he punched the officer and pulled his gun. He said plenty about police brutality but nothing about Leo. He never came clean.

"Now, he expects you to believe that he came clean here at trial, for the first time ever? This double-cross story is just another lie, a clever, monstrous lie. The man is a pathological liar.

"We will end with this. The rifle and pistol belong to Lee Harvey Oswald. The fingerprints and palm prints belong to him. The aliases belong to him. The wrapping paper was his. All of the physical evidence points to him. Nothing in this case points to Leopoldo or to a double cross—save and except for the story told by Oswald himself, a proven liar many times over. This case is horribly tragic but exceedingly simple. This man murdered two good men and deserves to die in the electric chair."

WHEN THE JUDGE COMPLETED his final charge to the jury, he said, "The case is now in your hands." A power shift filled the room, palpably felt. Until then, all proceedings remained under the control of the judge and counsel. Until then, the jury had been an audience. But as they filed out, the jurors took charge. Now, they and they alone controlled the proceedings. They and they alone held the fate of Lee Harvey Oswald.

As Elaine packed her briefcase for the last time, Bill Alexander handed her a small wooden cross, the product of weeks of whittling, and said, "It's been a privilege to serve with you, young lady."

# 73  AS GODDAMN SIMPLE AS THAT

"Jack, I'm worried. That son of a bitch could get off. That Percy Foreman had me convinced."

Little Lynn sat, one leg draped over the other, on the corner of his gray, metal, war-surplus desk. She opened a new pack of Tareytons and pulled one out. He sat in his chair with his jacket over his lap, mindlessly rolling up his white shirt sleeves. They'd just returned from court.

"You're the bitch who had to see it."

The smell of fresh tobacco made him reach for her pack. She sent a plume through the light falling through the small high window. She leaned over, opened the drawer, retrieved her handgun, then pushed it into her purse.

"That part," she continued, "about how much of his story got proven by honest people, cops even, that part got me. The bald spot got me."

Ruby gazed at the plume.

"Jesus Christ, Jack," she exhaled, "I just hope we electrocute the right man."

"I watched Ted Kennedy," Ruby observed slowly. "So much sorrow. So much sorrow on that face. I saw him hold the widow's hand. God bless him and that family and forgive the fucking rest of us."

He had wetness in his eye. He couldn't find a match. She gave him one. He struck it, then pulled on his cigarette. He wiped his eye.

"These fuckass things are killing me. I feel it," he said as he waved out the match.

"But when the federal guy got up," she resumed, "he made sense too. He made a good point. If Leopoldo didn't pull the trigger, the whole story collapses." She tapped ashes into a grimy tray. "For that part, we just have the word of a complete liar. What word did he use? Pathological. A pathological liar."

"Listen," he slammed his fist on the desk, paused, then lowered his voice to speak one phrase at a time. "Now, listen to me—this is Texas. Texas. A man's responsible for his goddamn gun. If he loads his gun and hands it to some goddamn killer, then they both fry. It's as goddamn simple as that. Period. End of goddamn story."

He felt unwell.

She drew hard one last time, then stubbed it out.

"I love you, Jack, for going with me. It was history. We did it together."

She stood, leaned over, kissed him on the cheek, then left. He remained, watching smoke curl into the shaft of sunlight.

*As goddamn simple as that. Period. End of goddamn story.*

# EPILOGUE

ON THE THIRTIETH ANNIVERSARY OF THE KENNEDY ASSASSINA-tion, Bebe made a point to reflect on that terrible event and, as she often did, to reflect from the same bench she and Abe had shared in Audubon Park. She had become the grand dame of journalism in New Orleans. Her series on the Oswald trial, with its profiles of the attorneys in the case, had won acclaim.

Dallas had been her defining moment. Bebe ever admired the genera-tion that had endured the Great Depression, won the Second World War, swept the Kennedys into office, and stood toe-to-toe against communism. For her, all those currents had met in Dallas—in the assassination and the ensuing trial.

It had become a defining time for America too. Thanks to Kennedy and then Johnson, America had passed in 1964 the most consequential civil rights legislation in history. That generation had done it. Yes, it had taken the moral force of the civil rights movement to prod them. But, still, that generation had done it.

Her mind landed on Frame 313 of the Zapruder film—such horror, such everlasting horror. She closed her eyes. She tried to shake it off. The image persisted until, finally, it gave way to another gruesome scene, the electrocution of Lee Harvey Oswald. She'd attended at the request of Judge Brown. The stench of burnt hair and flesh remained indelible. Both deaths remained repulsive, she thought, but at least one death compelled the other. She shook her head and lit her one cigarette for the day.

In the runup to the thirtieth anniversary, a young reporter in Bebe's intern program had gushed over Oliver Stone's film *JFK*, a movie about New Orleans District Attorney Jim Garrison and his attempt to expose a supposed vast military-industrial conspiracy to assassinate Kennedy but got smothered by it in the process. The intern had particularly liked the scene in which Garrison (played by Kevin Costner) ridiculed what Garrison called the "magic bullet" theory of the Warren Commission, its finding that a single bullet had caused both Kennedy's neck wound and all of Connally's wounds. The intern had drawn sharp right angles in the air to simulate a magic trajectory. No, Bebe had answered her, there was no magic—just the simplest of simple geometry—a straight line. "I saw the proof myself, young lady," Bebe had told her. "Do your homework."

At most, in her unguarded moments, Bebe entertained the thought that, just maybe, someone had put Oswald up to killing Kennedy. If so, it had been Leo, the one with the bald spot who'd visited Silvia Odio that September (and who was never found thereafter). And, if so, then it involved one side or the other on the Cuba question, not the mob, not the Soviets, not the far right. Silvia Odio, Bebe felt, had been entirely credible even if she hadn't been able to pin down the exact date of the Leo-Leon-Angelo visit. The Castro people had an incentive to get Kennedy before Kennedy got Castro. On the other hand, the anti-Castro exiles might've hoped that an assassination would get blamed on Castro and lead to a retaliatory invasion. So, either side might've been behind it. But Bebe always returned to her certainty that Oswald had been, as Abe had always said, just a misfit, a delusional loner and loser looking to double down on failure. At all times, she remained rocksolid that he had been guilty as hell and that there had never been any grand militaryindustrial conspiracy of the type portrayed in *JFK*.

THE END

# AUTHOR'S NOTE TO READERS

IN CRAFTING A STORY IN WHICH LEE HARVEY OSWALD IS NOT killed on November 24, 1963, it became necessary to reverse three historical events that occurred due to Oswald's death. *First*, in the actual event, FBI Special Agent in Charge Gordon Shanklin placed the Oswald note to Jim Hosty in his "Do Not File" drawer and, when Oswald died, ordered Hosty to take it and destroy it (and he did). In our alternative history, however, Oswald remains alive, so the order to destroy the note is never given. Jim comes clean and tells Abe about it, so Abe is able to recover the note from Shanklin to preserve it for trial. Relatedly, Jim remains in the story, rather than, as actually occurred, being exiled to Siberia by the Director. *Second*, in the actual event, with Oswald dead, Marina testified without restriction before the Warren Commission, revealing items of importance, including Oswald's attempted murder of General Edwin Walker on April 10, 1963. In our alternative history, however, Oswald remains alive, so Marina dutifully invokes the marital privilege and remains silent. Elaine nevertheless solves the Walker puzzle without assistance from Marina. *Third*, in the actual event, Jack Ruby lived out his few remaining years behind bars, but now, since he fails to shoot anyone, Ruby (and Little Lynn) continue to rock out at the Carousel Club and find themselves in our story.

As indicated in the Preface, I have endeavored to remain faithful to the historical record to the degree possible. However, a few passages are necessarily my own estimates of how witnesses would have answered questions outside that record. For example, the direct testimony elicited from Arnold Rowland, the defense witness who saw two men, one with a rifle, the other possibly a "light-skinned Latin," as well as an "elderly Negro gentleman" on the sixth floor of the Depository minutes before the assassination, is all drawn from his actual testimony before the Commission. Some of the cross-examination, however, is my estimate of what his answers would have been to questions unasked by the Commission. Another estimate is Alexander's adverse examination of Earlene Roberts and the "brainwashing" line of questions. All of it is my estimate of how she would've answered, though the facts relied on, like the whereabouts of Car 207, are authentic. So too is the cross-examination of Amos Euins (and some of the direct) my own estimate of how he would've answered.

Another important example is Agent Frazier's explanation of the complications attending the first shot. Before the Warren Commission, for example, he wasn't asked about the swerve of the limousine noted by Roy Truly. Similarly, Frazier's Eureka moment on the sixth floor when he discovered what appears to be a bullet hole in the traffic signal is my own invention. That potential bullet hole was discovered decades later in reviews (by others) of photographs from 1963–64, long after the original traffic signal had been removed and lost to history. We cannot today be sure it really was a bullet hole.

The testimony of Lee Harvey Oswald, of course, is necessarily fictional and represents my own view of his best defense of the case in light of the best case against him, a line of defense that, surprisingly, seems to have gone undetected in the assassination literature. It illustrates how an accused can sometimes concede most of the prosecution's evidence and repackage it as a story of innocence, by exploiting gaps and curiosities in the record.

Marilyn Sitzman was not interviewed by the Warren Commission and her observations herein are drawn from later interviews by others.

All of the occurrences used as "corroboration" for Oswald's defense are anchored in actual testimony before the Warren Commission. These occurrences include Oswald's trip to the FBI office right after Armistice Day; Silvia Odio and "Leon Oswald"; Silvia Odio and Leopoldo's "bald spot"; Amos Euins and the assassin's "bald spot"; Evaristo Rodriguez and the recessed hairline in front (another way of saying "bald spot") on Oswald's drinking companion; Arnold Rowland and the two men at the sixth floor window, one being possibly a "light-skinned Latin"; Carolyn Walther and the second man on the floor; the first shot missing the car altogether; the pause after the first shot; a man dressed like a photographer being seen by Officer Mooney on the sixth floor; the "puff of smoke" on the grassy knoll; a man running out the back of the Depository; a man running down the hill from the Depository and jumping into a Nash-Rambler station wagon minutes after the assassination; and two "cops" waiting and tooting their squad car horn in front of Oswald's boarding house thirty minutes after the assassination. All of these accounts reside in the historical record complied by the Warren Commission and are not estimates.

The defense wrings all it can from these circumstances and does so without having to resort to the kind of half-truths, even down-right falsehoods that sometimes creep into the never-ending contest among dedicated JFK assassination adversaries. In our story, at the moment Oswald takes the stand, Foreman has already set up a respectable line of argument based on genuine witnesses and has done so without any cheating on their testimony. To be very clear, the story should in no way be taken as a suggestion that defense counsel cooked up Oswald's story. Rather, Oswald told him his story and Foreman brought in witnesses to corroborate it.

All characters (and Sheba) are real except for Abe, Elaine, Karen, Cox, and, of course, Bebe. For the real characters like Lee Oswald, Jack Ruby, Little Lynn, Jim Hosty, Gordon Shanklin, Henry Wade, Bill Alexander, Judge Brown, Barefoot Sanders, Percy Foreman, Jim Garrison, Jack Miller, Jim Lehrer, Bob Schieffer, Robert Oswald, Marina Oswald, Marguerite Oswald, Robert Kennedy, Sarah Hughes, and Ted Kennedy, I have studied them as related to assassination events but, of course, I have only offered interpretations. Lehrer and Schieffer all had important roles in reporting on President Kennedy's Dallas trip and the assassination, so they would very likely have covered the Oswald trial. Schieffer's story of how he landed a role in the case (answering Marguerite Oswald's phone call) and Lehrer's story of standing next to Jack Ruby that Friday night are authentic. Their fictional conversations with Bebe are, of course, merely my interpretations of their styles, based on decades of admiring them on television. The scene with Abe and Jack Miller at Kennedy's house is fictional, although Robert Kennedy was indeed at his home in Virginia that day when he learned the terrible news of the assassination. Percy Foreman publicly expressed interest in representing Oswald so, in our story, Foreman gets the assignment. Roy Vaughn was indeed the officer tending to the Main Street ramp and, due to a distraction in the actual event, allowed Ruby to slip down into the basement. Virgie Rachley, the witness who saw the first bullet hit the pavement, preferred her married name (Mrs. Donald Baker) by the time of her testimony, but for simplicity she goes here by her maiden name.

I relied on the Ruby trial as a template for court procedures then in effect, and to learn personalities that the Oswald trial would have involved, like Judge Brown. He did deny a venue change in the Ruby case and did want to stay with the case if it transferred. Wade did tell Brown that the case (the Ruby case) was "too big for him." Sanders did lock the front door of the United States Attorney's Office to keep out the press. Miller did attend the funeral for Officer Tippit but Abe does so in our story. KLIF was then at 1190, not 570 (as now). The weather really was close on point—and so on and on.

All of the locations are real. Jack Ruby left his dog and car in that lot across from the Western Union. The city jail and police headquarter building were as described, including the basement and exits. The county jail and courtroom are correctly described as to location and floor but I adjusted the layout of the courtroom and holding cell. The United States Attorney's Office was then on the third floor of the Post Office Building on North Ervay (and the federal court one floor up). The FBI was in the Santa Fe Building on Commerce Street (and did take over the seventh floor for the Warren Commission investigation). The Carousel Club was upstairs at 1312½ Commerce Street with red carpets, the boomerang-shaped bar, one-way mirror, and as otherwise portrayed. Andy Armstrong, an AfricanAmerican, was the bartender at the Carousel Club. The Texas School Book Depository, Dealey Plaza, the grassy knoll, and the Triple Underpass were as portrayed. A neon Pegasus did then rotate on an oil derrick atop the Magnolia Building. The boarding house in Oak Cliff (including the front room and how it was furnished and arranged) are portrayed as per an FBI sketch of the front room, including the furniture. Red Bird Airfield lay south of Dallas, and the boarding house was on the way. The hotels, restaurants, Sangers, and Neiman Marcus were as described. The First Baptist Church of Dallas enjoyed being the largest Baptist church in the world. Amazingly, General Edwin Walker's front yard did indeed sport a full-sized billboard calling for the impeachment of Chief Justice Earl Warren. Shamefully, The Bottoms was a shanty town of squalor along the Trinity River. In New Orleans, the Court of Two Sisters, Audubon Park, Saint Louis Cathedral, Jackson Square, the St. Charles Streetcar, the Jax Brewery, the Habana Bar, the Newman Building (at 544 Camp Street), Oswald's shabby "sidecar" apartment at 4905 Magazine Street (still the same until recently remodeled as a law office), the local library (still there)—all of them were real. So too for all the places in Mexico City.

For the sake of authenticity, our story observes actual custom and conversational usage at the time. "Colored," "Negro" and, to an emerging extent, "black" remained polite, accepted terms then, as were "Mexican-American" and "Latin." "The Negro problem" used by Bebe was commonly used by the mainstream press. Jack Ruby, in fact, did say that he'd be a "Jew with guts," his very own words. Some flavors of ethnic "humor" remained routine in ordinary conversation, even among progressives like Karen. Only decades later did all such strains become politically incorrect. In that era, women in the workplace regularly had to put up with (and exploited, as in the case of Bebe) comments about good looks. Smoking saturated offices, restaurants and public facilities.

I lived through that era, born and raised in Mississippi. I was eighteen and in my first year at Mississippi State University when President Kennedy died. I had visited both Dallas and New Orleans in 1963 (before the assassination). Later on, I enjoyed a career in the courtroom as a trial lawyer until 1999 when President Bill Clinton nominated me to the federal court in San Francisco. I have done my share of trials on both sides of the bench. In 1978–80, I worked in Main Justice as Assistant to the Solicitor General, walking the same terrazzo floors as Abe. My own view of the evidence, for what it's worth, strongly favors Abe and Bebe's view.

For reading and critiquing the entire manuscript, I am obliged to my former law clerk Gwen Stewart (now practicing in Chicago); my former law partner Peter Pfister and his wife Bonnie Stack, both retired San Francisco practitioners; the most excellent Bill Gardner, civil rights attorney at Main Justice in the seventies; my friends Randy Sue Pollock, criminal defense attorney; Vern Winters, civil trial attorney; Joe Garrett, recovering attorney and author; John Briscoe, environmental attorney and historian; Joe Turnage, nuclear engineer and roommate at the time of the Kennedy assassination;

Junior Feild, my longest friend (from age five); John Hendricks, librarian and student of books; David Bluhm, civil attorney and the finest of neighbors; and Victoria Shoemaker, literati suprema. My wife Suzan read it and kept me inspired. Our daughter, Allison Alsup, the best writer in our family, read parts of the work and relentlessly preached literary principles. Ruth Paine, now retired in Santa Rosa, graciously read those passages pertaining to her. Meeting with her (twice) became one of privileges of this project. Particular appreciation is due to editors Randall Williams and Joel Sanders for their skilled insights and critiques on the manuscript and to NewSouth Books for its consideration of this work. Most of all, I acknowledge and thank Kathy Young, my longtime and ever-able assistant who typed the manuscript, critiqued it, and encouraged the project at every turn.

~